DARKNESS & DEBAUCHERY

CAUGHT IN A WEB OF LIES, BETRAYAL, AND
HEARTACHE...WILL JANE FINALLY CONQUER THE
DARKNESS AND RECLAIM HER LIFE?

THE DESIRE AFORETHOUGHT SERIES
BOOK THREE

KYRA ALESSY

DARKNESS AND DEBAUCHERY
THE DESIRE AFORETHOUGHT SERIES

FIVE CRUEL SEX DEMONS WHO HAVE FALLEN HARD.
ONE WOMAN WHO MAY NOT BE HUMAN.
ENEMIES WHO KNOW SHE'S NOT...

I THOUGHT I KNEW WHO THE BAD GUYS WERE. TURNS OUT I WAS DEAD WRONG, BUT SO WERE THE IRON I'S AND NOW EVERYTHING HAS GONE STRAIGHT TO HELL.

VIC, SIE, THEO, AND PARIS ARE MISSING. METRO CITY IS A WAR ZONE. AND I'M STUCK WITH THE DEMON WHO HATES ME THE MOST IN THE MIDDLE OF FREAKING NOWHERE. OH, AND VIC'S CREEPY DAD HAS HIS SIGHTS SET ON THE HUMAN GIRL WHO RUNS WITH THE IRON INCUBI MC

KORBAN IS KEEPING ME IN A GILDED CAGE AND HE'S DECIDED I NEED TO BE PROTECTED AT ALL COSTS, BUT I'M JANE MERCY, MOFO! I'M A NEURO-SPICY HUMAN AND I DON'T STAY ANYWHERE I DON'T WANT TO BE. AS FAR AS I'M CONCERNED, MY CONTRACT IS NULL AND VOID.

THEY SAY I'M NOT HUMAN, BUT THEY DON'T HAVE A CLUE. I'M AS HUMAN AS THEY COME. I MEAN, I THINK I *MIGHT* HAVE ACCIDENTALLY KILLED TWO GUYS WITH MY MIND, BUT, TRUST ME, THEY TOTALLY HAD IT COMING AND I FEEL LIKE IT WAS JUST A COINCIDENCE...

BECAUSE, AFTER EVERYTHING I'VE BEEN THROUGH, I FREAKING DESERVE IT!

KYRA ALESSY

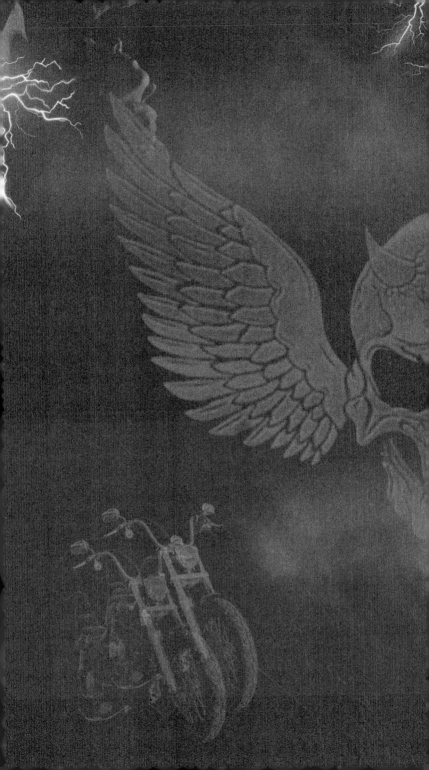

CHAPTER
ONE

Korban

My back hurts like a bitch. I don't think the bullet hit anything vital, but it needs to come out before it starts to heal over otherwise I'll have to open it back up later and practically torture myself to extract it.

Jane is trailing behind Maddox and I keep her in my sights as we follow him through his mansion.

'Where exactly are we?' she asks me.

'Europe, I think,' I say vaguely with a roll of my eyes, but hers widen.

'I always wanted to go to Europe,' she murmurs to herself in a wistful tone. Then, she frowns. 'Maybe I should have been more specific.'

I bite back a snort of amusement. She's funnier than I gave her credit for at first.

Maddox leads us down a grand staircase complete with white marble bannisters and matching floors. I glance up and find a v   nt mural of the heavens above our heads, cherubs with tiny wings and golden harps perched on fluffy clouds, gilded panels of gold and intricate plaster moldings that look like they've recently been painted.

And I thought our Clubhouse was ostentatious.

We walk down a wide corridor and through a solid, oak door that creaks loudly as it opens and looks like it's five-hundred years old. Jane winces a little. But I'm not Sie. I'm not covering her ears just so she doesn't hear a noise she doesn't like.

Suck it up, buttercup. I'm practically trailing blood around the house over here.

The room is cozy in comparison with the drafty hallway with a large, stone hearth and a roaring fire. I realize too late that Maddox's entire crew are in here too. Jayce and Krase – the twins who make me look sane – are both eating ... are those sundaes?

Iron is sitting in a huge chair, looking foreboding even to me. I've heard some very dark stories about him over the years that rival even my own. And there's Axel by one of the three tall windows. As far as I can tell, he's the equivalent of Sie. The dude is big and quiet, and I heard he's not all there either. But that's what they say about me, so maybe 'they' don't know shit.

'What the fuck did you bring her here for?' Iron spits.

'Hey!' one of the twins shouts, throwing the spoon in his hand at Iron. It bounces off the arm of his chair and the big man glares.

But I'm more concerned with how the twins are staring at Jane. The hungry looks in their eyes have a low growl leaving my throat. My glamour flickers, showing them my true form in all its pitch-black glory.

They glance at each other meaningfully.

Yeah. Do you really want to start something with me now?

Even with the hole in my back, I'll wipe the floor with both of them. Then I get a scent that almost brings me to my knees.

Jane. A very turned-on Jane.

The twins aren't scared of me, they can smell her arousal.

I move between them, cutting off their line of sight to her while trying to work out which of them has her excited. It seemed like a good idea to bring her here when the choice was a mansion or a war zone, but this place comes with its own dangers; ones I hadn't anticipated in my rush to leave Metro.

'I was hoping you'd made a deal for her,' the other twin complains to their leader.

Maddox ignores them both, glancing at Axel instead. 'Keep your ear to the ground in case the problems spread across the pond,' he says. 'I don't fancy being surprised by a mob of locals turning up at our doorstep wielding torches and pitchforks.'

Axel gets up without a word and leaves the room.

'Korban and Jane will be with us until their clan gets in touch.'

'And if they don't?' one of the twins asks.

Maddox looks back, but not at me. At Jane. He's half-hoping Vic and the others are dead so he can off me too and take Jane for himself and his clan. He truly believes what he said in the club. He really does think Jane's a succubus.

I think he just wants that to be true. I have no idea what a succubus looks like, but Jane seems human through and through to me. Besides, everyone knows he's been waiting with bated breath for a mate for him and his clan. I heard he's been actively searching for years for 'the one' and that it's

3

almost bankrupted him. I thought it was all bullshit, or at least something that was none of my business.

Until now.

Jane's face is blank as he stares at her. If she knew how much danger we're in if Vic doesn't reappear, she'd be freaking out right about now.

Damage control before this powder keg blows.

'You and Vic have known each other a long time,' I say instead of the insults I want to hurl at him.

I can be a politician if I need to be. I guess Vic has rubbed off on me a little over the years.

'Can you really see him being murdered in the street by those human scumbags?' I say casually.

Maddox's lips twitch. The Englishman is no fool. He knows what I'm doing in front of his clan.

'No,' he finally admits aloud. 'Besides, as you say, he and I have been through a lot together. I could hardly leave one of his own out there behind enemy lines.'

My eyes don't leave his. 'I could do with a med kit to get this bullet out.'

'Sooner rather than later I'd imagine,' he comments dryly. 'Wouldn't want you to faint while trying to extract it.'

The twins both snigger.

I ignore them, holding Maddox's unblinking eyes with my own.

'Wouldn't want that,' I echo.

'Show Jane to a room in the east wing,' Maddox says over his shoulder to one of the twins.

'She stays with me,' I say, almost hoping he argues.

There's no way she's going anywhere alone with either one of those twisted fucks.

'I can assure you she's perfectly safe here.'

'I've no doubt of that, but,' I glance at Jane who's looking

4

confused and tense, 'if she's what you say then you'll understand if I want to keep her close.'

'Of course.' Maddox's eyes are hard. 'The med room is down the hall across from the kitchen. I'll show you.'

'No need,' I say, putting my arm around Jane's shoulder and leading her from the room like a gallant prince.

As soon as we're out of sight, however, I let go of her and I lean against the wall for support. Jane tries to help me down the corridor, but I wave her away, feeling lightheaded. I tell myself it's because I don't want her hands anywhere near me. But, really, I'm afraid I'm going to fall on her and crush her, or something.

I hear footsteps and I straighten, gritting my teeth and walking in what I hope looks like a nonchalant gait, taking Jane's hand and making her have to step a little faster to keep up.

I get something from her for a second. Fear. And it makes me drop her hand abruptly. She's scared. How the fuck I know that, I have no clue because as usual she's not showing much of anything on her face.

I turn with a muttered curse. 'Everything's going to be fine,' I growl, half angry at my sudden urge to make her feel better.

She takes a step back, looking away from me, and the feeling remains.

I sigh, pinching the bridge of my nose. I try again, pushing the worry I feel away. It's not just Paris I'm afraid for, it's all of my clan. They drive me nuts, but they're my family.

'The others aren't dead. None of them are dead. Vic will get in touch with Maddox and Maddox will tell him we're here,' I say with forced calm.

She glances in the direction we just came from.

'You're right not to trust them,' I say extremely quietly. 'Not any of 'em.'

'I don't understand,' she says, but she lowers her voice to match mine. 'You need to give me more information.'

She sounds annoyed. With me? With herself? Who knows? This girl might as well be speaking another language most of the time as far as I'm concerned.

'I'll explain whatever you need me to, but first I need this bullet out.'

We find the kitchen and I turn my head. Seeing the door Maddox described, I open it and find a small medical room. I feel a pang in my chest, wishing Theo was here. Not because he's the medic and this is going to suck without him, but because he's my friend and he's missing in a battle-zone.

I glance at Jane. I'm not relishing having to do this myself, but I doubt she'll have the stomach for it.

I rifle through drawers until I find bandages and the other things I think I'll need. I strip off my shirt and sit down, then grunt in annoyance when I realize that I can't reach the hole where the bullet went in no matter how I twist and stretch.

I stand up and turn, sitting in the chair front-first and holding onto the metal back.

'You're going to have to help,' I mutter to Jane, thinking she'll probably balk, but she surprises me again.

She gamely steps forward, grabs the long tweezers from me, and pushes them into the bullet wound, widening it without me giving her any direction at all.

'Sorry,' she says at my hiss of pain in that bland voice of hers, but I get the distinct impression she's not sorry at all despite the fact that the lack of inflection in her tone is nothing to go on.

She takes the thin forceps and digs around in the wound. I grip the seat and clench my teeth together, trying not to make a sound. Something clatters onto the metal table next to me and I breathe a sigh of relief whilst trying to pretend to be the stoic demon that I am in front of this – for all intents and purposes – human ... despite what Maddox wants to believe.

'You did that quick,' I say out loud.

She shrugs. 'I like documentaries. I was pretty focused on the medical ones for a while. They gave me some good tips.'

'Were they like a special interest?'

She wrinkles her nose and I tilt my head, trying to figure her out. I get the impression I've insulted her somehow.

'Theo sent some website stuff before,' I try to explain. 'It said you guys get pretty focused on your hobbies and that's what they're called.'

'You guys?' she asks.

Why do I get the feeling I'm digging a very deep hole for myself?

'Uh ... people who have autism.'

She puts the tweezers down abruptly and they clang on the table. She winces and then looks angrily down at the things that made the offending sound.

'Look,' she says.

Yeah, she's really pissed.

'Thank you for reading whatever Theo sent to all of you to get to know the weirdo human neurodivergent sex slave.'

She stops talking, her jaw clenching.

'Firstly, yeah, they are called special interests, but calling them that makes it sound like I'm a little girl playing with Barbie dolls when I'm actually a grown woman with some hobbies. Do I enjoy documentaries? Yes. I liked the thing about the tiger guy, I enjoyed the one about the woman who went missing in the junk yard and the cops pinned it on that dude and his nephew even though there's like no real evidence that they did it. I love true crime and I listen to podcasts about it and I am pretty confident I could get away with murder, okay?'

I give a small nod, not saying a word to interrupt this tiny force of nature mostly because I want to see where she's going with her impassioned speech ... and because she's never spoken this much to me. I like the sound of her voice.

'Secondly, I don't have autism. I'm autistic. It's not a disease. It's just the way my brain works. And I'm not even that weird.'

Her lip wobbles and she sniffs.

'I'm sorry,' I say. 'I won't say it like that again if you don't like it.'

She nods once and turns away, shaking out her hands.

I don't ask in case I piss her off again. She's clearly upset. I can't blame her. It's been a helluva few days, that's for sure. We're both wrung out.

'There's some kind of wound filler here,' she says from the glass cabinet she's opening as if she's trying to change the subject. 'Do you need any? The bullet went in pretty deep.'

I shake my head. 'I'll heal fast enough.'

She shrugs and puts it back. 'Suit yourself.'

Then she comes back and wipes at the wound, causing my stomach to heave in the process. She dabs at it, making sure it's clean before she puts a thick pad over it and tapes it to my skin. She bandages my torso with relative precision, yet with clumsy movements like she knows what she's supposed to do but has never had any practical experience.

When she's done, I put my shirt back on and frown. The wound hurts more than ever, but it should have started healing at least a little by now. Maybe it was all the poking and prodding. I push the pain to the back of my mind. There are more important things to worry about.

'What now?' Jane asks.

I shrug. 'We rest up. We wait. We hope the others contact Maddox soon.'

'We can't go look for them ourselves?' she asks.

I shake my head. 'I'm not leaving you here with Maddox and his crew and you're not coming out there with me. It's too dangerous in Metro right now. So we wait.'

Her brow furrows but she doesn't say anything to contradict my plan of action.

'I'm tired,' she states in that abrupt way she tends to communicate.

'Me too. Let's go find our room.'

'Our room?' She asks. 'Like one room?'

I snort. 'I meant what I said to Maddox. I'm keeping you close.'

She looks hurt for a second. 'Because you still think I'm a spy or something for ... my ... for the Order?'

'No. I don't think that.' And it's true. I don't. It's something else and it's eating at me.

The truth is that Maddox will keep Jane as safe as I can. But that's because of what he believes she is and because he wants her for his clan.

What's bothering me is that she wants one of them back.

It hits me like I'm waving a key around on a hilltop in a lightning storm.

'Which one of them is it?' I ask calmly, knowing I'm going to gut whoever's name falls from her lips even if it's fucking Maddox himself.

'Huh?'

'You're sweet on one of them. I felt it in the other room. So did they. Which one is it?'

She blushes and the sight makes me freeze. She's never done that before. I'm right.

I let my glamor down, hoping it frightens her into

9

blurting the truth, but instead of fear, I smell that same sweet scent of her excitement.

Holy shit! It's me! She wants me ... in my demon form ...

I open and close my mouth, for once completely unsure if I should be angry or insulted in some way, mostly because I want to revel in what I now know about her. She thinks my demon is hot.

It doesn't matter.

I don my glamor and I see her swallow hard as she turns away from me.

'Come on.' I open the door and go into the corridor, stopping in my tracks when I find a human I don't know just waiting there.

He's dressed in a black suit complete with striped, satin waistcoat, holding a tray with refreshments.

Maddox has a fucking butler. Of course he does.

I take a bottle of water from the tray because I am thirsty.

'Good morning, sir. Madam. My name is—'

Jane is whispering almost inaudibly under her breath next to me. 'Say Jeeves. Say Jeeves!'

I choke on my water.

'Robertson. I'm Mister Maddox's butler. Please, allow me to show you to your rooms.'

He turns on his heel and walks slowly up the corridor, past the kitchen, and to the grand staircase. He takes us up it and I'm struck anew by the magnificence of what must be Maddox's family's generational wealth. I mean, I heard the prick was loaded, but I had no idea.

He leads us to the left when we get to the upstairs landing, down another hallway with wood paneling and past what is clearly a private art collection. I don't know much about art but I'm sure I hear Jane say something about Pissarro from behind me.

Jeeves (I mean Robertson) stops at a door and addresses Jane.

'Does the lady require a maid?'

Jane looks like she can't quite understand what this dude is asking her.

'No, thanks,' she says in a quiet voice.

'The lady and I will be staying together,' I say, drawing Jane close. She tenses next to me and looks surprised. It takes me a second to work out that it's because my arm is around her. Again. I make a conscious effort to let her go and not keep doing it.

Why can't I keep my hands off her?

I want to keep her safe ... for Vic. That's what he'd want me to do. That's all it is.

Jeeves nods. 'Of course,' he says and gives us a fucking bow at the waist.

He leaves the door closed and we travel up the hallway further to the double doors at the very end. He opens them with a flourish.

'Sir. Madam. The finest room in the chateau.'

Jane walks past him, saying a quiet 'thanks' and I trail in after her, practically closing the doors in Jeeves' face.

My back is aching and it's concerning me more than I'd like to admit. When it comes to getting shot, this isn't my first rodeo. Now that the bullet is out, it shouldn't still be hurting like this.

I look for the bed first because all I want to do is fall into it and sleep, but I still have the presence of mind to do a little recon first; make sure there are no pictures with moving eyes or random dudes pretending to be parts of the art.

I've seen Wild Wild West and Temple of Doom.

Nothing seems out of the ordinary though. It's actually a pretty decent room. Modern. Minimalist. The bed is massive and on its own dais in the middle of the floor. The walls are white plaster, and the cream carpet is so thick our shoes practically leave footprints in it.

Just as I'm noticing that fact, Jane takes off her Converses and then her socks.

I sit on the bed as I watch her, trying to figure out what she's doing now. She stands in the middle of the carpet and wiggles her toes.

'Oooh,' she exclaims to herself and then she sighs heavily, closing her eyes and I realize this is her relaxing.

I can actually feel her beginning to settle and, with unexpected mental clarity, I suddenly understand that she's been freaking out silently since we portalled out of the city. Not only that, but I've also been sensing her in this weird way the entire time we've been here.

What is happening? Is it Maddox's house? One of his fae tricks? I'm not sure when it started, but I think it's since we got here.

I frown at the thought, but I follow her example. I kick off my own boots and lay back in the bed, letting myself unwind a little for the first time since well before my fight. How many hours ago was that? I just need a little rest, just to close my eyes for a minute. Then I'll be ready to meet Maddox's bullshit head-on.

It's daylight.

Morning.

There are what sounds like a hundred birds chirping loudly outside the window.

Little Fuckers.

I groan as I sit up, my back is tight and feels like it's on fire.

I get up with difficulty, feeling dizzy, and staggering to the bathroom. My stomach revolts at the movement and I'm afraid I'm going to throw up. I don't, but I'm shaking from exertion and all I did was walk across the room. I throw some cold water on my face and take a few gulps from the faucet. I catch sight of my reflection in the mirror above the sink and have to do a double-take.

Shit. I look like hell.

Holding on to the door jamb, I move back into the bedroom. Jane is watching me from the bed.

'You don't look so good,' she says.

'No shit,' I growl.

She just stares at me as I lurch back to the bed and sink into it as gently as I can.

I feel her messing with my shirt behind me.

'What are you doing?' I ask, wanting her to leave me alone yet, weirdly, craving her attention.

Get your head on straight!

'Taking a look,' she replies.

She peels off the gauze and I eye her over my shoulder, trying to guess from her face if my body is healing the way it should be. Turns out I don't need to see her expression, or lack thereof. I can actually feel her concern. That in itself is disconcerting, but whatever is going on under the bandage, it's not good.

'Call Maddox,' I say, wishing it hadn't come to this, but I can't protect her if I'm incapacitated. 'There's a phone by the bed on your side.'

She turns away and messes with it for a second.

'Hi,' she says into the receiver. 'Can I get Maddox up here? Korban is ... not too good. Bye.'

She puts the phone down and I add speaking on the phone to the list of things that Jane does not enjoy.

There's a knock at the door about five minutes later and Jane pads across the room. I don't miss how she wiggles her toes in the thick carpet as I watch her. She opens the door and one of the twins strides in.

I assumed Maddox would come. Shit.

I struggle to sit up, to not look as frail as I feel. Maddox seeing me like this is one thing. He has a code of honor that he lives by to a point, but I'd sooner drink acid than have any of his clan see the same. There's nothing to stop them finishing me off while I'm down for the count.

'Where's Maddox?' I grate out.

He shrugs. 'I dunno, dealing with actual problems like the war between the supes and the humans maybe?'

'Which one are you?' Jane asks, ignoring his words.

He turns to her, his expression softening. 'I'm Jayce, darling.'

I don't like the way he's looking at her. I struggle to my feet only to fall back with a grunt.

He gives me his attention again, looks me over, and narrows his eyes.

'The bullet,' he mutters.

'Yeah,' I reply, gritting my teeth because I have to ask this asshole for help. 'Have something for it?'

'Nope.' Jayce shakes his head. 'But seen it before. It's a fae bioweapon, but it's not made specifically to kill our kind. You'd be able to fight it pretty easily... if you had enough reserves.'

Looking me up and down, he smirks. 'You don't though. Haven't been feeding enough lately? I heard that was your problem.'

He takes a step in Jane's direction, and she backs up towards the bed.

'Here's a clue. You want to heal? Get the fuck over whatever it is and feed.'

But when he casts his eyes to Jane, he looks as unhappy about that suggestion as I am.

I stare him down, hating that I'm so broken that I'll probably take my chances rather than put any woman at risk, especially Jane.

'There must be an antidote.'

'If there is, we don't have it.' He shrugs, still watching Jane with an intensity I hate. 'Don't feed then. Make my life easier when your clan doesn't return.'

He winks at me, and I resist the urge to fling the closest object at his smug face.

I'm not dying here in this house.

He leaves, giving Jane a wink too as he exits the room and Jane turns back to me.

There's something coming off her that I'm not quite understanding.

'What is it?' I ask.

She looks down and I see her swallow hard. 'If feeding is the only way that you're going to survive this, then you have to do it.'

***

Jane

He's surprised. He didn't expect me to say that. But then he locks it down and the feeling disappears. His expression turns hard.

'I can't,' he says, and turns away.

15

'You have to. You said it yourself.' I step closer. 'I can't trust them,' I whisper. 'I don't want to be left here by myself. You have to survive, so take one for the team and feed from me.'

He rolls around, goes rigid, and turns back quickly, clearly having forgotten about his wound that looks so much worse today that I literally almost heaved a few minutes ago when I uncovered it.

I know he's not feeling well, but maybe it's me. Maybe I'm the problem.

I look down at myself. Maybe I smell. I'll take a shower, I decide, and I start taking off my shirt and unbuttoning my jeans.

'What the hell are you doing?' he chokes from the bed.

I roll my eyes and don't answer him. Instead, I go into the bathroom in just my bra and undies and I turn on the shower. It gets hot and steamy quickly and I'm almost tempted to draw this out. The way I'm feeling right now, I could really use some actual relaxation. But there isn't any time for that, so I'm going to have to suck it up and deal with the mental fallout later.

I get in the shower and wash off the last 24 hours or however long it's been because I have no idea how long we were asleep for. There aren't any clocks in the room and my phone is dead.

Luckily, besides their lack of timekeepers, this place is five-star, so the shampoo and conditioner is top-notch and smells divine. There's decent shower cream too, the kind with lotion in it so your skin feels slippery after you wash it off.

I turn off the water after I'm rinsed and I step out, wrapping myself in a big towel and wringing out my hair.

In the bedroom, Kor is still on the bed. He looks like he's asleep. His breathing is shallow. I take a deep breath. It's now or never.

'I know you don't like me,' I start in a small voice, 'but ... I don't know ... just don't look at me and think of somebody else.'

One of his eyes cracks open and he reminds me of Smaug. He doesn't sound like Bandicoot Thundersnatch though. His growls are lower. They make my bones vibrate. They're hot as hell too.

'What are you doing?' he asks as I take another deep breath and let the towel slide away.

'I took a shower,' I say. 'I smell good.'

His brow furrows. 'Huh?'

I lay on my side in the bed next to him, but he doesn't make any move to touch me.

'Would you like me to do something?' I ask.

'I don't know what you're thinking, but I'm not in the mood for this,' he says.

I try not to feel the sting of his rejection.

He doesn't feel well. This isn't about you, Jane. Keep going.

'Sorry,' I say. 'I'm not very good at the whole seduction thing, but if you give me some direction, I can try.'

He just stares at me and I frown, wondering what it is that I'm doing wrong. I glance over at the phone. I don't like the idea of it at all, but if this will save his life ...

'Maddox and his clan have on-call girls too, right? Do you want one of them instead?'

He just stares at me.

That must be it.

I'm blinking back ridiculous tears as I reach over to grab the phone receiver. I shouldn't take it personally. I know how he feels about me. In fact, I'm eighty percent sure he actively despises the very air I breathe, but even my trusty Jane logic doesn't make the hurt dissipate. As I pick up the handset, though, he moves faster than I thought him capable of at the moment and he pins me under him.

The phone falls from my hand and thuds to the thick carpet.

'Don't you understand?' he growls, the sound of it making my stomach flip around. 'I need Paris here to do this.'

'Why? Didn't stop you in the woods,' I retort, remembering when he had me under him just like this on the forest floor.

'That was different. I thought you were an enemy. I didn't care if I lost control.'

'So ... you're afraid you're going to hurt me?' I ask slowly, trying to make sure I get it straight.

'I will hurt you. I'll kill you, Jane.'

'Why?'

'It doesn't matter why. Just trust me, okay?'

I huff out a long breath. 'Is there anything I can do to make it easier for you?' I ask.

'Like what?'

Remembering what Paris had me do that first time, I raise my arms until my hands are by the side of my head. 'I could leave my hands here. I promise I won't mov—'

I squeak as his fingers close around my throat just a little.

'Is this what you want?' he asks in my ear, grinding into me and I'm not sure what to say because I feel like maybe it is.

He swears softly.

'What is this?' he asks, but I have a feeling he's not really talking to me.

I feel the need to answer anyway. 'I don't know.'

'Fine,' he says, 'but don't say I didn't warn you and, if we're going to do this, there have to be rules.'

'I understand,' I say.

'No. You don't. Put your hands right here.' He takes them

and he puts them high over my head. 'If you move, I won't be responsible for what I might do.'

'Okay,' I say quietly.

He moves his hands away and I leave mine where he's placed them. I feel a little vulnerable, but I can do this. I have to. I don't want him to die and leave me here alone in this den of wolves.

That's the only reason, right?

His eyes darken as he looks down at my naked chest and his tongue flicks out. I start wondering what he's going to do and fear begins to creep in.

Maybe this was a mistake. I shouldn't have offered myself first. I should have just asked one of Maddox's clan for an on-call girl and one of them could have kept her safe while I went for a walk ...

'Just relax,' he says.

'I'm trying,' I mutter, feeling shaky as the adrenaline kicks in.

His lips close over one of my nipples and I let out a squeak, not really feeling aroused now that we're getting to the nitty gritty.

He draws back and frowns.

'Okay,' he says. 'Close your eyes and just take a breath.'

I do as he asks and when I open them a few seconds later, the sight that greets me is of him.

Demon him.

He's massive and hulking and so black that light just gets absorbed into his hide. But the sight of this other, even more dangerous side of him doesn't make me more scared. It makes me less. The tension leaves me. I don't know what that means, but if his demon form somehow makes this easier for me, then I'm all for it since their lull doesn't work on me.

This time, when his tongue flicks out, I can't help the

shudder that runs through my body and he grins in a very wicked way, showing me his sharp teeth.

Yes, I'm turned on by these brutish creatures. No, I have no idea why because I sure as shit wasn't into the Boogey Man before I met the Iron I's.

He moves against me, and my legs don't just part of their own volition, they eagerly wrap themselves around his torso like vines with a will of their own.

He looks surprised for a second. 'Shit, you do like the demon side, don't you?'

I assume he'll just fuck me the way he did before when Paris was hovering, but he doesn't. He doesn't thrust into me suddenly either. He eases himself in slowly, making me feel every hot, thick inch of him.

I bite my lip, trying to keep quiet but he stops me, putting one clawed finger between my lips.

'Don't do that,' he practically coos. 'I want to hear every fucking sound you make for me, princess.'

My eyes widen and I'm struck with inspiration. My tongue flicks out at his finger, and I surge up, taking the sharp digit into my mouth and sucking on it hard.

His entire body tenses and he lets out a groan as he slams the rest of the way into me.

I cry out at the force of him, but not in pain or fear, but because it just feels so right.

'Does that feel good, princess?' he asks in my ear.

'Yes!' I whimper loudly.

'I knew it would. You think my demon side is dangerous. Hot.'

He eases out slowly and pushes back in. 'You like the way my demon cocks wring pleasure from your body.

Wait. Cocks?

With an S?

He rotates his hips slowly and I forget his words as I writhe under him, wanting more because the ache inside is not nearly satisfied and he knows exactly what he's doing. I can feel it.

'Touch yourself,' he orders.

'But my hands. You said no—,' I mutter-moan.

'I don't care what I said. I'm telling you this now,' he growls deep and my muscles clench.

Watching his solid black eyes, I slowly move my hand down.

'I'm not good at it,' I murmur, wishing I had my trusty, pink, sparkly dildo-vibe to bring me home.

I glance at the backpack I brought. It's just by the bed. It's so close. I reach towards it, but he slaps my fingers.

'No naughty toys,' he growls. 'Don't worry, my little demon-loving human,' he murmurs, peering down at me. 'I'll make sure you come with me.'

My fingers begin to circle my clit gently, but the feeling of him moving in and out of me makes me wish I could peak right now and, instead of starting slow like I usually would, my hand goes in hot. My legs widen and I pull myself up towards him, trying to meet his slow, steady thrusts to make him go faster. But all he does is chuckle and force my hips back down to the mattress.

'Patience,' he growls, kissing my neck, licking down the valley of my breasts to my navel and then back up again. He thrusts a little faster but despite how awesome his dick probably is, it's not enough.

Then, I feel something nudging my ass and my eyes fly to his. Both his hands are on me. What is it?

It eases into me, and my eyes roll back into my head.

'Is that your tail?' I ask with what may turn out to be my last coherent thought.

He chuckles low. 'No, baby. It's not my tail.'

As if to emphasize his words, I see his forked tail flick up behind him.

My eyes widen and I groan.

'You actually have two dicks?'

'When I want to.'

He groans, moving them both in tandem and making my body bow under him.

My fingers have lost their rhythm and I stop what I'm doing with a sigh. Even with the two demon dicks, it's not going to happen. I'm too strung out and I can't relax enough.

He makes a sound of disapproval and licks two of his fingers, drawing them down to my mound and between my legs. He moves them across my clit in circles, pressing just the right spot at just the right ... Fuuuuuuuck!

I come suddenly and it's so intense that I'm afraid I'm going to make a mess on the bed.

And how does that work with servants anyway? Sorry, Jeeves, but while impaled on two demon cocks, I came so hard I squirted all over the place. Pretty please, could we have some clean sheets?

Embarrassing!

Korban thrusts into me one final time and tenses, his entire body freezing, his muscles bulging. All I can do is stare as he comes apart. I can feel him still inside me. Both of his dicks pulsing, releasing into me at the same time. He shudders and his hand goes back to my throat. He squeezes. The look on his face should scare me, but instead it excites me beyond measure.

I come again with a cry.

'Good girl,' he growls and his glamour flickers back on, hiding the demon once more.

He already looks a few steps back from death's door and, to be honest, I feel kind of better too.

He rolls off me, his movements more relaxed – like he's no longer in the pain he was in before. Guess feeding did what it was supposed to.

'How are you feeling?' I ask.

'Me?' He chuckles. 'I was going to ask you the same thing.'

'I'm fine,' I say, stretching languidly, basking in my post-pleasure haze.

'Want to call the laundry room and ask for some new sheets?' He smirks and I sit up, to see the massive wet patch in the middle of the bed.

'I'm pretty sure that's your mess,' I deflect with a wrinkled nose, 'double dick wonder.'

He laughs at the nickname. 'Nope. That was all you, princess.'

'That's never happened to me before.'

'Maybe you haven't been fucked good enough before,' he mutters.

I scoff. 'Well, at least you didn't try to kill me,' I say, changing the subject.

Wrong thing to say.

He clams up so fast, I wince at the speed he draws in the feels and I comprehend how open he just was ... until I ruined it.

'I know,' he says like he's wondering why he didn't.

'You do look a little better,' I observe aloud.

He nods. 'I feel better. It'll take a few hours, but I'll be a hundred percent in no time.'

I sigh with relief, realizing that I was actually very anxious and while I might have sworn up and down that it was just because I'm scared to be left here alone, that's not exactly the whole truth. That was part of it, but I was really worried about Kor too.

I kind of hope he doesn't know that.

'So,' he says, 'you find the demon hot.'

Something has changed in his demeanor, in what he's feeling. He's more arrogant all of a sudden.

Warning bells go off in my head.

'What are you, some kind of demon groupie?' He smirks nastily. 'Is that why you came to us in the first place? Was the stalkers thing just a cover?'

He laughs and the contempt he throws out at me feels like a slap to the face.

I scowl at him.

He must be feeling better. He's being a dick again.

'No,' I say truthfully and oh-so-calmly, pretending not to realize that he's trying to be mean even though I'd love to pull a Jane and hurl a dildo or a glass at his dumb face. 'At least not before I met you guys. The stalkers were ... are real.'

I get up slowly and go into the bathroom, afraid of what he's going to say to make me feel bad next because he's really good at it.

I close the door and turn on the water. I know I just had a shower, but I don't really want to be around him right now and this is the easiest way to stay in here without it being obvious that I'm avoiding him. Plus, he's made me messy and it's uncomfortable.

I sit underneath the spray for a while, zoning out and trying not to let all the things that have happened get to me.

But it's hard. I could really use ... something. A hug? Yeah, I want Theo or Paris to hold me. Someone I feel safe with, who actually at least pretends to give a shit about me. I sniff, letting a few silent tears fall.

I hear a noise and I know he's come in. I'm not surprised

when I look up – hoping the water is hiding my tears like the coward I am – to see him standing there staring down his nose at me.

He doesn't say a word. He turns around and leaves, closing the door behind him. I'm relieved, but also disappointed.

I shut my eyes and, as usual, cry alone, the water washing my tears away like they never existed.

Some don't think people like me feel anything because we so often don't or can't show it, but it's a lie. We feel things. Deeply. Agonizingly.

And it sucks.

CHAPTER TWO

Vic

I hear another gunshot in the distance and we all crowd back, hiding in the shadows of the alleyway and hoping no one looks too closely. Thankfully, it's still dark enough to hide us now, but dawn is fast approaching and there will be no safety at all out on the street once the sun comes up.

I hope for the millionth time that Jane is safe.

I saw her with Kor for a split second before we were caught in the panicking tide of supes who were trying to escape the Order and by the time we could fight our way out of the crowd, they were both gone. The portals aligned a few seconds later and when the doors opened, there was no way we were getting back through to find them in the frenzy of bodies trying to escape the slaughter.

I don't know how many supes died last night, but it's safe to say we never saw the Order coming for us like that, especially not in the numbers they did. I'll remember that sea of red robes executing people all my life and it didn't end in the club either. As far as I can tell, Metro has gone straight to hell overnight.

I think back to what Maddox told us last night in the spa, that Foley had been seen meeting secretly with one of the highest of the fae lords, one of the Ten, a few days ago. Could the fae really be behind this? And, if they are, why did the Order bother stealing our shipments of fae artifacts when the Ten could have just given them whatever they needed for their campaign of terror? It makes no sense.

Humans are now roaming the streets with weapons. Some are in robes, but many others aren't. They're just regular people with guns and bats, destroying supe businesses, breaking into supe homes. They're killing anyone who looks even remotely non-human and interrogating their own kind. Even in our human forms we aren't safe because we're too tall, too easy on the eyes. They'll know exactly what we are if they find us out here.

'This is a warzone,' Theo mutters behind me.

I turn to glance at him, catching Sie's eye in the process. This isn't Theo's first time doctoring in these kinds of conditions and he'll do what he was trained to do. He'll keep himself as safe as possible, so that he can help others. But that means making tough choices that he'll beat himself up over later. If things were different, he'd stop and help every person we came across who's injured or afraid. But the danger is very real and, if he does that out here, odds are that we'll all die tonight.

He knows that as well as we do, but his fists are still clenched as we watch a supe teenager stagger down the street. The boy can't be more than seventeen. Blood pours down his face from a wound on his head.

'He's just a kid,' Sie whispers behind me. 'We can't leave him out there in the open.'

'You know the stakes. Keep it together. Just keep it to-fucking-gether for a few more minutes.'

Theo's next to me, his stethoscope in his hand. He's clutching it like a lifeline.

I look back at the kid in the street. He's close, but he hasn't noticed us. Fuck. I give Paris a silent command to get the kid over here.

Paris is pretty fast and, with us down one Korban, he's the next best thing. I know he can make it out there and back without getting a bullet through him for his troubles. In fact, he'll be welcoming the order to take his mind off where the others are.

He's worried about Kor, but I'm not. If anyone is going to survive tonight, it's that unkillable fucker. I just hope Jane is with him.

Paris runs to the front of the alley and calls out in a low voice to get the kid's attention, but the young shifter is out of it. He staggers, one of his knees giving out and he falls to the side.

I can hear cars. Yelling. They're coming and they're going to find us all unless we get out of here.

Paris gives me a long-suffering look followed by a chuckle as he opens his arms with a shrug and runs out into the open.

Shots ring out almost immediately, the bullet ricocheting off the asphalt of the road. Small pieces of debris fly out of a tiny cloud of dust right next to Paris' shoe. He grabs the kid, loops an arm under his shoulder blades, and drags him towards us. Another bullet narrowly misses.

I hadn't anticipated that anyone would be lying or, in this case, standing behind their living room curtain in wait so close-by, but at least whoever's trying to gun Paris down has terrible aim.

I can see where the shots are coming from too. I take a couple of steps just outside the alley and pull out my Glock. But I make sure to shoot wide, hitting the brick wall a foot away from the window where the sniper is. There's a veritable frenzy tonight and no one's in their right mind. I don't actually want to kill anyone right now. Don't get me wrong, I will if I have to to save my clan, but it's not a priority. I'm not on a revenge mission. I just hope I don't find myself on one before we can get to safety.

Paris makes it to us. The kid is looking around with a blank expression.

'He's in shock,' Theo says, easing him to the ground on his back and kneeling beside him. 'Get his legs elevated.'

Paris grabs a box from by the dumpsters and puts the kid's feet on top of it to keep them high. Theo shucks his jacket and puts it over the shivering boy.

'Hey, kid, what's your name?'

'B-Brian,' the kid stutters. 'They killed them.'

'It's okay, Brian,' Theo says in a calm voice. 'Everything's gonna be okay.'

'No ... no, nothing's gonna be okay now. They killed them. They killed them.'

He keeps saying that, mumbling it to himself.

I take my eyes off him and look out from the alleyway. We still need to get to the house and it just got harder. I can hear the trucks that are patrolling the streets, picking off anyone who's dumb enough to be out there. Human. Supe. They don't give a shit. They just want to destroy anything that moves.

The distant sound of a gunshot bounces off the buildings

around us followed by whooping and hollering. They're celebrating another kill. They're probably only a couple of blocks away now. They're getting closer.

I turn back to the others and see that Brian is on his feet again. Before I know it, he's running from the alley, mumbling to himself. I try to grab him and pull him back, but all I catch is Theo's jacket.

He's too fast and then I see why. He's already shifting.

'No!' Theo yells, but it's too late.

The watchful sniper above us sees his chance and gets a lucky hit. Brian is on the ground a second later. Paris tries to run to him, but he's not as fast as a shifter and he doesn't get past me. I snag him by his shirt collar and pull him back.

'He's dead,' Theo says from next to us, squeezing Paris' shoulder. 'He's gone. There's nothing we can do for him now.'

Despite Theo's strong words, he deflates and draws a ragged breath, leaning heavily on the alley wall as he stares at Brian's half-shifted form.

I shake him a little to get his attention. We don't have time for anyone to fall to pieces. 'Come on. We need to go.'

Thankfully, he snaps out of it and gives me a nod.

'Where?' Sie mutters, looking angry. 'We're pinned down. Sitting ducks.'

'He's in the third window.' I unholster my gun again. 'You guys go. I'll cover you.'

I don't give them a chance to gainsay me before I run out into the street like I have a death wish, and it gives them no choice but to follow my orders.

I aim my gun at the window and I see a shadow inside, the silhouette of a rifle. I shoot first. This time, it's not a warning shot and my aim is better that his.

We run.

Three blocks.

That's all it is until we get to our house. And then ...

'What are we going to do?' Sie asks from next to me.

Fucked if I know.

'Let's just get to the house first,' I pant.

We make our way down the street, trying to stay in the shadows of buildings as much as possible so we don't get picked off by opportunists. By the time we bound up the brick steps of our townhouse, I feel like I've run a marathon.

We get inside.

'Lock the door and bar it with something,' I say over my shoulder as I stride into the living room and then to the kitchen, hoping to find Kor and Jane waiting for us.

They aren't there.

It was always a longshot, I think even as my spirits plummet.

'Keep away from the windows,' Sie says from the other room. 'This may be a supe neighborhood, but we don't know who's occupying the adjacent buildings now and it's been a decade since our true natures were a secret.'

Paris comes into the room a second later. 'If someone wants into the house, they'll find a way, but we should have some warning if they try now,' he says, looking around. 'They're not here?'

I shake my head. 'Send a comm out to all the human Iron I's and the prospects to hide their patches and leave the city. We'll let them know when we're back.'

I look up at Paris who nods and I realize belatedly that he's clutching his arm.

'Will do, boss.'

He sees where I'm looking.

'Got a bullet on the way,' he says, looking a little apologetic.

'Shit,' Theo says, moving Paris' hand away from where

31

he's pressing the bloodied sleeve of his shirt. 'It's a graze, but it's deep.'

'Just a scratch.' Paris gives him a half smile. 'It'll be fine in a few hours. Just wrap it up tight, so I don't bleed everywhere.'

'I'll be the judge of what medical treatment you need,' Theo replies, sounding a little more himself. 'Come on. I'll do it in the clinic.'

They go upstairs while Sie and I take a look around.

'What if Jane—'

'Jane is fine,' I growl. 'She's smart.'

'But what if—'

'I can't listen to 'what ifs' right now,' I say. 'We need to get out of Metro. We need to figure out where Jane and Korban are. Those are our priorities.'

Sie gives me a nod. 'I know. I'm just …'

I want to tell him I'm scared too. But I can't. I'm the Club President for a reason. I have to keep my head. I can't let emotion in right now.

'Look around,' I tell him. 'See if they've been here. If they've already come and gone, Kor will have left us a bread-crumb somewhere. You know him.'

Sie goes into the living room to see if he can find anything and I glance around the kitchen. There's nothing out in the open, but Kor wouldn't have just left a message on the counter telling us where he was.

I take a look in the cabinets first and, finding nothing, I check the fridge. And that's where I find it; a slip of paper between the bottles of beer that he and Paris always drink.

'Got something,' I say, snatching it out and scanning the hastily written scrawl. 'He's with Maddox. Jane's with him.'

Sie sinks down hard at the kitchen table and it's only now that I realize how worried he's been. And not just about Kor.

'You like her,' I say.

'You don't?'

I give a mirthless chuckle. 'Doesn't matter what I think about her. Doesn't matter what I say to her. She hates me.'

'I think she's probably right to hate all of us right now,' Sie says, 'but I owe her no matter what. She might not have meant to save me, but she did. That means something.'

'But it's not just that, is it?' I prod.

He shakes his head but doesn't say anything else about it, instead he gestures to the note in my hand. 'Where did they go with Maddox? Does it say?'

'No, but that's not an issue. He'll be at his main estate far from the fighting. The problem is getting there.'

I'm quiet while I think, pacing the kitchen.

'Pack some stuff,' I say finally. 'I think I have a plan of how we're going to get out of the city. We leave in ten.'

'And then what?' Sie asks.

'And then we get to Maddox the human way.'

Paris and Theo come back downstairs a little while later and I slide the note across the counter.

'Thank fuck,' Paris mutters, looking relieved.

I sigh deeply. Sometimes I forget he has the least experience out of all of us.

'They're safe with him for now, but we need to get there. I doubt they will be for long.'

'What do you mean?' asks Theo.

I eye him. He's not himself at all and I need him to be.

'Get your head together,' I sneer at him, not bothering to sugar-coat it, not even for Paris. 'You think he took Korban with him out of the goodness of his heart? No. He just figured Jane wouldn't go willingly without him. You've seen how he and his clan look at her. If we don't get in touch with Maddox,' I do glance at Paris a little apologetically now, 'Maddox will make damn sure Kor doesn't leave his estate alive and then he and his clan will take Jane for themselves.'

'I don't get it,' Paris mutters after a moment. 'What is it with her?'

Theo frowns at him and he shrugs.

'Look, I care about her too, but what is it about her? Why is everyone going nuts over this human girl? Don't get me wrong, I am too, but what is it?'

'It's not everyone,' Sie says quietly from the doorway. 'Just the incubi clans.'

'What do you know?' I ask, my eyes narrowing.

'Only that something else is going on here,' he answers, but I feel like there's more he's not telling me.

There will be a reason and now isn't the time to be forcing the issue, but if he won't give it to me straight, I'll get it out of Maddox easily enough when we get across the pond. My hands tighten at my sides. I'm looking forward to having a visit with my old friend, asking him a few things … like how the Order got into his sealed club.

'Where are they?' Theo asks.

'Lausanne.'

'How the fuck are we getting to France?' Paris exclaims.

'It's in Switzerland actually, and you're going to get us a jet.'

He throws up his arms. 'How are we even going to get to the airport?'

I give him a smug grin as I pull one of Maddox's portal links from my breast pocket.

'I lifted this from Maddox's club. One of those crazy twins left it in the men's room in the spa.'

I turn it over, taking a closer look.

'It's not a very good one. We can't use it to realm-jump, or

34

even to go more than a hundred miles maybe, but it should get us to the airport, so pack your shit.'

I glance around, feeling a pang. We've lost two houses in the span of a few weeks.

'I don't know when we'll be coming back here.'

~

Jane

I'M STILL in the bathroom with the water on. I feel better in mind if not in body as I uncurl from my spot in the shower, stand up, and stretch.

I watch the door as I towel myself dry. I'm not looking forward to going back into that room and facing Korban after he pretty much called me a thirsty, demon groupie. I wipe the steamy mirror with my hand and look at myself.

What if I am a thirsty, demon groupie?

I crack the door and peek out, doing a quick, secondary survey when I don't see him immediately. He's not out there.

I breathe a sigh of relief and walk into the room, the thick carpet under my toes a balm on my very soul. I'll bet it's expensive as fuck. Most nice things are so I've come to understand during my time with the Iron I's.

Something blinds me for a split second and I see a tiny disco ball hanging by the window. The sun shines off it and sprinkles light around the room. I frown at it. That's like the one in Metro that appeared in my room the other day. In fact, I'm pretty sure it's the same one I woke up to a few mornings ago and spent over an hour practically in a trance, just staring at the little prisms that were dancing over the walls.

Did Kor take it? Why? Is this an apology for him being such a dick? Even more confused now than I was before, I grab some fresh underwear from my backpack and throw on my clothes.

I open the door into the hall quietly. I want to explore. I want to plan my avenues of escape. That's what I always do in a new place. But I have a feeling Korban is going to want to keep me in this bedroom and away from Maddox's clan completely. I glance at the door itself. If it had a lock, he already would have secured me inside but lucky for me there isn't one.

Thinking of Kor again has me wanting to climb back into bed and hide under the covers for the rest of the day. I thought I was helping him but ... I freeze with a brainwave I don't like at all. Maybe I made him do something he didn't want to. Maybe he wasn't in any state to consent to anyone and I took advantage of him. I mean there are other options here besides me and when I tried to call for one of those options, he stopped me. He didn't want one of the on-call girls, but maybe he didn't want me either. Am I the bad guy?

That thought echoes in my brain and I shut it down as fast as I can, but the damage is done. My morale is shot to hell. I messed up again because I couldn't read the signs.

My shoulders sag and I hang my head, letting all the air go out of my lungs before I pick myself back up and put everything away. I look normal on the outside now, but inside I feel like nothing will ever be good again. I know it's just a trick my brain is playing on me, a chemical thing because everything is hard right now. I try to remind myself that things aren't as bad as they seem as I walk down the hallway, but it's difficult.

I distract myself by taking in my surroundings and committing them to memory. There are cameras watching me. They don't even try to hide them here. But I don't care if anyone sees me right now. This is only recon. I just don't want Korban putting me back in that room.

I go slowly down the grand staircase, almost missing a step as I stare up at the ceiling.

'That's dangerous,' I mutter.

Why have a painting above you that you can't help but look up at while you're going down the stairs? Someone did not think that through at all.

I rest my hand on the cold, stone railing as I descend because I can't actually stop looking up. I know we're still in the human realm, but it might as well be a whole other world.

My stomach twists. What if I'm wrong? What if this is a whole other world? What if we never left the club and I'm still lost in there?

No way.

I'd know … right? Yeah! I'd know. I'm not an idiot, I tell myself, but the horrible feeling lingers.

The white staircase has a delicate curve at the bottom and the banister follows it, gliding around into a ring that I slide my hand all the way around to the very end.

I peer down the two hallways in front of me and decide to begin my scouting mission in a spot I already know, retracing Jeeves' steps when he took us upstairs … Was it yesterday?

I find the door that led into that first room Maddox brought us to when we got here, where his clan was hanging out. I guess it's like a Drawing Room or some other room name I don't even know. I thought the Iron I's clubhouse was glitzy before it, you know, burned to the ground, but this one takes it to a totally different level. I'm afraid to touch anything in case I break a priceless artifact or irreplaceable heirloom that's a billion years old or something. The whole place reeks of old money. I didn't even know that had a smell, but it does.

I listen at the door and I hear noises, voices coming from inside. I nope out of there pretty fast because I don't feel like dealing with any of Maddox's crew. After what happened in the club the first time I met them when they tried to lull me, the way those twins were messing with me the last time, I don't trust them at all. I mean, that's what Korban told me too, but I'm not going to just take what he says at face value. I like to make up my own mind about things ... it just happens that we're on the same page this time. Maddox, Jayce, Krase, Axel, and Iron are sketchy dudes, and I don't like 'em.

I pad down the hallway a little further to the end where a massive window looks over a manicured garden with feature fountains and seating and ponds and shit. I squint at the horizon. Is that a maze out there? Not a maize maze, but an actual hedge maze like the kind from Alice in Wonderland? I promise myself right then and there that I'm going to visit it and lose myself in it. I mean probably not today because it looks like rain and it's frosty out too. But before I leave here, I'm going to that maze.

'How are you, Miss Mercy?'

I jump with a squeal and find Maddox skulking up behind me like a creepy creeper.

'I'm good. Thanks,' I murmur, trying to go past him because I feel trapped with him in this dead-end corridor.

I don't want to be near him. I don't like the way he talks to me, the way he looks at me. I don't really get it, but everything in me tells me to get away from him like we're opposing magnets.

But then he follows me, walking next to me. Thankfully, he doesn't grab me or anything, but, seriously, leave me alone, guy.

I stop in the corridor abruptly and swing around to face him. I just decided we're opposing magnets, jackass. Fuck off already!

'Stop following me,' I say plainly, so there are no misunderstandings.

'I'm not following you. I was just going over there,' he replies, but he doesn't move and his nostrils flare.

'Korban is better I take it?'

I just look at him.

'I heard from Jayce that he wasn't feeling too well last night,' he adds.

The way he looks at me ... I feel like there's some subtext going on that I'm not getting.

'Yep, he's feeling fine today,' I say, pretending that I've seen him this morning and that I didn't spend the entire night in the shower being pummeled with water because he was mean to me.

'Come. I want to show you something.'

I don't move. 'Is it a good something or a bad something?'

'Good, I think,' he says over his shoulder and keeps walking.

'Good, he thinks,' I mutter to myself, but I follow because I'm curious and I want to see more of his house.

He leads me to some more French doors. This place is full of them. Is that because this is a chateau or are all mansions in Europe like this? I sort of want to ask, but I also don't want to engage with him anymore than I absolutely have to. I'll bet he's the kind who'd get the wrong idea and then say I was giving him signals when I was just attempting to be friendly.

He opens the doors and goes into the room beyond. I trail behind, ready to run the other way just in case. My breath gets stuck in my throat and I almost choke as I see what's in the room. It's a library. There are books covering every surface and wall. Everything's decorated in white and baby blue. I gaze around in wonder.

'This is some Beauty and the Beast shit,' I say.

Then I glance over at him. 'You aren't giving it to me, are you?'

'Would it make you stay here with us?'

I frown at his words. 'Look ... are you ...' I shake my head. 'I'm sorry. I don't get nuances of meaning all that well,' I try to explain because he's thoroughly confusing me.

I start again. 'Are you trying to make me stay here as an on-call girl because I already have that job with the Iron I's.'

'No,' he says, 'not as an on-call girl, Jane. As our mate.'

My mouth opens but I don't speak. Instead, my torso moves forward because I figure I must have misheard him.

'Excuse me?' I ask, listening hard.

'What are you doing in here?' a voice from behind me says and I turn to see Korban in the doorway.

There's some more Beauty and the Beast vibes.

I'm not even in the west wing! Why are you yelling at me?

'Go back to our room,' he snaps.

He's not even looking at Maddox.

Only me!

It's like I was caught doing something wrong and whatever's going on right now is entirely my fault.

Like Maddox propositioning me to stay here is on me!

Like I was asking for it by leaving the bedroom.

My teeth grate. That's some misogynistic bullshit right there!

None of this is my fault! I didn't ask for any of this!

Everything I've been feeling this morning, the sad, morose pity party I've been stuck in, melts away and something else starts taking its place.

I don't care anymore if Korban doesn't like me. I don't give a shit if I made the poor baby do something he didn't want to. I saved his life and I deserve a little thanks!

The change inside me is sudden and catastrophic.

ANGER!

Full and furious; the kind I couldn't reign in even if I wanted to and I don't want to because it feels good. It's righteous and deserved and cathartic.

I round on Korban.

Wrath pulses through me, hot and powerful.

I literally feel like I could rip him apart.

'You don't tell me what to do!' I yell.

I cringe a little on the inside because I sound like a petulant child, but I press on.

'I'm a grown woman and I'll do what I fucking want!'

I tense, ready to stand my ground, fight him tooth and nail. I'll lose but I'll do some serious damage to this total a-hole no matter what.

Fucking demon groupie.

I'll show him 'demon groupie'. By the time I'm done with him, he's never going to call me anything but ma'am!

Yeah, I like that.

I take up a wider stance, ready for him to come at me, but he stays where he is. He doesn't attack me, or try to subdue me, or make me do what he wants me to do. He doesn't seem to be planning to drag me back to our room and put the on-call girl back in her place. Instead, his mouth falls open and his eyes snap to Maddox. He's surprised, no shocked by something.

'Believe me now?' the clan leader drawls from behind me.

I'm trying to hold onto my fury, but it's evaporating almost as quickly as it appeared. I have a right to be mad, but that level of pissed-off was ...

That was weird.

'Calm down,' Maddox says, and I look back at him, expecting him to be talking to Kor but he's talking to me.

'I am calm!'

I'm also feeling weirdly vulnerable and kind of embarrassed at my outburst. I don't usually lose it in front of people like that.

I put my hands out in front of me and turn away, removing myself from the scene entirely. But as I do, I catch my reflection in the window and I scream because what's looking back at me isn't me.

It's a monster.

CHAPTER

THREE

Theo

'Are you okay?' Paris murmurs next to me as I wrap his arm upstairs for the second time.

Damn thing soaked through the first bandage. I'm off my game. I should have done it right and put stitches in the first time.

'Yeah, sure,' I say because I don't want to talk about it.

The truth is I'm as far away from okay as I could get right now. There were so many people I needed to help out there. But I couldn't and it's going to be awhile before I can get them out of my mind.

'Be careful with it,' I say, pretending everything is fine. 'I'll bring some supplies with us, but we have to assume that we're going to be in the wind for a while and we don't know when we'll next get to feed.'

Paris nods, moving his arm around a little. 'It's starting to heal, just a little slower than when I was feeding every day.'

'And don't get shot again either. Kor will have my head if you aren't a hundred percent when you see him.'

Paris grins. 'At least we know they're safe. I was starting to worry when we didn't find them here.'

'Yeah,' I mutter.

There's a pregnant pause.

'You think Vic's right? You don't think Kor and Jane are okay?'

The edge in Paris' voice makes me internally grimace.

'He'll be fine,' I backtrack. 'They both will. You know Kor. Maddox or his clan step wrong and he'll take them down without a second thought. We just need to get there. It's too bad that link Vic picked up wasn't one of the good ones. If it had been, it could have taken us the full distance in seconds.'

Sie messages our phones from downstairs, asking if we're ready to go.

'Done in a sec,' I text back.

Paris leaves me in my clinic, closing the door behind him and I take a few seconds to myself. I'm trying to keep my head in the now, but it's hard. I triple check that I have everything I might need packed in my old-fashioned doctor's bag before I grab my backpack from by the door where I've stashed some clothes.

As I come up the hallway to the upstairs landing, I hear pounding on the front door.

Fuck. Time to go.

I race down the stairs and into the kitchen.

'You fucking ready now?' Vic hisses, the link already in his hand.

He closes his eyes and focuses on where he wants to go, and, when he opens the closet door, on the other side I can see a men's room.

I don't question his choice of locale as the others go through. I'm last and, as I cross the threshold, I hear glass breaking and the front door splintering. Heavy bootsteps pound through the house. They're looking for us. This isn't just some human neighbors taking their shot with the supes next door. This is the Order coming for us. Maybe even for Jane.

Fuck them and what they've done here.

I'm through the breach and I close the door just as I see masked figures in SWAT uniforms with AKs burst into the kitchen. A laser sight points at my chest. I hear the shot echo through the portal just as the door closes and I smile.

Too late, assholes.

The connection has already been broken.

I turn and take stock. I'm standing in the men's room in front of a cubicle.

'Did we make it to the airport?' I ask just as we hear an announcement for final boarding at Gate 12.

'Sounds like it,' Vic replies, looking in the mirror and straightening his stripey, silk tie like a reputable businessman.

We're all dressed in nondescript suits to blend in like we're a normal group of human guys on a work trip. I don't know how well that's going to work to be honest. It might have before when the humans were ignorant of us, before the world knew supes existed, but not these days. I'm not trying to be an asshole, but we don't look like human guys at all. I stare at our reflections. We look like extremely virile wolves in budget sheep costumes from a party store.

I dig out my human passport in case I'm asked for it.

'Hopefully we won't even need those until we land,' Vic mutters as he turns away from the sink. 'We should be airside already, so we don't have to worry about security either.'

He opens the door to the men's room and goes first. I follow a few seconds later, each of us exiting at a different time so we don't draw more attention than necessary.

'Which Gate?' Vic murmurs to Paris who checks his phone.

'Should be Four. We need to go to the concierge desk since it's a private flight. Come on.'

Paris takes point because he usually deals with anything public-facing. Vic walks next to him. Sie and I trail a little ways behind.

We get to the desk without incident, and Paris sorts out the details. We're asked to wait in a small lounge away from the prying eyes of the public, and we're ushered into a room overlooking the runways with contemporary décor and a staff-less bar.

There's no one else here, just us. I sit down, nervous energy making me mess around with the stethoscope that's, as always, in my jacket pocket. I'm trying to stop, but I'm nervous as shit and I keep thinking something bad is going to happen. My fears are realized when the woman from the concierge desk returns a few minutes later.

'I'm so sorry, gentlemen,' she murmurs, 'but I've just been informed that all flights are grounded until further notice.'

'Any idea why that is?' Vic asks, not moving from his chair and looking completely relaxed.

'I wasn't told, sir, but I would assume it's because of all the troubles.'

She looks uneasy and I see Vic and Sie glance at each other.

'No problem,' he says easily. 'We aren't in any massive hurry. Do you know when we might be able to fly out of here?'

'I don't know. I'm so sorry for the inconvenience, but I've been ordered to help clear the airport.'

'Of course.' Vic stands. 'I just need to confer with my colleagues.'

She leaves us with a nod.

As soon as the door closes, he kicks the seat he was just sitting in.

'Fuck!' he grinds out between clenched teeth before turning to Paris. 'We need to get on that jet.'

'But if there are no flights—'

'You know as well as I do,' Vic interrupts, 'it's not going to be all flights. We just need to talk to the right person, offer the right incentive.'

Paris nods and gets on his phone. If anyone can figure out who we need to bribe, it's him.

'What are we going to do in the meantime?' Sie asks, eyeing the door.

'We pay her to let us stay in here and we wait.'

$$\sim$$

Korban

I CAN'T BELIEVE Maddox was right. I'm blown away. Is this actually happening?

'How is this possible?' I murmur, staring at the door Jane ran through.

It hasn't been long since she fled and I know I should go after her, but I have no idea what to say, what to think.

I turn to Maddox. 'She really is a succubus?'

Maddox nods.

'How did you know?'

His eyes flick to a shelf of old books that look like they've been handled a thousand times, but he doesn't say anything out loud. The message is clear though. He's put a lot into learning about them and has been searching for one, probably for years.

He takes a step towards the door and I laugh aloud, the

sound cutting. As if I'm going to let him go after her, go anywhere near her.

'No fucking way,' I growl as I practically push in front of him and go upstairs to our room.

'She's not there.' Maddox is behind me.

I let my glamor down. It's a reflex.

'Relax. She won't listen to me anyway,' he says.

'Where the fuck is she?' I snarl, my claws lengthening.

But the crazy English fucker doesn't bat an eye. He walks to the window and gestures with his head out at the gardens.

'I think she needs some time alone.'

'You don't know her!'

He smirks. 'It's blatantly obvious, my dear chap, that neither do you. Perhaps do a bit of reading in my library before you make things worse with her.' He raises a brow. 'Actually, don't. The more you upset her, the more she's likely to seek solace with me and mine.'

I let out what can only be described as an inhuman roar in his general direction, but the asshole just grins and leaves the room.

I look out the window. She's outside, no jacket on, and heading towards the outer edges of the garden where the massive maze and no security cameras are.

'Awesome.'

I go downstairs to the kitchens where there's a door to the outside. There are a bunch of coats hanging nearby and I grab two off the hooks, throwing one on and taking the second for her.

The air outside is bitter but at least it's not raining anymore. I trudge down gravel paths past skeletal trees and old stone lawn ornaments weathered by time. There's a weird little gazebo by a stream and I go over a small stone bridge towards the entrance to the maze.

It looks massive, way bigger than it seemed from the house. The evergreen hedges are overgrown and at least fifteen feet high.

I enter, taking a deep sniff of the air and turning left when I smell her. I'm wondering what I'm going to say to her because right now I have no fucking clue. Maybe Maddox was right. Maybe I should have done my homework first. I've never met a succubus. I thought they were just stories; that maybe they hadn't even existed at all.

I keep going through the maze. The ground is wet and spongy under my boots and I errantly think her Converses weren't a good idea out here. She's probably soaked to the bone.

I walk for a few minutes, noticing her scent getting stronger, and I turn a corner and find myself in the center of the labyrinth; a big square with a fountain in the middle. She's sitting with her back to me on one of the four stone benches that form a diamond around the font. She's back in her human form.

I sit next to her without a word and I pull out the coat I brought for her, putting it around her shoulders.

She doesn't look at me.

'I'm sorry I yelled at you,' I begin, trying to think of what to say that won't piss her off even more since anger is usually the catalyst at the beginning, for incubi at least, and I don't want her changing again out here in the open. Who knows who might be watching.

I'm guessing from her reaction when she saw herself in the library that she's never changed before, which means she's not developed fully yet. At least she has me with her. My first change was the night I got jumped in the ally I was living in by a guy who wanted my shoes. I was terrified and confused and made some terrible choices afterwards. I don't want that for Jane. I need to make my presence count.

I hesitate though because I'm not sure how to do that. I need to apologize properly for how I treated her yesterday. I really messed up, but instead of fixing it then and there, I was a coward and left her upset in the shower. I put up the disco ball to say sorry, but that's something a kid would do to make things right. Am I really that emotionally stunted?

Maybe the reality is that I have no business being here right now. One of the others would be a more suitable choice, but I'm all she's got. Maybe her introduction into this life can be better than mine was.

'I'm sorry about last night too. I was a dick and you didn't deserve that,' I say, my words almost tumbling over each other. 'Thank you for letting me feed from you.'

'Did you know?' she asks, ignoring my apology completely. 'I mean, yeah Maddox said it when we were escaping his funhouse club. But I figured he was making a mistake. I didn't say anything about it at the time because I was afraid you were going to leave me there.'

She turns her head to look at me. 'But did you know about this?'

She doesn't wait for me to answer, just shakes her head.

'I don't get it. I didn't even know there were succubuses,' she mutters. 'Succubi?'

Then she frowns. 'If there are succubi, what do you need on-call girls for?'

'There aren't any ... succubi, I mean,' I say, glancing in her direction. 'Actually, it might be succubae. I'll have to look it up. But, no, I didn't know.'

'I don't understand how this is possible.'

'Me neither. I don't know much about it,' I mutter.

The truth is that I'm completely out of my depth here. Vic

should be the one to talk to her ... if there's anything to talk to her about. But I don't tell her that Maddox knows more than I do. I don't want her anywhere near him or his clan.

But she's already a step ahead of me anyway. 'Maddox has that great, big Disney library. Bet he knows some stuff. I mean, he knew what I was before I did.'

I shift on the seat. 'Just make sure I'm with you if you talk to him. Please,' I add at the end.

'Hmm,' she says absently. 'I don't like him much.'

'Good. Come on. It's freezing out here. Let's go back to the house.'

She doesn't move. 'I'm not a demon groupie.'

'What?'

She's looking at the ground. 'You thought I wanted you because of your demon side. I know you don't ... I didn't want you to feed because ...' She goes quiet. 'I'm saying this wrong.' She stands up. 'Just give me a minute to think.'

I sense her embarrassment and I hate myself for making her feel like that after she helped me, but I don't know how I can fix it.

We walk back through the maze in silence and head towards the chateau. She finally starts talking again as we get closer to the house.

'I know you didn't want to feed from me. I'm sorry that I made you. I didn't want you to because I'm addicted to incubus sex or whatever. I'm not attracted to your demon side—' She stops at that, her cheeks going pink. 'Not just your demon side, I mean.'

I scowl at her back. There's a lot to unpack besides the laughable fact that she believes she made me do something I didn't want to do. She thinks I don't like her, don't want her, that I'd rather have had another girl. Maybe that was partly true before, but it was only because I didn't want to hurt her.

I hate that I don't know what to say to her to make her feel better. And I want her to feel better. I want to undo the past, how I've made her feel. This is new to me. I don't think I've ever given a shit before.

'Want to play pool?' I ask, feeling like I'm failing her already.

'Okay,' she says.

I decide to count that as a small win.

We walk in the direction of the games room they have here, except they don't call it that. I think I heard Jeeves talking about a Billiards Room. I let out a sigh. That probably means there's a billiard's table in there and no pool table. Maddox and his hoity toity bullshit, acting like he's better than the rest of us because his family were rich as hell. Vic's rich too, but he just doesn't go in for all that crap.

I scoff to myself. Maddox and his clan probably play in smoking jackets while drinking 500-year-old brandy out of diamond glasses or some shit.

But when we go in the room, there are actually two tables. One has no pockets. And Jane looks at it in confusion.

'Billiards,' I mutter at her unasked question, happy to see that the other one looks more like what I'm used to.

'This table is huge,' she says, walking around the second table slowly.

'Yeah,' I say. 'It's for snooker. I think it's an English game. It's something like two feet bigger.'

'Can we play pool on it though?' she asks.

'Basically, if we take some of the balls away. I'll have the six colored ones and you take six of the red ones.'

I push the few remaining red balls into the table's pockets and set up the balls we'll be playing with into a triangle. I grab a cue, getting a shorter one for Jane too.

'Do you know how to play?' I ask.

She shrugs. 'I've played before a couple times. Where's the blue stuff?'

'It's here,' I say, taking the cube of chalk and rubbing it on the end of my cue. 'You do it like this.'

She watches me and then takes the cube and rubs it on the end of her cue. Then she rubs her finger in it like she can't help herself and wipes it on her jeans. She looks at me expectantly.

'You going to set up the table?'

'It's already set up. I'll break,' I say, smirking at the beginner as she stands there watching me.

I take my shot and two colored balls go in. She looks delighted. I shouldn't take advantage of this situation ... I know I shouldn't. She just found out she isn't human. She seems to be taking it well, but ... it's wrong.

I am a demon though.

'Maybe we should make this interesting,' I say casually.

She gives me a tentative smile. 'Interesting how?'

'Have any money?'

She shakes her head. 'Nope. Not a dime. Oh! Like to bet with, you mean?'

'Yeah.'

'I guess that would be more interesting.' She looks at the table, clearly thinking. 'Well, how about instead you can ask me a question and I have to answer it truthfully. If I win, I can ask you a question.'

'Okay.' I nod slowly, thinking how easy it's going to be to make this work to my advantage.

I try to think of a good question that will embarrass her. How did she lose her virginity? Has she ever taken two cocks at once? What does she do to get herself off? This is meant to be fun, but she deserves to sweat a little for agreeing to this wager. I mean, how exactly does she think she's going to beat me when she just saw my first shot? She clearly doesn't have any real understanding of how naïve she can be. Maybe someone needs to give her a friendly lesson.

I put the next ball in, but I miss the one after and I curse under my breath – force of habit from playing in bars, I guess. I grin at her. It's her turn but I'm not worried in the slightest.

She goes up to the table.

'Do you need some help?' I ask.

'No, thank you,' she says. 'You might sabotage me.'

She narrows her eyes at me and my lips twist upwards because I actually have no idea if she's serious or not, but I'm also not above using underhanded means to win.

She takes her shot, holding the cue at a really awkward angle.

I take pity on her. 'Like this,' I say, showing her with mine.

She tries again, but she misses the ball and lets out a small noise of disappointment.

I frown. I wanted to help her feel better, but now I wonder if maybe this wasn't the right thing to put her in a good mood.

I take my turn, knocking a couple more balls in their pockets.

'You're better than you were before,' she mutters. 'Oh!' She shakes her head. 'I forgot, that wasn't you. It was that other guy.'

I put my cue down on the table to pause the game, a little confused. 'What are you talking about?'

'Nothing.'

'Is it something that happened in Maddox's club?' I ask, a nasty feeling coming over me.

I haven't asked her what went on while she was lost in there yet and clearly I need to.

'Lots of stuff happened,' she says cryptically.

'Like what?'

'Uh, well Vic's dad pretended to be you and we played pool.'

I feel my blood go sluggish in my veins and I go cold all over. 'What?'

Why would Lionel Makenzie set his sights on Jane? He can't know what she is, can he?

But ...

'How did you know it was him? How did he know you?'

'He was at your fight. I didn't meet him, but we saw each other there.'

'Yeah, I remember. He was in the box.'

But I didn't take much notice of him. I was too busy trying to keep Jane away from me by kissing that shifter girl in front of her.

She gets a weird look on her face and turns back to the table and I know she's remembering it too.

'Look, Jane, I—'

She interrupts with a flinch away from me. 'He found me in the club. He was really weird. I think he needed to feed.'

I'm clenching my jaw so hard my teeth are going to start cracking any second. Now it makes sense.

'He tried something with you?'

Jane nods. 'He wanted me to go with him and then he tried to ...' She visibly shudders. 'I kept throwing glasses at him and running off. He tried to trick me. Then I found Theo, but I lost him again. I thought one of those twins was going to help, but he ended up just messing with me. I only found you when the attack began. It was not a fun night even before all the death and danger.'

'You should have said something before,' I tell her.

'Why? What do you care?'

Then her eyes flit around the room, a look of uncertainty coming over her face.

'I keep thinking ... We're not still in there, are we?' She looks like she's going to throw up.

'No,' I say firmly. 'We are definitely not still in his club.'

'But how do we know that for sure?' she whispers as if she's afraid someone's listening. 'How would we know we weren't still in there, Kor?'

I swallow hard, my name on her lips making me want to help her feel better another way entirely.

'There are clues when you're in there. You just have to figure out what they are.'

'Like what?' she asks, stepping closer.

'I don't know, it's just ... well, all doors lead somewhere, so if you open one without a clear picture in your mind of where you want to go, you'll end up somewhere really weird. Have there been any doors leading to random places here?'

She shakes her head a little.

'See? We must be in the real world.'

She looks somewhat mollified.

'You're taking all this well,' I say.

'The demon thing?'

'Yeah. The first time I changed, I freaked the fuck out.'

'You thought you were human too?'

'Yeah.' I chuckle. 'And that was a few years before the supes came out. I didn't know about any of that stuff. I didn't even know what an incubus was.'

She nods a little, her eyes getting a faraway look.

'What else happened in the club?' I ask.

She frowns. 'A lot of strange stuff. First, I was walking in a summer field and went through a forest to a cottage. That was kind of weird.'

'And then what happened?'

'I opened the door and I walked into the cottage and it was a different room to the one I saw through it, and that was when Vic's dad ...'

She makes a face and, not for the first time, I want to find Lionel Makenzie and slit his throat. I should have done that years ago. Too bad he's one of the most influential supe leaders. I'd never get away with it working on my own. Even Vic has to tread carefully around his father and his father's temper.

Jane stops talking and gets ready to take her shot. She looks a little more relaxed. Maybe she's getting into the game.

But then I notice that she holds the cue completely differently to the first time and I narrow my eyes. She shoots and the red ball goes into the corner pocket, smooth and easy. She does it again and again and again until all but one of the reds are gone. I feel my eyebrows rising higher and higher on my face until her last ball goes in and I still have three on the table.

'You fucking hustled me,' I say, feeling like an idiot for the way I spoke to her, how I tried to help her when she's easily a better player than me.

She flashes me a grin.

'Yeah,' she says without a hint of apology in her voice. 'I hustled you real good.'

She puts her cue back and claps her hands. 'You have to answer my question now. Them's the rules,' she says with unmistakable glee.

I roll my eyes. At least she does seem like she's in a much better mood now even if it is at my expense.

What dumb question is she going to ask me? Maybe why I gave her the disco ball or why I kissed that shifter girl at the fi—

'What happened to you in the house?'

I freeze, wondering if I misheard, feeling the color leaching out of my face. I take a step back from her like that's going to help.

'How do you know about that?' I ask in a barely audible whisper, unable to keep my eyes from staring into hers.

She flinches and rubs her chest. 'I overheard Maddox say that he heard that 'the house' is the reason you are the way you are.'

She knows about the house. What else does she know about me?

Stomach churning, I turn on my heel and I leave the room without a word, my head in a whirl of confusion, but, on the way past the kitchen, I have the presence of mind to at least grab the bottle of scotch that someone has left out on the countertop amongst some other random groceries.

I head up to the bedroom. Fuck Maddox. Fuck this house. Fuck that house. Fuck the assholes that put me in that house.

And fuck Jane.

CHAPTER
FOUR

Jane

I'm left holding my cue in the Billiards Room, feeling like I've done something awful, but I don't know what. I might as well have driven the cue through his heart if that mess of feelings that rolled up out of nowhere like an emotional sandstorm is anything to go by.

Miss Mercy in the Billiards Room with the shitty communication skills.

I stand by the side of the snooker table for a long time, trying to figure out why Korban is mad. Is he angry because I hustled him? Sometimes guys get upset when you make them feel stupid. Or was it my question? Whatever it was, I know it was my fault. I should tell him I'm sorry.

I put the cue gently on the table and walk towards the door. In the hall, I look both ways, but he's not there. Maybe he's gone back to our room. I make my way upstairs, thankfully not seeing any of Maddox's clan on the way. They all make me uneasy and I can't figure out why, but I feel like there's always someone watching me here.

I did get used to that with the Iron I's and I don't mind it with them, but I don't like it with these other guys. It's feels as if they're trying to force a connection with me that's just not there. They don't know me and they don't get to unless I say.

But they lost their chance to ever be bosom buddies the first time I met them.

That thought gives me pause. The Iron I's have done worse to me than Maddox and his crew have, but I want to forgive Vic and the others despite how they've treated me. That isn't right. Why do I have such a soft spot for the Iron I's even after everything? It doesn't make sense. Usually, once the trust is gone for me, it never comes back no matter what. But I can safely say that I've trusted Paris, Theo, and Sie with my life for a while. In their absence, maybe I've started trusting Korban too. I've let all four of them in in a way I've never done with anyone. The jury is still out on Vic though. In my mind, he's separate from the others. Maybe it's because he did the worst things.

I'm so deep in thought, that I'm surprised when I reach our rooms because I hardly remember getting here. The French doors are shut but that's not necessarily meant to be a deterrent. All the doors in this place are closed most of the time.

I open it slowly. I can't see inside, but I step in anyway. Kor is my only ally here and I don't want things to fester between us. I mean what if the other guys never – I break that line of thought immediately because it makes my stomach flip and my heart pound.

Inside the room, it's too dark. It's the middle of the day. Even with the curtains closed, there should still be a little light coming in.

'Kor?'

'I'm right here.' His voice is coming from deep in the black.

He's talking to me at least.

Relieved, I take a few steps into the room. I leave the door open though because there's nothing to see by at all.

'Look ... I wanted to say that I'm sorry.'

He doesn't say anything.

'Kor?'

The door shuts with an ominous creak and bang behind me and I turn with a cry, running to it. But it's not there anymore. No door. No nothing.

I hear echoing laughter and whirl around, breathing hard.

I was right. I'm still in that club.

Fuck!

I stand in the darkness. All I can hear is my heart pounding, thumping in my chest so hard I feel like it's going to explode.

'Who's there?' I cry.

Is this Kor messing with me? Is this retaliation for making him so mad? There are tears falling down my cheeks and I close my eyes as the darkness gets to me and I start to panic.

I feel something brush against my face and I throw myself back. There's more laughter.

I clench my jaw, forcing myself to open my eyes because I can't just stand here in ... wherever this is.

I'm met with a grotesque face inches from my own, lit up by a flashlight under his chin. I scream and turn to run, but his hand slides into my hair and wrenches me back.

It's not Kor, I realize. It's one of those twins, the one that fucked with me in the club. I'm pulled against a hard chest, his head towering over mine and growing taller as he lets down his glamor.

'I heard you like demons filling you up,' he murmurs in my ear from behind me, holding me tight against him.

He twirls us around in some weird, fucked-up parody of a dance and smacks me against the wide edge of what I think is a table. I hit it hard enough for it to grind across the floor a couple of inches and for me to definitely be left with a long, straight bruise along the front of my thighs. The wind is knocked out of me as I'm pushed down over it hard, my head knocking into the cold, smooth veneer.

I try to get up but he holds me down, his other hand skating down my spine and over by ass, which he grabs and then brushes against my core through my jeans.

What the hell is this?

'You like that?' he whispers.

'No,' I growl strong and loud through my teeth. 'I don't fucking like it.'

'You don't?'

Does he sound confused?

He doesn't move and he doesn't touch me again, though he's still holding me by the base of my neck. There's more laughter. It bounces off the walls around me, but I realize I'm not afraid anymore. This guy is just a pathetic asshole using tricks to mess with my head.

I feel a change in my body. Strength. Energy. Anger. Is this the demon? My demon? Fury is coursing through my veins like molten lava. This is exactly how it felt before in the library.

The twin is pissing me off with all his manhandling; him and all the other guys, supe or otherwise, who think that touching me or attacking me is okay. I don't have to take this. I don't have to pretend to go along with anything so nothing worse happens anymore. I don't have to give him or anyone else what they want.

What about what I want?

Ok, so I don't know what I want, but I know what I don't want and I'm a fucking demon. That means something.

I rear back as hard as I can, using the table as leverage and smashing him in the nose with my head. I hear the crack and his grunt of pain.

I stretch. I think I might be taller, but I can't be sure. It should feel weird, changing like this, but it doesn't at all. It's like every time I've ever looked in the mirror, she's been staring back at me. I just couldn't see her. I don't feel alien in this skin. I feel like I've come home. I lengthen my spine, my wings.

OMG, I have wings! They feel huge.

I beat them hard, driving the twin away, and making the air whirl around me but, disappointingly, my feet don't leave the ground.

Maybe I have to exercise them, I think errantly as I fold them away and I turn to deal with this mofo who thought he could touch me.

I don't see him, but he's still in here somewhere. I can actually smell him.

I hear him bang into something and I lash out in that direction. There's no more laughter now.

'What's the matter?' I taunt, echoing his words to me. 'Don't you like this?'

I stalk him through the darkness, feeling powerful and I realize that I'm not blind in here anymore. I can see better in this form.

It just keeps getting better and better.

He's by the wall, still as a statue. He's watching me, thinking I can't see him back.

I walk that way, pretending to head for the door out of his little funhouse. I go right past him, but, at last moment, I grab him by the shoulders and I kick him right in the balls so fucking hard I wouldn't be surprised if he coughs up a couple of walnuts.

I'm so strong now. That and the power I feel is a heady combination. This demon body is pretty awesome.

He makes a strange little whimper as he cups his junk and sinks to his knees, his body falling to the side and thudding to the floor.

I could have taken him down another way, but this seemed more fitting. Plus, he clearly didn't expect it at all.

I stand over him. 'Don't touch me again. Don't talk to me. Don't even look in my general direction. To you, I don't exist.'

'I fucking knew you'd be magnificent,' he hisses through the pain, ignoring my words completely. 'Choose my clan, Jane. We'll give you everything you've ever wanted, everything you need.'

Confused and disgusted, I turn away, replaying this whole sequence of events in my head from the moment I walked in this room to now, trying to work out what the point of this was because that sounded like some kind of proposal. And I thought Maddox's was weird.

What is wrong with these guys?

He grabs onto my ankle and tries to pull me back towards him. I wrench myself away with a curse and kick him in the face. Then I kick him in the stomach too, just for good measure.

'I said don't fucking touch me. I don't want your clan,' I say. 'Stay away from me or next time I'll kill you.'

I'm pretty sure I can do that. I've got mad demon skills.

I wrench open the door and leave the room, finding myself out in the hallway again and somehow in the complete opposite wing to where I thought I was.

I'm sure I went the right way before.

Fucking trickster asshole.

I stalk down the hallway, my heavier body thudding across the landing where the grand staircase is to the other side of the house.

I pass a mirror and I stop. Of course! I'm still in my newfangled demon form!

I have a demon form.

It's going to take some time to get my head around that, I think as I take in my appearance. I am taller and ripped as hell. I put my arms up and kiss my guns. I'm beautiful. Not in a human way. Any human who saw me like this would be terrified, but I love the way I look as much as how I feel. My skin is smooth, a lavender color that shimmers in the light. My hair is wavy and dark, almost black, but if I look closely it's actually a kind of a deep, midnight purple.

I watch my own reflection as I try to make the demon recede at will the way the guys can. They don't have to get mad every time they change, so maybe I won't have to either if I can get the hang of it. I gasp, feeling giddy as it works, the demon melting away and leaving me in my human form. I go back and forth a couple of times just to make sure I can do it whenever I want. I thought there'd be some kind of learning curve, but it's actually really easy when I'm focused.

Wax on, wax off. Wax on, wax off.

I feel powerful for the first time probably ever. Nobody can fuck with me. I'm a big, bad demon, bitches! I grin in a self-satisfied way as I twist around to look at my back.

I realize belatedly that the clothes I was wearing disappeared with my human body. I'm naked in this form and my ass is so toned! I don't have a tail like Vic and Sie though.

That is a little disappointing.

I wrinkle my nose, but I open my wings instead and just stand there in the middle of the hall, gazing at them in awe.

I flap them a little, knocking over what is probably a Ming vase or something equally as valuable from the little table in front of the mirror. It falls to the floor and breaks in two.

I grimace.

It's not too bad. A little superglue would probably fix that right up ...

I look around and back away, hoping there's not a camera on me right now as I put the demon back in the box and walk from the scene quickly.

I get to our actual room and go in tentatively just in case there are any more surprises lurking.

The curtains are drawn just like they were in the other room, but I'm not scared. After what I did to that twin just now, I know that if anyone else messes with me I can totally just rip off their arms and beat them to death with 'em.

I see the top of Kor's head peeking out from over the side of the bed where he's sitting on the floor.

I watch him take a long draw from a bottle, which puts me on edge even though I'm a badass bitch. Historically, I've been even less able to predict the actions of drunk dudes than I have sober ones and that's saying something. Drinking usually means danger, but, and maybe it's because I know my demon is strong as hell or maybe it's because I'm starting to realize that where Kor is concerned, I kind of like the danger, I step forward. There's a little voice in my head telling me this is a dumb idea, but I hush it like a baby.

Fear of bodily harm is in the past now. New Jane is way too awesome to care about that stuff.

But I still throw myself into my apology headfirst, the words tumbling out of my mouth as if I'm afraid I won't be able to say them if I don't rush, or I'll get interrupted. New Jane still has the social anxiety, I guess.

'I'm sorry. I know you're upset, but please could you tell

me what I did? I don't actually know and I don't want to keep doing it so ...'

Suddenly, I'm close to tears, but that can't be right. I'm a badass.

'Are you angry with me because I hustled you?' I ask low so he won't hear if my voice does break.

I draw closer so I can see him better. The feelings coming from him are raw and gnarled, despair tinged with rage and self-loathing. Maybe I should ...

He rubs his face and lets out a nasty laugh that makes me wince and third guess being in here with him.

'No, sweetheart, I'm not mad because you hustled me.'

He's hurting. I can feel it inside. I can't leave him like this. Tentatively, I sit down on the plush carpet in front of him. I figure if he's calling me sweetheart, he can't be that mad. But if it wasn't the hustle, it must be something else.

'So it was the question?'

'I don't want to talk about it,' he says.

I sit back a little. He's the kind of person who keeps all the bad stuff inside. He pushes it down and lets it fester and grow. I know how all that darkness is making me feel, so it must be way worse for him.

Poor Korban.

'But you lost the game,' I say, deciding that logic is the best way to do this, not emotions.

I have to at least try to help.

He looks at me, his eyes cutting. Anger bursts up and out of him like a geyser and makes me shuffle back. Where Theo's emotions were like an unstoppable tidal surge of gooey, nice feels, this is an eruption of noxious gases.

'I don't have to answer you,' he snarls.

I manage a shrug. 'I don't make the rules.'

I hold my ground under his intense stare. I feel the confusion he feels. He doesn't know what to make of me. But I press on. Even if he doesn't want me, he's still my friend and sometimes you have to be cruel to be kind, use the tough love. He needs to deal with whatever is making him feel this way because he clearly hasn't. I mean others in the supe community have noticed and talk about him behind his back. No one likes that happening to them, not even Kor.

'I won the game,' I continue. 'I got to ask the question. You have to answer and you have to tell the truth.'

He surges to his feet and I look up at him as he towers over me. He's trying to scare me ... and it's working.

Shit, he's big and he's not even in demon form.

I hastily get to my feet too. Maybe this wasn't a good idea after all. I was on a high after putting that twin in his place, but Kor is way more intimidating to me than anyone on Maddox's crew.

'It's okay,' I say, backtracking like a pro. 'You don't have to play by the rules if you don't want to.'

I turn to leave, but he grabs me by the shoulder and wrenches me back hard. Before I know it, I'm pushed onto the bed. I lay there for a second, stunned, not sure if I should try to run.

I decide not to. I doubt I'll get far anyway.

That time Kor caught me in the forest comes to mind again. This isn't really the same though and not just because I'm on a bed, not a pile of leaves. Maybe it's because he doesn't feel like a stranger anymore.

Whatever the difference is, my body is responding to him already and he knows it.

'You like this, don't you?' he hisses.

I don't say anything, not sure what he wants to hear, but wishing he didn't know how my traitorous body seems to crave him when he is clearly not attracted to me in the same way.

I lay there watching him. He snatches up the bottle and drains it. How much of that has he drank? I know shifters find it really hard to get intoxicated because of their fast metabolisms, but I don't know about incubi and I wonder if he's going to keel over and pass out next to me in a minute.

Would I be relieved or disappointed if he did?

He throws the bottle down on the bed beside me. 'Don't move,' he orders and I swallow hard, but I do as he says and I stay still as he slowly unbuttons my jeans and pulls them off me.

'W—What are you doing?' I stammer.

'Whatever I want,' he growls low. 'Nobody's going to help you here.'

AAAAANNNNNND I've made it to another kink level. Holy shit! Am I into this?

Yes. Yes, I am. It's scary, but so, so hot!

He surges forward with a snarl, pushing me down into the bed with his forearm.

I struggle to get up, but he pins me easily, anchoring me with his weight. I look up at his face and my eyes widen because I can't move and old Jane is starting to panic.

I shake my head a little and I open my mouth, but no words come out. I feel something cold at my entrance and I cast my eyes to the bed next to me.

The bottle is gone.

He can't—

I give a little cry as he pushes the neck of it into me as far as it will go in one swift move. I gasp as he draws it out and thrusts it back in again. It glides in easily and he notices that as well. He does it a few more times and when my only reaction is to moan, he pulls the bottle out and casts it to the carpet. It hits with a muffled thud.

'You like being threatened? You like being scared? It's time I showed you the real me, princess. The me who's going to make you scream and run just like you wanted to when I fed from you that night in Metro and Paris had to keep me from crushing your pretty throat.'

At first, I think he's going to let down his glamor, but he reaches into his jacket and pulls out his Colt 45 instead. I peer at it; sturdy and black, the barrel ridged in places.

I don't think he's going to kill me. But, the truth is, I don't know what he's going to do. I look away.

I jump with a cry when I feel it, the cold metal grinding against my slit and my eyes fly back to his.

He can't—

A moan bursts from my lips.

'Fuck,' he growls. 'You're so much more depraved than I thought you'd be.'

Our gazes lock.

'Maybe I just trust you,' I breathe.

'You shouldn't.'

But he doesn't stop like he did with the bottle. His gun keeps moving up and down, cold and hard, scary and hot.

'I've killed people like you,' he says low.

'Not like me,' I correct.

He lets out a breath and the gun leaves me. I'm equal parts thankful and frustrated, but then he takes the barrel and lines it up between my legs. The gleam in his eye makes me swallow hard in anticipation.

But, this time, he's gentle and I know it's because he doesn't really want to hurt me. He eases the boom boom end inside me, and I don't know if it's because it's his gun or because he's fucking me with A GUN!, but I've never been so turned on in my life.

He twists it, pushing it in further. Fucking me leisurely with a loaded pistol and I love it. I spread my legs apart, giving him more access and he looks surprised, but I don't care if he knows I'm kinky AF. I can feel my muscles clenching. I'm so close! My hand moves down, but he slaps it away hard.

'Don't you fucking dare,' he snaps and he turns the gun inside me so the handle is resting against my clit.

He uses it to massage in small circles that get bigger and faster.

He's getting me off with a weapon that can kill me.

I buck hard under him, biting my lip but the scream comes out anyway and I come all over his gun. My body is on fire in the best way and I feel like I'm floating in a sea of sensation.

As the pleasure ebbs, I flop back into the bed, my brain practically short circuiting as he takes his weapon out. He stares into my eyes and licks up the barrel with a dark grin. Then, he gives it a wipe and puts it back in his jacket.

'Don't you need to ... clean it properly?' I ask quietly.

'I just did this morning.'

'I don't think it's going to work right after that,' I mutter.

'Why don't you let me worry about keeping my weapons in good condition after I fuck you with them.'

My mouth goes dry. He's thinking we might do that again?

My head gets locked in that naughty ouroboros of thought. Guns, knives, batons, arrows – no not arrows. That wouldn't work.

'You want to know about the house?' he asks, clearly having moved on from the weapons thing. 'Fucking fine.'

He sits down on the bed and then sinks down next to me, his hand playing with my bare thigh in gentle touches that feel nice. He lets out a deep breath.

'I matured early for an incubus,' he begins. 'I was fourteen. I grew up in an orphanage. Never knew my family. Anyway, it wasn't a great place and I left one night when things got shittier than usual. Went out the window and I didn't go back.'

He's quiet for a minute, but I don't say anything. I get the impression that he rarely, if ever, tells this story and I don't want to break the bubble.

'I was on the streets for a while. Not doing too good. I met a woman. She was human. I'd been starving for weeks, dumpster diving for scraps near restaurants. But no amount of food eased the ache. I didn't know what I was. Like I said before, I didn't even know about supes back then. I didn't understand how she knew what I needed, but she did. She took me to a house. A nice house. She fed me good food and she let me shower.'

He lets out a sigh. 'And she came to me that night. She told me what I was. She helped me through the shock of it. She was ... kind to me. I thought it was okay. She made me feel good. I fed. I realized what I actually needed ... and she got high.'

He stops again and I slip my hand into his. He looks down at it, surprised I think because I so rarely initiate contact on my own.

'It was just her at first,' he continues, 'but then it was others too. I was kept in a room. They chained me up after I tried to leave on my own and got as far as the road. Usually ... usually it was human women, a little older and richer. They'd come. They'd do things. They'd make me do things. I'd feed even when I didn't want to. If I tried to resist ...' He goes silent for a second. 'Well, let's just say they had ways of making me do what they wanted. They could make me perform.'

'But you escaped.' I say.

'Yeah, turns out when you're an incubus feeding as much as I was, containing you is hard. I broke the chains a few months later during one of her parties of rich folk.' He smiles darkly. 'I killed them all and I burned the house to the ground.'

I'm quiet, taking in all he's told me. If that bitch and her friends were still alive, I'd kill them for him.

'I'm glad you got revenge,' I say.

He's surprised. 'You don't think it was wrong?'

'No. They sound like they deserved it.' I turn towards him a little. 'Is that why you don't like human women? Is that why you don't like me?' I ask.

'I like you just fine.' His hand grips mine a little tighter. 'And I think you like me just fine too.'

There's a change in his voice and I can't help but scramble up because I notice the difference, that darkness I can feel. His demon side is coming out to play.

He grabs me before I can choose flight and hauls me onto him.

'I think you're going to like this, succubus.'

I'm scared all over again, but I'm excited too.

'You do enjoy being made to submit. You're a very naughty, naughty girl, Jane.'

I shake my head.

'You pretend to be all innocent but face it. You like fucking demons. You love it. Admit it.'

I shake my head again. I'm not sure why I can't divulge it to him. I am a demon. Like, it makes sense ...

Suddenly, his hard cock is surging into me and I freeze at

73

the unexpected intrusion. My brain gets confused for a second, playing catch-up.

I can't stop what's happening.

But I don't want him to stop.

My body begins to move with his, and I ride him, using my new-found strength. I'm a little afraid that he won't like it because of what he's just told me, but I needn't have worried. He loves what I do and he returns it.

I scratch up and down his back, move my body roughly over his, hold him tightly between my thighs and I leave bruises where I touch him. He does the same to me and my body sings in pleasure and pain.

Gritting my teeth, I fight the urge to lock my mouth on him and taste his blood. I put my hands around his throat and I squeeze.

He comes hard, gripping my hips so tightly it hurts and, as he finishes inside me, I can't help coming again myself. My body spasms, every muscle clenching up tight, and I drop down to kiss him. At the last moment, though, I can't stop myself. I dip down further, sinking my teeth into his chest.

He's mine!

The thought is primal. Instinctual. Triumphant.

And then my head begins to clear and my eyes widen at the teeth marks I've left, at the trail of blood trickling down his torso, the pleasant tang of it in my mouth.

I scramble away.

'I'm sorry,' I say in dismay.

I don't really know what it is that I've done, but it's bad. I think I've taken something from him that he didn't consent to giving me. Again.

I did the same thing to Paris and Theo too, but I had no idea what I was doing ...

I feel sick.

'I'm so sorry,' I say again.

I jump off the bed and I run into the bathroom. I slam the door behind me and lock it.

I'm no different than the woman who found him on the streets and pimped him out.

Stupid, stupid, stupid!

What have I done?

I was so upset about him not wanting me, but this is much worse. He won't even want to be my friend after this. He probably thinks I'm even more fucked up than I was before.

My chin quivers.

I'm alone and it's my own fault.

There's a pounding on the door.

'Please leave me alone,' I call out brokenly.

'No.'

He kicks it in and I squeal as he bursts into the bathroom.

I back up, my teary eyes wide, wondering what he's going to say, what he's going to do.

Whatever it is, I deserve it.

But he just gathers me to him. At first, I'm afraid that he wants to fuck again, but he doesn't start anything. Instead, he takes me into the bed, tucks me in, and then gets in on the other side.

He puts his arm around me.

I snuggle against him because I can't help it. I'm weak where he's concerned and need comfort too badly to care where it comes from.

I grip onto him, my breathing hard and my body shaking a little.

'I'm sorry,' he says quietly. 'That was too much.'

'No, it's me,' I say. 'I'm sorry I pushed you into telling me your story. I'm sorry I did that to you.'

'Silly girl,' he mutters. 'You didn't make me do anything. I'm glad you know.'

'You don't understand. It wasn't just that. I bit you and—'

'So?'

He looks down at the crescent indentation of my teeth on his peck and I'm surprised when I feel pride coming off him. He's happy I did that on some deep, instinctual level.

He doesn't understand. Neither do I really, but ...

'It's not just a bite.' I look at him, just able to see his face in the gloom.

'What is it then?'

Permanence. Forever. A symbol that we're locked together or something like that.

But I'm a coward, so I say, 'I don't know.'

'I hope you're not sorry about everything we just did because we're going to be doing it again very soon.'

'I thought ... I thought you didn't ...' I break off, not sure how to say it without coming off as pathetic as I feel.

'I'm an asshole to pretty much everyone, Jane, and I'm not good with this stuff. But I like you. I like being with you.'

'So we're friends?' I ask, not wanting to misunderstand anything.

'We're more than friends, princess.'

Even though I'm still upset, his words calm something deep inside me that I didn't really understand was tense.

'Thank you for the disco ball,' I murmur.

'I'm glad you like it,' he rumbles.

I close my eyes and the smell of him, the feel of him, washes over me.

Who would have thought it would be Korban who made me feel like this?

~

Paris

I FEEL like I've been on the phone for hours. Luckily, the human woman, Marcie, who's working on the concierge today has nothing against supes and is a little short of cash these days, so she's been keeping it on the down low that we're hiding out in the VIP lounge.

There are people coming and going on the asphalt and I've seen planes landing. I've seen a couple take off too. Vic was right. It isn't all planes.

I end the call with a fist clenched in triumph.

'I think it's done,' I say to the others. 'There's a pilot who's willing to fly us out of here and across to Europe, but we only have a small window to leave. We need to go as soon as he sends me the details.'

I glance at Vic with a wince. 'And I just spent a fucking ton of money to make this happen.'

'The money doesn't matter. Only getting to Jane matters. Good job.'

Vic puts a hand on my shoulder as he strides past me to peer out of the large window. 'Where's the plane?'

'I'll know in a minute,' I say, trying to hide how much his praise affects me.

I know I'm practically glowing like a little kid though. I clear my throat and take a quick shot at the bar to man-up.

A message comes through on my phone, giving me the info on the jet and I look out across the asphalt.

'That's our plane,' I tell them, pointing to the sleek Falcon 8X that's by one of the hangers.

Vic nods. 'That'll do.'

'How are we getting to it?' Sie asks.

Vic goes out the door to the concierge desk to talk to Marcie. He comes back a minute later.

'She can get us over there, but we have to go now.'

Without a word, we pick up all our bags and go down in the elevator that takes us to ground level. The doors are all security locked of course, but Marcie comes out from behind a 'Do Not Enter' sign a minute later.

'You guys are lucky I still have the codes to these,' she says, punching numbers into the keypad by one of the doors, 'or you'd be shit out of luck. Management changed the policy last month and now only Security are supposed to have access, but the dumbasses haven't changed the numbers.'

She chuckles as the door unlocks and she eases it open.

'Come on. I need to walk you over,' she says.

'What if someone sees us?' Sie asks.

'It won't matter if I'm with you. I deal with all the high-profile guests so no one will think anything of it.'

'Thank you, Marcie,' Vic says.

'Like I said. No one will look twice,' she shrugs. 'Besides, you're paying me.'

Vic flashes her a grin and she blushes.

Yeah, money is not the only reason she's helping us, I think with a roll of my eyes.

She does what she says, walking us across the airport to the hangers where the jet we saw from the terminal sits waiting.

The engines are already warming up. The captain nods to us from the top of the steps leading into the aircraft. He's about to break a bunch of laws, and he'll probably never be able to pilot again, which is why it just cost us a shit ton to get him on board. But he and his plane will take us where we need to go.

'Can this tin can really get us all the way to Europe?' Sie mutters next to me.

'Further than that if we wanted,' I reply.

78

He gives a noncommittal grunt and climbs the steps, Theo following him silently. They each give a nod to the pilot as they disappear inside.

I scan the airport. Everything looks calm, as if a bunch of supes and humans didn't die in this city only hours ago.

'Well, thanks again,' Vic says, giving Marcie a small salute.

She gives him a thumbs up and turns away, but swings back.

'Look, I know what you are.'

Vic and I share a wary look.

'I want you to know,' she continues, 'not all of us agree with those red-robed psychos. There are problems, sure. But, hell, half my husband's family are part sprite and a lot of families are like that these days. Things are bad right now.' She looks away. 'I wouldn't have even come into work today if I didn't need the money.' She puts a hand on Vic's forearm. 'But the Order are going to realize real soon that people aren't just going to sit back and let their families get ripped apart.'

'Thank you,' Vic says, putting his hand on hers and giving her just a little euphoria.

Her lips part on a gasp. 'Shit,' she breathes, 'I can see why people get addicted to that.'

Her radio blares something I don't understand and she's back to business in a millisecond. She looks up at us sharply.

'Get on the plane and get in the air.'

'Security?'

'No, a ton of Humvees just busted through the west perimeter fence and they sure as shit aren't here for me.'

'Will you be safe?' Vic asks her.

She scoffs at him. 'Demon, please.'

She sets off back the way she brought us and we board quickly.

'Captain, we need to go now. The authorities know we're here.'

'Yes, sir.'

The doors close. There's no flight crew; just us, the captain, and his co-pilot. I requested that specifically. No point putting anyone else's lives at risk.

We both stow our luggage and take our seats. It's only a few seconds before the engines rev and we start to taxi towards one of the runways.

The captain speaks though the intercom. 'We're taking off in just a minute,' he says.

We sit in our seats, looking out the windows in silence.

'Shit,' Vic mutters, pointing.

There's a rush of vehicles coming down the runway towards us; black hummers and police cars. The Iron I's really are public enemy number one right now and, if they've got the human cops on their side, I guess that means the Order is fully in control of Metro now.

The captain eases up and the plane slows.

I get out of my seat, afraid he's going to change his mind.

I go to the cockpit door and knock. It opens.

'Get us in the air and I'll double your fee.'

The two humans look at each other. The co-pilot shrugs.

'I've been wanting to retire,' he says to his colleague.

The Captain gives a nod of agreement.

'Get back in your seat and send us our money,' he says, not even bothering to be polite.

I'm just sinking into the chair when the plane goes full-throttle, the G-force throwing me down into it. I fumble with my seatbelt, getting it on as the plane lifts and tilts.

And we're up in the air, flying over the line of vehicles like this is a fucking movie.

I breathe a sigh of relief and I see the others doing the same.

'Thank fuck,' Vic mutters, staring down at the SUVs that are sitting on the runway.

But as I look towards the ground, I notice something coming towards the plane.

Before I can warn the others, there's an explosion and we pitch to the side. I fold myself at the waist and brace as the plane lurches and then takes a nose-dive, pulling up at the last second. I feel the wheels thud into the ground and look around. There's smoke coming from the left engine. The whole thing's on fire.

We grind to a halt and I sit in my seat for a moment, trying to make sense of what just happened.

I glance around the cabin. It isn't broken apart, or anything. I guess we didn't get high enough. The others look mostly unhurt, but Sie's just staring out the window, his face blank and his hands clutching his thighs. Vic is looking around and taking off his seatbelt. Theo is already up and at the door to the cockpit asking the pilot if they're hurt. The door opens and he goes through.

I get up and peer out the window. They're already surrounding the plane and putting out the fire in the engine.

'Vic?'

He knows what I'm going to say, pulling the link key from his breast pocket and putting it on the door at the back that leads to the bathroom.

He opens the door, but all that's behind it is the plane's bathroom.

He tries again, but nothing happens. 'Shit.'

'Why isn't it working?' I grind out, clutching my laptop bag to me.

'I don't know. Fucking fae!'

He whirls around, taking out his gun and checking the clip. I do the same, but I shake my head. We're going to die out here.

'We aren't getting out of this if we start a fire fight,' Sie says, putting his gun on the table.

'What do you suggest then?' Vic asks with a sneer. 'Let them kill us in cold blood without even trying to defend ourselves? What about Jane? What about Kor?'

Sie puts his hand on Vic's shoulder. 'Look outside. Those are human cops. They still have to follow the law. I say we take our chances with them now and escape later.'

Theo comes out of the cockpit, wiping blood from his hands on a small, white towel.

'The captain and the co-pilot need medical attention,' he says.

Vic lets out a low growl. 'Fine. Put your guns next to Sie's and open the door.'

He looks at me, or, more specifically, at my laptop bag. 'They won't be able to get anything off that, right?'

I shake my head, putting down the bag and putting my gun on the table with Sie's. 'As soon as they fire it up, it'll be wiped. They won't get anything but gibberish.'

Theo pushes the door open and backs away. We all raise our hands as we're told to exit the aircraft slowly.

Vic goes first and Theo follows. I'm last and Sie exits in front of me with a slight spring in his step as if he's just glad to be getting off the plane. I trail after.

Outside, I go down the steps and see the others already in cuffs. Theo's telling them about the injured crew and we're bundled into separate cars with tinted windows.

So far, so good. It doesn't seem like they're going to gun us down. I errantly hope Marcie doesn't get into trouble for helping us as the cars start to move and we're taken back into the city.

I'm alone. My hands are cuffed to the table with iron strong enough to keep me bound even if I change. I narrow my eyes at the two-way mirror in front of me.

'You can't hold us here without charge,' I say at my reflection. 'Where's my fucking phone call?'

I don't know where the others are, but I assume they're in similar interview rooms to this one.

They got us here quick. Taking us off the plane and away from the airport with no more ceremony than reading us our rights. I thought they came for us at the airport because someone tipped them off that some supes were trying to leave, but now, sitting in the Metro PD, I think they knew who we were.

What I don't know is why we've been brought here and no one's been forthcoming about that so far.

The door opens and two very human detectives saunter in. Both are male and both look like they have something to prove to the demon cuffed in front of them.

'I'm Detective Davis and this is Detective White. We'd like to ask you a few questions, Mr. Deloitte.'

White drops a manila folder in front of me and taps his phone.

'Interview with Paris Deloitte, zero six-hundred hours. Detectives Davis and White in attendance.'

'What the hell is this?' I growl. 'I want to speak with Artic.'

'The Chief was killed in the rioting,' Davis says, not looking up from the folder as he sits down.

White joins him, grinning at me. He has the upper hand and he knows it. That puts me on edge.

'Where is my clan?' I ask.

'Right now? They're in holding, but they'll have their turn with us. Don't you worry.'

He turns the folder and opens it.

'We have reason to believe that the Iron I's have been engaged in illicit activities for a while now. Money laundering, racketeering, prostitution, arms dealing to name a few.'

I stare at him for a minute, wondering where they're pulling all this shit from because the Iron I's have never done any of that stuff. I mean we're not saints, but we deal mostly in black market fae imports, none of the stuff he's talking about.

'Let me make this easy,' Davis says.

He shows me his partner's phone and I see that the interview isn't being recorded at all.

'We don't need a confession. We don't need anything from you, demon. Everyone in this city knows the Iron I's are in the middle of some shady shit and, thanks to the riots and some key officers getting killed – may they rest in peace – the cops who actually care about doing the right thing in this city are able to get things done a little quicker around here when it comes to getting criminals off the streets.'

I'm getting a bad feeling that we're going to need our lawyers ASAP.

'I want my phone call,' I say.

Davis and his partner grin.

'How can you make a call, Deloitte? You aren't even here.' White laughs and stands up, leaving the interview room with Davis.

'I want my phone call,' I yell, but the door bangs shut on my words.

I wait in the room for another ninety minutes at least, getting more and more anxious as time ticks by.

I pull at the iron, but it's reinforced with magick too strong even for the demon to break.

The door opens and a couple of uniformed officers come in. They disconnect the cuffs from the table and lead me out into the hall, taking me down the corridor to the back of the building.

'You know what your superiors are doing here?' I try, but they just laugh.

'Finally cleaning up this city by getting rid of scumbag supes like you,' one answers, giving me a push through a door that leads downstairs to the cells.

They take me down in an old elevator with a flickering light.

'Welcome to holding until you get your ride out of here.'

I'm put behind bars and I see that Theo and Vic are already here, sitting on a bench at the back.

I look around. There are at least twenty cells down here. Most are empty, but I can smell death and blood.

'You guys okay?' I ask.

They both nod, but don't say anything until the guards leave.

'Jane said this place was pretty full when she was put down here,' I murmur.

Vic gestures with his head to the wall above his head and I realize that what I assumed was just years of grime and wear is actually dried blood splatter and bullet divots in the concrete.

'Looks like they took most of them out last night.'

'While they were trapped in the cells?' I ask out loud.

Vic snorts. 'Shooting fish in a barrel.'

'Shit. Is that what they're planning for us?'

Theo shakes his head. 'I heard one of the sergeants upstairs talking about a prison transport.' He stands up and walks to the front of the cell, looking down at the elevator at the end. 'They're moving us to the Mountain.'

My eyes widen. 'But they can't do that! What about due process? The Mountain is for the worst supe criminals, and not just from the human realm either.'

'Look around!' Vic says. 'They can do whatever they want. Didn't you notice upstairs? No supes anywhere. Every single cop was human. There's nobody here to fight our corner for us and none of those officers give a shit who we are.'

I hear the elevator ping and it opens. Sie is inside flanked by two guards. They bring him down the row and throw him in with us. They lock the door and turn to leave.

'You can't do this!' I yell, but the guards just walk back to the elevator laughing.

Sie lets out a rumble and sits on the bench.

'Did you get interviewed by the two cops?' I ask him.

He nods. 'White and Davis.'

'So what's your plan now that they're taking us to the Mountain?' Vic asks, lounging back on the bench and then thinking the better of it because he's just put his head in a bunch of dried-up blood spray from the supe prisoners who were killed in here last night. Instead, he leans forward, resting his elbows on his thighs and steepling his fingers.

Sie doesn't look happy at being called out. 'There's no time to try getting out from here. The transport has already arrived.'

'Then what are we going to do?' I ask, feeling panic rising. 'No one escapes from the Mountain. This was a dumb idea. We should have fought our way out of the plane.'

'And we'd be gone, Kor would be dead, and Jane would be Maddox's,' Theo says. 'There never was any choice and there isn't now either. We can't get out of here.'

'I'm guessing they took the link key off you,' I say to Vic.

He nods.

We hear the elevator ping again. The doors open and a man in a suit walks slowly down the row. Two officers are with him, but when he's about halfway to us, they hang back and he approaches by himself.

Even in front of our cell, we can't see his face clearly, but Sie's glamor is down and he's already reaching through the bars, snarling in rage before I can blink.

'I know it's you, Foley. I can fucking smell you, you son of a bitch!'

The man in front of us takes a ring off his finger and I can finally see his features as he tuts at Sie, waving back the guards that have started forward with their cattle prods.

'You always did have a decent nose, Sie.' Foley chuckles, looking him over. 'Too bad your ears weren't so good, or you might not have so many punishment scars from your fighting days, huh?'

Sie takes another swipe at Foley with a snarl, but he's just out of reach.

'Been putting all those fae artifacts you stole to good use, I see,' Vic says, standing and crossing the cell like he's taking a stroll.

'Told you I'd be seeing you, demon,' Foley sneers. 'Bet you didn't think you'd be on the wrong side of a jail cell.'

I eye the officers. 'How did you even get in here? Last I heard, the Metro PD hadn't officially allied itself with the Order.'

Foley shrugs. 'It's like your president said, I've been putting the artifacts I've stolen to good use.'

I look at the guards. Surely they can hear Foley admitting his crimes.

'Don't worry about them,' he says. 'They think they're in the break room. They won't even remember I was here.'

'What the hell do you want?' Vic asks.

'I heard you were caught at the airport trying to run.' Foley grins. 'Too bad we missed you at Julian Maddox's club, huh? But I guess you saw some of the fun when it spilled out onto the streets.' He looks at the empty cells around us. 'Looks like some purging was done down here too.'

'Killing innocents isn't really how we get our kicks,' I grind out, remembering the screams that echoed through the club when the Order began their slaughter.

'I also heard my girl wasn't with you,' he continues, ignoring me completely. 'Tell me, demons, where is my retarded whore of a daughter?'

I clench my fists and I see the others are just as angry at Foley's words as I am.

'Don't you fucking talk about her like that!' Sie snarls.

'She's mine. I'll talk about her any way I want!'

'She's not yours,' I growl just as angrily as Sie.

'Wow, you're a real Father Of The Year,' Vic drawls.

'Fuck you, Makenzie,' Foley hisses. 'You don't know me.'

'Why do you want to know where she is? You don't give a shit about her.'

Foley makes an effort to control his temper, running a hand through his salt and pepper hair and taking a breath.

'And you do?' he scoffs more calmly with a roll of his eyes. 'As if you hell spawn even have the capacity.'

His expression twists, full of hatred, and I grip the bars in front of me. If I could get to him right now, I'd rip him apart.

'She's not with us anymore,' Theo says, coming to stand next to me. 'She left.'

'Tell me where she is and maybe I can do something about getting you out of here.' Foley's eyes narrow. 'You're out of time. The prison transport is already here for you. You know where they're sending you, right? I hear most supes who get sent to the Mountain die within the first twenty-four hours. Give me my daughter, I unlock this cage, and your clan is safe.'

I look around at Vic. I'd rather take my chances in the Mountain than let Foley anywhere near Jane, and I know Theo and Sie feel the same.

Sie opens his mouth to speak, but Vic stops him and, for a horrible moment, I'm afraid our president is going to tell Foley where Jane is to get us out of here. The Club always comes first for him.

Vic approaches the bars, looking Foley up and down. Then, he shrugs. 'She left a couple of nights ago. Sneaked out of the house and we haven't seen her since. We can't help you.'

'You're a fool.' Foley shakes his head, giving a small laugh. 'But I already knew that. Anyway, it doesn't matter. I've found her before. I'll do it again. Have fun in the Mountain.'

I frown at his words about Jane. 'What do you mean, you've found her before?'

Has he been keeping tabs on her and, if he has, why didn't he help her? Why does the man hate his own flesh and blood?

But Foley is already walking back down the row to the officers.

'Fucking coward!' Sie roars, pulling at the bars with all his might, but they're solid and unmovable.

'Fuck!' he hisses, pacing around the cell and punching the concrete of the back wall as hard as he can. A sizable chunk falls out of it but there's just more underneath, and that's probably followed by iron. This place was built to keep supes like us incarcerated until our trials.

Vic is pacing the cell. 'What the fuck does he want with Jane? He didn't give a shit about her before.'

'She's safe with Maddox, at least from the Order,' Theo

says. 'One problem at a time. If the transport really is already here for us, then we're going to the Mountain no matter what. So how are we going to escape from there?'

'It's impossible,' Sie mutters. 'No one gets out of the Mountain.'

I shoot him a look. 'We won't need to break out. All we need to do is get a message to our lawyers and they'll get us out,' I say. 'It's literally what we pay them for.'

Our discussion is cut short as the elevator pings again and ten officers with rifles emerge.

They tell us to line up at the cell bars and put our hands through. We're all cuffed with iron and led upstairs to a long hallway.

A couple of the officers are laughing as the doors at the end open and prison guards marked by their tan uniforms enter the building.

'I heard White and Davis just deleted these guys' files,' one says to another in a conspiratorial tone he probably doesn't think we can hear. 'No one's going to know they were ever here. Once they're in the Mountain, they ain't never coming out again.'

'More supe scum that won't be back out on the streets.'

I hear their low-five as my stomach bottoms out and I glance at the others, who look grim.

'You can't just hide the fact that we were ever here!' I say, turning towards the officers at our backs. 'That's against the law!'

I'm pushed around the other way roughly.

'Look straight ahead,' one of the officers barks and I feel the end of a rifle push into my back.

We're walked forward, but I turn my head back to look at them.

'You can't do this! It isn't right. We aren't the bad guys.'

The officer closest smirks at me and pushes me forward hard enough for me to stumble. I see the others being taken outside ahead of me.

'White and Davis are fucking heroes,' the officer calls as I'm grabbed by two prison guards and pushed through the door.

I see the transport bus waiting.

'What the fuck is going on here?' I yell, struggling in their grips. 'You can't just pretend we don't exist!'

My demon rears up and I change, but they're waiting for that and I feel a pain in my shoulder. I see a dart protruding from the skin.

They haul me up a ramp and onto the bus before my legs completely give out and then they chain me into a seat, my head leaning against the window.

I'm almost unconscious, but I can hear them talking, saying that this transport isn't going to be on the books either and not to expect to get out of jail ever because once we're inside the Mountain, we won't exist anymore.

I try to struggle, but there's no point. Whatever they've shot me with has knocked me out good. Before my eyes close, my thoughts are of Jane.

How are we going to save her now?

Jane

As soon as I wake up, I know something's not right. My head hurts and my abdomen feels like a school of piranhas are swimming around in there and tearing pieces off my insides. Another cramp makes me groan, my entire body feeling weak. I curl into a ball. I'm vaguely aware that I'm alone.

The pain peaks and my stomach revolts. Trying to find some strength from somewhere, I roll out of the bed and trip down the dais the bed is perched on, running the few steps to the bathroom as fast as I can in case I either pass out in the middle of the floor or throw up all over the pretty carpet. That would be embarrassing to tell Jeeves about and also a travesty because I love this carpet.

I get to the toilet and dry heave into the bowl, but I haven't eaten in hours so nothing comes up. I turn and sit down, putting my head in my hands.

It's been a long time since I felt this bad at this time of the month. I mean it's always been a little iffy, but ugh. I feel like I'm dying. I do what I need to do and get up, rifling through my backpack because I've always got some lady products kicking around in the bottom.

I find the things and sort myself out in the bathroom. Waves of weakness-inducing pain radiate across my stomach and into my back and I sink down to the floor, leaning against the door jamb at the juncture between the two rooms.

The light coming through the windows is like knives sticking into my brain even though it's cloudy out. The carpet I loved the feel of yesterday is scratchy today and doesn't feel nice against my skin at all. Even if it did, I can't stay here like this. I'm naked except for my undies and I'm starting to get cold. I take a deep breath and claw my way up the wall to standing, choosing my moment in between cramps to walk to the window and draw the curtains quickly.

I get back into the bed in the gloom with a sigh of relief and pull the covers over me. Feeling sorry for myself, I sniffle a little. I thought I was a demon. Strong body and mind. Kicking ass and taking names and stuff. I don't even know what that means, but I guess I'm feeling more, flying high in April, shot down in May right now. Story of my life.

Yeah, I feel mopey.

I hear the door open and I freeze, making my breathing slow. I don't want to see anyone right now, not even Kor ... even if we are 'more than friends' like he said.

I don't move. If I stay really still, maybe whoever it is will just leave.

But then I hear the curtains being drawn open and I groan. 'The light hurts.'

'I don't care. We need to talk,' Korban snarls, sounding pissed again. 'Get up.'

The thought of leaving the bed makes me want to cry. In fact, I think a couple of tears do squeeze out.

The blankets are ripped off me and I whimper, curling into myself even more tightly and hiding my head in the pillow as light blinds me. The cold air makes me shiver. Even Kor's voice that I loved the sound of yesterday feels like a motorcycle revving next to me. I cover my ears. I'm in sensory hell.

'I said get up. Maddox wants to see you. Us. He's pissed about something. This might be him making a move. We need to be ready.'

I sit up, shivering. Without even looking at me, he throws some clothes in my direction.

'Get dressed. I'll meet you in the hall.'

He adjusts something under his jacket. The gun.

Yesterday, what he did with it was hot as hell, but today, the thought of even one innocuous touch of a finger on my skin anywhere on my body at all makes me want to go back to the bathroom and try throwing up again.

He leaves the room, obviously just thinking that I'll follow his orders.

And I do because I don't even want to talk, to explain why I don't want to leave the bed. It seems like less effort to get dressed, go with him, and come back later when Maddox is done with whatever he wants us for.

I pull on my pants and shirt, grabbing a hoodie because I'm shivering like a Victorian child with influenza. I get to my feet and pad across the room in my socks, not even bothering with shoes. The room spins a little and I swallow hard as I open the door.

Korban is already striding down the hall. I struggle to follow, catching sight of myself in the mirror by the table. A pale face and dark eyes stare back at me.

Ugh.

I look like a Victorian child with influenza too.

I also errantly notice that the vase I broke yesterday is gone. Is that why Maddox wants to see me? OMG what if it actually was a Ming vase? I'll need some kind of payment plan to reimburse him for damages.

Korban's already at the bottom of the stairs by the time I get to the top. He's pacing. I've never seen him do that before.

What did he say in the bedroom? That Maddox might be making a move? What does that even mean? Anxiety skyrocketing, I hold the banister tightly as I take one step at a time, my legs feeling like Jello by the time I get to the bottom.

Korban doesn't give me a moment. As soon as my foot touches the ground floor, he's pulling me along behind him. We stop outside a door; the door to the room Maddox brought us to when we first got here.

He knocks once and opens it and I find it a little strange that he bothered to announce our arrival at all. That's not really Korban's modus operandi.

Maddox and the rest of his crew are there looking bored, except for the twin whose ass I beat yesterday. He's sitting in a chair looking sorry for himself and I feel a little glimmer of satisfaction until I remember that I look worse than him right now and I didn't get my ass handed to me yesterday.

Maddox stands up as we enter. He doesn't beat about the bush.

'Do you know why I've asked you here?' he asks, looking directly at me.

I don't deny what I've done. I want to, but there's probably video evidence of my clumsy demon ass knocking that vase over.

'I think so,' I say quietly and quickly, cowed by the multiple pairs of eyes that bore unrelentingly into me and wanting this to be over as fast as possible so I can go back to bed.

'I'm sorry. I promise I'll pay for it.'

He glances at Korban who looks at me, and I can't read either of their faces.

'You'll take whatever punishment is decided on?' Maddox asks.

There's something in his tone. It puts me even more on edge. I'm missing something, but what?

'No, she won't!' Korban snarls, grabbing me and pulling me closer to him.

'Well, I ...' I close my eyes and swallow hard, my hands curling into fists. I'm glad he's close, but ...

Just get this over with and then you can go lay down.

'I thought it would be more like a 'you broke it, you pay for it' type of deal to be honest,' I whisper. 'I know it's probably a lot, but maybe we can work out a payment plan or something.'

He looks at Korban again. Kor looks at me.

'What is this about?' Korban asks.

'The vase I broke.'

'The attack on Krase.'

I take a step back, my eyes flying to the twin who's looking at me with a smug grin on his face.

'What?' Maddox and I say in unison.

'I broke a vase in the hallway upstairs,' I say, a very nasty feeling snaking up my body.

I know Kor wants me to stay close to him, but I don't think I can stand up anymore. I sink down into a chair furthest from Maddox's clan's unblinking stares.

'I'm talking about you attacking a member of my clan in my own house.' He gestures to Krase. 'By all accounts, the damage done to him was minimal, but the attack itself was injurious to my clan's hospitality.'

'Huh?'

I glance at the twin.

What is Maddox talking about?

My eyes find Korban for support, but he's looking at the blank wall next to him. He's not even paying attention.

'To put it in simple terms, Jane, you attacked one of us after I offered you safety here. That's against the fundamental rules we all live by. It's a big deal. So, succubus or not, you have to pay for your transgression.'

My mouth opens and closes. I can't find words.

'What the fuck is this?' Kor growls. He's back in the room again ... so to speak. 'Look at her! How could she have done anything to Krase?'

'She's much stronger than she looks ... especially in demon form,' Maddox says.

Korban looks at me incredulously. 'Did you attack him?'

I mouth is dry. The room is spinning in a slow circle around me and I'm just about keeping it together.

'I did,' I whisper. 'But—'

'But nothing!' Krase explodes. 'She admits it. Now she pays the price and I decide what that price is. Those are the rules, succubus.' He gives Korban a triumphant look. 'And you aren't allowed to interfere.'

Korban turns to look at me and what I feel from him scares me to my core. He's afraid. For me. Then he looks again at the wall, zoning out, his emotions unreadable.

What is going on with him?

What are they going to do with me?

I try to find my voice, but the words won't come. I'm shaking my head.

'What price does the injured party decide?' Maddox asks, sounding weary.

'I think an immediate, bare-flesh caning should do it.' He looks at the rest of his clan. 'Administered by me in this very room in front of all of you to witness.' Then his gaze cuts to me and his slow smile chills my blood. 'On that pert, little arse.'

This can't be happening.

Krase advances towards me and I send a pleading look to Kor, but he isn't coming to my aide. He's just staring at nothing, like he's frozen ...

Or someone's playing fae tricks on him.

That realization has me lurching out of the chair, moving around to the back of it, and keeping it between me and Krase.

'He attacked me first,' I grind out with a huge amount of effort and I doubt I'll be able to say anything else right now.

'I didn't attack you,' Krase says with a condescending chuckle.

I get the impression he doesn't even think he's lying.

I back away from him, shaking my head, my eyes swimming. My head too.

Then, finally, Korban gets between us.

He growls low and Krase stops.

'Get out of the way. You can't stop this from happening. The price has to be paid to ensure balance between the clans. The Law's the law.'

Kor looks at me over his shoulder just as I feel the wall at my back. I lean on it heavily.

'Tell Maddox what happened,' he grinds out.

But I can't. My eyes beseech him and he finally, finally looks at me properly for the first time today, feels me.

The room lurches and I can't stay upright. I crumple to the floor.

He gets to me too late to catch me but hoists me up in his arms as soon as he's within reach, concern for me coming to the forefront, surpassing his anger that I've been feeling since he dragged me out of bed.

'Jane?'

My head rolls in the direction of his voice. I want to tell him this is bullshit, but I can't make the words come out.

I close my eyes, tears tracking from the corners of my eyes into my hair.

I hear him swear and I'm lifted up into his arms.

'She's clearly not well,' one of Maddox's clan says, either Axel or Iron.

'Convenient,' I hear Krase say.

'Shut your mouth,' Axel or Iron says. 'I'm sick of you twisting our laws to suit your purposes.'

'You're the one who hates what you are but will use your fae magick for EVERYTHING!'

'Enough!' Maddox's voice cuts through his clan's in-fighting. 'Tend to your female. We'll conclude this matter when she's feeling better.'

Korban doesn't say anything, just takes me from the room, up the stairs and back to our room.

When we're inside, he kicks the door shut and puts me in the bed.

'I'm sorry. I didn't know what that was about until it was too late,' he says. 'Talk to me. Tell me what's going on.'

I burrow under the covers, shaking my head, wanting to be left alone.

I close my eyes and feel the mattress next to me dip, but he doesn't try to touch me, he just lays in the bed with me.

I curl up, trying to ignore the cramping that's come back

with a vengeance. It's like the worst period ever combined with the nastiest flu imaginable.

When I wake up, the curtains are closed and I'm feeling a little better. My back and my stomach each have a heat pad on them and it's making the pain more bearable.

Korban notices I'm awake.

'Here,' he says, handing me some pills. 'They're just regular painkillers, but they should help.'

I take them from him, gulping them down with some cool water from the glass he hands me next.

'Are you feeling any better?'

I nod and snuggle into the heat of the pads.

'How did you know where it's hurting?' I ask low.

'Turns out when I stop being a selfish asshole and think of your needs, I can read what they are in a roundabout kind of way. We need to talk about that sometime soon. But not now, don't worry.'

'I wouldn't know what to say about it anyway,' I mutter. 'It's pretty new to me too.'

'You can only do it with me?' he asks, and I feel this tiny spark of excitement that he might be special.

I grimace, not wanting to take that from him, but I also don't want to lie to him either.

'I can feel Theo, Sie, and Paris,' I admit, 'but that's all.'

'Not Vic?'

I shake my head a little and he seems slightly appeased.

He doesn't ask anything else about it, just turns his phone around and I see he's researching neurodivergence.

'You didn't defend yourself in there with Maddox's clan. That's not like you. I thought maybe it's because you're sick, but then I remembered something from what Theo sent me. I'm sorry I didn't put it together and help sooner. Maddox's clan likes to use fae tricks a lot and one of those dicks was keeping my brain occupied while Maddox was playing judge, jury and executioner with you.'

'What do you mean?'

'It's hard to explain, but it's like a daydream puzzle you have to find your way out of. You can talk again ok now?'

I nod. 'I'm sorry I ...'

'Don't,' he says gently. 'Just tell me what happened with Krase. His story is you attacked him in demon form without provocation.'

'That's not how it went at all. He tricked me. I was coming up here to find you yesterday after we played pool and he ... I don't know how. I thought I was here but I wasn't. I was in a different room. He was waiting for me in the dark. He wanted ...'

'He wanted what?' Korban growls.

'What everyone seems to want from me,' I mutter. 'I don't get it. No one ever looked twice at me before but now it's like every dude I meet wants a piece. Maddox practically proposed to me. So did Krase, but not in the same way. He's ... not right, all nasty tricks. He tried to assault me.'

'And you fought back.'

'Of course, and I'm not going to lie. It was awesome. I handed his ass to him.'

Kor gives a mirthless laugh. 'So he and his hurt pride decided to get even.'

I shudder. 'I'm not paying his dumb price. I feel like shit now, but as soon as I'm better I'm going to find him and teach him another lesson.'

'I'll take care of him, princess, don't you worry about that. But first we talk to Maddox.'

'Now?' I ask, my heart sinking.

'No, baby, not now.'

But there's a knock at the door right then and I groan, diving back under the covers.

The door opens.

'Get the fuck out of here. I'm not giving her to you.'

'I just came to talk.'

It's Maddox.

'I want to apologize for not realizing that you aren't well, darling.'

I scoff from under the covers at his endearment. It means less than nothing coming from him and I thank my lucky stars that Shar sent me to the Iron I's for help and not Maddox's clan of scumbag liars and tricksters. I mean the road has been a little rocky, but Maddox's clan would have probably thrown me off a cliff or something for shits and gigs.

I poke my head out from the duvet. 'Krase is a liar.'

'If that's the case, why didn't you defend yourself? Why didn't you say anything?' he counters.

'I ... couldn't.' I look away.

I don't want him and his clan to know about me. They'll exploit the way my brain works the way Vic did, but I just know they'll take it to a whole other level.

'She's sick,' Korban says by way of explanation. 'And you jumped on her as soon as we got in there. And don't think I don't know what you did, stopping me from helping her.'

Maddox looks sheepish. 'I knew you'd interfere and I wanted the truth. It wasn't me though. Iron is the one who's part fae.'

'He's fae and his family named him Iron?'

Maddox shrugs. 'His kin have odd senses of humor apparently.'

Kor looks calm, but I can feel him getting riled up.

'Can you give us a minute?' I ask him.

'You want me to leave you alone? With him? No fucking way, princess.'

'Just outside the door. You can leave it open if you want.'

'No,' Kor huffs, 'I'll stay over here and I'll keep quiet, but that's the best I can do.'

I nod, kind of liking that he's staying to keep me safe.

Maddox steps towards the bed. 'What did happen, Jane?'

'Krase attacked me. I defended myself,' I say as succinctly as possible.

'And you have proof?'

'About as much proof as he does that I attacked him first.'

I'm feeling a little more myself. I guess the painkillers are working. I sit up in the bed and stare Maddox down. 'I'm not going to let him do that to me.'

'It won't come to that. Can you give me some more details if it's not too much trouble?'

It is, actually!

But I give him the specifics ... in as few words as I can and when I'm done, he mutters an inaudible curse.

'I'm sorry that happened,' he says, 'with Krase and also this morning. You must understand, our information about succubi is second-hand at best. Few have ever met one. That has unfortunately meant that our views about you have been skewed through very old writings by, as I'm suddenly learning, many who had probably never met a succubus before. I believe your story and Krase will be dealt with.'

He pulls a small book from his pocket.

'An olive branch,' he says, placing it on the bed.

I eye it. 'What is it?'

'The diary of a succubus. It's very old and, as far as I know, the only copy in existence. You may find it useful as you begin to navigate your new reality.'

He turns away.

'Wait. Why do you believe me over your friend?'

He swings back, silent for a few seconds while he watches me, as if he's not sure that he should answer, but then he seems to decide.

He draws closer, lowering his voice. 'We've been searching for a long time for someone like you.'

'A succubus?'

He nods.

'But I thought they were ...'

'Everyone thinks they're gone.' He eyes Korban who's standing by the wall, pretending he's not listening when he clearly is. 'But they're not. I know that for a fact. Krase, like all of us, has wanted a true mate for a long time. But the years have twisted his mind. To meet you, to have you come here when we've never been so close to having our own mate before, but then to see you claimed by another clan, it's not been easy for him, nor for the rest of us ... I'm sorry you have borne the brunt of his madness.'

Claimed by another clan? He thinks the Iron I's are mine? I want to ask why, but this is a can of worms I don't want to deal with right now.

Are they mine?

Not now, Jane!

I think I understand what Maddox is saying. I was alone for a long time myself after all, but I never did anything like what Krase has done to me to anyone. It's fucked up, and what about the story he made up just because he was mad that I was stronger than him? How will Maddox explain that away?

'But what about after? I didn't do what he wanted, so he lied? Why, so he could tie me up and beat me while all of you watch?' I shiver in spite of myself. 'That's psychotic.'

'It's not exactly like that.' Maddox clears his throat.

'According to the books we've come across, a succubus was more powerful than any one incubus. That's why clans were made up of five incubi to one succubus – the females were kept in line by all of their mates. That was the only way to keep their power subdued and everyone safe.'

My lip curls. 'That sounds like some old-fashioned, sexist bullshit to me.'

'Perhaps. As I said, we only have old texts to understand the dynamic.'

'Bet they were written by dudes too,' I mutter.

A small smile plays on his lips. 'Most assuredly, but they're pretty much all we have to go on as no incubi clan has had a succubus in so long. The books say that the succubus and her power was usually kept in check by her mates.'

'And how did they keep her in line?' Kor asks, looking me up and down.

I frown. Maddox is going to give him all the ninja tips.

Korban is not keeping me in line!

'Corporal punishment. The cane was used ... among other implements. The way it's written, it seems as if the succubus needed the discipline but also sought it.' His eyes look away from mine. 'Enjoyed it.'

My eyes widen. 'Wanted to be ...'

Spanked?

I don't say that out loud, but I think about Vic. He's into that stuff ... is that why?

'I believe Krase thought that if you were made to submit to him, you'd change your mind about which clan you're allied with.'

'I'm not allied with any clan,' I say stiffly, not looking at Korban.

Maddox smiles. 'Aren't you?'

I frown at him. I don't know.

'What happens now?' I ask instead so I don't have to answer him.

Maddox turns away. 'My clan business is my own, but Krase will be dealt with. Permanently.'

I gasp. 'You're going to kill him?'

I don't know how I feel about that. I mean the guy is clearly mentally ill. He needs help, not a bullet through the chest.

'Of course not! But there are ways to keep him out of trouble until we can help him properly. Besides, at the moment with the way he is, he can't be trusted with your secret.'

What secret? The succubus thing? Is this why Paris got weird before when I told him I could read his emotions?

Maddox turns back and tilts his head at me. 'Darling, you do realize that if anyone finds out what you are, you're in danger, don't you?'

'Um ...'

'The Ten will have you executed if they learn of you.'

Korban growls from his corner.

He hardly gives Korban a look. 'You know what I say is true and your mate is ignorant of too much, enforcer. You should remedy that quickly, but the fae will not find out about you from this house. I give you my word.'

Korban nods. 'Have you heard from Vic yet?'

I perk up a little to listen to Maddox's reply. I miss the others and I'm finding that I feel weirdly adrift without them, even Vic.

Maddox sighs. 'I have had news. But it's not good, I'm afraid.'

My heart begins to hammer in my chest.

'Are they dead?' I whisper, hoping he'll just tell me straight if they are.

'No. They're alive for now, but they were incarcerated in Metro before they could leave the city.'

Korban pushes himself off the wall. 'Why didn't you tell us this earlier? We need to go get them!'

'Time isn't of the essence and I wanted to get our conflict out of the way first. And, no, we can't go get them. They've already been transferred.'

'Where?' Korban snarls.

Maddox steps away, putting some distance between Kor and him. 'The Mountain.'

'Shit!' Korban yells.

'What's the Mountain?' I ask, looking from one to the other.

Korban covers his face with his hands, the worry coming off him making me very anxious.

'It's like ... a super-max prison for supes. No one gets out, no matter what they are,' he says.

'And it's ... on a mountain?' I ask in a small voice.

'It is a mountain, Jane. The prison is deep underground.'

'We have to get them out!' I say to Kor.

'We will,' he says, taking my hand and gripping it. 'I'll contact the lawyers now and find out what's going on.'

'The fighting is still going on in the seven cities where the attacks began,' Maddox says, 'but it's waning and hasn't spread. This isn't the war we feared, but there are still people missing and parts of Metro are burning. You might not even be able to get in touch with anyone there yet.'

Korban grunts a response.

Maddox goes to the door. 'Please do let me know if you'd like me to send for a discreet doctor as you aren't feeling well ... although this should pass in a day or so.'

Despite my worry, I frown at him. He knows so much about my body that I don't.

'How do you know?' I ask.

He looks between Kor and me and sighs. 'You don't know what it is.' It's not a question.

I shake my head. 'I'm like this sometimes, but it's never been this bad before.'

'Incubi sexually mature in their late teens, but for succubi it's later, not until they're in their early to mid-twenties.'

'You think she's maturing now? Here?' Korban asks.

'I believe so. Proximity to your clan would have helped it along. I'll send up some of the more informative books for you to read while you're ... indisposed.'

Maddox moves to the door and gives a small bow. 'Apologies again, Jane.'

He leaves without another word and I glance at Kor.

'I'm going to try the lawyers now,' he says, picking up the phone by the bed.

'But what about what Maddox said about the fires and—'

'You can't trust what he says, remember?'

'But Vic and him are friends, right?'

Kor swears under his breath. 'Yeah, they're friends, but they're incubi too.'

At my blank expression, he continues. 'His clan has been looking for a succubus. YOU'RE a succubus.'

I shake my head, not getting it and wishing he'd just spell it out. 'So?'

He puts the phone down and comes around the bed. He takes my shoulders gently and stares into my eyes. When he speaks, it's slow and clear.

'If Vic and the others don't get out of there, Maddox's clan will slit my throat and take you as their own, Jane.'

I give him an incredulous look. 'Are you messing with me? You know I sometimes don't get jokes ...'

'This isn't a joke. This is your world now, sweetheart, and

you need to know these things. I'll protect you as best I can, but Maddox is desperate and desperation can make things turn nasty real quick.'

My eyes widen. 'Call the lawyers.'

～

Sie

I GAZE UP at the high walls of the outside of the Mountain. The barbed wire is rusted. The guard tower looks like it's been abandoned for years. I wonder at that for a few seconds, but I notice as the prisoner transport goes through the gates, that there are drones, cameras, and all kinds of other electronic surveillance on the outside, so I guess they don't need so many actual guards on watch these days.

I catch Vic's eye. He's sitting opposite me on the other side of the bus. Theo and Paris are behind us. I glance back to take a look at Paris. It's been a few hours since they shot him with that tranq. He finally seems to be waking up.

The bus comes to a stop and I play with the idea of making a run for it when they take us off the bus, but in addition to the guards and the drones that all have firearms, there are remote-controlled machine guns placed at strategic locations all around the place. We'll be stains on the ground before we've gone two steps.

We're offloaded quickly and are made to stand in a line at the bottom of a sheer cliff while a guard with a loud voice and stripe on his collar tells us that rules don't exist in the Mountain except what the other prisoners enforce themselves. Once we're inside, we won't see a guard, or daylight until our sentences are up at which time we'll be automatically pulled out by conjure. It's up to us to survive if we want out, he continues, because there's no one inside but inmates except when the food arrives twice a month. By the way he says food, I don't think he's talking about chow from the grocery aisle.

I glance at the others, making sure no one sees fear on my face. If the guards out here don't beat it out of us, our fellow inmates will.

I'm just beginning to wonder how we get in, vaguely imagining a massive archway with an iron gate or a huge, wooden door around the corner, when the guard bellowing at us takes what looks a little like a link key and puts it on the stone at the base of the cliff. A narrow opening appears and every guard eyes it with fear, their weapons trained on it. I guess they're afraid of something coming back out. That's probably the only way anyone can escape. But nothing emerges from the hole.

We're told to walk forward. Paris is in front of me and I feel for the kid. I can see the terror in his eyes and his knees are practically knocking together. He's probably still half-asleep from the drugs.

'Lock it up,' I hiss. 'You're an Iron I and you love danger every day of the week. Fucking act like it.'

He turns to look at me, his eyes wide. Then he nods and I see his game face fall over his features. I give him what I hope is a look of pride and turn my attention back to the tunnel.

Vic goes first, losing his glamor as he goes through.

Smart.

I do the same, letting my scars stand out and for once almost glad I have them because I know that they'll give even the most seasoned inmates pause. I nudge Paris and make sure he demons-up too, glancing behind to check Theo. Out of all of us, he seems the most composed at his core. Probably his medic training from when he was in the forces. He lets the demon out too and I hear a couple guards swear because he's almost twice the size of his human form when he changes. He's like a dangerous, giant, extremely ripped smurf.

Paris walks into the dark with only slight hesitation, even smirking at the guards like he doesn't give a fuck. There's the Paris I know!

I follow, the pitch black throwing my senses for a second until we materialize on the other side. I glance around, making sure I look mean, staring down the various supes who've come to gawk at the fresh meat.

We stand together, trying to appear as tough as we can, but as I look around, I mostly see dull eyes and hollow desperation. A lot of these guys don't look like hardened criminals, but I can pick out the ones I need to watch out for. My time fighting for the Order was good for something it seems.

I fume when I think of how easy it was for a bunch of humans to capture us. And those damned detectives ... As soon as I saw their smug faces in that interview room, I knew they were going to cause us trouble. Trumped up charges, false witness statements, unrecorded interviews. I didn't get what they were doing at first, but I caught on eventually. Now, we're stuck here and Jane and Kor are in a ton of danger if we don't find a way out.

I get that Metro is a mess after what happened. People are still missing and I'll bet a shit ton of paperwork has 'disappeared' from the Metro PD too. Locking the big, bad supes in here and making sure we get lost in the system is a good plan. It'll probably work and I'm all for cleaning up the streets.

But we aren't the bad guys.

No one approaches us, so we move around a little, taking stock. The lighting isn't bad considering this is basically a huge cavern in the rock with tunnels shooting off from it in all directions and heights like a rabbit warren. I look up and see a conjured sphere of light that keeps most of the vast chamber bathed in an icy glow.

I keep my eyes open, not shying away from anyone else's stare. I make others move out of my way and most do because I'm one of the biggest guys here right now, second only to Theo who's staying close.

Another demon approaches me. He's an incubus. He's alone, but if he does have a clan, I hope Theo is watching my back in case they decide to creep up and jump us.

He stops in front of me, not budging when I attempt to push by him. He's young ... and dumb.

'You're the Bear,' he says.

I sigh because I already know where this is going, but I give a small nod. There's no point in denying it. Everyone knows what my name was, what I used to do.

'They say you used to be a pretty good fighter.'

I give him a once-over. I can take him with both arms tied behind my back if it comes to it, but I hope I don't have to.

'I don't do that shit anymore,' I say, giving the kid one more chance to walk away.

But he squares up to me. 'Well there's a kinda hitch, old timer. If you're new, you gotta fight.'

Yep, young and dumb.

I look him in the eyes and, without even closing mine, I butt him in the face, hitting him in the nose. I don't give him a second to recover, I just grab him, punch him in the gut, and uppercut him right in the chin. He flies backwards and falls on the floor on his ass, slumping down all the way because he's out cold.

The room goes silent, watching me for a minute until they decide I'm not on a rampage and go back to doing what they were doing, the hum of conversation returning.

I see Vic and Paris watching, keeping out of the drama. Stepping over the incubus I just laid out, Theo and I make our way over to them.

We sit together at an empty cafeteria-type table that looks like it's seen better days.

'What do you think?' Vic asks.

'I think we stay together and get that incubus kid I just beat down to show us the ropes when he comes to,' I reply.

'What about his clan?'

I shrug. 'No one came to defend him. I figure he's alone.'

Paris looks worried and I give him a commiserating look. 'Keep it together,' I say. 'Remember who you are and remember your job.'

He lets out a breath and nods. 'I've never been on the inside before,' he mutters. 'It's a weird place.'

'You'll get a feel for it soon enough,' I venture.

Vic snorts. 'You intending on staying? I'm not.'

My response is a grunt. Vic is a typical Makenzie sometimes, thinking everything's going to work out in his favor despite the odds. Who knows? Maybe it will. I hope it does, but we also need to be prepared to survive in here until his miracle pans out.

Theo is watching a group of guys side-eye us and they aren't the only ones. Pretty much everyone is keeping us in their sights.

'This is going to be a problem, Bear,' Vic mutters.

I look down at the name. The mere sound of it makes me sick.

'Might not be,' I mutter.

'Everyone knows who you are in here now,' Vic scoffs. 'Look at them. Every last supe in here is sizing you up.'

I can see he's right. This is going to lead to trouble one way or another.

'We don't have time for this,' Paris snarls low. 'We need to get out of here and get to the others.'

'They'll be okay.'

'How can you say that?' he hisses.

'Because they will be! Jane isn't a push-over and Korban is a maniac. They'll be okay.'

'She's still human,' Paris persists. 'What if—'

'Our girl is tough as nails,' I say, knowing it's true and hoping it'll be enough to keep her safe.

'What if she's not our girl?' Paris asks, continuing to confess fears.

'She is,' I say quietly, refusing to look at any of them because I don't want to see the doubt in their eyes.

'What do you think Maddox will do when we don't appear at his Swiss estate? How much grace do you think he'll give us before he makes a move?'

'Look,' I say, 'I'm not saying we shouldn't be trying to escape, I'm saying we can't just sit at this table and hope for the best in here. That's all.'

Vic nods. 'Agreed. Do some info gathering and meet back here in an hour or so. No one leaves the cavern without the others though.'

I nod and stand, getting ready to take a walk around and go find that kid I smacked around. The others move away and I survey the room, taking everything in, sizing-up potential enemies.

Two big guys approach me and I sigh. Here we go again.

They incline their heads to me and I return the greeting warily.

'You're the Bear.'

'Was.'

'We want you to fight in the ring for us.'

'I don't do that anymore.'

One of them tries to look friendly. 'Look, you're a great fighter. You'll win hands down. Just come fight a couple rounds.'

'I said no.'

The first one pushes the other one away.

'Suit yourself,' he says, but I just know I haven't heard the last of this.

I know his type. They aren't going to take no for an answer.

CHAPTER
SIX
KORBAN

Korban

'Y ou were never going to let Krase follow through on what he wanted to do with Jane,' I growl at Maddox, catching him in the hall outside our room. 'It was all bullshit. Why? To scare her? What's your game, clan leader? Because I know you don't do anything on a whim. I thought you wanted her. Why these games to drive her away?'

I shut the door behind me so Jane doesn't hear our conversation. She's been through enough over the past few days. Hell, ever since she met us. Maddox keeps talking about Jane being ours like it's a foregone conclusion. The truth is I wouldn't be a bit surprised if she left us as soon as we give her a way out. She has no reason to stay. We haven't given her one. Far from it.

'No,' he says. 'It wasn't actually anything to do with either of you. Please accept my sincerest apologies for bringing you both into my clan's problems.'

Is he fucking kidding?

I narrow my eyes at him because I think I just figured it out.

'Did you put her through that because of Krase, you fucker? Is that what this was all about?' I growl low, vowing I'm going to give this asshole what's coming to him one day.

Maddox doesn't even look contrite. He'll do anything for his clan just as Vic would, even hurt the girl he wants to be his. He's even more dangerous to us than I thought. The lawyers better get back to me ASAP and tell me they're getting my clan out of jail today because I think we're quickly outstaying our welcome here.

'I've been seeing signs of the madness in him,' Maddox says, confirming my suspicions.

'And that was enough to warrant terrorizing her?' I ask.

Maddox shrugs. 'At least this way she can serve some purpose to my clan. Krase has been hiding his true mental state from me. I needed to push him to reveal himself.'

'Well, now you know how far gone he is,' I growl, not believing for a second that Maddox is actually giving up his claim to Jane, 'so take him outside and put a bullet through his brain and next time leave my clan's female out of your dramas.'

Infuriatingly, Maddox just gives me a nod and turns away, disappearing down the corridor.

I go back into our room and, for the first time since we got here, I try to relax a little. He's definitely double-bluffing where Jane is concerned. There's no way he's given up. But the lawyers will call me, tell me Vic and the others are out, and once the clan is at my back, Maddox won't dare try anything.

I gaze at Jane lying in the bed. She looks pale and is clearly feeling very sorry for herself. I remember when I came into maturity; the pain and the nausea, feeling like I was dying.

I've been hard on her. Too hard.

I notice she's asleep and turn down the electric heat pads I found in the med room so she doesn't get too hot.

To hear Maddox talking, she's a demon more powerful than us. But right now she's small and tired and scared. I can sense it and I'm glad that I can. It makes me feel close to her and like I can help. I've never had that before.

I wonder if the others feel it the same way. I'd guess Theo does. That would explain their familiarity before.

I pace the room. I miss my clan and, truth be told, I've had enough of being in charge. There was a time when I thought maybe I should fight Vic for leadership, but these last few days have been exhausting. He can keep the presidential mantle. I don't want it.

Jane stirs in her sleep and I turn my attention back to her, keeping watch over her as I sit on the bed and turn on the TV. I put on a movie to listen to while I close my eyes and try to rest. I may need to be at the top of my game very soon.

An hour or so goes by and I hear her get up. She goes into the bathroom. When she comes out, she looks at me through hooded eyes.

'How long it this going to last?' she asks plaintively, tears coming to her eyes.

I hate this.

'Shouldn't be too long,' I say, but I have no idea.

She gets back in the bed, sniffling, and I frown. She looks thinner. When was the last time she ate? I'm ashamed to realize I don't know. She hasn't asked for anything, but I need to step up and take care of her properly.

I glance over at the phone. 'I'll be back in a few. Answer the phone if it rings. It'll be the lawyers.'

She nods, shifting closer to that side of the bed, so she can grab it if they call.

I go downstairs to get her a hot chocolate, maybe a cupcake or something. I know she likes sweet things, so maybe that will tempt her even though her stomach is upset.

There are pain aux chocolat on the counter in the kitchen, under a glass dome like there are in coffee shops sometimes, so I grab a couple, throwing them on a plate before I open the fridge. There's nothing sweet in there though, only an array of French cheeses and bottles of champagne. I roll my eyes.

I look through the cabinets, but there's nothing to make hot chocolate, and there are no cupcakes.

'Can I help you find something, sir?'

Jeeves.

I turn to find the butler standing behind me. What was his real name? I've forgotten.

'Uh, I was trying to find something for … the lady.'

'Anything in particular, sir?'

'Uh … desserts. Maybe some pizza or fries. Do you have anything like that?'

If Jeeves is disgusted by Jane's food preferences, he's too *butlerish* to show it.

'But of course, sir. This isn't some backpacker's hovel. I'll have an array of dishes sent up directly. Is there anything else the lady desires?'

'Vanilla cupcakes.'

'Very well.' Jeeves bows at the waist and leaves the kitchen.

I haven't seen any other servants here besides him. I wonder where he's going to get the stuff I've asked for.

I leave the kitchen too. I want to get back to Jane as soon as possible, but I decide to make a pitstop in Maddox's library.

I go in and find the man himself. He's sitting in a high-backed chair in front of the fire, staring into the flames. I've seen Vic look like that a lot over the years, like the weight of the world is on his shoulders. I don't say anything. It's not my business. He's not part of my clan.

I move towards the shelf of books I saw before and tilt my head to the side to read some of the titles.

'Apologies for not sending them up,' Maddox says and I look back, but he's still just staring into the flames. 'The first two books on the left will be the most interesting to you. Since meeting Jane, I realize that the descriptions of succubi don't match up to how she is.'

'Thanks,' I say, dragging the two books out. They're old, but I have no idea how old. I try to be careful. Don't want them falling apart on me.

I go to leave, but turn back with a sigh, my conscience rearing its head for once. We're all incubi after all. That counts for something.

'I'm sorry about Krase,' I say.

Maddox nods but doesn't look at me. 'He wasn't always like this.'

'Sie came back from the brink. Maybe he will too.'

Maddox gives a small chuckle. 'Was it Jane who brought him back?'

I don't say anything, but he gives me a knowing look.

'I think, old chap, that, without a succubus, my clan is going to be up the proverbial creek without a paddle very soon.' His face contorts in anger. 'And I know just who to blame for that,' he mutters to himself, his jaw setting like he's decided something.

He goes back to sulking in front of the fire and I leave. As long as his anger isn't directed at me and mine, I don't give a shit who the hapless asshole he blames for his predicament is.

I'm itching to get back to Jane, I realize. I don't like leaving her when she's weakened like this. What if crazy Krase tries something else?

That thought has me practically leaping up the shallow steps of the grand staircase, the books in one hand and the plate of pastries in the other. But when I get to our room, all is quiet.

Jane's form is still visible in the bed. The movie I put on earlier has finished and now the screen is blank. I see the tiny book Maddox gave her open next to her.

I put the plate down, deciding to let her rest for now and I settle into a chair in the corner, turning on the nearby lamp. I crack open the first book Maddox gave me and begin to read myself. I want to know what to expect with Jane so I can anticipate her needs, any problems that might arise. I also want to know what's with this weird empathy we have between us. I've never experienced that with any of the other Iron I's. Why her? Is it a succubus thing?

Maybe I'll be able to get at least the bare bones of what Jane being a succubus actually means for her ... and for us. Maybe if we know enough about how to make her happy with us, she'll stay.

I didn't know I wanted a mate, maybe I didn't before we came here, but these past few days with just her and me have made me realize that I do. I never realized a clan needed a mate either.

It's going to be Jane. Maybe it already is and we just have to get her to see that.

I'm just getting into the book when the phone buzzes and Jane is already picking up the receiver before the second ring even begins.

'Yes?' she says, keeping it short as usual. 'This is Jane.'

There's talking on the other end that I can't make out.

'That's not possible,' Jane says, her voice devoid of emotion, but her fear and worry spiking.

I'm already next to her, taking hold of her hand.

'Well, check again. We know they were taken there.'

There's more chatter from the other end, but it's too crackly for me to make it out.

'You'll keep trying?'

She squeezes my hand, turning her blank face to me.

'Okay.'

She puts the phone down. 'There's no record of them,' she whispers. 'There's nothing about them being at the precinct, no record of their arrests, and nothing about them being transported to the Mountain. It's like they've disappeared.'

'Fuck,' I hiss, already knowing the game the cops are playing. 'What can the lawyers do?'

'They're going to keep looking, keep asking questions, but until they find something tangible, there's no way of getting them out of there because, to the Law, they aren't even *in* there.'

She's shaking a little. 'What are we going to do? How are we going to get them out?'

'There are ways,' I lie, trying to think unworrying thoughts, so she doesn't pick up on it.

But no one comes out of the Mountain and I can only think of one thing I can try, which means asking Maddox for his help.

I wouldn't if there was any other way because I can guarantee that this time I won't be getting another freebie.

Paris

WE'RE IN A CELL. I guess that's what it is, but the only door is a thin curtain that the previous occupant left. Whether he died or got out of here, the kid who showed us in here hasn't said. There's an old table and a stool, a couple of books and an infinity candle that's doing a decent job of lighting up the space. I found a knife amongst the bed covers in the corner too, and its already stowed on my person.

I survey the room again, trying to distract myself from the fear that's boring into my self-control. This time I notice a hole near the top of the wall at the back which seems to lead to another tunnel but it looks too small for any of us to fit through even in our human forms.

I rest my head against the wall, smoother in places from the many others who have probably sat here just like this over the years.

I hear Sie talking in a low voice outside in the passage. He's finding out what the rules are here, who's in charge, how we're going to survive. Panic claws at my chest, not just because Kor and Jane are out there alone, but because we're stuck in this place. What if we never get out? What if we die in here? What if I never see Jane and Kor again? I clutch my chest.

I can't breathe!

I struggle to my feet, my eyes searching wildly for Theo.

What's wrong with me?

He's there, just on the other side of the room flipping through one of the books from the desk.

The room is spinning. I lurch towards him, grabbing for him.

He turns around and his eyes widen.

'It's okay,' he says. 'I'm here. You're okay.'

'What's wrong with him?' Vic asks, but Theo just puts his hands on my shoulders.

123

'Feel my fingers squeezing your skin. Feel the ground under your feet. Look around the room and tell me five things you can see in here right now.'

'You,' I grind out, clutching my hands hard. 'The candle.'

I look around wildly. 'The blankets in the corner.'

'Good. That's three. Two more,' he says, not letting go of me.

'The- the table. The rags over the door.'

'Good job. Better?'

I nod a little.

'Touch your thumb to the tips of your fingers on each hand. Focus on the pattern. Forefinger, middle, ring, pinky. Let it ground you. Take slow, deep breaths.'

I do what Theo says and the feeling starts to go away, my body relaxing. I take a deep breath.

'What was that?'

'Just a panic attack.'

I cringe. I just had a panic attack? I'll never live this one down.

But neither Theo nor Vic say anything about it.

'You're fine,' Theo says, squeezing my shoulder. 'Just keep doing what I said and it'll ease off in a minute.'

'We're going to get out of here,' Vic says.

I just nod and go back to the wall, tapping my fingers together and hiding my embarrassment.

'What did the kid say?' Theo asks Sie when he comes back into the cell a minute later.

'Enough,' says Sie, sitting down heavily on the ground.

Theo rolls his eyes. 'Feel like sharing?'

He grunts. 'There are supes of all kinds here, including more than one arania.'

'What the hell is an arania?' I ask, trying to keep the rising unease off my face.

124

'Kind of like ... a giant spider,' Theo mutters. 'They're very old and, some say, sentient. They mostly keep to themselves unless they're hungry, but if you annoy one, you better have a decent escape route because when they come after you, they're relentless.'

'So stay in the well-used tunnels that have light and keep out of their webs,' Sie finishes. 'We have enough problems right now without pissing one of those things off.'

I shake my head, keeping my fingers moving. 'Fucking place.'

Theo leans back on the table. 'What else did you find out?'

'The guy in charge is a demon, but not an incubus. His name is Dante. He rules the Mountain like a king. He's been here a long time. Doesn't have a clan. We want anything here, we have to go to his guys to get it.'

'So, if anyone knows a way out of here, it's him?'

'Yeah, but we can't just go talk to him. He's royalty here. You have to get an audience.'

'Are you serious?' Theo scoffs. 'This is a jail, not a palace.'

Sie shrugs. 'I'm just telling you what the kid told me. But you best believe we aren't getting anywhere near him unless we prove ourselves somehow.'

'Iron I's!' a voice shouts from the tunnel outside. 'I come from Dante. He wants to see you.'

Sie's eyebrows practically disappear into his hair and, even in the state of fear I'm in right now, I can't help my snigger.

Vic opens the curtain. 'Why?'

The vampire outside opens his arms wide and the look he gives us reminds me of a petulant teenager. 'He wants you. I bring you.'

The others follow him. I get to my feet and hurry after them, not wanting to be left anywhere by myself.

'This is dumb,' I mutter at Sie's back.

'You got a better idea? We need to see Dante and he's making it real easy.'

'What if he wants to kill us?'

Sie snorts. 'Then we make sure we're too valuable to kill. What is up with you, anyway? Get it together, would you?'

I nod. He's right. I'm acting like a liability and that's not going to do me, us, or Kor and Jane any favors.

We're taken through multiple tunnels and into a cavern that's pretty big, though nothing like the size of the first one we were portalled into. There are some pretty big supes lining the walls and, as I look up, I notice some large holes in the ceiling. One of them is coated in white silk and I shiver. Is a giant spider going to come out of there and attack us? As I look, I swear I see a humanesque face peering down out of it, but when I look again, it's gone.

There's a large, wooden chair at the front of the room. A big guy dressed in faded jeans and an old-fashioned lace-up shirt lolls in it, one leg draped over one of the arms like he thinks he's Jack Sparrow. This must be Dante.

There's a motley group of supes in front of him armed with torches and a couple of candles. At his gesture, they nod as one and then leave the cavern like they're on a mission.

'What's that about?' Vic wonders aloud.

The vampire looks around at him. 'We believe there's a female in the mountain. Dante sends search parties out to find her every few days.'

'Is something like that even possible?' Theo asks.

He shrugs. 'Shouldn't be. There's only one way in or out and the authorities definitely wouldn't send a human woman in here, but he's not the only one who's smelled her. I've scented her myself more than once.' He closes his eyes, his fangs elongating as he thinks about it. 'What I wouldn't give to sink my teeth into a human woman again.'

'I'd have your head before the blood hit your tongue,' Dante drawls. 'Perhaps you should content yourself with the humans they send through at chow time. Don't want you getting grand ideas, Silas.'

I get stuck on what Dante has said for a second, wondering where they get the humans that feed the supes down here from.

The vamp opens his eyes and grins. 'A guy can dream.'

But before he can say anything else, he's taken from the ground by his throat. Dante is now right in front of us and in demon form.

Shit, he's about two times the size of Theo and he's fast as hell.

He shakes Silas like a maraca.

'The human woman is mine when she's found and let no one forget it,' he commands, his voice echoing through the chamber.

'Of course,' the vampire chokes out. 'Didn't mean anything by it, boss.'

He's thrown down to the ground where he lays motion-less, clutching his throat.

Dante puts his glamor down again and his eyes find us. 'I've heard of the Iron I's,' he says with a jovial upturn to his lips. 'I'm going to keep this short. I want the Bear in the ring.'

Sie steps forward. 'I don't fight anymore.'

Dante doesn't say anything for a moment, but the smirk doesn't leave his face.

I feel a guy coming up behind me and I have him in front of me with my new knife at his jugular before I even see him. I know there's more than one surprised face in here. Everyone assumes I'm the weakest because I'm the youngest ... until they see the real me.

Dante looks pleased though. 'You'll be useful.'

He turns his attentions back to Sie. 'Fight. Win. Or I kill the big, blue one.'

I see Sie's jaw tick. I know he used to fight in the Order's cages before he got out of there. But that was a long time ago. He hasn't been in a ring in years.

Sie grinds out one word. 'When?'

Dante grins, showing his perfect, white teeth. 'Soon.'

SEVEN

Jane

Maddox and Korban are in the room arguing by the door. I'm trying not to listen.

That's a lie. I'm totally listening, straining to hear every single word.

But I'm pretty sure it's about me and even I know it's rude to talk about someone behind their back right in front of them, so I figure listening to them do it is okay.

'The answer is no!' Korban hisses.

'Good luck getting your clan out of the Mountain without me then!'

'You're a real sonofabitch, Maddox.'

'Call me what you will, but we both know that asking this small thing is preferable to what I could actually do to you now that your clan is gone.'

'Fuck you ... and they aren't gone!'

Maddox crosses his arms. 'They are without my help and this is what I demand for it.'

I sit up in the bed, feeling a little under the weather still, but better than I did earlier.

'What's going on?' I ask.

Korban's lips thin and I look to Maddox. 'What's the price of your help?'

'He wants you to help Krase like you did with Sie.'

I scratch my head. 'How can I help Krase?'

'You brought Sie back from the madness that had claimed him,' Maddox says with conviction. 'I want you to do that for Krase. If you can, I know a way to get the Iron I's out of the Mountain.'

'How?' I ask.

'Let's just say someone owes me a favor,' Maddox mutters.

I look at Korban. 'How did I bring Sie back? When?'

'The night you chose him,' Korban mutters through gritted teeth.

'You mean I'd have to ... with Krase?'

But I don't want anyone besides the Iron I's. I wrap my arms around myself. The thought of letting Krase do that gives me the ick and lowkey scares the shit out of me after everything he did.

'Yes,' Kor growls.

'In truth, I don't know,' Maddox says, giving Korban a look. 'It may have been your presence or something else you did that made Sie's sanity return.'

'If I do this, you'll save Vic, Sie, Paris, and Theo?'

'Yes. You have my word.'

'Don't!' Korban snarls.

'I have to if it gives them a chance,' I argue. 'You said no one gets out of the Mountain. They won't be able to escape on their own.'

I get out of bed and throw on some clothes, ignoring

Maddox who turns away immediately and Korban who stares, practically licking his lips.

'I'll take you to him.'

Maddox leads me from the room and, when Korban tries to follow, I tell him not to. I just want this over with and I won't be able to do what I need to do if Kor is there. I can see he doesn't like it, but he does what I ask.

I figure Maddox is going to take me down to a dungeon or something, but all he does is close the door and put one of those link things on it.

'Krase isn't in the house?'

Maddox shakes his head. 'Too much of a danger now.'

He opens the door to a bright, padded room and comes in with me. I startle as he shuts the door, cutting off my connection to Korban and making me feel very alone all of a sudden.

'Can't have him getting out,' Maddox mutters. 'Who knows what he'd do.'

I look around the room, not seeing him at first, but then I spy him in the corner, blending into the white walls.

He's sitting, staring straight ahead like he doesn't even know we're there.

Maddox doesn't say anything as we slowly approach. I look back at the door, which probably no longer leads back to Korban, and I try not to give in to how scared I am. I know what I might have to do in here and I don't want it to go that far. But if Maddox doesn't think I'm going far enough, would he and Krase be strong enough to subdue me together to take what they want?

Krase emits a low growl.

I swallow hard.

'I'm not going to let anything happen to you,' Maddox murmurs next to me.

I give him and his platitudes a scathing look. 'Please stop talking.'

I take my mind off what's happening now, thinking back to that night when I was being made to play Vic's game, when he wanted me to choose which one of the Iron I's would feed from me first. I remember going to the gym that night. I'd chosen Sie, but I couldn't find him. I was trying to work my feelings out of my system on the bike, when Sie grabbed me. I'd been scared, but I'd liked it too.

I go through it again, thinking about everything I did and felt. I didn't know what I was then. But all I can think is that Sie fed from me. I don't even know if I fed from him. I was so out of it after, I hardly remember him taking me to my room.

'I didn't do anything,' I say to Maddox.

He looks at me sharply. 'Are you saying you won't help him?'

'No. I mean I think that feeding from me is what fixed Sie. I didn't do anything else.'

Except fuck him but let's hope it doesn't come to that.

'So let him feed from you then,' Maddox says, gesturing to Krase who still hasn't moved.

'Can he do that without touching me?'

Maddox looks me up and down. 'Of course. You need only feel sexual pleasure.'

I frown at him. 'By myself?'

'Yes,' he smirks. 'Though I'm sure neither of us would object to helping you if you need it.'

He grins like he knows what I'm thinking and is just itching to give me a hand.

'I don't need help,' I say quickly.

But I'm a little doubtful. I mean, I don't have my trusty, pink sparkly dildo and I'm not usually able to get there without it when I'm by myself. Plus, I'll be trying to get myself off in front of two guys I don't trust and am not into at all.

'Turn around,' I order. 'I can't do it with you staring at me like that.'

Maddox bows all chivalrous-like and turns on his heel.

I don't mess around, letting out a breath and sinking to the padded floor. I unbutton my jeans and put my hand into my underwear. I block out where I am and who else is here. There's only me.

I close my eyes and start slowly but think of things that have a very high hot factor. I picture Korban, the bottle, his gun as I circle my clit. I think about Theo in the club and how big he was. My fingers move a little faster and my other hand finds my nipple, pinching it when I remember Paris taking all my clothes off and fucking me on the kitchen counter. I think about Sie in the cleaning closet that night in Metro, how he shoved me up against the wall over and over and I moan at the memory. It morphs into Vic with his demon tongue between my legs licking me, feasting on my pussy. My fingers move over my clit faster, pretending it's him and I shove them into myself hard, crying out as it sends me over the edge and I collapse onto the padded floor, my body twitching in the throes of an orgasm I practically forced out of myself.

'Well, there's something you don't see every day,' a voice says from above me.

I shrink back when I see it's Krase. I take my hand out of my pants and try to subdue my body's shivering. That was intense and so quick!

Maybe I do have succubus powers ...

Maddox is staring at me, his jaw working and he looks a little euphoric. Guess he got a snack out of my pleasure too. I don't see lust in his face, but there is a tent in the front of his pants. I look away from it immediately, the evidence of him taking so much enjoyment in what I just did making me feel sick.

'It wasn't for you!' I want to scream, but I don't. Instead, I get up on shaky legs and notice that Maddox's attention is now firmly on Krase.

'How do you feel, my friend?'

Krase is still staring at me when he answers. 'Better.'

He tears his eyes away from me and gives his clan leader a small nod.

'I was very far gone even for me.'

'And you're well now?'

Krase frowns rubbing his forehead. 'I can still feel it at the edges of my mind. I think this may simply be a respite.'

He looks at me again. 'Thank you. That was ...' He closes his eyes and lets out a slow breath. 'I'm sorry about before, how I treated you ... but please believe me when I say I couldn't help it.'

I give him a faint nod.

'I can't believe you found one after all this time, Maddox,' he continues, surveying me. 'A real succubus. I always knew you were right, that they still existed.'

'Fat lot of good it's done. Years and a fortune wasted searching and it's all been for naught.'

Krase takes Maddox's shoulders and I feel like I'm intruding on a private moment. 'It's not been for naught.'

Maddox's eyes narrow on me. 'You've only delayed the inevitable,' he says. 'Do it properly and make it stick. Now.'

This was what I was afraid of. I shake my head, my gaze shifting from Maddox to Krase and my heartbeat begins to pick up speed. I demon-up because I'm not going down without a fight.

But it's Krase who pulls Maddox back around to look at him. 'It won't work. It doesn't feel right. She's not ours, Julian.'

'But that's only because of Vic's clan. Maybe if we—'

'Listen to me!' Krase gives Maddox a shake. 'She's allowed me to feed from her. It's given me back some time. I'm well enough to get my affairs in order, perhaps even for you to find the answer before it really is too late for me. But, however much you're used to getting your way, my friend, you cannot force a succubus to give anything she doesn't want to give. We know that.'

'Not everything from the books is true. If we could just ...' Maddox's words fade as Krase shakes his head.

'No more of this. Come, take me back to the house, let me see my brother. You do whatever it was you promised you would if she helped me. She's done all she can, all I would want her to do.'

Maddox's head hangs low and I can see tears in his eyes, but he eventually nods and heaves a great sigh as he pulls out the link key he used to get us here.

'My word is my bond, I suppose. I'll get your clan out of the Mountain.'

~

Vic

'I'LL SEND Silas for you when it's time,' Dante says, waving us away.

But when I turn to go with the rest of my clan, he stops me with a finger pointed right at my chest. 'Not you.'

Theo and Paris turn back to wait for me, but I shake my

head. I don't know what Dante wants, but I'd rather they were out of the line of fire.

'I'll see you guys later.'

They both give me wary looks before they sprint to the door to catch up with Sie, who's leaving without a backwards glance. As soon as my Second agreed to that fight, I saw his whole demeanor change. He'll go in the ring to keep Theo alive, but I hope he can get in the right headspace for it because right now all he's thinking about is the past.

I turn back to the demon in charge. He beckons me and goes through a curtain behind his chair that I hadn't really noticed. I see a room behind this one. I follow him in.

There's a real bed, a couple of candles, and a few seats. It's sparse and bare, but not as spartan as our cell.

'What is it that you want from me?' I ask him.

He gives a snort and then sniffs the air, turning his attention to the holes high in the roof of the cavern.

'Do you smell that?'

I breathe in through my nose, but all I can pick up are the other prisoners. The air is thick with the scents of the many supes who live down here.

'I don't smell anything.'

Dante laughs. 'No one can in here at first, but you will.' He sits down hard in a chair facing me, but he's still staring at the ceiling.

'There's a female in this place with us,' he murmurs. 'I know there is. Every asshole in here would gut his own mother for a female, but there's only one.'

'You will be mine!' he roars at the roof of the cavern.

I don't show my true thoughts, but it's clear to me that while the motor might be running with this guy, there's no one behind the wheel.

'I was contacted by your father. He told me to kill you and

your clan when you got in here,' he suddenly says and I find him looking at me again. 'But he was supposed to give me something and he hasn't, so you get to live another day, Alexandre. Congratulations.'

I stare at Dante, showing nothing outwardly. So Lionel wants me dead and it sounds like maybe he had a hand in getting us sent here. I always figured this day would come ... just like it did for Harris.

I push the memories away. I haven't thought about my older brother in years and now is definitely not a good time for it.

'Thank you,' I say, keeping as much control of this situation as I can. 'What was your deal? Maybe we can make a new one that benefits us both.'

'Doubt it unless you can find the female,' Dante mutters almost moodily. 'I'm going to die in here without one. Every demon, every clan is stronger with a mate. Even your asshole father knows that, the fucker.'

I frown at the implication. 'My father doesn't have a mate.'

Dante gives me a look. 'I've known your father a long time, whelp. I was there when his clan had a female of their own. I was younger than you, but I was there. A shifter girl.'

'My mother—'

He lets out an angry sound. 'This was long before he hired your mother to breed him you.'

I just stand and stare, wondering if he's lying, but I can't think of any reason for him to. Some clans do find a mate outside their species, it's true. It's rare and I've heard it's not the same, but no one ever mentioned my father's clan ever having one.

'What happened to her?'

'This was prior to your father becoming THE Lionel

Makenzie. He and his guys were just another incubus clan working their way up. They made enemies and they couldn't protect what was theirs. She was taken. Killed.'

I nod because I expected as much, but my mind turns to thoughts of Jane. I'm worried about her and Kor in Maddox's home, but I'm just as worried about Jane in Kor's company. He doesn't like her. I don't think he's even capable of being friendly to a human girl. What if he's had to feed from her? Without Paris there to temper him, what if he's hurt her or worse?

'They killed most of the males of the shifter pack who did it,' Dante continues, clearly in a story-telling mood, 'and enslaved the lower ranking members. It was a smart move. They rose in power and wealth because of it and started their clubs with what they stole.'

His eyes find me again. 'Her loss pretty much broke their clan apart though, from what I heard.'

'He's never spoken of her to me.'

Dante lets out a gravelly laugh. 'They had their memories cleansed of her. They couldn't talk about her even if they wanted to. That was the only way they could survive.'

I make a slow circle of the room, keeping Dante in my sights.

So my father had a mate who was killed and it destroyed him and his clan. Is this why my father's the nasty sono-fabitch he is; why his clan has always struck me as hollow and devoid of anything even resembling a brotherhood? Is this what would happen to us if Jane—?

I shake my head a little at the thought. Jane isn't our mate, I remind myself. She's our human on-call girl. She means a lot to me. I know that now and I need to keep her safe. But that isn't the same as having a mate.

'Why are you telling me this?' I ask him.

Dante shrugs. 'Talking passes the time until that female hiding here is found. That's all we got in the Mountain. Time.'

'Me and my clan need to get out of here,' I say.

Dante's eyes snap to mine and he starts laughing hard.

'Well, after you!' he sniggers with a flourish. 'You think if there was a way out I'd be here?'

I frown at him. 'I don't believe there's no escape.'

'Oh, there are two, Makenzie. Get killed or wait 'til your time's up and the automated system pulls you out. But that's it. Many have tried, spent their lives searching this hellhole and all they got for their troubles was a dark death down some forgotten tunnel or getting sucked dry by an arania. Go searching. Be my guest. But make sure the Bear is here when I call or I'll throw your boy Theo into the ring instead.'

'Theo can take care of himself,' I reply.

'No doubt. He's a big guy. He might even go for the full first round, but he's no fighter. He won't last long in my ring.' He cants his head as he smirks at me. 'I just have that feeling.'

Right.

Dante waves me out and I don't try to keep him talking. He's a little less nuts than I first thought, but I can still see it in him the way I used to see it in Sie. I thought it was an incubi problem, but it looks like other species of demon have the same affliction.

Would having a mate really fix Dante the way he thinks ... the way Jane fixed Sie? A nasty theory starts taking hold, becoming more and more tangible the longer I let it float around in my mind. Could Jane really be our mate? It should be impossible. She's human and I've never heard of a non-supe mate before.

I catch a whiff of a scent and stop.

Well, I'll be damned. There is a female down here somewhere.

Impossible clearly doesn't hold the weight it once did. But if a human is my clan's mate, where is that going to leave her – and us – in a world as dangerous as ours?

When we get out of here, I might have a difficult decision to make.

Theo

An hour. That's all the respite Sie gets before Dante makes him go back to a place he hasn't been since he escaped the Order's cages.

The ring.

I'm keeping an eye on Sie, but there's nothing to see. He's just sitting with his back to the wall. His face is blank and he's staring at nothing. I've tried talking to him, but he doesn't say anything back.

'Leave him alone,' Vic mutters as Paris tries again. 'If this is what he needs to do, let him.'

'What's the point of this?' Paris asks. 'Why Sie? Was he really that good?'

'Better,' I murmur, almost hoping Sie doesn't hear me. 'I saw him. Once.'

Vic looks up sharply. 'How? The cage fights were human spectators only, closed to everyone except the obscenely rich.'

I shrug. I thought Vic knew all my stories, but maybe I subconsciously kept this one back.

'I was doing my residency. It was a few months before the news broke about supes. I was still just a very pretty human kid with a secret. I had a friend whose dad was on the Board of Trustees at my hospital. He had an invite and asked me to tag along. I don't know what I expected, but it wasn't supes in animal cages being made to fight for humans' entertainment, that's for sure.'

Paris looks from me to Vic. 'I don't get it. The Order was around before the humans knew about us?'

'Yeah.' Vic leans up against the wall on the other side of the room. 'You see, some of the humans knew supes existed before it was out of the box, and they capitalized on the fact that there were no laws for us. The Order was already around. They just weren't what they are now. I don't know what they were into exactly besides the fights, but Foley was there from the beginning too.'

'Sie knew him?' Paris asks.

'Knew him?'

I shake my head a little. I'd forgotten that Paris was probably only sixteen or seventeen back then. He's probably never heard people talk about the underground fighter who wiped the floor with demons, vamps, and shifters alike.

'Sie was Foley's number one fighter. I think he lost maybe five fights?'

'Three,' Sie corrects from the wall and I wince. 'Four years. That's how long I was the Order's cash cow. That's how long Foley kept me shackled.'

He stands up and stretches, his body cracking and popping.

'I'm going to the ring.'

He leaves without another word and Vic and Paris move to follow.

'Are you coming?' Paris asks.

I nod. 'I'll be there in a minute.'

I'm left alone and I make a show of slowly walking over to the desk and sitting at it.

'I know you're here,' I say quietly, not looking up. 'I can smell you.'

I don't hear anything.

'You don't have anything to fear from me,' I continue. 'I have my own female. I'm not interested in you like that.'

There's a moment of silence before I hear a sound. I look up and see a face peering out of one of the smaller holes in the ceiling.

From what little I can see of her, she's pretty short and slight of build.

She doesn't come down into the room, just stays in the tunnel above, watching me. She must be a pretty good climber, I concede, to be able to stay up there like that.

'Dante sent a party out looking for you,' I say, thinking of the group I saw leaving his throne room earlier.

She nods.

'Guess you're used to it, huh?'

Another nod.

'How did you get here? How long have you been here?'

She makes a weird movement and I realize she's shrugging upside down.

'Look,' I stand up and she immediately tenses.

I sit back down again. 'Sorry, I didn't mean to scare you. I'm just ... I need to know how you got here because you didn't come through the main portal, right?'

She shakes her head.

'So there's another way out? Another portal? Can you get out of the Mountain?'

She looks apologetic as she shakes her head and my spirits plummet.

'Shit,' I sigh, putting my head in my hands.

Paris is heading for another panic attack, Vic is more taciturn than I've ever seen him, Sie is about to do something he swore he never would again, and I'm going to be used as leverage to make him fight until one of us dies.

'I'm sorry,' she whispers just loudly enough me for me to hear. 'It was a one-way ticket.'

I lift my head up and look at her. 'You chose to come in here? Why?'

She offers me a grin. 'It's more dangerous for me out there.'

And then she's gone.

I can't help my chuckle as I stare at the space where she just was. I just had what amounts to a conversation, albeit mostly one-sided, with the woman Dante wants more than anything but can't find.

I leave our cell and follow the noise that has been steadily growing over the past few minutes. Sounds like the fights have started.

Sie

THE SIGHT of the ring sickens me. The smell makes me want to fold in half and spew all over my shoes. But the sound is the worst. The roars and the cheers make me cringe on the inside and I wonder, errantly, if this is what Jane feels when it all gets to be too much for her. If it is, I understand her affinity for closets.

But I don't let anyone see any of it as I stand there in my human form. I put it all away deep in my mind as I watch my opponent with unblinking eyes. He's a shifter. I take a whiff.

Dragon shifter.

That's why the ring is so big. And that means that changing in the fight isn't against the rules.

Good to know.

I size him up, see him doing the same. He yells something at me with a grin on his face that's probably meant to rile me, but I don't listen to his words. There's only quiet now as I take that part of me I buried so deep the night I escaped the Order's cage and let it out.

As soon as the bell rings, I'm on him, my hand wrapped tightly around his throat, and I know my speed has surprised everyone.

When he can't throw me off, he shifts, just like I knew he would. The big ones always go for the shift first.

His neck elongates and grows in girth like the rest of his body, but I lock my fingers in their hold, keeping a tight grip on the area that becomes his fire glands as he changes. I twist the handful of flesh and scales that I'm holding like I'm taking the lid off a jar of pickles, making sure this part of him can't form properly. I hear him choke as I let him go, grinning as he opens his huge jaws to incinerate me and nothing comes out but a puff of smoke.

Someone shouts something about Puff, the Magic Dragon and the crowd roars with laughter.

I see the surprise in the shifter's eyes, the uncertainty as I uppercut his reptilian jaw no differently than I would a man's. A couple of his massive teeth fall out of his mouth and bounce on the floor of the ring.

His arms encircle me, trying to crush me like his constrictor cousins might. His tail whips around to break my neck, but my own un-glamors and entangles with his, keeping the appendage at bay as I hunker down and push his arms away from me, forcing them back and giving me space as my fingers move over the scales of his torso quickly, seemingly at random, but looking for something very specific.

I look into his eyes and see them dart nervously to Dante who I know is sitting in his chair behind me at the ring's edge, but I don't follow where they lead. I never take my focus off an opponent in the middle of a fight.

I find what I've been feeling for, a scale that feels bigger than the others, and I rip it out. The dragon roars in pain and I flick the scale away as hot blood pours from the wound I just made.

He shifts back into a man immediately and I lower my own glamor, now taller and stronger than he is. I don't hesitate now that I have the higher ground. I hit him in the face over and over, not letting up, not giving him a moment to recover until he's on the floor unable to defend himself, his face unrecognizable from moments ago.

The fight's over.

Only now do I look out of the ring and not at the dragon shifter who's laying unmoving in the puddle of his own blood. He could be dead for all I know, but he would have killed me if he'd had the chance. There's no place for mercy here.

Dante is still sitting in his chair. He looks a little surprised.

'Hope you enjoyed the show, motherfucker,' I say as I walk past him and I see him grin.

I make my way back to our cell slowly, ignoring the inmates who give me a very wide berth. I get into the room and only then do I look down at my hands that are covered in blood. I sink to my knees and vomit on the floor next to me.

I was a natural talent, I was told whenever anyone saw me fight. I was an amazing fighter, able to see the weaknesses I could exploit. But I never wanted that to be my skill. I escaped that life. I left it far behind me, I thought. But here I am back again.

The room goes dark and I feel a light wind dancing on my skin. I know this feeling. I'm portalling out.

Gratitude fills me. I don't care if I end up in a lake of boiling lava so long as I'm not here for a second longer.

$$\sim$$

I'M EJECTED from the dark abyss a moment later and left standing on a gravel driveway in the cold sun. I blink as my eyes adjust to the light. I've been pulled out of the Mountain.

How?

I whirl around. Vic, Paris and Theo are here too. I try to make sense of what's happening even as I struggle to put that part of me I let out in the prison away again as fast as possible. I'm as much a danger to others when I'm like this as I was when I was going crazy.

If Jane is here, I'm a danger to her too and, more selfishly, I really don't want her to see the darker side of myself that just beat a dragon shifter probably to death and felt nothing.

I try to get a handle on it as I look around me. This is Maddox's house.

House. Yeah right. This is a castle complete with turrets and gargoyle statues.

The door to the castle opens.

It's a butler. An actual butler.

I don't wait. I should give myself more time, but with nothing now in my path to Jane except the small man at the door, I rush past him, ignoring the affronted noise he makes as I run through the house calling for her. She better fucking be here or I'm going to kill every single person inside these walls.

I find Jayce. I can always tell those two fuckers apart.

'Where's Jane?' I snap, hoping he doesn't tell me so I can crush him. 'I can smell her.'

'Charming.' He makes a face. 'Upstairs to the right. For fuck's sake. I don't want a mate if she makes me as pathetic as you. Go and find her. Take her away. She's outstayed her welcome just like your brother has anyway.'

At the mention of Kor, I freeze. 'Is Jane okay?'

He turns away as if I'm no longer worth talking to and I curse at his back, sprinting down the corridor and up the stairs. I call her name at the top of my lungs and a door opens.

Korban emerges. He's well fed, practically glowing.

My heart drops into my stomach.

'You know you're running around with your horns out, right?' he mutters, then looks me over. 'You look like shit.'

I'm still in demon form. I'd forgotten. I don my glamor, the blood disappearing from my hands as they turn human in a very welcome side-effect.

'Where's Jane?' I yell more loudly than intended.

He hushes me, stepping out and closing the door behind him.

What doesn't he want me to see?

I grab him, throwing him into the wall. 'Where the fuck is she?'

He pries my hands away from his throat where I'm threatening to choke him.

'Would you keep it down? She's asleep!'

'I want to see her,' I thunder.

'Fine!' He rolls his eyes. 'She's in there, but she's tired. Shut the fuck up or you'll wake her.'

I push him away from me and go into the room. There's only one lamp on in the corner. It smells of her and of Kor. I glance back at him standing in the doorway, a growl emanating from deep in my chest.

But he only gives me a look, points at the bed, and then puts a finger to his lips.

'Fine!' I hiss, moving forward quietly.

She's in bed. I can see the shape of her body. I'm already starting to relax just knowing she's in front of me, but she's hidden under the covers.

I go closer and peer at her face. Her skin is pale and grey. She looks sick.

I whirl in Korban's direction. What has he done to her?

But he only turns and walks out the door, beckoning me. I don't want to kill him in her presence because I'm going to do it slow and it's going to be bloody, so I exit the room.

'What did you do to her?' I ask, my anger quickly becoming unmanageable.

I feel like I did before, when madness had me in the dark, unable to control my fury as I lash out at him. I hit him square in the jaw with everything in me. He thumps to the floor and stays there, conscious but not bothering to get up.

'It's not like that,' he says with a groan. 'Would you listen?'

I lunge at him, but he rolls away from me, picking himself up and high-tailing it along the corridor. And then the fucker mounts the banister and slides down like he's in a cartoon.

I can't do that. I'll break my demon neck.

By the time I get to the bottom, he's hiding behind Vic like a little bitch.

'He's been feeding from her,' I snarl. 'He hurt her.'

'No, I didn't!'

'You're telling me that you look healthier than you have in months, and you haven't fed from her?' I scoff.

He gives me a look. 'Must be the European lifestyle,' he goads, laughing when I lunge forward and Vic stops me.

'She's upstairs in a room they've clearly been sharing! She looks half-dead!' I say to Vic who turns around to confront Kor, his expression darkening.

'Explain,' he says.

He doesn't raise his voice, but the force of his power has Korban's knees hitting the marble floor hard.

'It's not what you think,' he grinds out. 'Yeah, I fed from her. I didn't want to but I had no choice.'

'You selfish sonofa—'

'You made it through. Goodie,' Maddox drawls, appearing in a doorway that seems to lead to a library. 'You can give me your eternal thanks for getting you out of the most secure supe prison ever after you've settled in if you like, but there is a lot we need to talk about. May I suggest we do it by the fire after you've checked on your female?'

He turns, walking back into the room and leaving the five of us standing a little awkwardly in the wide hallway.

Korban picks himself up off the floor and follows Maddox immediately. I scowl at his back. Vic gives me a concerned glance as he, Paris and Theo walk past me, all looking pensive.

'Show us where she is.'

I climb the stairs slowly.

'Are you okay?' Theo asks me.

I nod. 'I will be, but I don't want to talk about it now.'

He puts a hand on my shoulder, but, thankfully, doesn't ask me anything else about how I'm feeling.

I return to the room where I saw Jane and we all shuffle inside. She's still curled up in the bed.

'See?' I whisper, angry with Kor all over again.

'She's breathing fine,' Theo says, looking at her closely.

'And I don't see any injuries where ... where I'd normally expect to see them. I don't think this was Korban. She looks like she has the flu or something.'

'But he admitted he fed from her,' I argue. 'He always hurts them if Paris isn't with him.'

Paris gives me a look, but I meet his eyes unapologetically.

Jane stirs in the bed, making a tiny noise of distress in her sleep that has me yearning to take her in my arms, but she doesn't wake.

Vic ushers us out of the room. 'Let's leave her to rest and speak to Kor.'

Theo's still standing by the bed looking confused.

'What is it?' Vic asks.

Theo sniffs the air. 'Her scent is different. Can't you smell it?'

'It's probably the house.'

Theo shakes his head, but comes along, shutting the door quietly as we leave.

'What do you think?' Vic asks Theo.

'I think we need to go downstairs and speak with Kor and Maddox.'

'Speak to them? We need to go downstairs and fuck them up,' I growl low, but I'm ignored.

We trail back down, my body feeling more and more tense the longer I'm not beating Korban into a bloody and unidentifiable pulp. I'm vaguely aware that this is the price of fighting and that these penchants for violence will fade into the background again soon, but it's difficult not to act on them.

Vic leads us into the library and we find Maddox there. Axel, his second, is standing next to him. Kor is staring out the window. He turns when we enter.

'How is she?' he asks Theo.

'Until I examine her properly, I can't be sure, but she seems fine for now.'

Korban nods. 'Good. I gave her something to help her sleep.'

'You drugged her?' Theo asks, his eyes flying to Vic, no doubt remembering the last time one of us slipped her something.

'Relax, it wasn't like that. She asked me for it when we heard where you guys were ... she's been worried.'

I can't help the growl that comes from deep within me. Kor and Jane are friends now? I don't buy it.

'Are you going to tell us what the fuck is going on?' I growl, stepping forward, but Vic stops me.

Kor looks at a loss for words. 'A lot's been going on,' he begins and then breaks off, pacing around the room. 'I didn't hurt her. I promise you that. I fed but,' he looks at Paris, 'it's not like how it was with the others. I didn't lose control. At least ... not like that.'

Paris steps forward, enveloping Kor into a hug that he returns with enthusiasm.

'We missed you,' Paris whispers.

I don't fail to notice that Kor takes Paris' hand and squeezes it. He's relieved that Paris is here, that we all are.

'She's not what we thought,' he says.

'Stop speaking in riddles!' I step towards him, fists clenched. 'Give us some fucking answers!'

'You're not going to believe me,' he says simply.

'Jane is a succubus,' Maddox says.

'Bullshit!' Vic laughs. 'Trust you to make jokes when we've been put in jail, stripped of our civil liberties, and then thrown into even worse jail.'

'It's not a joke, nor is it a trick or a powerplay or whatever else you may think. She is what I say.'

'That's not possible,' Theo says. 'They're extinct … and that's if they ever did exist as anything more than a fairytale.'

'You're wrong,' Maddox says, striding to the bookshelf and ripping one of the books from it.

He holds it in the air in front of us and chucks it on the table. It slides across and all the eyes in the room track it's journey.

'They hide with the humans. Sometimes they don't know what they are. Sometimes they figure it out and go looking for help and the fae disappear them before anyone finds out.'

'What?'

'That can't be tru—'

'It's all here,' Maddox says, cutting through everyone's words, 'mentions of them in the rare, surviving copies of books banned by the Ten.'

'The Ten are powerful and ancient fae, it's true. But even they wouldn't have been able to—'

'Wouldn't they?' Maddox interrupts again. 'If succubi are somehow a threat to the Ten, what wouldn't that denary of the highest and most powerful fae lords do to protect themselves? Perhaps they wouldn't exterminate half a race in secret. Perhaps they wouldn't drive the few survivors into hiding amongst the human populations, forcing them to be very careful when they fed, who they fed from, never letting the demon out in case someone realized what they were. There's a reason the Ten have been the highest in the pecking order for so long, and it's not luck.'

'This is absurd,' Vic mutters. 'Your search for a mate has made you start deluding yourself. Jane is a human and our on-call girl. You aren't keeping her.'

'I couldn't keep her if I wanted to,' Maddox sighs. 'Not

without a great deal of effort and time we don't have. She's already decided who her mates are. She's bitten half of you! Didn't you notice or did you think that was a human custom?'

He laughs and he actually sounds like he thinks it's hilarious.

All of this makes sense.

But Vic just rolls his eyes. 'Even the Ten couldn't have hidden such a genocide. This is ridic—'

'No,' I say, stepping forward and trying to find some of the Zen I had before the fight. 'It's not ridiculous. You know it's not, Alex. There's been something off about her from the start. I thought it was the human part, but it isn't. I had my suspicions about what Jane was, but nothing came of them and the idea seemed so outlandish ... especially as she didn't exhibit any real signs that you'd see in a young incubus, so I second-guessed myself. But there was something; something I couldn't put my finger on.'

I look at the others and see Paris nodding.

'You've sensed it too,' I say to him.

'No, but she told me she could feel my emotions ... and I started feeling hers.'

'And you didn't think to tell me?' Vic hisses.

'It wasn't like that,' Paris says, looking at the ground. 'I've heard stories about succubi and I've seen stuff down rabbit holes online. If she was one, I knew she'd be in danger if anyone found out, so I told her to keep it to herself.'

I wave a hand, getting impatient. 'There's no disputing Maddox's claims about Jane. And the Ten do whatever they want. We all know that.'

'As some of the only beings with such longevity who actually concern themselves with the mortal realms, they can practically rewrite history at will,' Maddox adds, his tone angry.

I glance down at the old book with its frayed edges and faded, cracking leather binding.

Theo speaks up. 'If it happened long enough ago, and all those who remembered were dead and the fae destroyed as much of the evidence as they could find, they could make their story whatever they wanted. Everyone would believe it and that's if anyone even cared one way or the other. It's happened within the human histories more than once and none of them even live all that long.'

My clan are quiet, thinking it over.

'Have you actually seen anything to prove this?' Vic asks Korban. 'Or is it just conjecture. She might be a tiny part fae or something else entirely.'

'I've seen her demon,' Korban says. 'Both Maddox and I have ... and Krase,' he adds with a twist of his lips that I make a mental note to ask him about later.

'You've seen her change?' Theo asks.

Kor nods. 'Her first time. It was amazing,' he mutters with a grin. 'But that's what's wrong with her.'

'She's maturing into a full succubus,' Theo guesses and Kor nods.

'But she's in her twenties,' Paris says. 'We mature in our teens. If she really is a succubus, why is it so late?'

'A succubus reaches sexual maturity later,' Kor says.

'How do you know?' I scowl at him again.

He didn't even like Jane a few days ago. How does he know everything about her now?

'I've been reading up about succubi,' he says smugly, making me want to pummel his self-satisfied face again.

'Where's this book?' Theo asks and I'm glad that he seems more himself now that we're all back together again.

'Up in the room,' Kor says. 'I'll show you.'

'If her transformation is anything like mine, she feels like shit,' Vic says. 'Let her rest for now. The book can wait.'

'What are we going to do about this?' I ask.

'About what?' Kor says, looking confused.

'Jane is a succubus,' I say to him slowly. 'That's a massive fucking problem or am I wrong? We already have enough issues with the fae; their rules, their taxes, Torun's black market shipments that went missing from our warehouses. Now we're going to be on the Ten's radar too if we aren't already. Do any of you really think they're going to let us keep her?'

No one in the room says anything.

'How the hell are we going to keep her a secret? Keep her safe?'

'We'll find a way,' Korban says. 'There's no alternative.'

I turn away from them, shaking my head. I care about Jane and don't want to lose her, but if what she is becomes common knowledge, the Ten will have us all taken out as easily as blinking.

CHAPTER
NINE

Vic

'What do we know about the fighting in Metro,' I ask, trying to move the subject away from Jane. Our mate. 'Is it spreading?'

'Not as yet,' Maddox replies. 'I've had Iron keeping tabs on it. It's still going on, but only within the borders of the seven cities that were attacked.'

'Is no one else going to ask how the fuck Maddox got us out of the Mountain?' Paris asks suddenly. 'No one gets out. Ever. So how did you pull it off?'

My gaze find's Maddox's. 'More to the point,' I say, 'what's the price of your help?'

Maddox grins. 'You'll be happy to know that the debt's already been paid, my friend. As to how I did it, well, I have many favors owed to me. I simply called one in.'

My eyes narrow and I look over at Korban. 'You paid it?'

'Not exactly,' he growls.

'Jane?' I ask, unable to keep the snarl contained as I focus back on my viperous friend. 'What did you make her do, Julian?'

'Nothing she wasn't willing to do,' Maddox says, clearly enjoying how enraged I am. 'Just a small issue I had, that's all.'

'A small issue?' Korban growls. 'Krase lost his mind and Maddox had him feed from Jane in case it cured him.'

'Like Sie,' I growl, stalking forward and taking Maddox by the neck.

I let my glamor up at the same time. 'You shouldn't have brought Jane into this. It's not up to an on-call girl to settle debts between clans.'

I let my power out. All of it and he grunts as he feels it drive him down, but he's as strong a leader as I am. He stands his ground, not letting his knees buckle under the force of it.

'Are you still going to pretend she's an on-call girl?' he goads.

I squeeze harder.

'It's not what you think,' he grinds out finally. 'She only gave him what she wanted to give him. I didn't make her do anything.'

'If you didn't, it's only because forcing her wasn't necessary to get the outcome you desired,' I say low, trying to keep some semblance of control.

I finally let the power wane and push him away from me.

'Don't pretend to be magnanimous, Julian. It doesn't suit you.'

'Touché,' he says, rubbing his throat and breathing heavily. 'I can see you're overcome with worry for your female, so, though you attacked me in my clan's own home, I'll take this no further.'

I don't say anything more. I leave the room immediately. Regardless of what Korban said, I hope that Jane really wasn't forced into more than she'd bargained for just to get us out of that place.

Why did she agreed to help at all?

I sneak up the stairs, hoping none of the others catches me. I want to see Jane properly for myself.

By myself.

I don't want Theo worrying next to me, Paris' jokes to lighten the mood, Sie breathing down my neck. I just want to see Jane, make sure she's okay.

I've been burying my feelings and my worries since the attacks because I needed to keep everything together. But she's here.

She's a succubus.

Did I know? I didn't think so at first, but now … maybe I did connect with her on a deeper level. She always felt different to me, and not just because of her human diagnosis.

'I guess we know how her mother got ahold of an orc stone,' I mutter to myself. 'Hell of a family heirloom.'

I halt outside the door. Why do I feel like a dumb kid about to be torn a new one?

It's now or never.

I enter the room, not knocking, not giving her the chance to turn me away.

She's awake and sitting up in the bed. A tray of food has appeared and the tantalizing smell of pizza and fries wafts towards me.

She's staring at me. 'Is it really you?' she asks, looking wary and I wonder what's been going on if she's this suspicious.

'It's me. I promise.'

'You guys are here and you're all okay?'

I nod. 'Korban told us what you did, what Maddox's price

for getting us out of the Mountain was. Are you okay?' I clench my fists. 'You shouldn't have done that for us.'

She shrugs. 'I'm fine. Besides, how else would you have gotten out of that place?'

'We wouldn't have,' I state plainly.

'Well, there you go. Just say thanks and we'll call it square.'

'Thank you,' I say, but we're so far from square.

I owe the woman in front of me. A lot. I don't know what I can do to actually make things up to her, but I know how I have to start.

I take a deep breath.

'I'm sorry, Jane. I'm sorry for losing you in the club. I didn't keep you safe and that's on me. And I know I said it before but I'm sorry for putting you in that cell and for all the other things ... I promise I'll make it up—'

She looks away and I know she wasn't intending on all that being brought up again, but I need her to know that I'll fix it, that I'll fix all of it.

She opens her mouth and takes a breath. Her next words come out in a rush as if she's afraid she won't be able to get them out. She's staring at the bed.

'You've been an asshole since the beginning, Vic. Some-times, I don't realize at the time how shitty someone's being to me. Not just you, but other people too. People I thought were friends, people I worked with.' She frowns but doesn't look up. 'I think because I don't say anything at the time, maybe they don't think I realize what they are, maybe they think I'm naïve and stupid because I don't understand the games they play. Maybe some part of me is so used to it that it takes me awhile to see how different things can be when someone cares about me.' She glances up and stares at me.

I'm frozen, my heart beating erratically.

'Maddox's club was terrifying and I was lost in it all alone.'

I take a step towards the bed, but she cringes away, moving to the opposite side from me.

'No. I need to say everything now or I won't,' she says, settling back down into the bed again. 'I've been thinking about all the other stuff a lot too while I've been here, and I think I understand your reasons. You thought I was an enemy and this is a war ... I could probably forgive a lot of it.'

She looks up at me again. This time there's steel in her eyes. 'But you used my senses to torture me in Metro. You used my own brain against me to make me miserable. You left me in the dark and you knew—' She wraps her arms around herself. 'You knew how much I hate it. You were so casually cruel. The things you said ... what you did. The worst part of it is that it was so easy for you to turn on me and tear me down, make me feel whatever you wanted me to. You were so good at it.'

She breaks off with a wince, a shiver, and shake of her head all at once like she can't even face the thought, but shame slithers into my chest and I look away from her.

She's right. At the time it was easy for me and I congratu-lated myself on my success. How quickly I became my father, I think with an inward, self-loathing sneer, scraping my fingers through my hair hard enough to hurt.

'I'm sorry,' I say again.

She gives me a mocking smirk the likes of which I haven't seen on her before.

'I'm sorry,' she says in a customer service tone that sounds like a learned mimic from that kind of work, 'but I don't actually care if you're sorry.'

Korban comes in, looking concerned and rubbing his chest as though it pains him.

'What are you doing?' he sneers at me.

He goes to the bed and gathers Jane into his arms and she lets him. I just stand there, struck dumb.

Korban has gained a lot of fucking ground while we were stuck in the Mountain.

Maybe it's too late for me to try and make amends. Theo tried to warn me, but I thought I could fix the things I did later if I needed to. I thought ...

Kor picks something up from beside the bed and chucks it at me.

I catch it.

A book.

He gestures at the chair in the corner with his chin. I look down at the book.

'Read it,' he mouths as Jane curls into him with a long sigh.

'Do you want something to eat, princess? I ordered all the best things from Jeeves. There's even cupcakes,' he whispers. 'Vanilla. Want one?'

'Cupcakes?' Jane looks over at the tray. 'Yeah, okay,' she concedes.

He gets her one and then stares at me from the bed while she takes little bites.

I pretend to ignore him, taking quick glances at Jane when she doesn't notice me looking.

I wish I could go back and stop myself from doing all that shit I did. But I can't.

And now our human on-call girl is a succubus.

I scan the pages of the book in my hands, but I can't concentrate on the words. Dread coils deep inside me. Sie was right about what he said downstairs. We have nemeses and so does Jane, more if anyone finds out the truth about her.

At the end of the day, I couldn't keep her safe when she

was human. I think about what Dante told me about my father and his clan. Their mate, their family was taken from them by their enemies.

I'm more like my father than I ever thought. Jane's in danger from more than the fae, the Order, and her stalkers. I'm a threat to her and my clan is a threat to her too. She doesn't deserve a life like that. When she was human, I planned to keep her with us so that she'd be protected, but she's in more danger with us than she is without us now.

What if Jane was taken from us and hurt or worse? The reality is that that is a lot more likely now.

I need to keep her as safe as I can. I glance up at her. She looks content with Korban but it won't last. Nothing good ever does. But maybe there's more than one way to make everything up to her.

I leave the room with purpose. I know what I have to do.

~

Paris

I'VE ALWAYS WANTED to visit this estate. Maddox's main home is practically legendary in supe circles, but it's by invitation only, so I figured I'd never get the chance.

Then we were pulled here. As soon as I realized where we were, I put our time in the Mountain behind me and focused on the fact that I'd finally see the amazing place everyone always talks about. Wide open gardens with privacy, and even ancient woodland somewhere on the grounds where Maddox lets shifter guests hunt deer and camp.

It sounded like supe paradise, but now that we're here, I'm seeing that the brochure left out some key points.

The reality is that this place is a sprawling museum and

that's about it. Their cameras are outdated, their security system, laughable. There are no games consoles. The house has like two TVs ... in the WHOLE thing. The nearest town is hours – HOURS! – away.

What do Maddox and his clan do for fun? Maybe they just go out and patrol their borders on horseback like this is the year 1245 since they're living in the actual Dark Ages! I mean there's a decent magickal defense around the house. Korban would have got Jane the hell out of here as soon as they arrived here if there wasn't, but ugh this place is sooooooooo boorrrrrriingg.

I walk around aimlessly, checking my phone for signs of life outside this place but getting very little other than the occasional ping because the WIFI is so damned patchy.

I ultimately find myself outside Jane's door.

Jane. An actual succubus.

I still can't quite get my head around how we could be so lucky. I've already started planning for it, though, because no one can find out what she is outside these walls. She'll have a great, big, glowing target on her back if anyone knows.

I stand in the hall, wondering if I should go in. I was going to leave her be for a little while, but I find I can't. Now that I'm this close, I need to see her.

I open the door and go in slowly, finding her sitting up in bed, reading silently from a tiny book.

Korban is in here too, and I frown. He's hovering over her, making sure she drinks the rest of something from a cup. She's a little annoyed, but he murmurs something about more cupcakes and she perks up with a nod.

He smiles indulgently and I just stand there in the door-way, gaping. Who is this guy? I've known Korban for a long time and I've never seen this side of him. EVER.

They finally notice me and Jane gives me a smile that I take to mean she's okay with me being in here.

'How are you feeling?' I ask her.

'A little better.'

I sit on the bed next to her. 'Can I get you anything?'

'I have it covered,' Korban says, smirking as he pours Jane another steaming cup of tea from an actual bone china teapot with flowers painted on it.

'I see that,' I say, getting up and going to him.

I hug Kor around his torso from the back. I've hardly spoken to him since we got here. I squeeze him hard and he turns around in my arms, hugging me in return.

I give a contented sigh, letting out all the worry I've been harboring. 'When we couldn't find you ...'

'I know,' he says, tilting my chin up to look into my eyes. 'I wanted to tell you I was okay, but I couldn't get through and then we heard where you were ...'

I nod. 'I'm just glad we all made it out.'

'Were any of you hurt?' Kor asks.

I hold up my arm. 'Bullet grazed me in Metro, but that's it.'

'Kor got shot too,' Jane pipes up from the bed and I realize that her hearing is a lot better than it was because I was being very quiet on purpose.

I look accusingly at Kor, drawing back from his embrace. 'You got shot?'

Korban gives Jane a look.

'In the back,' Jane adds.

Korban scowls at her now.

'In the back?' I raise my eyebrows at him. 'When were you going to tell me?'

'I hadn't got to it yet. It wasn't bad—'

'He's lying. It was really bad,' Jane says, her eyes still on the book.

'Quiet!' Korban thunders, 'or do I need to do the thing Maddox was talking about, succubus?'

Her eyes focus on him and widen. She goes quiet, shaking her head.

'What thing?' I ask.

Korban points to a book on the bureau. 'Read it and see.'

Intrigued, I pick it up, but a scent in the air has me putting it back down gently and turning back to Jane.

'Whatever it is, it just made Jane more excited than scared.'

Korban grins. 'It did, didn't it?'

He stalks towards the bed and Jane cowers back into the pillows, her face blank.

'You can't hide from me,' Kor says gently. 'I can read you, princess. You're scared, but more intrigued than you'd like to be. Maybe just a little taste?'

She shakes her head. 'No, thank you,' she whispers. 'I didn't like it.'

Korban sits on the bed. 'Has someone given my princess a spanking before?'

The image that appears in my head of a bent-over Jane fisting the covers with a glowing red ass has me hard in two seconds flat and my eyes flick to Korban, excited to see what he does next.

Kor looks back at me with a lascivious grin on his face that doesn't bode well for Jane.

'Who was it, Jane? Who tanned that little ass?'

Jane holds his gaze. 'Vic.'

'Ah, well Vic can be a little heavy handed when it comes to discipline,' Korban coos, his voice lowering to a throaty growl that makes Jane shift on the bed. 'But maybe Paris and I ...'

She looks from him to me. 'Um, well ... but I'm ...' she looks down at herself. 'I'm still ...'

'Bleeding?' Kor chuckles and I can't help but join him.

'We're demons, Jane. Think we care about a little blood?'

She shakes her head.

'What will you do?' she asks.

'What do you want me to do?'

'I want to watch you two,' she breathes.

I wince, remembering when Jane saw Kor and me kissing after the hospital and he almost throttled her because she liked it.

But Korban throws back his head and laughs. 'Nice try, princess, but we'll do that another time. Right now, it's all about you.'

'But—'

Korban hushes her and pulls the comforter away. My eyes take in her panties and tank top and I groan. Fuck. I don't think I've ever seen anything hotter.

'The book says that sex with her clan will make the maturing faster, so she won't feel bad for so long,' Korban says. 'What kind of clan would we be if we didn't at least try?'

He flips her over with ease and she lets out a sound of annoyance.

I don't move, watching him dubiously. 'I don't think we should—'

'Of course we should,' Kor interrupts. 'We need to take care of her needs. All of her needs.'

'I can look after my own needs,' Jane says, her angry tone muffled by the sheets.

'You don't even know what you need,' Korban scoffs, bringing his hand down to slap her ass.

She squeals and tries to rise, but I can smell her arousal. I can feel her excitement too, and Korban gives me a triumphant look.

Turns out all I needed was to know that she really wanted it and I grin in anticipation as I jump onto the bed. I lie next to her and caress her back. 'Just relax into it,' I advise. 'This is going to be fun.'

'Not for me!'

'Yes, for you,' I laugh, slipping my hand between her body and the bed and under her panties.

She stills as my fingers delve into her slit and play at her entrance. Korban gets impatient and rips off her underwear, throwing it over his shoulder and staring down at her ass.

He slaps it again, not very hard, but she bucks forward, impaling herself on my thick finger. She squeaks and freezes and Kor and I share a dark grin. He gives her another whack and I make sure two of my fingers are lined up and ready to go in a little deeper.

I can't help my chuckle as she valiantly tries to keep her body away from Kor's hand and mine, but fails every single time, her ass cheeks getting redder while my fingers are getting more and more drenched by how turned on she is … even if she won't admit it.

Korban halts and licks his finger, giving me a wink as he parts her cheeks and eases a lone finger into her ass.

She pulls forward, trying to escape the intrusion, but sliding completely onto my waiting three fingers in the process. I use them to stretch her tight pussy, hardly able to wait until I can fuck her properly.

She whines, breathing hard.

'It's okay, baby,' I whisper. 'Let us make you feel good.'

Korban works his finger into her while she pants and mewls, but he's relentless, adding another digit and pushing her to the brink of what she can take right now.

She comes suddenly, arching back with a loud cry as Korban's hand and mine pump into her without mercy.

When she finally relaxes under us, Korban draws his touch away and I do the same.

'There, see, baby girl? That wasn't so bad, was it?'

She turns over onto her back, still panting hard. Her face is red and there are tears on her cheeks. For a second I'm afraid we've hurt her, but then she gives us a small, tremulous smile and shakes her head.

'And do you want more?'

She gives a tiny nod.

'Good girl.'

Kor eyes me. 'Fuck her pussy,' he orders me, 'but do it gently.'

I don't need to be told twice. I let out a groan as I lick the fingers that were just inside her and I'm on my knees and easing myself into her while Korban holds her legs wide.

'That's right, princess,' he says, slapping my ass hard so I startle forward, thrusting into her hard and fast. 'Take it all.'

She moans as I seat myself in her completely and then I feel Korban behind me, his hands parting my cheeks and lining himself up.

'Good boy,' he murmurs and he sinks into me.

I let out a hoarse cry. It's been awhile since I saw this side of Kor too. Fuck, I've missed it.

I lean over Jane and try to make love to her as ordered, but Kor, the fucker, drives into me like he hasn't seen me in a year and it takes all my strength to keep his thrusts from becoming mine and ravaging the beautiful succubus under me. My movements are smooth and gentle as I take Jane, and I'm gratified when she comes again, her back bowing and her lips opening on whimpered gibberish. Kor thrusts into me hard and grips my shoulders tight as he nuts in me and his release becomes mine. I plow deeply into Jane, throwing back my head with a roar as I spill inside her.

Kor pats my ass like it's a horse's flank and I can't help my smile, shaking my head. He's incorrigible.

I hear him turn the shower on as I ease away from Jane. She's practically a boneless puddle on the bed, not even bothering to close her thighs.

I caress her leg as I get off the bed and go into the bathroom. Kor's already in the shower and I join him. We soap each other up and take some time together in private before Jane wanders in, looking a little lost.

Kor gets out and urges her in with me. Then he grabs a towel and leaves, closing us into the bathroom alone.

Jane's shivering a little and I turn up the temperature of the water.

'Are you okay?' I ask, a little worried.

But she nods. 'I feel better after that.'

'Feeding will do that.'

She gives a sheepish smile and I pinch her sore ass. She squeals and bats my hand away.

'Fucker.'

I laugh and grab the soap, but she stops me.

'Not that one.' She grimaces and points to another bottle. 'That one's nicer.'

I throw the offending soap out of the shower completely and she lets out a startled laugh. I lather us both up with the one she likes best and she smiles at me at little shyly while I do it.

I press my lips to hers while the water pelts down on us.

Fuck, I've missed this girl.

I get out a while later and towel off, letting her stay under the water alone. I know she uses the shower to relax, so I leave her to it in case she needs to decompress from her Paris-Korban time.

In the bedroom, Korban is dressed again. I wrap my towel around my waist and look back at the bathroom. I close the door quietly.

'You guys have gotten close,' I say.

'Jealous?' he says giving me a glance, one eyebrow raised and his lips turned up into a ghost of amusement.

But his bravado doesn't fool me. He seems a little worried.

I grin. 'Not even a little. She works pretty well with us, doesn't she?'

He snorts. 'Maybe it's us who work pretty well with her.'

'You and I haven't really talked since we arrived. What do you think about all this?' I ask. 'What she is, I mean.'

'I don't give a shit what she is so long as she's safe and she's with us.'

I sit on the bed. 'What happens when she decides to leave?' I say, finally voicing the fears I've had since I started to care about her.

I say the words as inaudibly as I can because I don't want her to hear if she is listening. I don't want her to know she can leave us. Her contract as an on-call girl was for her as a human. I doubt she's bound to it as a succubus.

Kor pulls on his shoes. 'We have to convince her not to,' he says simply, giving me a once-over like I'm not thinking things through.

As if it's that easy.

'But if she wants to go, we have to let her, or at least make sure she knows that she can leave if she wants to. Otherwise, she's just our prisoner, Kor.'

Kor turns back to me. 'She is what she is and she shouldn't be out there alone as a new demon. It's too dangerous.'

'What about what Sie said? If anyone finds out about her, the fae are going to kill us all including her. She needs to know how to hide, how to protect herself,' I persist. 'I mean, her mother must have been the same as her.'

'Her mother's dead,' Kor growls, 'and we aren't having this pointless conversation.'

He leaves the room quickly and I heave a sigh.

Kor can bury his head in the sand all he likes, but we all need to have a talk, Jane included. We need to decide what happens next, where we're going to go, how we're going to stay safe.

CHAPTER
TEN

Jane

I don't spend all that much time in the shower. At least I don't think I do, but when I emerge from the steam, both Korban and Paris are gone. I'm wondering at the sensations I felt while I was in the bathroom. They were muted, maybe because I wasn't trying to feel them or because we weren't in the same room, but Kor and Paris were definitely having a heated discussion about something.

I put my clothes on. I'm going stir crazy in here and I feel well enough to leave. I put on my shoes and head downstairs. Kor brought me French pastries and now I have a taste for them. I want more.

At first I think the kitchen is deserted, but then I hear a noise in the pantry and, upon further investigation, find the butler wrestling with a live bird.

'Jeeves?'

He turns when he hears me with a grimace. 'Once again, it's Robertson, Madam.'

Oh, yeah.

I need to remember that. He just looks so Jeevesy!

The bird flaps in Jeeves' face and he loses his grip on it. Feathers flying everywhere, it fall-flies to the floor and scrambles under one of the shelves.

'Bugger,' he mutters and turns with a bow. 'Apologies for my language, madam.'

He glances at the shelf the bird disappeared under, his jaw clenched.

'What's with the ...?'

He gives me a rueful smile and ushers me out into the main kitchen.

'The pheasant, madam? An accidental purchase. I was attempting to catch him and return him, but he's proving to be less than amenable to the idea.'

Jeeves goes to the other side of the island in the center of the kitchen, standing behind it like it's a bar and he needs my order. 'Can I get you something, madam?'

'Well, I was hoping there were some more of those chocolate pastry things.'

'I'm afraid you aren't the only one who enjoys a chocolate pastry thing,' he says, 'but there will be more tomorrow morning.'

'Oh,' I say, not able to hide my disappointment. I was really in the mood for one or five.

'Can I tempt you with some macarons instead, perhaps?'

'Macarons?'

He snaps his fingers and a small plate appears under a glass dome on the counter between us.

'You're a fae!' I exclaim, taking a step back, my heart flipping as I wonder how I didn't know and whether or not I'm in danger.

'I am, madam.'

'But ... I thought the fae and the supes didn't get along.'

'Some don't, but I'm a Low fae. Some of us look more human than others. We tend not to bother with the politics of the high lords and the Ten. Like the rest of the supes and humans, it never ends well if their exalted eyes drop down to us either.'

I think about this for a second and then I frown at the macarons. 'If you can make those appear, why not chocolate pastries ... and how come you can't just make that bird go poof?'

'My gifts don't work like that I'm afraid, madam. I only have authority over the estate and articles therein as part of my station here. I can't make things appear from nowhere as much as it may look like that's what I'm doing. The macarons were already on the grounds, so I brought them here to us. There really aren't any pastries in the house, as I said. And the pheasant isn't from the estate itself, so I have no magickal influence over it.'

'That's a lot of rules,' I mutter.

With a small smile, he lifts the glass cloche off the plate. 'Care to try one?'

I look at it dubiously. 'Okay,' I say, choosing a pink one and taking a bite.

My eyes widen. 'Wow! Crunchy, but chewy too!'

'Indeed, madam.'

'Can I have them?'

He puts the plate in front of me. 'Of course.'

'Thanks, Jeeves!'

He doesn't correct me this time as I snatch up the plate and practically run out the door.

I freeze in the middle of the hallway. I can feel Theo close by.

That's new.

If I can tell where the guys are when they're close by, that's pretty cool, but what if he wants my new-found sweet treats and there aren't any others on the grounds for Jeeves to make appear?

My eyes narrow. This could well be the cereal debacle all over again if I'm not careful ...

Not today, demon!

I start walking slowly, keeping my eyes peeled and I see him as I round the corner. I almost turn on my heel and creep away before he notices me, but I stop. Something isn't right. He's just staring at a painting of a woman in a room. His face is blank. At first I'm afraid Maddox's clan has put him in one of those puzzle daydreams Kor was talking about before, but it doesn't feel the same as when Kor was stuck in one. I can feel Theo and he's ... upset.

His emotions are so different from that first time I felt him at Maddox's club, that I decide to share my macarons with him at once. Sweet things make me feel better after all, so maybe they'll work on Theo too.

'Theo?'

He turns to look at me.

'Are you okay?'

He offers me a smile, but I don't buy it.

'I hold out the plate.'

'Macaron?'

He shakes his head and I frown.

'Ok, what's wrong? You don't seem like yourself and if I'm noticing, well then it's probably way worse than I think.'

'Nothing's wrong. I'm glad to see you though.'

I'm not convinced at all.

'I'm glad to see you too,' I say.

I move closer, suddenly craving his arms around me. But

it's not coming from me. It's coming from him. He wants me to hold him even though he's not saying it out loud.

I put the plate on the floor by the wall so I have my arms free before I turn around and hug him fiercely.

There's a moment of surprise before his arms come around me to hug me back.

'What's wrong?' I whisper again.

'Nothing.'

'Don't lie,' I say. 'Lying is naughty.'

I feel a rumble of laughter. 'It's been a difficult few days. The night of the attacks just brought back some old memories that I'm finding it difficult to shake. I'll be okay.'

'Sure you don't want a macaron?'

He eyes the plate on the floor. 'Okay. For you.'

Ha! I knew he'd come 'round!

But when he takes one, I frown in the knowledge that he isn't like me. This isn't really going to make him feel better.

But I bet I know something that will and I've been wanting to try it for a while.

I take Theo's hand and pull him down a hallway to one of the rooms I know.

The Billiards Room.

'Do you want to play?' he asks and I delight in the fact that he sounds more naïve than I do most of the time.

'Sort of,' I grin and I sense his confusion as I sink to my knees in front of him.

His puzzlement quickly evaporates as I look up into his eyes and my hands flutter to his pants.

I try to undo them, but my clumsy, shaky fingers fumble around with them until he takes pity on me and unbuttons himself.

'Thanks,' I whisper.

'Are you sure? You don't have to—'

He closes his eyes on a moan as I take down his pants and touch him.

'I've only done this once or twice,' I tell him, 'so, sorry if I suck ... no pun intended.'

He chuckles and caresses my cheek.

'It's already amazing,' he breathes and I almost start preening like a bird at his words even though they're bull.

But I try to keep my mind on what I'm doing. This isn't for me. This is to make him feel better.

He's still growing as I put him in my mouth and lick him, taking the shaft as far in as I can because he's huge and soon I'm not sure I'll be able to.

I gag a little and draw back, taking a breath.

I take him again, going a little further and focusing on relaxing, becoming attuned to my inner sex demon.

I should be freaking epic at all things sex!

But I gag again when it goes too far and, a little disappointed in myself, I have to grip the base with my hand. I begin bobbing, and he grips his legs like he's afraid to touch me.

I move back a little. 'Is this okay?'

'It's more than okay.'

His fingers are flexing on his thighs, digging into his skin.

'You can touch me,' I murmur and then gasp as he immediately tears my shirt down and starts kneading my breast.

He takes his other hand and entwines his fingers in my hair, moving my head to the rhythm he wants.

I let him.

This is for him.

He goes too far and I choke a little.

'Sorry,' he whispers.

He rocks me faster and I focus on the sucking part, my jaw

aching from how wide my mouth is. I swirl my tongue around him and he erupts in my mouth suddenly.

My eyes widen and I try to pull back, but he doesn't let me.

'Swallow it,' he commands. 'Every drop, Miss Mercy.'

I try, but there's just too much. It leaks from my mouth and drips down to my chest, feeling cold and sticky. I don't like the sensation of it, but I resist the urge to jump up and find something it wipe it away immediately because I don't want him to think it's him.

He finally pulls out and stands in front of me. I must look a mess. My eyes are swimming, so I can't see him properly, but I hear the sound of his phone.

'Did you just take a picture?' I ask, a little scared that he has evidence of me on my knees without a top on and covered with his jizz.

'Don't worry, beautiful, it's for my private collection. No one else will ever see it ... except maybe Paris,' he admits.

I blink my eyes clear. I look up at him. I'm okay with Paris seeing it. I know he was watching me that time in the Clubhouse over the cameras. Guess it's a thing Theo and Paris are into together.

'Who else is in this collection?' I ask, not sure if I really want to hear the answer.

'Only you, Jane.'

He leaves the room and I stand on wobbly legs, looking for a tissue ... or several.

But he comes back a minute later with a damp towel.

'Here.'

He cleans me up and fixes my shirt for me while I stand still and let him.

'Was that ... okay?' I ask, cringing a little.

He steps to me and tilts my chin up to look at him, kissing

me hard on the lips, his tongue invading my mouth and making my knees feel weak all over again.

'That was amazing,' he says.

I give him a look. 'You don't have to say that.'

'Jane.' He pulls back and takes my face in his hands. 'Truly, you were magnificent.'

'But I wanted to take you deeper. I thought because I'm a succubus it would be one of my powers.'

He smiles. 'One of your powers?'

'Yeah, duh. Sex powers!'

He laughs outright. 'There's a learning curve even for us, sweetheart.'

I frown. 'That's very disappointing.'

'Well, that,' his eyes move down to my mouth, 'wasn't disappointing at all.'

Ha HA! Miss Mercy in the Billiard's Room with the awesome BJ skills!

I allow myself a small smile because I have made him feel a lot better and that was the point after all.

I grab a macaron because of course I didn't forget the plate in the hallway – I'm not an idiot! - and growl at him when he tries to take one.

'The invitation to share has expired,' I say through narrow eyes, pulling the plate closer to me and out of his reach. He lunges for it and I run, clutching it to me with a cry.

'They're not yours! Jeeves got them for me, not you! Get your own!' I yell over my shoulder as I run through the house, up the stairs, and to my room. When I get there, I can hear him just behind me.

No time!

There are five left. I push them into my mouth all at once just as he comes into the room.

I frisbee the plate onto the bed and raise my chin at him in triumph, my cheeks full like a chipmunk's.

'Did you just stuff your face with all of them?'

I nod. 'They're mine,' I garble.

He laughs and grabs for me, but I dance away, giving myself enough time to chew and swallow.

'Ha!' I say. 'I win!'

He jumps at me and this time I can't evade him. We land on the bed, laughing and wrestling, and I can't remember the last time I had this much dumb, giddy fun.

But then there's a noise.

Theo and I freeze like we're two kids caught doing something wrong. Vic is in the doorway and he's exuding nothing but adult seriousness.

My laughter evaporates and so does Theo's.

He gets off me slowly and pulls me up to standing.

'We need to talk,' Vic says.

It sounds so ominous. That combined with how Theo's now feeling because of those words makes my stomach clench.

What does Theo know that I don't?

'All of us,' Vic continues. 'Come downstairs. We're meeting in the Drawing Room.'

He goes to leave, but at the last moment turns back.

'That's what Maddox calls the living room here. The one with the sofas and the big fireplace. Be there in five.'

Sie

SHE LOOKS like she's coming to her death. What the hell did Vic say to her upstairs to get her down here? She's anxious and that's worrying me. I'm still feeling on edge from the fight and the events of the past few days that have led us here.

I try to catch her eye, but she's looking at the floor. I frown at Vic, but he just ignores me.

Theo comes into the room last. He looks a little better than he did the last time I saw him at least. As he comes to stand next to me, I smell him and I know why.

Someone's had a little Jane time.

I quietly seethe with jealousy. I've spent hours since we appeared here trying to get myself under control and bringing myself up to speed on what's been going on in Metro, but it smells to me like everyone's been around Jane today except me and, I sniff, maybe Vic. That's not surprising. It seems like she can hardly stand to look at him. That's his own fault, though, and only he can fix it.

She sits away from us in the small turret window that boasts a built-in bench covered in plush cushions, looking out over the dormant garden. That in itself is telling. She doesn't feel like she's one of the clan. Her posture is stiff and uninviting. She's locked up tighter than a rusted wheel nut.

'We need to decide some things as a clan,' Vic begins.

She doesn't look at him, but she seems to get smaller in the seat as he talks. I feel her anxiety, but I don't know the cause.

Then I wonder ... what if she's picking it up from me? What if I'm upsetting her?

'Jane, are you listening?'

I glare at Vic. Why is he goading her?

Now, she does look at him, giving a single nod before she turns her head to look out the window again. I'm pretty sure that's Jane speak for 'don't fucking talk to me'.

I think I see a vein in Vic's forehead throb, but he doesn't let his annoyance show. Maybe he's finally thinking with his actual brain instead of his ego ... or his dick. Although maybe in Vic's case they're the same thing.

'Maddox has had some intel. There are still some clashes going on, but the fighting in Metro and the other cities is largely calming down. There's talk of a ceasefire between the supes and humans.'

'Already? Short war.' Theo murmurs.

'Why would the Order allow that when they put so much into starting this?' Paris asks.

'They wouldn't, but Metro and the other cities are now under Martial Law and the Order has all but disappeared in the wake of the supe and human authorities taking control.'

Vic paces the room. 'Foley's secret meeting with one of the Ten indicates that the Order is working for the fae now. If that's true then it wasn't just the Order attacking the supes, it was the Ten as well. They're just hiding behind the humans.'

'Then their plan is the same as what Maddox said they'd done before. They make us fight each other so that we're weaker and then they broker a peace between us to be our saviors,' Paris says, jumping to his feet.

I sit back in my seat. 'That doesn't explain why they'd end the fighting so suddenly when they put so much into killing as many supes as they could that first night? Why would they just stop?'

'Perhaps they misjudged the modern human and supe communities. It's been a long time since they pulled this stunt and since the humans learned of us, things have been better between us, not worse. There are so many supe-human families these days. The various species are a lot more inter-twined than they were a decade ago.'

'Social media had an effect too,' Paris says.

'How?' I ask.

'Well, everyone was on the socials, supes and humans

alike, even a ton of fae,' Paris answers. 'There were videos of humans and supes helping each other, of prominent figures from both sides condemning the fighting.'

'Looks like the High fae and the Ten are behind the times,' he continues. 'They didn't realize that these days a war has to be waged in virtual spaces as well as on the actual battlefield. There was almost no propaganda in favor of the fighting at all. The conflict has blown itself out before it even peaked. Now everyone's trying to figure out what happened, who was behind it in the first place.'

'So the Order pulled out,' I mutter, 'because they were told to. They're working for the Ten and those high-born fae fuckers don't want eyes looking in their direction.'

Vic nods. 'Seems that way. Maybe that's what the secret meetings between Foley and the fae were about.'

'When will we be returning to Metro?' Theo asks.

He doesn't look overly enthused by the prospect.

'It's going to take time to rebuild the city,' Vic says. 'Our enterprises have taken a hit and they'll continue to until the city is back on its feet. We will go back eventually. It's too close to the Clubhouse not to. But Paris will need to liaise with the lawyers before we do. Don't want to end up back in jail.'

He looks thoughtful. 'Maybe it's time we fold up shop and find other opportunities elsewhere. We still have to square things with Torun and his guys regarding all those stolen fae artifacts that never made it to him. There's no way we're getting them back from the Order now, but I guess now we know why they stole bunch of black market fae objects. Their campaign wouldn't have gone nearly so well without them. Anyway, it's only a matter of time before Torun tracks us down and demands his due.'

'Why did you want me here for this?' Jane says from the window.

Her tone is soft as if she doesn't really want to ask, but feels she has to.

Vic regards her for a moment before taking out his phone. He hesitates for a second, but then flips it and crosses the room to hand it to her.

'Here. This shows your friend Shar's personal bank account. That amount was deposited into it today. She'll never have to worry about money again.'

Jane looks at the screen, her eyes widening. 'Why?'

He doesn't answer. Instead, he pulls some folded papers out of his breast pocket.

Jane's on-call contract.

I recognize the documents immediately and dread pools in my belly.

I know what he's about to do.

I glance around the room. The others look confused at best and, at worst, kind of bored. They don't see what Vic is doing.

But I do.

NO!

Fear turns to anger even as my blood runs cold. The fucker hasn't spoken to any of us about this. He's working alone and he's going to ruin everything with Jane before we've had a real chance to fix what we did and ask her to stay with us.

I lurch up to stop him, but it's already too late. The paper is in the fire, burning to nothing.

I stare at it open-mouthed. No.

I didn't want her bound to us ... but at the same time, I did. At least until we could make amends for how we acted and the things we let happen.

'You're free of us,' Vic says.

Sanctimonious ass!

Jane stares at the flames. 'Was that—'

'Your contract? Yes and I've put the same amount of money in your account. If you need more, you can have it. No strings. Paris will still find your stalkers and we'll take care of them when he does. You don't need to worry about them anymore either.' He pulls something else out of his pocket. 'This is yours. I wouldn't feel right keeping it. It was your mom's after all.'

He dangles the orc stone from his fingers.

I'm rooted to the spot by his power. The fucker has thought of everything. He's keeping us all from saying or doing anything to stop this. I see the others getting angry as they realize what he's pulling, but I know why he's doing it like this. He's trying to make it quick, like ripping off a Band-Aid. He thinks that'll make it easier on all of us. But he's going about this all wrong.

Jane doesn't look happy. She doesn't look anything, but what's rolling off her like a heavy mist coming in from the sea makes me inwardly wince.

She's been blind-sided. She wasn't expecting this and she's unsettled. Adrift. Anxious. Scared.

And I can't do anything but watch.

I look around at the others, trying to figure out if they can feel what I'm feeling from her right now. Paris is shuddering a little as he's looking at her, Theo has his eyes clenched like he's in pain, and Korban ... well, Kor is lot like Jane in some ways I've come to realize. He doesn't show much on his face when he doesn't want to, but he's watching her, staring unblinkingly, his eyes never moving away. One hand is clenching and unclenching covertly at his side. Oh, he feels it all right.

But Vic is just standing in the middle of the room, calm and stoic. He gives me no indication that he's suffering the way we are.

Because he isn't.

He really can't feel her the way we can. The realization is like a punch to the gut. If this is still a clan, then Jane is on the inside of the circle and our President is on the outside.

And he doesn't even know it.

Jane doesn't look at any of the rest of us at all, only Vic. She stands up and walks towards the door, taking the orc stone from his outstretched hand as she goes by him.

'Okay.'

That's all she says before she calmly exits the room, closing the door with a soft click behind her. Vic stares after her, a look of resignation on his face.

'It's done.'

His power that's stopping me from acting disappears and there's a millisecond of utter silence before the room erupts into chaos.

'What were you thinking?' Paris demands, in Vic's face and pushing him hard in the chest.

Vic staggers back a step and the rest of us advance towards him. I don't know what we're going to do, but the darkness in me is chomping at the bit for me to let it out and pound Vic into the floor.

I could fight him for control of the clan.

I hear a growl from Korban and I know he's thinking the same thing.

Vic is about to have at least one battle for leadership on his hands right here in this room. I don't even want it but if I win, I'll make sure Jane stays with us.

But Vic is too experienced to let this even start. His power flows out and locks our dissent down fast.

Paris grunts, falling to his knees first. As he's the closest to Vic, he bears the brunt of the pressure.

'Leave the kid alone,' I grind out, trying to stay upright as Vic's magick attempts to make me submit.

I pick up a small table by the couch with one hand and hurl it across the room. It crashes to the floor and splinters in half.

'Enough, I said!'

Miraculously, Vic's power recedes and the weight pushing at me lets up. I can breathe again.

'What the fuck did you do?' Theo bellows.

'What I had to,' Vic replies without an ounce of remorse.

'We're your clan, Alex. You should have spoken to us first!' I explode.

'Why, so you could argue with me and try to get me to change my mind? She isn't an on-call girl, Sie. She can't belong to the club. We have to let her go. She isn't safe with us.'

'So, what? You send her out there on her own with no protection?' Kor snaps. 'Might as well tie a ribbon around her and give her to Foley, her stalkers, the Ten, Lionel Makenzie.'

Vic's father? That's news to me and from the look on Vic's face, he's as surprised as I am.

Kor stands in front of Vic, his fists clenched, breathing hard.

'Yeah. Daddy wants a piece of Jane too. Major players know she exists. Maybe they don't understand what she is. Maybe they just want her because they're male and she's a succubus like that book says, but that's a stretch to believe where they're concerned. They're powerful as shit and they didn't get so far by making decisions with their dicks. They all want her for something and they sure as hell don't have her best interests at heart!'

'I make the hard decisions—' Vic starts.

'But we didn't ask you to!' I yell.

He throws his hands up in the air.

'What do you want me to do? We can't keep her, Sie. We're dangerous to her. Without us she has a chance at least and she needs to be free to make her own choices. Paris! You said the same thing to me earlier. You know I'm right.'

Paris backs up, wilting a little under our combined hard gazes. 'I said she should be able to choose for herself without having to worry about her friend and how she's going to live. I didn't say you should ... cast her out like that without any discussion. You didn't even ask her what she wanted. She won't be okay out there alone.'

'She's not safe with us either!' Vic says.

'You think it'll be better for her out there than with us? Do you really think that or are you just angry that she can hardly stand the sight of you?' Paris asks. 'Because that's all you, Alex, and we shouldn't all pay because you don't give a shit about her. The rest of us do!'

My eyes widen a little and I see Kor's do the same. Paris is pissed. He doesn't speak to Vic like that. EVER.

Vic's jaw clenches, but he doesn't rise to the bait. 'If she's careful, she'll have a better chance without the Iron I's,' Vic says stubbornly. 'She lived fine before us.'

'She wasn't living, she was surviving!' I say. 'Barely! And that was before the Order and her transformation into a thought-to-be-extinct supe.'

Vic heaves a sigh, pulling his fingers through his hair. 'We can't keep her.'

'We aren't letting her go!'

'Yes, we are.'

'You don't have a say,' Kor growls. 'We chose her. Sie,

Paris, Theo and me. And she chose us.' He brandishes a bitemark. 'I can feel her with me. Even now.'

I watch as Theo and Paris show their marks too.

Vic is trying to hide his shock, but he can't. He had no idea it was all three of them and neither did I. I'm wishing I'd let her do it when she wanted to that first time I fed from her now.

'We can all feel Jane,' Paris says and I nod because that I do have even without her mating bite.

'She hasn't bitten me,' I confess aloud. 'But I can feel her the same as you can.'

'But he can't,' Korban growls at Vic. 'Maybe it's because she doesn't trust him,' he adds with a sneer, 'and I can't say I blame her. It's not our fault she hasn't taken you as a mate.' Korban's eyes narrow. 'But she is ours and we are hers. You can't change that, Alex. So, no, we aren't letting her go.'

I nod, for once in complete agreement with Korban.

'You should have spoken with us,' I say. 'You're the clan leader, but you can't make a decision like this without speaking to all of us, Alex.'

I stride forward, trying to ignore the fact that she hasn't bitten me for now.

I ignore Vic now too. We'll discuss this again when we've all calmed down, but now we should find Jane and tell her not to go. Her pride will have her trying to leave without seeing us again, but maybe we can convince her it's better for her to stay with us for now.

'We need to find her,' Theo says. 'You know how impulsive she can be.'

'And how resourceful,' Paris adds.

I nod. 'The fastest way out of here is by link key. She'll go to Maddox. We need to find him before she does. He won't consult with us, he'll just deposit her wherever she wants to go with a shit-eating smile on his face, the petty bastard.'

We abandon Vic in the living room, branching out around the house to find Jane.

She'll be trying to leave, I know it. She wouldn't just wait for us to find her and kick her out. She'll leave on her own terms in her own way and we need to stop her before she does because once she's in the wind, finding her is going to be nigh on impossible.

CHAPTER
ELEVEN

JANE

Jane

I leave the room quietly, trying not to draw any more attention to myself than necessary. I understand the reasons they want me gone, but a little warning would have been nice before they threw me out on my ass. The truth is I'm in turmoil. I was just starting to relax here, content that the guys were all okay and that we were together. I even thought that maybe Vic and I could bury the hatchet. But I was given less than a day before they collectively decided to get rid of me.

I feel sick to my stomach. Where am I going to go? What am I going to do? I'll take the money Vic gave me. It's a cold comfort, but I consider it compensation for all their BS and because they wasted my time and never did solve my stalker problem. I know what Vic said in there, but they're just words. I doubt they'll bother once I'm gone. Out of sight, out of mind. I can't believe I thought ...

Do you blame them for wanting you gone? You're difficult and high-maintenance with a bad temper, a shitty attitude and the emotional range of a wet sponge. Of course, they want to cut you loose and find some beautiful human girls who put on makeup for them and wear cute clothes, normal girls they can feed off without all your demon drama.

I go upstairs, dragging my feet, trying to silence that nasty voice, but failing because it's all true. I'll go to Maddox, I decide. He can use one of his link keys and send me somewhere. I won't have to see the guys again either if I do it like that.

But where will I go?

Maybe to Hawaii. I can find Shar and spend my days on a beach in a cabana sipping cocktails. We can all live our best lives then.

I grab my backpack and start throwing my stuff in quickly.

But what about feeding?

I pause.

Will I need to like the others do? I have no idea, but if it comes to it, I'll try going to clubs. Maybe lust from others will be enough to keep me alive. Then I won't have to take from anyone in particular.

What if someone finds out what I am? And there are still the stalkers. They always find me. It's only a matter of time before they track me down again and I don't want to lead the wolves to Shar and her kids' door. The whole reason I went to the Iron I's in the first place was to keep them safe. What's the point of everything that's happened if I go there now and put them in danger all over again?

I need to go out alone, have no contact with anyone.

I throw the last of my stuff in the bag and zip it up quickly, looking around to make sure I got everything. I'm about to go, but my eyes notice the disco ball. I mean that was a gift so I should really take it. I use a chair and am just able to reach the top of the window to unhook it, realizing after it's in my hand that I should have just demoned up to get it.

I put it carefully in the bag and I don't wait around, leaving the room and keeping my eyes open as I walk quickly down the hall. The last thing I want is to run into any of the guys before I go.

I take the back stairs down to the ground floor. What did Jeeves call them? The servants' stairs. Apt for a former on-call girl, I guess. Conscious of Iron I's potentially lurking, I try to stay stealthy when I get to the bottom.

Maddox is usually in his Beauty and the Beast library so that's where I go first, but he isn't there. Instead, I find Jeeves putting books away.

He turns when he hears me come in and offers me a friendly smile.

'Is there something I can help with, madam?'

Already my plan isn't going to plan. This is turning out to be such a shitty day and it started out so well too. I feel my eyes going misty.

Get it together, Jane.

'Um, is Maddox around?'

'I'm sorry, madam. He was called away on some urgent business. He'll return this evening.'

Another crushing blow to the plan. Shit.

'Can I stay in here until then?' I ask hopefully.

The last thing I want is to drag this out, have to hang out with the Iron I's until I can get Maddox to transport me elsewhere. That would be awful.

'But of course, madam, but might I suggest a turn in the gardens if you're feeling out of sorts?'

'A turn?' I sniff, still blinking back traitorous-eye tears.

'A walk, madam. The sun is shining and some communion with nature might be just the thing to settle your nerves.'

He knows I'm nervous?

I look outside dubiously. It's a winter's day but it does actually look kind of inviting. It's dry and crisp, which is a change from the other days of damp gloom. I guess it would be nice to visit the maze again before I go.

'Maybe you're right. Thanks, Jeeves.'

'Of course, madam.'

I think he knows I'm teasing him now because he doesn't correct me, just lets me out of one of the French doors that leads onto an impressive stone terrace.

I descend the worn steps down to the gardens and walk the gravel paths towards the maze slowly, taking in all the nature as Jeeves advised. It's quiet except for chirping of the little winter birds flitting around, landing in the dormant bushes and trees for a second and then flying off again. He was right. It is making me feel a little better.

I get to the maze and start the walk through, knowing that it'll only take me a few minutes since I memorized the pattern of the turns the first time. But then I turn left and find myself at a dead end a minute later.

I frown. This is right. I'm sure of it, but when I backtrack and turn left, the way is clear and leads me through to the next part. My mouth opens on a silent gasp.

No way! I rush to the next bit and find another way closed that I know was open before. It's irrefutable. This maze moves itself around.

I'm in a magickal maze!

Feeling giddy, I try to forget why I'm out here as I skip down the next couple of paths, learning the new sequence as I go. When I get to the center, I do a little dance, but I freeze in embarrassment as I notice a lone figure standing by the fountain, peering into the water.

Jeeves?

How did he get here before me?

I walk closer and look into the water to see what he's staring at. There's nothing in it.

'How'd you get here so fa—'

He doesn't look up, but I trail off as he makes eye contact with my reflection.

A feeling of impending doom settles over me like a death shroud.

Jeeves finally raises his head. 'I'm sorry. I had no choice.'

I feel the charge in the air before I see anything and it rachets up my fear from 'creepy kids' party clown' to 'dead ghost child watching me sleep'.

Fae.

High fae.

Fae magick.

Out of the corner of my eye, I see a portal shimmer open inside the maze itself. Two fae emerge from it and one of them immediately throws a spell out. It hits the seat right next to me, sizzling against the cold stone.

NOPE!

I turn tail and run, forgetting that I'm a badass mofo with demon wings and beach-wavy hair as I'm slipping all over the place and internally screaming 'fuck fuck fuck fuck fuck fuck fuck!'

I'm still cursing Jeeves' sudden betrayal as I slide through the wet grass and escape back into the maze. I mean, seriously, isn't this against the Butler Code or something?

I flee down the paths, imbued with a false sense of success and I realize too late that the maze has changed again when I get to a dead end that wasn't there before.

I try to power through the hedge, but it ejects me onto the path again, throwing me out on my ass.

Guess the magickal mystery maze doesn't like cheaters.

I get up and turn to go the other way, but it's too late. The two fae are already closing in on me and there's no way out of here.

'Look, guys, I don't know what Jeeves told you but—'

They don't even let me finish. One of them just zaps me, laying me out on the ground.

At first I think I'm winded, lying on my back in the cold, wet grass, gasping for air. Dude just zapped me. He didn't even let me get him monologuing.

I mean, who does that? Assholes, that's who!

But then I find I can't move. Not even my head. I'm paralyzed. Panic sets in quickly. There's no holding it back.

This is so much worse than being tied up and a million things are going through my head. The most important ones I want to ask because one of them just might tell me.

Is this a spell? Is it permanent? Or was it the fall? Have I broken my back? Severed my spinal column?

But I can't ask because I can't even use my tongue to talk. Tears are sliding from my eyes into my hair as they come into my vision, the two fae whose faces I'm going to do my best to memorize because I'm getting revenge for this even if they kill me.

'Well, that was easy. I thought she'd be way more powerful than that.'

'I know, right? Her clan are dumbasses letting such a weakling out of their sights.'

One of them takes a look at his watch. 'Oh, hey we can still catch the game probably if we get her offloaded in the next few minutes.'

'Awesome!'

I'm picked up by the biggest one. He puts me over his shoulder and slaps my ass with a laugh and I'm half outraged, but also half grateful because it makes me realize that even though I can't move, I can still feel. That means it's a spell and that means it'll wear off. I mean I'm still going to get these assholes back because fuck them, but at least this isn't a forever thing.

And also I'm not a weakling. I just forgot I'm all powerful and shit!

It's new!

They trudge back to the middle of the maze. Jeeves, that betraying jerk, is gone, but the portal is still open. They take me through without hesitation, and I close my eyes in the tunnel, my stomach revolting at the sensation of what I think indoor skydiving probably feels like.

It's different than the other times I've travelled by portal and, I'm no expert, but I'm wondering if it means we're going further. Fae took me, so maybe they're working for other fae.

We arrive at our destination and the smell is the first thing I notice. Rot. Decay. Damp. It's cold too and there are echoes.

Is this a...

I open my eyes.

Ugh, I was right.

A dungeon.

An actual, real-life dungeon. Trust the fae to be this behind on the times.

I'm carried through a dingy, low-ceilinged stone hallway and to a lone cell. I'm flung onto a soft-ish surface and the two fae back up.

'It's weird. I'm not usually into supe chicks, but I sort of want to ...'

The one who was carrying me steps forward and runs his

hand down my chest to my breast. I still can't move, but I stare at him like I'm burning him from the inside. Maybe I can. Like Superman. No one really knows what Succubi can do. I've been reading the diary that Maddox gave me, and I have learned a couple of things about focusing my power so I keep trying just in case it works.

'Hey,' the other guy says, pulling him away from me. 'C'mon. Get a handle on yourself. They warned us we might feel that way.'

His friend just stares at him with a blank look on his face.

'... because of what she is, dude, remember?' The nicer fae facepalms. 'Man, you need to start listening at debrief. I can't keep covering for your ass. Come on. You know it takes ten minutes to get to the main portal AND we have to go past the arena which you just know we'll get stuck around because it will be crazy busy with gawkers today.'

They leave the cell and the nicer one locks it with a huge, old-fashioned key. He looks me over and glances back at his friend who's already leaving.

'I'm sorry,' he says quietly. 'It's nothing personal, but orders are orders. The spell should wear off in a few.'

Minutes? Hours?

They leave me sprawled on the grimy mattress, staring up at a shadowy ceiling of rock that looks more cave than castle.

It's not all that dark, just gloomy, which I'm thankful for. I don't want to think about where I am or who had me brought here. But I can't help it. It all just keeps going around and around in my brain. I thought it was the fae because of the henchmen and after what Maddox said, but maybe that's too easy or like a red herring, so I expand my list of the possible suspects.

I don't know what it says about me or my life that I can actually make a list like this though. I definitely need to make better life choices going forward. Maybe then I won't meet so many psychos.

I close my eyes, trying to relax with calming mantras since rocking and whatever other moving stims I subconsciously do have been taken away by the immobilization spell.

I'm a badass. I'm not in immediate danger. I just need to think things through.

Badass. No danger. Think things through. Okay.

My dad? None of this really has his MO. He made it pretty clear when I saw him what he thinks of supes and it's not a leap to assume he thinks the same of the fae. Plus he is the Order according to know-it-all-Maddox. I strike him off the list.

I think it's pretty safe to suppose that it's not the stalkers from my old life either, just because if they'd wanted to kidnap me, they'd have done it before now. Plus they never showed any magickal capabilities so why would they suddenly start using fae lackies? They're gone too.

Lionel Makenzie. Vic's dad. The creepy sex pest. I discount him as well. He seemed more ... fancy old money restaurant, rich people sex dungeon to me. I get the feeling the nasty, cold jail is too icky for him to put his stamp of approval on.

OMG is that a puddle of dried blood over there?

I look away.

Focus!

Who else would have had me taken like that? Who else even knows about me?

There's only the fae left and there's only one reason they'd give two shits about a bottom feeder like me. The High fae, the Ten know what I am. If that's the reality then I know why I'm here. They're going to kill me like Maddox said they would if they found out about me, which I guess they did from evil Jeeves.

I mean I might be wrong, but now I kind of wish I'd taken a nap instead of thinking everything through ...

How the fuck am I going to escape the fae? They're like the most powerful beings. EVER.

Will the Iron I's save me? Why would they? They cut me loose like I was nothing to them at all. Why would they bother trying to find me? How would they even? No one has a clue where I am. And no one stands up to the High fae. Not even them.

My heart sinks lower and lower with every revelation.

No one's coming for me.

They won't even know I'm gone. And when it turns out I am gone, they'll assume I just left like they wanted. Fuck, they'll probably be glad I disappeared without a clingy-girl drama for them to have to deal with.

I find my jaw can move a little and I clench it together as tightly as I can, which isn't hard because my muscles feel all juddery and weak.

Ugh, this is bullshit!

I swallow hard and try to move my fingers. One of them shudders a little.

Ok, it's wearing off, but very slowly and I need to decide my next step for when I can move again.

No one is coming for me, so how am I getting out of here myself?

Because I am not rotting in this cell or waiting for whoever ordered those two fae jerkoffs to kidnap me to come kill me or whatever.

I'm Jane Mercy, last of the succubi (maybe), goddess of female sexual awesomeness and autism as a fucking superpower in humans. I'm a badass motherfucking demon and I don't take any shit!

A loud noise echoes through the cells, making my body jerk as I squeak like a tiny rodent.

Oh, hey, my voice is coming back too. Super timing ...

Footsteps reverberate through the jail. More than one set.

I wish I could sit up, not meet my enemies while lying awkwardly on a bed like this. It's demeaning and also I think it sends the wrong message. But when I try to hoist myself up, I'm nothing but a ragdoll and all I succeed in doing is lodging my head against the bars really uncomfortably.

It's easier to look up the hallway now though and I see figures walking through the shadows towards my cell.

There are three.

They look like they're in their mid-thirties, but they're fae – High fae – so there's no real way of telling because they don't age after a certain point. They're impeccably dressed in very expensive, bespoke suits.

Thanks, Paris.

They stare at me imperiously like the three vampires from that really massive vampire franchise ... complete with the outrageously long hair.

'This is the she demon?' one asks aloud with a chuckle.

Another looks in his direction. 'Don't underestimate her. You recall how our numbers suffered before we subdued the clans and obliterated the females.'

Guess I know what happened to the succubi however long ago. Fuckers. They're so casual in the way they talk about it. It makes me sick.

'Yes, but,' the first one gestures at me, 'look at her! She still can't move and it's been at least two hours. Her forebears would have thwarted such a spell within minutes. They did if I recall.'

'Perhaps you aren't remembering it properly,' the third one drawls, looking at me for a moment and turning away as if repulsed. 'Ugh! Her pheromones work upon me even now. She can't control her own lust for anyone in her vicinity.'

He looks back at me, surveying my body prone on the nasty cot, his gaze lingering. 'I won't be letting you feed from me, demon!'

Um, ew. Like you're fooling anyone.

I want to tell him to his self-righteous, fae-dick face that I would never stoop so low as to feed off him and also that whatever lust he's feeling is so not coming from me, but my mouth won't make words yet.

All I can do is watch and listen to them, which I do in case I learn anything that would be useful while I'm escaping later.

They speak about me like I'm not there, like I'm too stupid to understand them. I remember the times people talked about me and to me like that and I seethe silently on the bed.

Easy with that chip on your shoulder, Jane. They probably have no idea you're autistic. They probably wouldn't know or care what neurodivergent even is.

'How long until we're ready?'

'A few hours.'

'Still?'

'It's been a decade since we found one. These things take time.'

'Well, we do have that in spades.'

They all laugh a little like that's a joke and then they turn and leave me alone.

A few hours before I'm guessing I get obliterated.

I start trying to move, make the spell wear off faster. I keep mulling over that one comment about the succubi from the middle one too. How did they thwart fae spells? I've never heard of anyone being able to do that and that sounds like the ultimate badass power.

Maybe my demon form?

I concentrate. Wax on, wax off.

My skin changes and my wings grow under me, propping me up a little, but I still can't move.

There must be more to it. I think about the diary Maddox gave me. It's mostly the daily writings of a woman who'd just become a succubus and she talks a lot about directing energy and focusing power. I keep my thoughts on moving, trying to work my body. A few minutes later and I can twitch a little more than I could before, but slowly and sluggishly. I'm basically in slow-mo.

I hate it!

I scream through my teeth, anger and frustration getting the better of me, pooling in my chest like lava, radiating heat. My legs stamp on the ground and my body lifts up to sitting.

The first time my demon form came out to play was when I was severely pissed off.

I am a demon. Historically, we're angry and wrathful creatures. I'd like to think I'm a little more evolved, but maybe fury is what it takes. I need the fire of rage to … to burn the magick away?

Worth a shot.

I try to make myself mad. It isn't hard. Turns out I have a shit ton of repressed anger floating around under the surface.

I think about the customers who treated me like shit over the years, the loud buzzing of the fly-zappers in every kitchen I worked in that I had to pretend didn't bother me because no one else even noticed them. I remember the times I had to walk back and forth to work with the freezing rain pelting into my face because I hadn't received enough in tips for the bus, the co-workers who would stand in a tight circle and talk about me like I was too stupid to realize, the ones who would go out of their way to make sure I felt like an outsider even though I already did, and the numerous managers who saw a vulnerable girl and decided to try and exploit me any way they could. I recall Angie and her death, and the social workers who acted like I had done it because everyone said I was a 'weird' girl, all the times I made a little life for myself and then had to abandon it at the drop of a hat – even though I HATE change – because I got a note or a text telling me to leave.

I think about today when Vic told me to go, how he doesn't care about me at all.

I'm standing and shaking with anger, my fingers clenching and my wings batting in the confined space before I even realize it.

I'm back, baby!

I do the first thing you always have to do. I try the cell door without much hope, but you just have to do it.

It swings open.

I look at the padlock. It's undone. The door was never locked. Nicer fae guy didn't secure my cell. He also told me where and how far the exit is ... and when to escape I realize, thinking back to what he said to his soon-to-be-dead friend.

Ok, I might rethink my rage vengeance and only kill his handsy buddy because it looks like he's not the fae's lackey at all.

He's my boy.

~

Theo

'SHE'S NOT HERE. FUCK!'

'I know she's not here! Her backpack is already gone. I can't feel her either.'

'Does that mean she's *gone, gone* or just that she's not close?'

'How the fuck should I know? I never had a succubus mate before. How 'bout you?'

I fidget with my stethoscope. 'Arguing is just going to delay us and give her more of a head start.'

Korban lets out a breath and rubs his temples. 'I know. I'm just ... All these feelings and shit. How could she be gone already?'

I draw back a little, looking at Korban, the real Korban, perhaps for the first time. He thinks he loves Jane ... but does he actually? I've been there when the on-call girls have been freaking out because he threatened them or worse. I know what he has to go through every time he feeds from a human girl. What if he only cares for her because of what she's not instead of who she is?

'Did you decide you cared about Jane before or after you knew what she was?' I ask, not bothering to tread carefully.

His features darken. 'I know what you're thinking, but I promise you it was before. I cared about her when I still thought she was human. I didn't know what to do with that either,' he mutters. 'I love Jane, not the succubus.' He grins. 'I mean it's a plus.'

I let out a hard breath and he smiles a little. 'Bet you won't be quite so indifferent about it after you see her for the first time.'

'Won't matter if we can't find her before she leaves the estate,' I say.

Kor lets out a growl. 'Thanks to Vic, we can't even use the contract she signed in blood to find her location since he decided the burn the fucking thing. He could have ripped it up, but, no, he had to go for maximum drama.'

He walks around the room slowly. 'Vic needs to get his head on straight before one of us takes control of this clan.'

I nod absently. I don't disagree, but the first matter is the more pressing one. If Jane leaves Maddox's estate, I don't know where to even start looking for her. She won't go to her friend Shar. She won't want to put her and her kids in danger. I don't think she'd bother going to Metro either. It's not like it's her home. She doesn't have ties there that would entice her back.

We give the room another cursory inspection.

'She's taken all the stuff she brought,' Kor says and then he turns and looks at the window.

'What is it?' I ask.

'I got her something. Looks like she's taken that too.'

'You bought her a present?'

Korban shrugs. 'It was only a little thing and technically I stole it, so I didn't buy her anything.'

'She does like gifts,' I say, 'but I'm pretty sure Paris is in the lead on that front.'

That drags a laugh out of him. 'That's for sure. Come on. Let's see if the others have had better luck in the search.'

We go back downstairs, looking in the other bedrooms on the way, but she's not up here and neither are any of our hosts. Come to think of it, I haven't seen any of them since we got here.

'Where is Maddox's crew?'

'Haven't seen 'em today. Why?'

'I just wondered if maybe she went to one of them for help to leave if she couldn't find Maddox himself.'

'Doubt it,' Korban mutters. 'She doesn't like them.'

My eyes narrow on Korban's back. 'What did they do?'

He keeps walking. 'Same shit they pulled with her at the clubs. They wanted her for their clan. They messed with her, played mind games. You know she doesn't get those too well. Then Maddox made her agree to let Krase feed from her in return for getting you out of the Mountain.'

I stop in my tracks. 'What did they do to her?' I snarl.

'Relax. She only smelled like her when she came back, but you can guess what she had to do in front of them and you know she's shy when it comes to that stuff.'

'Yeah,' I mutter, feeling somewhat mollified as I catch up to Kor.

He lets out a sudden chuckle. 'She went demon on Krase and laid him out real good before that though.'

'She did?' I grin, feeling proud of her.

When she first came to us, there was a spark in her, but her vulnerability was easy to see and even easier to play-on. Now that she's come into her own, I'll bet she's doesn't take any shit.

'So you said before that you saw her demon?' I ask.

'Oh, yeah.'

'What does she look like,' I can't help asking.

'Fucking gorgeous,' Korban breathes as we go down the stairs. 'You'll lose your fucking mind.'

In the corridor at the bottom I see Robertson, Maddox's butler, carrying a silver tray up the hallway.

'Have you seen Miss Mercy?' I ask him.

He stops and turns, giving a small bow with just his head. 'I did, sir. Not long ago. She asked me the whereabouts of Mister Maddox. She appeared to be in some distress and went into the gardens for a walk. To the maze, I believe.'

'And where is Maddox at the moment?'

'He was called away on business earlier today, sir. He should be back this afternoon.'

'Thank you, Robertson.'

I get another head bow and the butler goes on his way just as the others meet us at the bottom of the stairs. Vic is trailing behind them, looking determined. Whether that is to find Jane or stop us from finding her, I don't know.

'She's not downstairs,' Paris says.

'The butler just told us she was looking for Maddox, but he isn't here. She went outside to the maze,' I say.

'We check the grounds then,' Sie says.

Sie gives me and Korban a pointed look and I realize what he's afraid of. He thinks Korban is trying to get me on his team, conspiring against Sie for leadership. I roll my eyes.

'Vic and I will go to the maze,' I say. 'You guys check out the other gardens and the stables.'

Sie nods, looking pacified, at least for now, that he and Kor will be together so he can keep an eye on him.

Vic and I leave the house by way of the side door near the kitchens and make our way towards the looming maze ahead of us. The supes who Maddox entertains here rave about the thing with its moving hedges and changing fountain. Apparently it plays music by itself sometimes too.

I don't see what the big deal is. It's only an enchantment. The fae use them all the time. Give me good, old-fashioned pumpkins and a corn maze over this any day.

'How are you feeling?' Vic asks.

His words come as an unwelcome surprise even though I suggested he come out here with me, so we could talk privately.

'I'm fine,' I say. 'Feeling better.'

With a little help from Jane, I think, remembering the impromptu and amazing blow job she gave me earlier. That sure as hell took the edge off.

'What about you?'

'What about me?'

I swear under my breath. 'This is me, Alex. Talk to me. You've been pulling away from us since we first made the deal with Jane. What is going on with you?'

He doesn't say anything and we walk into the maze. I think he's not going to answer, but then he speaks in almost a whisper.

'I don't know.'

'Look,' I stop and turn to him. 'I'm your friend. The others are your friends.'

He scoffs and I shake my head at him.

'This is about the challenges from Sie and Kor this afternoon? Fuck. Nobody even wants the presidency, no one wants to be the leader, Alex. We just want Jane!'

He doesn't speak and we continue through the maze, turning back every so often when we reach a dead end.

I fucking hate this thing.

We finally get to the middle. She's not here.

'Fuck!' I mutter, sinking down onto one of the stone seats around the dumb fountain. 'She can't be gone. She has to be on the grounds somewhere, right?'

Vic nods. 'The butler would have told us if she'd ordered a car and she can't have just walked. The estate is massive and there are warnings in place.'

He sits on another seat. 'Can all of you really feel her?'

'Yeah.'

'How?'

I consider for a minute. 'I thought it was the bite at first, but Sie said he can read her and she never bit him. I think maybe she decides who she lets in, who she trusts. But it's not a conscious thing, it's more ... intuitive, maybe. I don't think she knows she's doing it.'

Vic lets out a breath and I know he's thinking about how she doesn't trust him and all the reasons why.

'What's it like?' he asks.

'Well, you know how she doesn't show much? Well, when you can read her, it doesn't matter. There's this connection and everything comes through it. I think it's the same for her too.'

'You think she can feel what you feel?'

I remember how she was when we were in Maddox's club, when she took me to my room at the clubhouse. She was a little freaked out after we slept together there and I didn't get why at the time, but maybe ...

'She hasn't said it to me, but, yeah, I think she can.' I stand up. 'You need to get it together. Figure out how to gain her trust and connect with her. She is our mate, Alex. We need to protect her and that means keeping her with us regardless of the dangers. We're the first clan in a thousand years to have a succubus and we aren't giving her up.'

I turn back towards the tall hedges. We've wasted enough time here. We need to find the others and regroup.

'None of us want to be the leader,' I call behind me. 'I doubt any one of us could win against you. Not one of us is strong enough, not even Sie. But all of us together? It's just a matter of time before this clan turns on you. I don't want that to happen, but, if it's the only way we can have Jane, I won't be standing with you.'

I leave him by the fountain, hoping I've talked some sense into him. He has issues ... like everyone else. Lionel Makenzie is a real piece of shit and I know a lot of stuff happened when Vic was a kid before I knew him. Before the Iron I's. Stuff he hasn't told anyone about. But, also like everyone else, his problems can be overcome if he works on them. I just hope he does.

I'm walking briskly back through when I see something out of the corner of my eye, down another path. Whatever it is, it looks familiar, but it's in the grass and half-under the hedge.

I take a closer look, hearing Vic coming up behind me.

Jane's backpack.

I pick it up. Everything's still inside. A tiny disco ball falls out when I unzip it.

I look back at Vic and his expression is as grim as I'd imagine mine is right now.

'She'd never have left her stuff.'

'Not unless she had no choice.'

I grab the disco ball off the ground and we get out of the maze as fast as we can, running for the house. We see the others walking through the gardens on the way.

I hold up her backpack. 'This was in the maze, but there's no sign of her.'

'Where the fuck is she?' Korban growls, snatching the disco ball from my hand and holding it against his chest protectively.

'You know as much as we do,' Vic says.

'This is your fault,' he snarls. 'If you hadn't pulled that shit earlier, she'd be here right now or we'd at least be able to use her blood signature on the contract to find her!'

'Enough,' Sie says. 'Fighting amongst ourselves is the worst thing we can do right now. We need to stop wasting time. Who could have taken her from here and how?'

'We need to speak with Maddox. Now,' Vic says, at last sounding like his authoritative self once more. 'Where's that butler? He should be able to contact him in an emergency no matter where he is.'

'We won't need him,' Paris says. 'Look.'

He points at the house and I can make out Maddox in the library with Jayce and Axel.

We sprint across the lawn and up the steps to the library doors. Maddox opens one of them when he sees us coming.

'What's going on?'

'It's Jane,' I pant. 'She's gone.'

'That's not possible,' he states in that smug, British way of his.

'Look, you self-important, English bastard, she isn't on the property and we need to find her.'

'Her bag was in the maze,' I say, lifting it to show him. 'Could she have gotten off your grounds from there somehow?'

'No. There's no way out that way. The estate goes for twenty kilometers in every direction and if she's somehow reached the boundary, I'd have been notified. No one gets in or out of here without my knowledge.' He turns to Jayce. 'Get Robertson. He should be able to shed some light on what's going on.'

Maddox retreats into the middle of the library floor and we follow. 'I don't see how she couldn't be here,' he continues. 'Are you sure she's not ...' he glances at Axel, 'playing silly beggars?'

'This is no game,' Paris says.

'Jane ISN'T HERE and you better start taking this seriously,' Sie growls.

Maddox puts up his hands in placation. 'Well, she can't have left on foot and no one can create a portal within the confines of this estate except for me and my clan. Only one of them was in the house until about five minutes ago when the rest of us got back.'

That's news to me. 'Which one?'

Maddox hesitates. 'Krase.'

The sound Korban makes has me taking a step back so I don't get caught in the crossfire.

'You left him here?'

Maddox looks a little uncomfortable. 'He's been taking care of his affairs. He's locked in his room at his own request. He can't have—'

'It's Krase! He's fucking Houdini when he wants to be. What the fuck, Maddox?'

'She can take care of herself pretty well from what I saw,' Maddox argues back. 'Let's see what Robertson has to say. He may well have ordered a car to take her into Lausanne.'

I frown. There's no way that's what happened. Jane has few creature comforts, but the ones she does have she would never have left. Even her earphones are in the bag and she goes almost nowhere without them.

Jayce returns a minute later, bringing with him the butler and Iron. All of Maddox's clan are here now except for Krase.

'Have any of you seen Jane today?' Maddox asks his crew.

All of them shake their heads except the butler.

'Robertson?'

'As I told Mister Wright earlier, sir, the lady asked me where you were and, when I explained you weren't in and that you wouldn't be returning until later this afternoon, she became distressed.'

I hear Korban and Sie curse under their breaths.

'What happened next? Did you order a car for her?'

'No, sir. Miss Mercy decided on a walk outside to pass the time and I believe I saw her going in the direction of the maze.'

Maddox eyes Jayce. 'Would Krase have ...'

'Why?' Jayce scoffs. 'You said she gave him some time. He's using that to tie up loose ends,' he finishes with a bitterness that Maddox pointedly ignores.

Maddox looks out the window and lets out a short breath through his nose.

Then he looks at Robertson, disappointment in his eyes. 'They got to you didn't they, old friend?'

I swing around to look at him in shock.

The butler did it?

Robertson looks grim, but he doesn't deny it. 'I'm afraid so, sir. I was contacted yesterday. I won't bore you with the details, but they ... have leverage over me that supersedes my position here.'

He reaches into his pocket and I see Korban move very slowly for his gun.

But Robertson just pulls out a tiny, wooden box. 'They had me put this in the maze.'

'What is that?' I ask.

'It dampens the spells around the perimeter that limit portal travel except with my own link keys,' Maddox says through clenched teeth.

'Quite so, sir. Two mid-level fae entered and pursued Miss Mercy through the maze. I was told to leave, which I did.' He glances at Vic. 'They probably took her to the Meridian. The Ten will be congregating there for the equinox.'

Robertson delves into his jacket pocket and holds an envelope out to Maddox. 'My resignation, sir.'

How British.

Maddox snatches the letter with a sneer. He's shaking with anger and I can feel his power struggling to be freed, but he keeps his control.

'As if you'll be in a position to receive references after this. Tell me, was it worth betraying us?' he asks the butler who looks at him sadly.

'I'm afraid I can't answer that, sir. Not yet at any rate.'

'This isn't over.'

'I'm afraid it is, sir.' He looks at Vic and the rest of us. 'My best on finding the lady. If I could have helped her, I would have. Delightful girl for an American.'

There's a puff of smoke and a scuffle I can't see, I'm thrown out of the way as someone barrels past me and when the room clears, Robertson is gone.

Vic turns on Maddox as his clan go after the butler. 'How could you let this happen under your own roof? What the hell kind of shit show is this, Maddox?'

Maddox just shakes his head. 'If she's been taken to the Meridian, it means she hasn't got much time. It's where the Ten hold their private executions.'

'Here.' He hands Vic a link key. 'This will get you there, but neither me nor my clan can set foot in the fae realms on pain of instant death. This is all I can do regarding that place. But my word is my bond and it's been broken. My clan is at your disposal in any other way needed.'

Vic snatches the link from Maddox's hand.

'I trusted you.'

'I know and I'm grieved to have let you down.'

'You owe us,' Vic growls.

'And, when this is over, I have no doubt you'll come to collect sooner rather than later, old chap.'

Vic's eyes narrow on Maddox. 'If we're going to save Jane, we need weapons and whatever magickal fae baubles you have.'

He strides to the door and looks back at the rest of us. 'Get ready,' he says to the Iron I's. 'We're going to go get our mate back.'

CHAPTER
TWELVE

Jane

I got out of the deep, dark dungeon without much problem and I was flying high, metaphorically speaking anyway. Escape Plan Part One: Get The Fuck Out of Here was going great until I got to the top of the steps and saw two nasty-looking fae soldiers guarding them.

How am I going to get past these assholes? They're probably going to notice a non-fae prisoner just walking between them.

I hide between the open oak door and the grimy wall that's behind them as I wait and hope an opportunity presents itself. Some people say you make your own luck, but I'm a firm believer that sometimes luck pats you on the back and other times it flicks you on the forehead really hard. I'm hoping this turns out to be a back-patting moment. Today could be going better, but it also could be going a lot worse, so it could go either way right now. Fingers crossed.

I actually cross them — on both hands — and hope for some

kind of miracle as I look beyond the doors to the busy floor beyond.

Fae are going this way and that. It looks like a mall or a market, a center of commerce, but I can't really work out what they're commercing. It's all old-fashioned handshakes and rich-looking fae peering down their noses and nodding at each other. Once in a while, a small package is handed between them as they pass one another. The wealthier fae are sometimes followed by drab ones who carry their bags and look miserable-poor. Some are in wizardy robes and their servants are dressed in sacks. It's sooooo wizarding world on one hand, but on the other, plenty of fae are wearing modern and expensive designer brands that I can pick out because ... Paris.

I wonder what he and the others are doing right now. I push the pang away and focus on the modern fae's servants who are wearing ... well the budget clothes I used to before the Iron I's, I guess.

Stop thinking about them!

I watch for a little while longer, trying to relax in my hiding place in case I'm here for a while, but unable to help feeling like a coiled spring. How far would I get if I ran for it right now? Even a few steps would be better than this wait-ing. I know that's a ridiculous idea and it's only been like five minutes, but just standing here is driving me crazy. It's torture and it's making my brain want to make some very impulsive and very dumb decisions.

'Someone help! HELP!'

The cry rings out through the crowd and comes from pretty close by. There's a scuffle and a crowd forming a few feet away and the guards are moving from their posts because they're the nearest soldiers. They take a few steps and everyone's eyes are on what's happening. No one's watching the doorway.

I don't rush, just calmly walk out from behind the door and onto the concourse, melting into the crowd's flow. I've put my hair down and pulled my jacket hood up to cover my ears. I'm a little short height-wise, but I don't look too out of place I don't think.

Part two of the plan, Find The Way Out of This Dump, has started. Nicer Fae said it would be about a ten-minute walk to, I'm hoping, the main portal because everyone knows the fae's key travel gates are never shut down.

There are signs dotted around, which I guess tell the fae where to go like on a city street, but they're not in English. I think back to what he actually said in the cell. It would be crowded and I'd go past an arena, so I follow everyone else, hoping for the best. I'm relying on luck again, but it seems to be a pretty good day so I'm just going to go with it for now.

The hallway is wide, but it clogs up as we round a bend. I keep my head down, but no one looks at me twice. Everyone's busy going about their business.

I get to a massive room, more like an ancient amphitheater and I'm sure this is the area that Nicer Fae was talking about. Curious, I look up and into the center, immediately wishing I hadn't because it looks like it's Execution Day in fae land.

I study the ground like it holds the secrets of the universe as my stomach revolts, the image of a hundred dead fae in rags, crucified on wooden crosses religious -style seared into my brain forever.

Why would they kill so many of their own?

I try not to think about it and I keep walking, staying with the flow of the crowd as we leave the arena again via the next opening and willing no one to notice me.

A few more minutes pass and I'm starting to panic a little as I walk because I don't see anything that looks like a main portal anywhere. I also need to make sure it doesn't look like I'm a lost tourist. That's just inviting trouble. Rule Number One in a new place: look like you belong there and always as if you know where you're going.

Then I see it and I roll my eyes at myself because it's right in front of me. It's freaking huge with a Stargate circle and everything. It's literally right in the middle of the room I'm walking through.

I allow myself a quick glance around, looking for guards and I see some in the far corner, but they're just standing around socializing.

They're going to be in sooooo much trouble if I make it out of here ...

I step out of the foot traffic, watching as fae materialize and de-materialize at the same time. They just walk in and out like they're crossing a road.

Confident that I'm not going to do something wrong, or break the portal, I gather my courage. I need to look confident, like I belong here, like I do this all the time.

Hey, guys, I'm just a normal fae girl going to work. I do this everyday. Totally normal! Don't even give me a second look.

'Are you Jane?'

I jump with a 'hoOOLY shit!' as someone links arms with me.

There's a girl standing next to me with pointed ears and dressed in a pink sweatsuit. 'Who the hell are you?'

'Shut the fuck uuuuup,' the fae girl whose arm is locked with mine mutter-sings, her eyes scanning the room.

'I'm Gisele and I'll be your partner in crime today,' she says in a flight attendant voice as she keeps her eyes moving.

'Next stop, getting you the hell out of here before your date with the secret executioner.'

My eyes widen. OMG, I mean I sorta knew, but it sounds so much worse when you hear it out loud!

'Okay, the Fae Guard are looking over. Just act cool.'

'I am acting cool!' I say through clenched teeth, starting to freak out and trying to hold it together.

'Chill, girl. Look at me and laugh like I'm your BFF and I'm freaking hilarious.'

I do what she says, channeling what I hope is my inner Valley Girl.

'Tone it down a little annnnd we're good. No more talking .... and walk with meeeee ... now.'

She pulls me forward to the portal entrance and we just stroll into it. The tunnel starts out calm with little golden stones underfoot like a yellow brick road, but it changes suddenly, getting dark and ominous. A loud noise makes me cover my ears and flinch.

I look at Gisele, who I'm hoping really is my savior, in alarm.

'It's okay,' she yells over the roaring that's getting louder, but she takes out a rope with a freaking hard-core, Everest-climbing carabiner on the end and hooks it around me.

'This happens sometimes,' she shouts in my ear.

She takes out what looks like one of the link keys that Maddox carried around with him and it starts to glow. She gives me a smile and a thumbs-up. 'We're good!'

And then we fall through a hole in the floor and I scream as my organs push up into my throat. I think I hear her yell 'Geronimo!' and everything goes black.

'Hey, I think she's coming around. Cool, cool. See? She's fine. Give me the cash.'

'You're one lucky fucking fae, Gisele. I thought Ada was going to rip your throat out.'

I recognize the two voices. One is the fae who helped me escape. The other I can't place.

'Ha, me too! Good thing she didn't, huh?'

'Get out of here before you run out of luck.'

I open my eyes and find myself lying on a long seat at a table. I blink in confusion.

Pretty lights.

I sit up with a groan and look around me. I recognize the place. I was here with the Iron I's.

The strip club?

I swing my legs around so I can sit in the seat as I take stock of my surroundings.

I notice a woman behind the bar a short distance away.

The girl who helped me get out of fae land gives me a wink and makes a gun with her thumb and forefinger Shooter McGavin-style. With an audible click of her tongue, she leaves via a portal in the doorway that disappears after she goes through.

'I know you,' I say. 'Fiona, right?'

'Fi is fine,' the beautiful woman who helped us escape the bar before says.

I think she's a vampire. She was drinking that blood-looking stuff last time I saw her.

'What am I doing here?' I ask, getting to my feet and walking to the bar, wondering if she's going to try to snack on me.

'Um, well, we have contacts in the Meridian and heard they'd brought in a succubus all hush hush-like. Figured it was you, so we had you extracted.'

She tilts her head at me, looking me over thoroughly. 'It

was kind of a slap-dash thing, so great job getting to the portal on your own.'

'Thanks' I say faintly, rubbing my face and trying to make my brain catch up faster, figure out my questions because there are a lot of them. 'So you're what? Resistan—'

'Whoa there,' Fiona darts forward and leans over the bar, putting a hand over my mouth. 'That's a no-no word, princess.'

I blink. 'Princess?'

Fiona grimaces. 'Sorry.'

She fans herself with her hand and looks away, taking a deep breath.

I didn't even know vampires got hot.

'I enjoy the ladies and your pheromones are ...,' she shivers, 'off the charts right now.'

She takes a few steps back.

'So I've heard. Sorry. I can't seem to turn them off,' I say, moving away from her too, wondering what I'm going to do if she takes a running leap across the bar and tries to bite a chunk out of my throat, but she only waves a hand.

'It's fine. I have self-control and Ada warned me that you probably wouldn't be able to help it yet.'

'So you know I'm a—'

'Oh, yeah.' She gives me a dark grin. 'I knew it the night you were in here. That frenzy you induced was insane.'

My eyes widen. 'That was me?'

'I'm afraid so.'

'I'm really sorry,' I say, 'I had no idea ... I didn't know I wasn't human until a few days ago.'

'You got out! Great!'

A guy strides into the room.

'You're Nicer Fae,' I exclaim.

He laughs. 'Nicer Fae?'

'Yeah. That's your nickname because you stopped your handsy friend.'

'Wow. Yeah, sorry about him. Uh, my real name is Ged.'

'Hi, Ged. Thanks for all that info you gave me and for not locking the door to the cell. Full disclosure though, I'm going to have to revenge kill your friend. You, I decided, I'm just going to smack around.'

His eyes widen and he looks to Fi for help. I see that I've waxed on without realizing it from my reflection in the mirror behind the bar.

My wings open wide. Fi stares at me, mouths the word 'wow', and knocks back a shot.

'Hey, come on!' Ged says, backing away. 'I got the orders to take you and I had to go with it, or they'd know I'm not on board with the Ten. That's like my whole job, lady! I left the cell unlocked and I stopped Billy from giving into the pheromones ... which was really hard by the way. You're smokin' hot and they're crazy potent.'

'They are crazy potent,' Fiona mutters.

'Right?'

My eyes narrow on him and I lose the demon. 'Okay, I'll give you a break ... and I won't kill your asshole friend even though he touched me totally inappropriately and should definitely suffer at least a little bit.'

'He's not a bad guy. He's just been fed the line. He doesn't know any better. He thinks the Ten are awesome. He's kinda dumb, but his hearts in the right place.'

I wrinkle my nose at the plethora of excuses, but he's already turned his attention to Fi.

'Am I cool to get out of here?'

'Yeah,' Fi answers, 'but don't portal straight back to the Meridian from the bar though.'

Ged gives Fi a mock salute. 'Sure thing, boss. Later, sex demon.'

I find myself waving and frown, putting my hand back down to my side.

'What's the Meridian?' I ask.

'It's like the capital of fae-town,' Fi answers, coming around the bar. 'They do all the big stuff there. It's on a magickal fault line, or something.'

'That's where I was?'

'Yeah ... Look, you sort of can't leave the club. Not right this second anyway. They're searching for you already. Now that they know there's a succubus running around out there, they're getting a little verklempt about it. The Ten see you as a massive threat, you know?'

'Not really. I'm a threat? To the High Fae?' I shake my head at the idea of it. 'That's crazy. I was a human a few days ago.'

Fiona shrugs. 'I'm only telling you what I've heard. I'll take you up to Ada. She'll be able to fill you in better than I can.'

'And Ada is your boss.'

'Yeah, I guess you could call her that. I mean I prefer the term 'life partner', but she does own this place and I do work here so technically yeah.'

I frown as I'm ushered to a door that says 'PRIVATE' and follow Fi up some narrow stairs.

'And is she a vampire too?' I ask Fi's back.

Fi cants her head. 'Vampire? Oh, we aren't vampires, sweetie.'

She laughs a little and turns around. 'Vampires,' she titters to herself.

What is she if not a vampire, I wonder, hoping this isn't going to turn out to be a frying pan-fire situation. Can I ask her? Or is that rude, like when the guys didn't like showing me their demon forms?

Ugh! Stop thinking about them!

We get upstairs to a large landing and I frown, looking back at the cramped staircase and how it opens out into this much larger space. It doesn't look right.

Fiona notices where my eyes are trained and smiles at me.

'Yeah, it's a space displacement. Don't worry, we're still in the club. This just takes us to my apartment and that,' she points at a closed door, 'is Ada's office.'

I assume we're going to Ada but she leads me past her door to the other one, which she unlocks. She all but pushes me over the threshold and I find myself in an elegant, and very feminine apartment.

'The bathroom is that way. Shower,' she commands. 'You stink like fae dungeon and you can't meet Ada like that.'

I nod a little as I look around. It's nice and it feels ... cozy. I like it a lot. I do as Fi says mostly because I feel like half the dungeon is on me and it feels très icky.

I lock the door and strip off my clothes, getting into the shower. And that's where I finally break. I can't keep it together for even a second more. Sobs come hard and fast and choke me, all the emotions I've been holding back take me down. I sink to my knees and cry on the floor of the shower, trying to be as quiet as possible because I don't want to be heard. I don't want to talk about it. I don't want a well-meaning, touchy, love conversation.

I miss the Iron I's and I'm devastated that Vic banished me when I was just beginning to feel welcome. I thought they liked me. Who am I kidding? I thought it was more. I'm such an idiot. I should have known better. I do know better. But the truth is I'm in love with five – yeah, five because even Dick Vic who I don't trust has a place in my ridiculous heart apparently – demons who don't love me back.

Pathetic. As usual.

But the tears quiet as they always do and I'm left marinating in the water, feeling exhausted and empty. My tummy is hurting. It's a gnawing sort of pain. Like hunger, but this is the first time I've felt it.

I need to feed.

That unbidden thought sends me into panic-mode.

I can't feed! I can't have sex with some random stranger! Even if I could, isn't that against the law anyway? Isn't that why the guys had on-call girls? Do I need to find on-call boys? How do I do that? If I don't feed, what happens?

I stand up and turn the water off. My freak-out is over and I need to figure things out now.

I'm angry, I realize. At Vic. At the all the Iron I's actually. Once again, Vic turned cruel and once again none of them stepped up to save me. I'm out on my ass with a bunch of enemies looking for me, and potentially no one who knows what a succubus needs, or how to help me.

I have to help myself. I know that, but I don't even know where to start. I'm overwhelmed and the guys who I thought would help me through this aren't here. I mean, yeah, I was taken and they probably have no clue, and, yeah, I don't have my phone so even if they were trying to contact me, I wouldn't even know ... What if they're trying to call me but they can't?

I catch a glimpse of myself in the mirror.

'You know that's not what's happening,' I mutter to myself. 'They aren't trying to contact you, Jane. You need to forget them if you want to survive.'

I can do that. I've been doing that since dad abandoned me to spearhead the 'We Hate Supes' Society, since Angie died and I had to run. I can survive. A part of me is asking why I'd want to without the men I love, but I silence it. Fuck them. They don't deserve the magick that is Jane Mercy. I can make this work. I'll build my life again like I have a hundred times. Okay, like ten times, but that's still a lot for a girl in her twenties! I can do this again and this time when the stalkers find me, I'm going to fuck their shit up and make sure they never bother me again. I finger the orc stone around my neck. I don't need them. Maybe one day I'll find a clan of incubi who actually gets me ... who actually wants me.

I exit the bathroom and venture out into the hall.

'Do you have something I can wear?' I ask, as I wander through the apartment in a towel looking for Fiona.

'Sure,' she says, poking her head out from the kitchen. 'Take a look in my closet. Something in there should fit you.'

I look where she gestures and go into her room. Again, it's very feminine but elegant and understated. I rifle through her closet, but every single item is practically an evening gown. I take a look in her drawers too, but there's nothing but underwear.

'If you need undies, look in the bottom of the bureau. That's all new stuff,' she calls as if sensing what I'm looking at.

I pull open the bottom drawer and let out a sigh. It's a sea of black lace. I take out a thong and a matching bra, looking at them dubiously before I bite the bullet and enter sensory hell, but they're silky high-end and not scratchy. I shimmy a little to get a feel for them and decide they aren't too bad.

Then, I tackle the closet again, trying to find something that isn't overly shiny or sparkly. There are a few black dresses in the back and I choose the one that reveals the least, a bodycon black and grey leopard print that reaches my mid-thighs with a square neck and no sleeves.

I take a look at myself in the mirror. I don't look half bad. She's right. We aren't much different size-wise.

I wander to the kitchen. 'Hey, what happened to my clothes?'

'Ooh, you clean up nice. Dirty stuff goes to the laundry automatically,' she says, sipping something off a spoon. 'It'll come back when it's clean. Are you hungry?'

I nod. 'Yeah, but I don't think soup is going to cut it,' I say, clutching my stomach. It's hurting worse now.

'Ah, I see.'

'I'm not sure how to ... how I can ...'

'It's okay,' Fi says. 'We'll go see Ada first and then you can come down to the club for a while and feed.'

I look at the floor. 'I don't want to feed from anyone,' I mutter.

'You won't have to,' Fi says, opening the apartment door. 'The lust will be palpable in the air down there. It should be enough to keep your hunger at bay for a little while. At least until your clan comes for you.'

I frown, but she's already leaving so I can't tell her they aren't coming for me.

She takes us up the hall and knocks on the door.

'Come in,' says a muffled voice from the other side.

Fi winks at me and leads me inside a chic office with a view overlooking a mountain range. I blink at the massive window. It must be an illusion, but it looks so real.

'Jane, this is Ada,' Fi says. 'Ada, Jane.'

'So this is the illusive succubus who almost destroyed my club?'

Uh oh.

'I'm really sorry about that,' I say contritely. 'I didn't know it was me.'

I'm staring at the floor and I can't seem to make myself raise my eyes.

'Look at me.'

I glance up. A woman as beautiful as Fiona sits behind a desk. She exudes power.

Ada's eyes find Fi. 'She certainly does have a kick,' she murmurs.

Then she gives me a tiny smile. 'But you'll learn how to control it.'

I forget my shyness. 'Did you know other succubi before the fae ... you know?'

Ada snorts. 'How old do you think I am, girl?'

'I don't know,' I say. 'I'm not even sure what kind of a supe you are.'

I get a look I can't decipher.

'I've known a few,' Ada concedes while still somehow giving nothing away. 'I assume you'll need to feed soon.' She stands. 'You're aware you can't take anyone in particular in the bar, yes? You understand you must stay incognito until the Iron Incubi come for you?'

'Yes, I understand,' I say, 'but I ...'

'She is a submissive little thing, isn't she?' Ada says with a smile to Fi. 'I'm half tempted to keep her. Wouldn't that be something? A pet succubus?'

Fi chuckles. 'I'm not sure she'd be on-board, mistress.'

Mistress?

My impossibly wide eyes fly between them.

'The succubus blushes!' Ada laughs, clapping her hands. 'I've never seen that before!'

'Don't tease her!' Fi says, grinning herself.

Ada winks at me.

'Um. I ...' I shake my head. 'I'm sorry, but I'm not ... I'm pretty sure I'm only into dudes.'

Yeah, five of them who go by the names Vic, Sie, Korban, Theo, and Paris.

Shut up!

'I don't want you to tell the Iron I's where I am,' I blurt and then cringe.

Fiona and Ada share another look.

'Of course. We'll let no one know you're here if you don't wish it,' Ada assures me.

'Thanks.'

I feel my chin wobble and clench my jaw so I don't start crying like a little bitch.

'Oh, darling girl.' Ada comes out from behind the desk and stands in front of me.

She doesn't touch me and I'm thankful. I don't know her and I'm not really sure about her. I wish I knew what she and Fiona were.

'A succubus is strong,' she says softly and I think she's trying to make me feel better. 'You'll feel more yourself after some food.'

She turns back to Fi. 'Take her downstairs for a little while, but you keep her behind the bar and you watch her. If there are any signs of another frenzy starting, get her up here as quickly as you can.'

Fi nods. 'Come on,' she says to me. 'You can snack in the club while you pour drinks behind the bar with me.'

'Okay,' I say, figuring bartending can't be that much different to waitressing.

'Oh, and Jane.'

I turn to Ada who's back behind her desk. 'Try to keep the pheromones to acceptable levels, would you, pet?'

I nod, wondering if it's a wax on, wax off kind of thing.

Fi takes my hand and pulls me away. 'If you're a good girl and rile up the customers just enough so they start spending more money but not so much that they tear the place apart, I'll take you out for some fun later.'

I give her a doubtful look, but she's already tugging me downstairs.

When we get there, she procures me some flat, black sandals from the changing room where the dancing girls get ready and installs me behind the bar.

I think about my pheromones as I familiarize myself with where everything is while it's quiet. Learning to control my glamor was simple, so I'm hoping it won't be much different to get the hang of the other stuff.

I try to visualize them as tiny little love hearts with messages on them like the chalky candies you get on Valentine's Day mostly because thinking about them like that just makes it more fun. I make them float around and draw them in and out, wondering if they're real or I'm just making stuff up.

I guess to be sure, I need a test subject. I look around for someone a good distance away who I can still see easily. I choose a shifter who's sitting by himself in a booth. He's wearing a suit and playing on his phone. He's all buttoned up and he doesn't look like he wants to be here at all.

I envisage my tiny love hearts floating towards him. They say stuff like 'HARD 4 U!' and 'LET'S FUCK!' and I snigger a little as they smack into his head like miniature dive bombers.

I only do a few, but he puts his phone down immediately. He swallows hard and tugs at the collar of his shirt. He adjusts himself in his pants and I feel it.

No, not THAT!

Ew!

I feel his lust coming off him. I can actually see it if I look hard. It wafts out of him, a shimmering fuchsia mist and comes right to me, settling on me. The ache in my stomach recedes and I close my eyes on a contented sigh and more than a little pride. I did it!

I wonder if I can use the pheromones for other things like happiness or anger, but when I try it, nothing happens. My guinea pig in the suit just stays lustful and starts booking private dances. Looks like my pheromone powers are limited to lust only.

An hour later, the place is hopping and I'm pouring drinks with Fi while we dance around and have a little fun. I get the feeling she's trying to make me feel better because of the 'breakup' and it's kind of working unless I specifically think about them, which I'm trying very hard not to do.

'You okay?' Fi asks and I nod.

'Yep, all good.'

'You're doing a great job,' she says.

Her praise makes me grin. I do like being good at things.

But as I'm making a cocktail, my stomach clenches, cramping without warning. I double over with the pain of it, so much worse than it was before at Maddox's chateau and I try to cover it by pushing a pen off the counter and bending down to get it. The cramp eases off and I straighten only to gasp and almost drop the glass I'm holding a second later when it comes back with a vengeance.

What is this?

'Go out back,' Fi whispers, pushing me towards the Fire Exit. 'I'll be there in a minute but watch for Hell Hounds, okay? There's a pack around this area right now. They're freaking everywhere and they'll rip your face off if you give 'em the chance.'

I try to walk normally, but mostly stagger to the door that leads to the alleyway out back.

I glance around for Hell Hounds, remembering the loping,

red-eyed monster I saw when I was here with the guys that night, but there's nothing out here but a very under-the-weather succubus.

I try to use my pheromones to feed some more in case it's hunger causing this, but when the lust dust comes at me from inside the club, it makes me feel worse and I end up throwing up in the street.

'What is it? What's wrong?' Fiona asks when she comes out to check on me a minute later and finds me curled up next to the wall.

'I don't know,' I groan. 'Is this what happens when Incubi get hungry?'

'No clue. I don't think they ever let it get this far. That's why all the good clans have enough on-call girls close by.'

I put my head in my hands. 'I think I need an on-call girl then.'

'Thought you didn't swing that way.'

'I don't.' I look up at her. 'But beggars can't be choosers.'

'Gee, thanks. I feel so special.'

I chuckle in spite of the hideous pain I'm in.

'I fed more than once while I was behind the bar,' I say. 'Why didn't it work? It did once before,' I murmur, thinking about the two Order guys I drained in the closet of Maddox's club when they came for me.

But now I'm remembering that time and the one with the Frat guy in the alley did feel different to how it does tonight somehow. May it was because they were human, or maybe I wasn't feeding from them at all if lust is needed.

'I don't know,' Fi says, sitting down next to me. 'Maybe you can't feed off just anyone? I mean, the incubi vet their on-call girls for months before they decide. I always thought it was because of all the legal stuff and because they had so many to choose from that they couldn't make up their minds, but maybe there's more to it. I'm sorry, Jane. I don't know.' She bumps me with her shoulder. 'Come on, let me take you back upstairs.'

I double over with a hiss as she helps me up, leading me inside.

What am I going to do? How am I going to survive as a succubus if I can't feed?

~

Korban

THIS IS SUICIDE. We all know it, and yet here we are standing in Maddox's house, suited and booted and ready to attack the Ten. Maddox and his guys left as soon as they'd given us all the information they had on the Meridian and every single weapon in their arsenal. They can't set foot in fae land, they refused to even be in the house when the portal to that place was opened and I've never considered them cowards.

I almost laugh. This is insane. We are so fucked.

But we can't leave Jane in the Meridian. We can't let the Ten execute her. Fucking Jeeves, I seethe when I think about that turncoat butler.

I watch our indomitable leader barking orders to Theo and Paris and I suppress the growl I want to let out telling him I want control of this clan. I don't want control of this clan. Neither does Sie, but Vic is doing a shitty job of keeping Jane safe. I blame him for what happened. If he hadn't done what he did, Jane wouldn't have been in that maze by herself. If he hadn't burned her contract, we'd have had the blood we need for a locator spell to find her.

I search inside myself for her, but that feeling in my chest that I'd grown accustomed to, that told me what she felt, is gone. I'm hollow and bereft and I've never felt so alone. Fuck, I miss her and I know the others do too, even Vic. We need to get to her. I need her safe beside me. I want her laughter and her touch. I want her silly jokes and weird conversation. I need her in ways I've never needed anyone. I never knew what a mate was for an incubus.

'We can't lose her,' I growl aloud.

'We aren't going to.' Vic eyes me. 'Five minutes to go-time.'

He prods at a crudely-drawn map. 'She'll be here. These are the Ten's personal dungeons. We can use Maddox's master link to portal straight in, but he said it can be a little temperamental, so we need to be fast and not let the portal shut behind us. We'll only have a few seconds before their defenses kick in and it locks the entire Meridian down. If that happens and we're still inside, it's over.'

'Is no one else going to ask where the fuck Maddox got a master link key?' I mutter. 'That shit is reserved for the Ten and the Ten only. How do we know he and his crew aren't in on Jane being taken? He makes deals with those immortal bastards all the time. Maybe he just acquired a shiny, new, fae club and Jane is the payment for it.'

'I've known Maddox a long time,' Vic says. 'I would never trust him completely, but he wouldn't turn against his own to ally himself with the fae. He has his own code and his own reasons to hate them. If I'm wrong, I'll let one of you take leadership of this clan.'

I see Sie's eyebrows rise.

'We believe you,' he says and I snort.

'Whatever. Let's just get this done, get our mate back, and get her somewhere safe before we give her the dicking down she needs to know what she is to us.'

'Do you think that's all it's going to take?' Paris asks. 'You know how she felt when she left.'

'Betrayed,' Theo says softly.

'Betrayed?' Sie shakes his head, rubbing his heart. 'That's the understatement of the fucking year.'

Paris picks up another knife and sheathes it at his belt. 'Do you think it's really going to be as easy as, 'Sorry, Jane. We fucked up again. Let's go to bed and feed.'?'

'No,' Theo says. 'It's not. Trust is one of the things she values most and we keep breaking it.' He looks at Vic. 'I warned you about this in Metro, but you didn't listen.'

'I know. I will fix this. I'll tell her I stopped all of you from interfering at Maddox's.'

I roll my eyes. He doesn't get it. Even I get it.

'You might not be able to fix this.' I say what everyone else isn't. 'And if you can't, we're leaving with her. All of us.'

Vic doesn't look surprised. Instead, he just nods.

Maybe he does get it after all.

'Two minutes,' he says as his watch beeps.

I ready myself for the fight of a lifetime just in case things don't go to plan. I'm going to kill as many of those fae fucks as I can before they take me down.

Vic's cell phone starts buzzing.

He looks at it, frowning. 'What do they want?'

'We don't have time for this,' Sie says. 'We have less than ninety seconds before we portal out.'

'It's a resistance number. They wouldn't call without a good reason.'

He answers it and I try to hear the other side of the conversation, but I can't.

He doesn't say much, but when Paris tries to ask what's going on, Vic hushes him.

'When?' he asks. 'And she's okay? Where is she?'

I see sudden relief in his eyes and I frown.

What is happening?

'Thirty seconds.'

Vic ends the call. 'She's safe. Jane's safe.'

'How?'

'She's not in the hands of the fae anymore. The resistance got her out of the Meridian.'

'And she's okay?'

'Yeah, but they wouldn't tell me where she is.'

Vic's phone beeps and he curses, pressing a button on the link key and stopping the countdown.

'Then we're back to square one,' I snarl, 'with no way of finding her.'

Vic puts down his phone and looks at all of us. 'Are we all operating on the assumption that Jane is our clan's mate?' he asks.

No one answers for a moment.

'She chose us,' Sie says stubbornly.

'But she didn't really know that's what she was doing,' Vic argues. 'She wasn't even a full succubus until a few days ago. What if it's not what she wants?'

'What do we want? Is that what you're really asking?' Theo says. 'Because I already consider her our mate.'

Sie and Paris begin to nod and I do too.

Vic sighs. 'I just want her to be safe and I don't think she will be with us.'

'She could take care of herself when she was human and you haven't seen her since the change,' I tell him. 'Besides, she has enemies with or without us. I think she'll be safer with us than she is alone.'

'What if someone took her from us?'

'Someone did take her and we weren't there to protect her because of you!' I growl. 'I'm not talking about this anymore.

Jane is our mate and I care about her too much to let her go. When we find her, I say we do what we should have done before and ask her what she wants. Then we pray to every god there is that she wants to be with us.'

'What if she does want to leave?' Paris asks.

'Then we make sure we do it right. We get her a new identity and everything, so she's as safe as possible without us,' I answer.

'And if she wants to stay?' Theo asks.

I grin. 'Then we take her home and make her a part of our clan officially. We keep her with us every moment of every day and night. We make sure she's happy and that she has everything she wants and needs so that she never wants to leave us.'

Vic nods. 'Okay.'

I frown at him, not sure I heard him right. 'Okay?'

'Yeah.' He pulls out the master link key. 'I want that too. So let's find her and ask her.'

CHAPTER
THIRTEEN

Jane

'What happened to her?'

'She was making drinks behind the bar with me,' Fiona pants, still out of breath from helping me up the stairs. Her pheromones were under control, I promise! But she just keeled over. She had to go outside and I found her on the ground.'

I stare up at the ceiling and groan, clutching my stomach. 'Did you feed, girl?'

I nod. 'Yeah a bit. I felt better for a little while, but then it got a whole lot worse.'

Ada stands over me, looking down and I flinch under her stare. 'Why didn't you want me to contact the Iron I's?'

I frown. 'Because I think they broke up with me,' I whisper, sniffling like a little bitch.

I wish they were here. I'd give anything to have Kor hold me like he did when I was in transition.

'Foolish girl!' she snaps, her voice as powerful as a whip

I cringe, rolling into a ball on the floor.

'You're mated to a clan. Why didn't I feel it? How were you able to hide that from me before? Answer!'

'I didn't!' I cry. 'Or at least I didn't mean to. I don't know how it works!'

I succeed in sitting up and get to my feet gingerly as Fi hovers close by and Ada goes back behind her desk, picking up the phone.

I sink into a nearby chair. 'What does it matter anyway?'

Ada looks up at the ceiling for a moment and closes her eyes, saying something clearly long-suffering in a language I don't understand.

'It matters,' she says very slowly in a way that gets my back up, 'because a succubus who has chosen her clan cannot feed from just anyone. And neither can your mates. You'll need either your clan or more than one suitable human that meets a variety of criteria.'

'Why not just any human?' I ask.

'Because feeding from the wrong human could kill them after you've chosen a clan, which creates a problem if you keep doing it and the bodies start piling up ... and no supes or fae at all either!'

'Oh, shit,' I mutter.

Guess I know what happened to those two guys at Maddox's club and I guess that means I'm not just going to be able to feed at random in clubs like I'd planned.

'That really narrows down my options, huh.'

'Indeed,' Ada mutters, dialing a number.

'But I didn't know,' I argue. 'I mean I didn't even know I was choosing them when I chose them. I sure as hell didn't know we needed to stay together forever so we wouldn't starve to death!'

Ada sinks into her chair, putting the phone to her ear when an alarm begins to sound.

She slams the phone down immediately.

'Get her into the panic room in your apartment! NOW!'

Fi hoists me up and drags me out of Ada's office.

I cover my ears at the piercing noise. 'What is it? What's going on?'

'It's a fae raid!' Fi shrieks, practically throwing me over the threshold and slamming the door after me.

She runs to the closet door in her hallway and taps at something I can't see on the wall. The door opens and it looks like a small pantry with a bed inside. She comes and gets me, hauling me into the room with her and shutting this door too.

There are monitors on the walls that link to the cameras I've seen in Ada's office and the club itself.

I see blasts of white powder coming down from the ceiling.

'What's that?' I ask.

'Scent obliviates.'

At my questioning look, she shakes her head.

'They like ... destroy smells.'

'So the fae won't be able to track me?'

Fi nods. 'Nor anyone else who's been here since the last time we got raided.'

I watch the monitors as a legion of fae soldiers pour into the bar. They tear the place apart, breaking bottles and glasses, cutting the seats open, shattering the mirrors and lights.

Ada stands calmly next to a very built fae soldier with a gold helmet tucked under his arm. Not a hair is out of place on her head and her suit looks spotless. Her arms are crossed and she's looking more annoyed than anything else as she surveys the damage they're doing to her club.

'This happens a lot?'

'They pull this shit once or twice a quarter,' Fi says. 'We have insurance for it and magickal cleaners and stuff. It'll be back to normal by tomorrow. They just like to show us lowly supes what they can do to us.'

'Who's that guy?' I point to the big fae who's standing with Ada.

'That's Kaliq, the captain of the Ten's guard. See him out anywhere and you run the other way. He's a real piece of work.'

'So this is them looking for me?'

'Well, they're looking for something. Safe bet to assume it's you since the resistance got you out of the Meridian.'

I give her a tight smile. 'I thought resistance was a bad word.'

'In the panic room, no one can hear you scream,' Fi says dramatically.

'So do they know that you guys are part of the resistance?'

'Kaliq suspects we have ties, but he doesn't have any proof. He basically just comes here to fuck with Ada. They have a history. She hates him.'

I watch as the fae continue to wreck the bar and then I see them making their way up the stairs.

'They're coming,' I say quietly, my heartbeat spiking as one of them busts into Fi's apartment, splintering the door-frame and almost knocking the door off its hinges.

'They're clearly looking for someone. They usually just destroy the place and they don't usually come upstairs, but don't worry. They won't find us even if they check the closet.'

'I don't hear them,' I mutter.

Fi keeps staring at the monitors. 'You won't. Ada had this room put in. It cost a ton! They'll never find it even with magick.'

We keep our eyes on the monitors as three fae pull every-thing out in Fi's home, basically making a huge mess.

'Fuckers,' she mutters. 'I wish I could go out there and beat the shit out of those uppity fae assholes.'

I picture her melting out of this room armed with a bottle of Jack and a cocktail stirrer and kicking their asses. I chuckle a little despite my fear.

'Are you feeling better?'

'A little.'

After the fae have created as much chaos and caused as much damage as possible, their captain gives them an order and they stop what they're doing, filing out of the club via the portals that brought them in the first place.

Fi heaves a sigh as she goes to the door and opens it.

'Safe now,' she says brightly.

I leave her panic room and we make our way back to Ada's office.

Ada's already there. 'Fucking fae assholes,' she mutters. 'That Kaliq is more of a cunt now than he ever was before. Mark my words, one of these days I'm going to forget my reasons for doing this entirely and I'm going to show them who I truly am and each one of those little fae children are going to shit themselves.' She keeps ranting, mostly in another language, muttering to herself.

'Take the rest of the night off,' she says to Fi.

'And you,' she points at me. 'I'm calling your clan. Take this.' She tosses me a small box with some pills inside. 'Take three of those and that should keep your hunger at bay for a few days. Don't try to feed from any supes besides your clan or you'll get sick. No humans or they'll likely die.'

'But ...what am I going to do after that? The Iron I's—'

'The Iron I's will come for you,' Ada mutters adamantly.

'What if I don't want them to?'

244

'Then you're a fool. If you didn't want to mate them, you shouldn't have mated them. They're yours, girl, and even if there was a way to undo it, what self-respecting demon clan would rid themselves of a rare succubus?' She laughs. 'It's absurd, too ridiculous to even contemplate seriously. Now, leave so I can make some calls, sort out the damage the fae have done to my place.'

She starts muttering to herself again as she picks up her cell and starts pushing buttons in an angry manner. Fi leads me out into the hallway.

'Come on,' she says. 'It's best to leave her to do her thing when she's like this. I know where we can have some fun and kill some time before Vic and the others get here.'

~

Vic

It's been hours since we portalled out of Maddox's estate intending to return to Metro after Ada called me and told me Jane was with her. But this piece of shit link key overshot our destination, bringing us out in a town three-hundred miles inland from where we wanted to be.

I stare out of the train window at the frozen landscape as it goes by, wishing we could get there faster.

I try the link key on the nearby bathroom door again and let out a harsh breath when it still doesn't work, swearing as I put it away. Pacing down the aisle, I try to ignore the curious looks. The train is busy, even in First Class.

'Sit down,' Theo mutters from behind me. 'You're making the humans nervous.'

'When are we going to get there?' Sie growls from the seat next to him.

'Another hour or so.'

'The link still isn't working?' Paris asks, looking up from his laptop.

'No.' I fling myself into my seat like a petulant child. 'When Maddox said it was temperamental, I didn't think that meant it was a piece of shit.'

Paris shrugs. 'They're not made for the human realm.'

At my expression, he gets a little defensive. 'What? I looked it up when it didn't work on the plane. Our sun messes up their magick, so they're not very reliable over long distances in this world. They don't work at all near the North Pole because of the solar flares.'

'Thank you for that,' I mutter.

'I just mean if we used it to realm-jump, it would have worked fine.'

I go back to staring out at the snow, listening to Paris tap away on the keys. I hate this waiting. I want to get to Jane. I need to make sure she's okay. I also need to figure out how I'm going to explain my reasons for hurting her. Again. The others want to speak to her first and I get it. My every interaction with her seems to take things from bad to worse, but I've been thinking about things a lot and I want to tell her everything.

'Did you ever get those video files fixed up from Vic's study?' Sie asks.

'Still trying,' Paris says. 'I looked through the ones my software was able to rebuild so far, but there wasn't anything there.'

'Keep going,' I order. 'I want to know who all our enemies are. No more surprises.'

CHAPTER
FOURTEEN

Jane

I sigh with relief as the pills Ada gave me start to take effect and the pain eases off.

Fi leads me back to her apartment.

'I'm feeling better,' I state and it's true. 'Where are we going?'

Fi looks back through the door and then at me, clearly thinking twice.

The thing is, I don't want to be here when the Iron I's get here. I still intend to leave with these little pills Ada gave me and not look back.

'C'mon,' I say, 'you said you'd help me pass the time. I mean unless you want to stay here and bond over cleaning up this massive mess.'

'Ok,' she mutters finally, 'but only because you're begging me and I feel so sorry for you. But you have to stay with me. Ada will stake me out and pussy-whip me if something

I must look shocked at her candor because she winks at me. 'See? You're missing out.'

'I don't think so.'

Fi makes a noise of dissent. 'What the fuck those boys been doing with you? Not much from the sounds of it!'

'The usual kind of stuff, I guess.' But my cheeks heat.

'Ah ha! I see! You're holding out on me. You're a dark horse, Jane Mercy.'

I smile, looking away in embarrassment.

She shuts the door to her apartment, leaving us in her dark hallway.

She puts something on the door.

'We're using a link?'

'Yeah. Now, shh. I need to concentrate.'

'Where are we going?'

Fi taps her chin in the glow of the light from the kitchen. 'Somewhere where the supes are hot and the wine is expensive.'

She opens the door and takes the link off it, stuffing it in her bra. The sound of lounge music comes through the void beyond her and I guess I look dubious because she grabs my hand with a roll of her eyes and drags me through into the light.

'Come on! Live a little!'

She pulls me along through throngs of people to a long, polished bar. The décor is golden and bright. We sit down and Fi orders a vintage from a year that makes the barman's eyes widen.

With a charismatic 'Yes, ma'am', a bottle is uncorked with a pop and two glasses of white wine are poured for us. He puts the rest in an ice bucket and sets it on the bar in front of the stools we're sitting on.

'Ok,' Fi says, twizzling around on her seat to face the room. 'Let's take a look at the talent here tonight, shall we?'

'Do you ever ...you know ... with guys or is it just girls?' I ask, wondering if she'll answer.

'Sometimes I do it with guys,' she admits. 'Ada likes to surprise me with a couple once in a while, watch me get tag-teamed.'

My eyes widen. 'Do you like that?'

Fi laughs. 'Yes, I like it. Hasn't your clan done a little DP with you yet?'

'Um, well, only once or twice and it wasn't all that long ago.'

'Ooh, which ones did it? No, let me guess! Theo and Vic. No, Vic's too uptight to let go with anyone like that and from what I've heard, the doctor's interests are a little more niche.'

She waggles her eyebrows and I can't help the laugh that bubbles out of me.

'I give up. Who?'

I decide not to tell her about double-dicked Korban.

'Paris and Korban.'

'NO! Oh wow, I'll bet that was intense.'

I blush and clam up. Guess I'm not really a kiss and tell kind of girl, but then I wonder why Fi is telling me these things about Ada. I frown. Maybe she's trying to signal me for help. Maybe she's in a bad relationship and doesn't know how to get out. I should probably find out more just in case. Maybe Fi will want to come with me when I leave here tonight.

'What if ... when Ada surprises you ... what if you don't want to?' I ask carefully.

Fi leans back a little like she's trying to figure me out but can't quite do it.

'On the rare occasion I'm not into it, I just safe word out. Ada and I have been together for a VERY long time, Jane. We like to mix it up.'

'How long is a long time?' My head tilts. 'Are you going to tell me what you guys are?'

'Okay but keep it on the down low. Not many know the truth.' Fiona leans in close. 'Ada's real name is Hecate.'

'So she's named after a Greek god?'

Fiona laughs. 'No, Jane, she is a Greek god?'

My mouth falls open. I didn't even know that was a thing. 'Are you one too? Is that why you were drinking blood the night we met?'

'Nope. The blood is a necessary thing for me. Ada doesn't need it. I'm just considered a devotee, so I get a couple powers and to live as long as she does so long as I stay topped up with 'ze blood',' she hisses, putting on an Eastern European accent.

I sit back in my chair. 'Huh.'

'Okay, so are you satisfied that I'm not in an abusive relationship with my goddess girlfriend?' she chuckles.

'Yes,' I say, taking a sip of my wine.

Ooooooh that's nice.

I plot my escape while I polish off the rest of my glass and watch all the people talking and laughing around us. It'll probably be easiest just to go to the bathroom and slip out from there. But as I hear couples talking and see others dancing and having so much fun, my mood turns.

My heart is broken and I just want to curl up on a couch somewhere and cry like other girls do when they get the break-up talk. I've been trying to put it to the back of my mind so I can function, but I'm so, so desolate. I'm glad I can't feed from anyone. Even though it doesn't need to be sex if I'm snacking, the idea of anything like that with a stranger just doesn't really do it for me at all.

Ugh, worst succubus ever.

Fi frowns at me. 'Are you okay?'

'I don't know. I don't get it,' I say. 'How could I mate with a bunch of guys and not realize that's what I was doing?'

Fi takes a long drink from her glass. 'I have no clue. Must be a demon thing.'

I make a noncommittal sound. 'They treated me like shit, but I still want to be part of their clan. How dumb is that?'

Fi shrugs. 'It's not that dumb. You're lonely. I can tell. But you're sort of bound to them. If they're treating you like shit, you'll have to either make them treat you better or probably kill them to break the bond or whatever it's called.'

'Really?'

'It's likely. That's usually how all that shit works. But I'm not really an expert. Sorry. Maybe ask Ada.'

I nod, but I won't be able to. I won't be seeing Ada again. Besides, she creeps me out. I wouldn't want to talk sex and mate bonds with her. I'd probably find myself tied to a bench in a gimp suit while she paddles my ass and tells me I've been a naughty slave girl.

Goddess or no, that's just the vibe I get from her.

'Who's that?' I ask, gesturing to a guy not far away who catches my eye.

I'm mostly drawing this out a little so I can have more wine before I make my getaway, but the more I look at him, the more there's something about him that feels familiar. He's dressed in a crisp, white shirt and tailored suit jacket ... Oh, maybe it's just the expensive clothes. They make me think of the Iron I's. Vic in particular.

This is ridiculous. Surely not everything can remind me of them!

I realize I'm accidentally staring and he notices, his blue eyes turning towards me with interest and I immediately look away because, even though he's half-way across the room, meeting his eyes is too intense.

How would I ever have let go enough with a stranger to feed properly … even if I could?

I can feel his eyes on me still and Fi grimaces when she realizes who I was talking about.

'Oh no. Not him. He might look cute, but, trust me, he's a walking, talking problem. Ugh, now he's looking at us,' Fi murmurs into her drink. 'You sure know how to pick 'em.'

'What is it?' I ask, getting alarmed because he's staring right at me still.

'He's an incubus. Can't you feel that he's the same as you? What was his name? Used to run with Maddox's crew before they kicked him out. Daemon. Dumb name for a demon, huh? Like, who would name a human kid 'human'? Oh, shit, he's coming over. That's exactly what we don't need. You don't want to be in his sights, that's for sure.'

I glance at him again, realizing that what I felt before was a kind of camaraderie because we're the same.

I know when he's in front of me even though I'm staring at the floor.

'What do we have here?' he drawls and I feel his eyes on me again.

I glance up and then down again quickly.

'Sorry, we were just leaving,' Fi says.

She slides off her stool and I do the same, still not looking at him as I lament the wasted wine and wonder if I can just take my glass with me, when he grabs my hand hard. He doesn't let go.

I gasp, pulling away and looking up into his piercing eyes. He's handsome as fuck, but I'm utterly and completely repulsed. My body wants to get as far from his as possible. This was how I felt when Maddox and Krase touched me.

Anti-magnets.

'Holy shit,' he breathes. 'You're a—'

'Come ON!' Fi says and hauls me away from his trapping gaze.

'Wait!' he calls, but I'm full-on running away, dodging people and waiters like my life depends on it.

Then someone else is in front of me and I stop abruptly.

Vic!

He sees me too and smiles. 'I'm sorry about everything. Come outside with me and we'll talk.'

I'm tempted to run from him too because he's a jerk and, even though my stupid, betraying heart sings like he hasn't broken me multiple times, I'm not just going to fall into his beefy arms and forgive him. But if he's here, then the others will be close by. Maybe they don't want me gone. My plan to leave melts away like the rice paper wrapping on a candy.

He takes my hand in a gentle grip and I wonder for a second why his is gloved. I've never seen him wear them before. But it is chilly outside, so maybe he's cold.

Fi sees who I'm with and waves goodbye to me from a few feet away. I wave back, letting him lead me through the crowds and losing her in them.

We get outside and it's dark and cold. We're in a part of Metro I don't recognize.

'How did you find me?' I ask.

'Wasn't hard.'

He's looking at me weirdly.

'What?' I ask.

He doesn't answer. His gaze shifts to something over my shoulder but before I can turn to see what, strong hands grip my upper arms, hurting me.

'Do it quick before she can bring the glamor up,' says a gruff voice from behind me.

Why are they doing this? Are they intending on locking me in their garage again? I thought they'd come for me. I thought ...

I change almost without meaning to, like it's a new defense mechanism for me to add to my arsenal. I rip away from the hands holding me.

With a sob, I take off down the dark street, staying out of the glow of the lights and trying to keep my speed up. I hear them giving chase and they don't sound like the Iron I's at all.

Who are these guys? What do they want me for? Did I just wax-off in the street?

A shot rings out and a biting pain in the back of my thigh makes me trip. I go down hard, but pick myself up as fast as I can, limping into a dark alley and hiding behind a dumpster. I try to keep my breathing steady as I let my glamor back down and become smaller, more easily hidden.

I touch my leg just below my ass where it hurts and my fingers come away wet.

'She's down here! I can smell her.'

I hold my breath as I sink down, pushing myself into the space between the dumpster and the wall, but the light from a phone momentarily blinds me.

They've found me!

I try to get to my feet, but before I can do anything, Vic comes forward with a syringe in his hand and jabs me in the neck.

I go limp immediately and I'm hoisted up and cradled against a solid chest.

'Lucky I saw her when I did,' says Gruff Voice.

'I can't believe it,' a third guy says. 'Our own succubus.'

Just before I lose consciousness, we exit the alley and I'm enveloped in the glow of a streetlamp for a moment. I look up, but it's not Vic's eyes that stare into mine, it's Lionel Makenzie's.

'She's not ours yet, boys, but she will be.' He smiles. 'And she is going to make us more powerful than the Ten.'

Vic

WHEN WE FINALLY MAKE IT to Ada's bar, we go in the back way. We've been keeping our presence in Metro as lowkey as possible since we got here so the cops don't swoop in and cart us back to the Mountain before we can get our lawyers earning their money.

We walk into the loud and crowded strip club, but instead of the usual dancers and clientele, we find cleanup crews and handymen.

'Was this from the other night?' Paris wonders aloud, turning in a slow circle to view all the damage.

'I'll bet Ada's pissed,' Theo murmurs.

I've lost track of the days, but I think it's a Friday or a Saturday. Ada's club is never closed on those nights, no matter what. It's clear that Metro is already recovering from what I keep hearing media types, who weren't even there, call 'the unpleasantness' like it was a barge of garbage that made the city stink and not a massacre of families by terrorists, but if this had happened during the fighting, it would be fixed already knowing Ada. She runs a tight ship.

'This is from something else,' I say, my heart beginning to hammer in my chest.

'Jane might be down here helping to clean up,' Sie says.

'Why do you say that?' I ask.

'She's like that.' He gestures to the poles. 'Plus, she enjoyed watching the dancers.'

'And the disco lights,' Korban adds, his eyes following the colors that move around the room.

They know more about her than I do. I shouldn't be surprised. It's my own fault I'm on the outside of the succubus mate circle.

We take a quick look around, hoping that Jane is down here somewhere.

Fi isn't behind the bar, so we find one of the bouncers to tell Ada we're here. Luckily, he knows us by sight so we don't have to waste time trying to explain who we are or getting the 'Ada's not here right now' speech.

I want to see Jane, hold her, tell her I'm sorry. But I'm nervous at the thought. What if she pushes me away? She has every right to. A part of me hopes she does because she deserves so much better than a fucked-up Makenzie like me.

The door upstairs is opened for us and we race up straight to Ada's office.

I'm the first at the door, the others crowding around me to get through. We can't go in there like this. At best Jane will freak out. At worst, Ada will and I don't want to see that.

I let my power out to force them back.

'Fucking relax,' I growl. 'Remember where we are. Just because Ada did us a solid, doesn't mean she'll be okay with us busting in on her.'

I take a breath, make sure I look okay. I see the others do the same. I knock.

'Come in.'

I open the door and go inside Ada's office, the others following silently and exercising restraint. I don't know exactly what Ada is, but every single supe knows not to piss her off.

She looks surprised to see us, glancing at Fi who's standing next to her.

'Alexandre. To what do I owe the pleasure? Do you come to offer me a gift for keeping your wayward succubus safe for you?'

'Of course,' I say. 'I'll give you anything you want. You only need to ask.'

Ada looks even more surprised. 'Anything I want? Well, that is a fine promise. I'll take you up on it one day, I'm sure. For now, I suggest you keep her close lest she slip through your fingers again.'

She and Fi share a look and then their eyes fall on us and Ada tilts her head a little.

'Was there something else?' she asks.

I glance back at the others. What game is she playing?

'We've come for Jane,' I say.

'I'm afraid the joke escapes me,' Ada says, her eyes flicking to Fiona.

Fiona shrugs at her, shaking her head a little and looking just as confused.

'But you already took her,' she says to us. 'In Café Vino.'

She shakes her head at me again like I forgot.

'No,' I say slowly. 'I didn't.'

Ada's hand shoots out and grabs Fiona's arm, making her wince.

'You told me Vic came and got her,' Ada says, her voice dangerously low.

'He did! I mean it looked like him. He said he was sorry and that he wanted to talk and Jane went with him. She—'

'Be silent!' Ada hisses in a tone that has tears coming to Fi's eyes.

'I'm sorry, mistress,' she whispers. 'I didn't know.'

'Go to the anteroom and wait for me,' Ada says, sounding

calm, but then she pulls their faces close. 'You and I are going to make sure you can still be trusted, pet. It will not be a funishment,' she says through clenched teeth. 'Go.'

Fi nods and leaves the room quickly, tears already falling from her eyes.

Ada turns back to us. 'Sincerest apologies, Alexandre. But I think you can guess who has her now, no?'

I nod, not trusting myself to speak because I'll get us all eviscerated and then who will save Jane?

I turn without a word, pulling Paris along by the scruff of the neck when he tries to ask Ada the question. Out in the hall, after the door has closed behind us, he wrenches away from me angrily.

'What the fuck, Vic? Where is Jane?'

'Lionel has her,' Korban guesses.

I nod. 'Sounds like his MO to me. He knows what she is. It makes sense he's trying to use her somehow.'

'But for what?' Paris asks.

Theo gives him a disgusted look. 'What do you think?'

Vic shakes his head. 'Lionel makes decisions based on two things: leverage and power. He might be an incubus, but sex has never been first on the list.'

'But it is on the list,' Theo says quietly.

'Who gives a shit why he took her?' Korban growls. 'We're standing here with our dicks in our hands while our girl is in danger.'

'So what are we going to do about it?' Sie growls.

I look around at the others, storing my anger deep for when I face my father. I've let him take a lot from me over the years. He and his clan have gotten rich and powerful off the backs of me and my clan. They've taken from us a hundred times and I let them because I still yearned for that familial approval he'd promised my brothers and me if we were obedient.

No more.

I'm the leader of this clan of powerful incubi and I'll be damned if I'm going to let him have Jane.

I take out my gun and check it's fully loaded.

'I think it's time we paid dear old dad a long overdue visit.'

FIFTEEN

JANE

Jane

My foot hits something hard that clangs, and I open my eyes with a quick breath as I curl my leg back under me. The back of my thigh throbs.

I'm in a dark room. All I can see are cracks of light coming from windows that are covered by shutters, I think. I try to stand up and hit my head hard.

Another clang.

I groan, rubbing my head and using my other hand to reach up as I sit back down on my ass. About a foot above my head, I can feel a thick lattice of metal.

Am I in a cage?

But I got out of the dungeon, didn't I?

I sit there for a few seconds in the dark second-guessing myself. Did I dream up Ada and Fi and the nice wine bar? Am I still in fae land?

I hate their tricks. I never know which way is up or what information is real. It's such a mind fuck.

The vision of Lionel Makenzie's eyes before he jabbed me with a needle comes back to haunt me and my fingers move up to touch my neck where he got me. It hurts a little, but that's it.

So I did get out but then I was taken again. Seriously? I've never particularly thought of myself as a hapless individual, but two kidnappings in as many days really seems like too many times. I really need to start checking my decisions because this is ridiculous.

Wait, I got shot!

I feel my leg and it seems like the wound has already closed over. Remembering what Kor told me, I hope one of Lionel's cronies has already dug the bullet out or that's going to be a pain later.

Letting out the breath I've been holding, I tremulously move my hands out beyond my body to see how wide and long this thing is. My knuckles brush the metal before my arm is straight. Same on the other three sides. Under me is a blanket, like you put in a dog crate, and I can feel the ridges of the cage's frame through it.

I'm in a cube, which means I won't be able to stand up or stretch out. My muscles immediately start to complain while my head starts the freak out I know all too well.

Panicking right now would be bad.

I push it all down as far as it will go as I feel for a latch, keeping my mind focused on a solution. It's unlikely that this door won't be locked, but maybe there's a Ged who wants me to escape here too.

My fingers find the hinges and run along the cold, rough metal. The whole thing feels rusty.

There it is.

It's a thick, heavy-duty padlock, but its metal is smooth and there are parts that are clearly molded plastic. I'm not sure what that tells me but information is information at this point. I'll take what I can get.

My legs and back are itching to be straight, so I sit down on my ass and sit up tall with my back against one side of the cage, stretching my legs out in front of me at the same time, but there's not enough space to do that. I take in a quick breath, feeling dizzy.

I'm trapped in a tiny box!

No you're not. You can get out anytime. Just demon-up and this cage will bow like it's made of reeds.

I wax-on and tense a little, expecting to break out like the Kool-Aid pitcher breaks through walls.

But nothing happens.

It's okay. It's okay. I'm a noob. These hiccups are bound to happen.

Maybe it's because I'm scared. I take a deep breath and sit cross-legged, trying to relax and imagine myself somewhere else.

I try again, but no demon comes out to play.

'It won't work,' says a voice from the darkness and I give a surprised yelp.

Sounds of movement come from behind me and I scramble to turn around and face my captor.

'Who are you? What do you want from me?' I ask, fumbling for my bravado, but it falls flat because my voice is scared and squeaky.

A light comes on, a fluorescent flickering brightly from above, and I close my eyes, covering them with my arm.

He doesn't answer my clichéd questions.

Instead I hear him coming closer and move away from the sound, squinting through the light to figure out exactly where he is, who he is.

Except there's a noise from the other side.

There's more than one.

I blink rapidly, trying to make my eyes adjust faster.

'She doesn't look all-powerful.'

'Read the files on her. Even as a human she had deficits. It's like Foley said. Some brain issue.'

Someone snorts. 'It doesn't matter if she's not all there. We'll create the narrative. The fact that we have a succubus mate will entitle us to power. Whether or not she's actually as strong as she's supposed to be makes no difference.'

'What about the fae—'

'Enough.'

Vic's dad's cold, calculating voice rings out through the room and every one of them shuts up.

I've heard five different voices including the one who helped Lionel grab me.

That makes this Lionel Makenzie's clan.

My eyes finally start working and I peer out of the box.

There are five massive guys standing way too close, staring at me like I'm part of a freak exhibit. They're all older, but like silver fox, not toothless miner. I mean, they're incubi. No matter their ages, they have to look hot. It's in the job description. Not one of them does it for me though.

I'm trying not to get even more scared than I was before, but being in the middle of them, in a freaking cage … well that's tough to take and not lose it a little.

I try to demon-up again, pushing upwards in case it helps to let out the rage, but there's nothing to tap into. All I do is smack my head into the metal hard enough to see stars.

'That won't work in here, little girl. Did you hit your head? Want to tell daddy where it hurts?'

OMG ew!

I stare at the guy who said it with wide eyes as I rub my

head. His eyes bore down on me, making me feel small and very, very vulnerable in the worst way ever.

I can literally feel my budding daddy kink withering and dying here and now.

I try to change again in desperation, but it's like I can't get to it. This isn't a 'me' thing. This is a conjure. It's got to be.

Vic's dad laughs at my disgusted expression. 'You'll learn to love it,' he says to me, but then looks back up at his clan-mate. 'You can play daddy dom with her once she's ours, Stoke. I told you, if you try anything with her too soon, you'll both get sick. She's another clan's mate.'

He looks back down at me. 'Aren't you, honey?'

I just glare at him.

One of them to the left of me holding a tablet nods without looking up from what he's doing. 'It says no feeding from her forcibly. We can't take from her unless she wants us to and she can't feed from us at all until she's ours.'

Stoke sighs, stepping back and very clearly adjusting himself in his slacks. 'But how are we going to—'

'Hugh? What does it say?'

'Catch the succubus. Check. Put her in a conjure cage of iron. Check. Okay, uh ... here it is.'

He's silent for a minute while his eyes scan the screen. The others wait for him to speak, all of them staring at me.

I huddle into myself, trying to escape their eyes any way I can.

'Basically, to change a succubus' allegiance from one clan to another, we need to make her dependent on us completely. We don't give her food or drink unless she takes it from our hands. If she wants clothes, then she lets us put them on her after she's earned them. If she wants to be clean, she lets us bathe her. If she wants out of the cage, then 'yoke her as if a mule and lead her'. Don't allow her to speak until she shows submission.'

'So we treat her like one of the human slaves. Simple.'

'There's more,' Hugh mutters. 'It literally says not to try to hurt her physically. 'Do not beat the succubus, do not sodomize her, but do cover her in your essences whenever you see fit. Let all smells be of you.' But that's about all the info there is besides the feeding thing.'

I don't let them see my reaction, but holy shit! Every word out of this guy's mouth takes this situation from bad to worse. I mean what the fuck is he reading?

I look up at Lionel, just Lionel, trying to block out the others. 'What do you want from me?'

He squats down so he's eye level and he grabs the cage, making me jerk back.

'Everything,' he says softly with a smirk that chills me.

He looks me over, his eyes scanning me, before he stands smoothly.

'Get her out of there,' he orders.

The key is in the lock almost before he stops speaking and grabbing hands enter the space. I try to evade, but I'm literally in a little box. There's nowhere to go as fingers drag me out.

I'm held between two of them by my arms and shoulders and although a part of me is grateful that I'm able to stretch, the feeling is short lived.

'Well, you heard Hugh. No clothes until she earns them, gentlemen.'

The irony of him calling his clan 'gentlemen' isn't lost on me, but it's my last coherent thought as his words register with them and they literally begin to pull the dress off my body.

I scream and struggle and kick, fabric tears and it's only a few seconds before I'm standing in just the black lingerie from Fi.

My eyes are clenched and I'm trembling as I hear a laugh and I jerk away as I feel a finger run along the edge of my bra.

'Very nice,' murmurs Vic's dad. 'I think we can safely say that breeding her isn't going to be a chore. What's this?'

My necklace is ripped from my throat.

'Where did you get an orc stone?' he chuckles.

I don't answer.

A knife cuts off the rest of my clothes and the pieces of fabric fall to the ground at my feet.

I don't open my eyes. Maybe I'm a coward, but I can't face seeing them looking at me. It was hard before, but this ... I struggle to contain my tears ... this is awful.

He orders me put back in the cage quickly, and I'm practically thrown through the door like they're afraid they'll lose all self-control. I smack my shoulder on the way in and let out a cry of pain as the tiny cell is slammed shut.

'When do you think she'll need to feed next?' one asks breathily.

I curl into a ball in the cage, trying to hide as much of my body as I can from them.

'The pills I found on her will keep it under wraps for a few days if she took them. By then she'll have submitted and be ours. She'll be able to feed from us after that,' Lionel says, 'and we from her.'

Fuck. You.

'What do we do now?'

'Well, we have that meeting in ten, so I suggest we scent her, get cleaned up, and we should be right on time for it.'

Scent her?

I don't have to wait long to discover what he means as I

hear flies unzipping and the unmistakable sound of hands pumping flesh.

The first jet takes me by surprise, hitting me on my back and hair. I uncurl and scramble back with a cry of horror, realizing what they're doing just as another hits my cheek.

I wipe it off with the back of my hand immediately, trying to keep sobs at bay. It's sticky and the ammonia smell of it hits my nose, making me gag.

Another gets me on the thigh at the same time as my side.

I'm shaking, tears running down my cheeks as I try to keep my mouth shut.

Lionel is last and he gets close, practically poking his dick though the lattice so when he comes, every single drop lands on me, catching my shoulder, hair, and neck.

I feel it slide down my chest and try to brush it away, but all I succeed in doing is spreading it around.

One by one, I hear them leave, speaking in low tones with each other. I can't make out the words ... or maybe I just don't want to hear them.

Finally, it's just Lionel and me.

'This will go easier if you don't fight.'

I blink back my tears before I look at him, but I find I can't even do that, I stare past him like I used to do with the Iron I's.

I want to tell him to go fuck himself, but I already know that trying to force words out will be useless. I'm too upset. My eyes hurt from the lights. My skin and hair feel sticky, and I'm cold.

'I'll bring you some food later,' he says.

Then he smiles and his eyes move over me. 'But consider this your first meal, Jane. I wouldn't waste the protein if I were you.'

My jaw sets and he chuckles low. 'You in a cage covered in

our cum is the sexiest thing I've seen in a very long time.' To my horror, he takes out his phone and snaps a pic. 'Breeding you is going to be fun and the plans I have for you after ... Well, you aren't just going to make us the most powerful clan, honey. You're going to make us the richest one as well.'

He leaves, turning off the lights, and as soon as I hear the door close, I start to sob in the dark. They've taken my dress, my demon, and my dignity as easily as snapping their fingers.

Breathing in fits and starts, I ineffectually wipe at the cum they've covered me in before remembering the blanket under me. I use one side of it to wipe myself off and another to wrap my body up, giving me a little warmth and tiny bit of my self-respect back.

I huddle into myself, closing my eyes and trying not to think about what's happening, but it's impossible. The reality is that no one except Lionel and his clan know I'm here. Even Fiona thought Lionel was Vic so she won't even think there's a problem. As far as she's concerned, I'm back with my clan and probably happy as a clam. No one's coming for me like last time. I'm a lone succubus without her supey mojo, surrounded by brutes.

I don't want to yearn for the Iron I's, but I can't help it. More tears fall as I wish that Theo or Paris was holding me, warming me instead of this scratchy blanket, that Sie and Vic were pacing around thinking of a way out of here and Korban was tearing this fucking place apart.

But it's quiet and dark and I'm all alone.

Even my mantra that everything was to keep Shar and her kids safe no longer has any power to make me feel better.

I grip my knees tighter, sobbing quietly, wishing that my clan would come.

But they won't. They don't care about me.

~

Sie

I FEEL like I'm going to lose it as we leave Ada's club, Vic practically dragging me out because I want to go back in there and break every single thing the handymen have fixed.

Lionel has Jane.

It's almost too much for me to comprehend.

'We have to get her out of there,' I say, grabbing onto Vic hard. 'They'll treat her like one of their other girls. They'll—'

'No, he wants her for something else,' he says tightly, gripping me back and I wonder who he's trying to convince.

'What does he and his clan want with Jane?' Theo says, staring at me like he's in a daze.

'They have to know what she is,' Korban snarls. 'That's what they want her for. They want their own mate.'

'No,' Vic says. 'They had their own mate. She was killed before I was born. That's not what it is, not really.'

'What then?' Paris asks, looking like he's going to throw up.

'This is Lionel,' I say. 'He chases power. That's all he's ever wanted. That's what a succubus is to him and his clan.'

'But she's already ours. They can't just pretend she's not. It doesn't work like that,' Kor says.

'You read more of the books on succubi than we did,' I say to him. 'What else did you learn?'

'Nothing that would be useful here. But ...'

'But what? Think! Anything you remember could be helpful now,' Theo says.

Korban pulls a hand through his hair. 'All the books were very old and Maddox said that there was this idea in a lot of them that succubi were too strong and needed to be tamed. Kept weak.'

'Kept weak? What the hell does that mean?' I growl at him.

'I don't know, but Lionel and his clan are known for their abilities to break slaves wills. If they're taking advice like that to heart, it sure as hell doesn't sound good for Jane.'

Various scenarios start running through my head, making my whole body clench tighter and tighter with anger and fear. 'We need to find her.'

Vic starts pacing the sidewalk. 'There's more than one place she could be. We need to recon them all and once we know where she is, we go in and get her.'

'We can't wait that long! We don't even know what they're doing to her!'

'I know!' Vic snarls. 'But they own countless properties, Sie.'

'Slave houses and brothels, you mean!'

Vic goes silent.

'We need to find her,' I tell him. 'Fuck you for burning that contract. We would know exactly where she's being held if we still had it.'

I push him hard and he bangs into the bricks of the building.

'I know, okay?' he hisses. 'Fuck! I know.'

He pushes himself away from the wall. 'There are five likely places, the ones that have the best security. She'll be at one of those. Each of us will take one and report back. Then we'll find a way to get her out.'

'And if she isn't at one of those?' I ask.

Vic gives me a hard look. 'We tip off the fae that Lionel Makenzie has the succubus they're looking for and they'll find her for us.'

CHAPTER
SIXTEEN

Jane

Despite the blanket, I'm shivering and crying still, and not just from the shock of what they all did.

I don't know how long it's been since they left, but my skin is crusty and the smells of them still pervade my nostrils. Unlike the scents of the Iron I's that I find comforting, these other incubi's aromas don't elicit the same reaction in me at all. The soiled blanket doesn't help either, but without it, I'm so cold.

I've been thinking and thinking and I don't really know how this could get much worse. I'm naked and locked in a cage and Vic's dad and his clan want to brainwash me into taking them as mates so they can use me for ... I don't know. Evil?

From the words they used, it didn't sound like my kick-ass demon is gone forever, but it ... she is definitely not here right now. I've tried a few times to change, but nothing has happened. I don't want to say I'm useless without her, but I want her back. I felt so much less afraid when I could demon-up.

I try to keep it together. Escape is my only priority. I was literally a human for all of my life before this. I can survive without being a supe. I can deal with fear and anxiety. I can't fall apart or I might as well just give up and tell Lionel I'll be his and his clan's mate.

Not happening!

I try to remember everything I heard them say because it seemed to me that they weren't being all that careful around me, much like the fae I met. That means they'll underestimate me.

And, like the fae, they took me because I'm a succubus. Not for the same reason though. They don't seem to want me dead. Putting aside the fact that everyone seems to know what I am when I only found out so recently, I try to work out their motives. Lionel's clan want me to be theirs because a succubus equals power. So that must mean that ... I am more powerful than an incubi clan like Maddox's books said. So is that why the highest fae want me dead too? Is that how I'm a threat to them?

Noooooo, that's nuts.

How could I hurt the Ten? They're the most powerful of the fae and they're old as dust. All the bazillion years they've lived and I come and take them down?

C'mon! That's even more ridiculous that being kidnapped twice in two days.

But I keep coming back to it. There's something to this. The Ten tried to get rid of all of the succubi. I heard those three High fae literally say it in the dungeon. That's a hell of a campaign for no reason. They must have been afraid of something and they did say that during the war with them all that time ago that many of their numbers were lost.

The door opens and the light comes on.

I hide my face under the blanket and hope he'll go away, but I hear him come towards the cage.

'Wakey, wakey, little succubus. I brought you some food.'

I peer out a little, staying under the blanket and keeping my eyes away from the fluorescents. It's one of the ones whose names I don't know. He has a plate in his hand and it looks like plain pasta.

'Are you hungry?' he asks.

My stomach twists. I am hungry. I nod once, hoping he'll leave it and go, but he doesn't. He stands in front of the cage, staring down at me.

'Get near the bars and kneel in front of me,' he orders.

I do what he says because food.

'Drop the blanket,' he says, with a smirk.

I narrow my eyes at him.

'I'd rather starve,' I say.

He chuckles and goes down on one knee.

He holds out a piece of pasta and find that I'm just hungry enough to take it from his hand with my fingers, but he draws it back.

'No, no, not like that. Open,' he says, grinning.

I shake my head, remembering what the one with the tablet said. There is no way I'm taking food from them like an animal.

'Do you want it?'

I nod.

'Then give me the blanket or open your mouth. Obedience is the price for a meal.'

I seethe. I'm not giving him my blanket. No way!

But I'm hungry and I'm not going to be able to escape this place if I'm too weak to run.

I scrunch up my eyes and I open my mouth.

'Very good,' he coos and I clench my fists in the blanket.

Fuck this guy.

A piece of pasta is put in my mouth and I chew it. It's bland and tasteless, not even any salt to season, but I don't care, opening my mouth again like a hungry bird. I hate myself for this, but I hate him more.

He keeps putting pieces into my mouth, his fingers brushing against my lips on purpose and I try to ignore it, keeping my eyes firmly shut.

When there's no more, I open my eyes to find him very close and I scramble back, but not before he grabs the blanket, pulling it through the lattice before I can stop him.

With a self-satisfied grin on his face, he peers down at me.

'Sorry, pretty girl, but how can we see your beautiful body if you cover it up?'

I clench my jaw and hug my knees. My belly is full, but I'm starting to shiver already.

He notices my shaking though and walks across the room to the thermostat on the wall, which he twizzles.

Guess it would be less fun for them if I froze to death.

I think he's going to leave, but then he comes back and unzips himself.

Not again!

'Don't,' I say, wincing at my own pleading voice.

'No talking unless you're told you can. You'll thank us when this is over,' he says, already beating his dick to the sight of my body.

'No, I won't,' I promise him, looking away and vowing that I'm not just escaping when the time comes, I'm going to kill these assholes.

It's not long before he's done, grunting as his stream of cum hits me, dripping down my back.

He doesn't turn the light off when he leaves and I have a

chance to look around the room for the first time without anyone here.

I survey it, using it to forget about what's on my skin, what I just had to do.

There's faded wallpaper and what looks like a door to a bathroom. I figure this was a bedroom once, but all the furniture has been removed so it's just the cage and, I squint at the light that isn't in-keeping with the rest of the room. Why fluorescents? Is it because they're the brightest, most horrible flickering lights imaginable? Did they just install them here to add to my torment?

I take a closer look at the cage door, trying to pry up the pins in the hinges with my fingers, but all I do is break my nails in the process and they don't even budge so I turn my attention to the padlock.

The lock is for a key and I have nothing to even try to pick it with. I scan the floor, but besides an errant piece of pasta, it's completely clear. No screws or nails. Nothing.

At least the room is getting a little warmer now that the thermostat has been turned up. I'm still a little cold, but at least I'm not bordering on hypothermia now.

The last things I notice are the windows. It's bright outside, but there are old-fashioned shutters over them so not much gets through. Why would they bother covering them? Do they not want me to see out there, or do they not want others seeing in here?

The door opens again and I hug my knees to hide as much as I can again.

'Being a bad girl already?' Lionel asks with a snigger.

I glare at him as he comes and sits in the chair by the cage. He doesn't speak, just watches me.

'They'll come for me,' I say even though I don't really believe it deep down.

He laughs. 'I'm afraid not, Jane. They cut you loose, remember? No one's coming for you. The truth is, the Iron I's gave you to us. You were just payment for a debt and you're ours, so you might as well get that pretty, fucked up head around that. We are your masters now.'

He moves the chair closer and I make myself stay where I am.

I'm reeling internally. He's got to be lying, right? The Iron I's might not want me, but they wouldn't let Lionel have me ... right? He's just messing with my head, trying to break my spirit faster. I can't trust anything he or his clan says.

'Did my son tell you what I do?'

I shake my head, not sure I want to know.

'I have clubs like Maddox does and mine are for a certain demographic just like his. But whereas his clubs cater to the young supes who want to experience the fae's entertainments, mine are for an older, very different, and very discerning clientele.'

I stare at him, not really sure where he's going with this.

'My clan and I buy and sell girls, mostly human. They're taught to please supes and then they're placed in rooms like this to service men like me.'

I feel sick and I don't even think I can hide it at this point.

'Don't worry,' he says. 'You're a special little bird. You won't be serving anyone here but me and my clan, at least not until after we're able to breed you, but you will be learning to be an obedient slave just like the rest.'

I don't say anything, just stare at him, looking him in the eyes as he takes out his dick and does what the last one did, but this time I don't look away. I stare into his face and I make sure he sees how much I loathe him.

Little bird.

I'm going to find the part of me they've stolen and I'm going to kill Lionel Makenzie last.

He doesn't look at my eyes while he works himself, but when he comes, he aims at my face and I have to move or get hit. I lurch away at the last second, but he steps forward and there's nowhere for me to go. He groans as his seed falls from the top of the cage and onto my head.

I freeze, not letting him see how what he does affects me both bodily and mentally. I don't try to clean off my hair. I have nothing to wipe it with and it won't make any difference. My body is already covered in their scents and I don't want it on my fingers too.

Lionel winks at me and gets up. He goes to the door, turns off the light again, and leaves me in the dark. I huddle in the cage and close my eyes, falling into thoughts of the Iron I's comforting me.

~

Paris

It's been two days and I'm only just finishing my recon of the house that Vic gave me to watch.

Virtually, of course. I doubt I'd have made it in there physically. Not my skill set.

This place is locked up as tight as the Mountain it seems like, and I have it on good authority that they only just beefed-up security very recently. There must be a reason for that, I think as I tap the feed from the last of their cameras.

I sit back in my chair. Now, I can see everything pretty much as it's happening in the house judging from the time stamps on the recordings.

I watch all the comings and goings, everything that goes

on in the house. I have photos of every John who's gone in there over the past two days and I'm giving them to the authorities as soon as we find Jane. There are twenty girls housed here, some clearly much too young to be anywhere near a place like this. I've seen them being trained as slaves for rich supes and I've been sickened by what I've witnessed.

I frown at one of the many screens and bring up the camera, seeing a flicker of movement in a room that's been empty since I started watching. The door is thrust open and a hooded girl is pushed inside the room. She's struggling and, as the door closes, she beats on it with her fists.

My heart's pounding. Is it Jane? She's the right height, her movements are similar. But her hood falls down and I see blond hair.

I close my eyes for a moment in disappointment and relief. I thought for sure it was her, just for a second.

The others have already checked three of the houses and I'm waiting to hear from Theo on his, but there's no sign of her anywhere in this one and the others haven't had any luck either.

I text the clan the bad news and I get up from my desk, wandering into Theo's room. I go into the closet where all of Jane's clothes still hang on the hangers.

I thought it would be weird being back here for the first time since the night we ran, but it's actually just comforting. If I close my eyes, I can feel her here, her smell permeating the air. I see her backpack by the bed. One of the others must have slung it up here when we were trying to clean up all the glass and other damage left behind from the fighting that had left the downstairs unlivable.

I open the bag, finding the headphones I gave her to say sorry for being such a dick on the top. Does she need them where she is right now? Are they treating her well because she's a succubus? I put them by the side of the bed, plugging in the charger so they're ready for her when she gets back. If she gets back.

WHEN!

I hear the door and leave the room before I'm overcome with emotion.

I can hear talking and I know it's the guys returning from their meeting with the lawyers.

'How did it go?' I call down the stairs ahead of me.

'Good. They found some footage of us on one camera they must have missed when they were deleting evidence, so the Metro PD is pretty fucked if they bother us at all.'

'That's some good news, I guess,' I mutter.

'Well, we have a better chance of finding Jane if we can move around town without worrying about the cops snatching us at least,' Vic says. 'Have you heard from Theo?'

Theo walks in the house at that moment. 'She's not there. She's not in any of the houses on the short list.'

Korban kicks the door closed. 'What now?'

'I meant what I said,' Vic replies. 'We tell the fae where she is. They have the resources to find her much faster than we can.'

'That's insane.'

'Is it? We make them do the work for us. They get her out, take her to the Meridian, and,' he pulls out Maddox's master link key, 'we go in and grab her right out from under their noses.'

'Breaking her out of the Meridian was a dumb plan in the first place,' Sie says. 'It wouldn't have worked then and it won't work now.'

'You have a better idea?'

There's silence as he thinks and I look away from them.

We can't afford to argue now. Every moment she's with Lionel's clan is another moment they could be hurting her.

A shadow falls over the glass of the front door that miraculously survived the other night. There's a knock.

Korban pulls the door open roughly. 'What do you—'

He breaks off. 'What the hell are you doing here?' he growls instead.

'I'm here to see my brother.'

CHAPTER
SEVENTEEN

Theo

K orban looks over his shoulder with a sneer. 'Looks like you got a family drama to deal with, Alexandre.'

Kor leaves the guy at the door like he doesn't give a shit who he is, and goes into the living room by himself, shutting the door behind him.

Paris and I are rooted to the spot.

'I thought Vic's brother was dead,' Paris whispers to no one in particular.

'Harris, his older brother, is dead. This is the younger one. Daemon,' Sie murmurs very low.

'What are you doing here?' Vic says, not going to the door. 'We don't speak for a reason. Leave.'

'I know where your succubus is.'

'How?' Vic scoffs without missing a beat. 'Look, I don't have time for your games. We need to find our mate.'

'I'm telling you, Alex, I saw her.'

Vic snarls. 'Fine. Come in and tell us what you think you

know, but I swear if you're playing with us, I'll gut you like I watched Lionel do to Harris.'

He comes into the house with a scoff, shutting the door behind him. 'I'm not playing.'

'How do you even know about her?' Sie asks.

'I smelled her the other night in Café Vino when she was there with Ada's pet. I saw you there too.'

My eyes narrow. That's what Fi said she saw as well.

'Go on,' Vic says.

'I saw him. You. Lead her out onto the street. That's when I saw dad's crew waiting. She went demon and ran as soon as she realized it wasn't you. They shot her.'

'What?' I can't help the snarl that rips out of me and I hear similar sounds from the others.

'They shot Jane?'

'Yeah, Hugh got her in the leg. She went down but she didn't give up. She kept going. They still got her though. They put her in a car. I followed in a cab until I realized where they were going.'

'Where?'

Daemon's mouth closes for the first time since he got here. He looks at Vic with a gleam in his eye. 'Well, I'll tell you, big bro ...'

'What's your fucking fee?' Vic roars.

Daemon doesn't hesitate. 'I hear Krase doesn't have much time left. I want you to get Maddox to let me back in his clan.'

'Impossible. You know that once you're out, you're out.'

Daemon chuckles. 'I remember what the fucking rules are, Alex. But he'll listen to you, and I hear he owes you a favor. That's my price. Take it or let your girl be bloodied and broken by our sick, twisted father and his clan.'

'Apple doesn't fall far from the tree,' Vic grinds out, but

Daemon only shrugs. 'Fine. I'll talk to him, put in a good word as your brother. But that's all I can promise.'

'That's all I need.'

'Where is she then?'

He barks out a laugh. 'I know I'm the youngest, but I'm not stupid, bro. You talk to Maddox first. When he calls me, I'll let you know where she is.'

Vic grabs him by the jacket and throws him against the wall, making a visible dent in the plaster behind the wallpaper.

'Tell us where she is!' he thunders, but Daemon just laughs.

'Kill me and you'll never find her, Alex.'

Daemon extricates himself from Vic's grasp and Vic lets him go. He doesn't say anything more, just gives us a wink and leaves the house, closing the door quietly behind him.

We stand in the hall for a second, staring at the space where Daemon just was.

'That sonofabitch!' Vic yells.

Jane

I DON'T KNOW how long it's been since one of them was last here. They come at intervals, usually one at a time. They watch me with creepy, unblinking eyes, making me take food from their hands, touching my face with their fingers. And then it ends with them whipping their dicks out and beating them violently until they spurt cum on my body. It's happened a few more times, but I've lost count of the exact number just like I've lost count of the days. They're getting restless too, impatient.

Whatever they want to see, it's not happening. I'm not developing succubus Stockholm Syndrome. I'm just retreating further and further into myself. I haven't spoken, I hardly move. I haven't been like this since the worst times in foster. I can feel my mind losing its grip on reality. Sometimes I even think I see the Iron I's. I can't stop it. I don't even want to. Better to be crazy.

My body is tired and dirty, caked with their dried fluids. My skin is red and flaky and its started burning when their cum gets on me. I try to wipe it off with my hands now, sluice it off my skin and throw it out of the cage, but they noticed and now if they see that I've done it, I'm punished.

What could they possibly do to make this worse? I didn't think there was a way either, but kudos to them, they did it. One of them, I think his name is Hugh ... He noticed me cringe when he banged the door closed, so he reread my file and came in with a bunch of things to see what sounds would affect me the most from babies crying to heavy metal music. He decided on high pitched screams and nursery rhymes on repeat, so now that's what I get to listen to.

It goes on for hours and hours. I'm a quivering mess on the ground with my hands ineffectually covering my ears and bruises all over my body from hurting myself when Hugh finally shuts it off and comes to stand over me. His cum splashes across my stomach. All I do is lay there, long past flinching away. I'm covered in it anyway, so what's the point?

'Just give it up,' he says not unkindly.

I turn my head away and start to cry, not caring if he sees.

A little while later two of the others come in and look in at me, talking to each other in low voices.

'... not going to matter if she's dead,' one hisses and I catch the tail end of his words.

The door is opened and hands come in. I bat them away

weakly, but they drag me out and I vaguely wonder what fresh hell they've thought of to torture me with now.

One of them picks me up, but I buck enough even in my weakened state to make him think twice and put me down. I sway on my feet, but I stay upright. He points at the door.

'Go to the bathroom,' he says.

I look at it with trepidation, wondering if this is a trick. They haven't let me go before. I usually have to direct everything through the bottom of the cage and one of them moves it and scoops my business up out of a pile of kitty litter.

Yeah, actual kitty litter. It's so fucked up.

I go slowly, half because I feel so weak and half because I'm afraid of what awaits me on the other side of the door. I slowly push it open and it squeaks loudly, but it's just a dated, yellow bathroom with a toilet, a sink, and a small shower.

I glance back and see the two incubi coming. I leap into the bathroom and try to shut the door, but my sluggish mind hasn't thought this through and it turns out I'm too slow anyway. One gets his foot in the door and after that it's easy for them to overpower me.

I back up to the wall, wondering how I'm going to be punished for what I just tried. I can't tell if they're mad, or not.

Neither of them say anything, and only one comes into the bathroom.

'Bad girl,' he growls.

He pushes me under the shower and turns it on. Freezing water pelts onto me and I scream, trying to escape, but he holds me there, not budging as I yell and cry and plead with him to let me go.

Finally, it gets warm and I surrender, going limp under his

grip and relaxing in the stream. I pretend I'm not here, that these two incubi aren't watching every move I make.

There's a cracked bar of soap on an old shower caddy. My eyes flick to it.

I refuse to talk to them, but I don't want another punishment like that.

He gives me a nod and I grab it, washing my body and my hair. The soap, thankfully, smells of nothing.

The guy waiting at the door protests. 'We're supposed to wash her the book said.'

'It's been days and all that's happening is she's getting weaker,' the one who was holding me argues. 'I think the book is full of shit.'

'Well, Lionel—'

'Lionel can suck my dick. I didn't sign up for this.'

His friend takes a step into the bathroom. 'You don't have a problem training the humans.'

The guy's hand leaves me and I breathe a sigh of relief.

But the other one grabs me. I gasp, as he snatches the soap from me and begins to lather my arm.

He's actually intending on bathing me. My body freezes. The combination of the shower, something I use to relax, and this man touching me, which is one-hundred and ten percent the opposite, has my brain unable to form thoughts.

I sink to the floor, curling up and rocking, pulling at my wet hair.

They're systematically taking everything from me and now they have their sights set on one of my favorite things. They'll ruin it, and I'll never be able to enjoy the shower again once I get out of here.

I tug my hair harder, the pain almost grounding me as I laugh out loud, finding it suddenly hysterical that any part of me still thinks I'm ever getting out of here.

'What's wrong with her?'

'I fucking told you something like this would happen! Get Lionel. NOW!'

I'm dimly aware that he's moved to the door, then he sighs and comes back.

He speaks to me slowly and loudly like he's a really dumb tourist who's trying to talk to a non-English speaker and doesn't understand how different languages actually work.

'If you can hear me, the water is going to go cold soon. You need to finish up or you're going to be stuck with semi-washed-off cum all over you.'

Few things would break through the fog, but that does and I make a concerted effort to stand up and finish cleaning myself.

It's hard and it takes a lot of effort, but I do it, eyeing him in case he tries to touch me, but he doesn't make a move.

I wash my hair as many times as I can before the water starts to turn and I flick the switch. It shuts off and I'm handed a small, cardboard-like towel that feels as if it's been in constant use since 1982. I rub my body with it, hating the sensation. I wrap up my hair with it before they take it away and leave me with nothing to cover myself.

His eyes move over me and he opens his mouth, but as he does, the door bangs open and I cringe away.

Cold air from the other room wafts in making me shiver and I wrap my arms around myself.

'What the fuck is going on in here?' Lionel thunders. 'Griff says there's something wrong with her.' He looks me over. 'She's fine.'

'I swear,' Griff says. 'I tried to bathe her like Hugh said and she was suddenly on the floor pulling out her hair and rocking.'

Lionel looks at me again, his face contorting. 'The bitch is playing you and you both fell for it hook, line, and sinker.' He looms over me. 'You might be able to pull the wool over these two idiots' eyes, but you don't fool me with your nonsense.' He picks the towel off my head and drops it to the floor.

'Go back to your cage.'

I look past him at the tiny metal cell and shake my head, taking a step back. I don't want to go back in there. I try to plead, to my everlasting humiliation, I open my mouth to beg him not to make me go back in, just about ready to promise him anything he wants if he just lets me stay out here, but nothing comes out.

He grabs me by my wet hair and drags me out of the bathroom, throwing me at the iron crate, bending me over it. I scream and claw at his hand, trying to make him let me go.

His clan mates are telling him to stop, but something comes down hard on my back.

I screech in pain and twist, almost succeeding in getting away, but the fingers in my hair tighten, keeping me steady as he hits me again.

I see it out of the corner of my eye.

His belt.

He hits me seven times in total so hard that by the end he doesn't even need to hold me in place. I'm gripping the metal of the cage as hard as I can, tears streaming down my cheeks. I'm sobbing hard, still bracing for more.

But I see him leaving, going to the door while threading his belt back through the loops of his pants.

'Get in the cage or I'll do worse,' he calls over his shoulder to me and then adds to his clan brothers, 'Don't forget to scent her.'

A hand touches my arm gently and I tear away from it with a snarl, feeling more like an animal than ... whatever I am now.

I go to the cage and I get inside, curling up and ignoring them as they get themselves off and shoot their loads on me again. Their cum hits the welts on my back and makes them burn even more, but I ignore the pain. The music and the screaming flicks back on, tearing into my senses and my brain, but I'm too far gone to care.

My tears dry up and something new takes their place, something I've been missing since I was brought here.

Cold, hard rage.

It makes me hope. Maybe whatever is keeping my demon at bay is failing because I can feel a sliver of her in the back of my mind that wasn't there before, trying to break out.

I'm going to get out of here.

Then I'm going to ... I don't know what I'm going to do. All the time I've had in here to think and I still don't have a plan, but I'm going to live. I'm going to experience every last thing that life has to offer. Even if it's by myself.

EIGHTEEN

Kor

I come down the stairs quickly, thinking about everything I need to take with me to make sure we save Jane.

That fucker, Daemon, finally text Vic about five minutes ago to let him know where our female is. The sonofabitch made us wait over twenty-four hours.

FUCK!

As I enter the living room, I see that Paris has his monitors set up in here so we can all easily watch them for signs of Jane. Vic, Sie, and Theo are in here too, just watching the screens as Paris jumps around from camera to camera.

'What is that place?' I ask.

'The Lakehouse. One of Lionel's properties.' Vic lets out a breath. 'I never even thought of it as a possibility. It was a wreck last I saw it.'

'It still is from what I can see,' Paris murmurs, 'but looks like they made it habitable. Just.'

'You got into their system already?' I ask, putting my hand on his shoulder and squeezing it gently. 'Good job.'

He nods, eyes still focused on the computer in front of him.

'Yeah. It took less than a minute. It wasn't as difficult as the other house. These cameras are older and their software isn't up-to-date.'

Vic nods. 'Second-hand from one of their other properties. Plus, it looks like they've only done the bare minimum to make the house weathertight. Probably wanted to keep it looking as derelict as possible. That way no one would think there's anything going on there. Are we sure she's there? My asshole brother could have been lying about everything.'

'Hugh and Griff are in the hall, but I haven't seen her on the feed yet.'

'What are they doing?'

Paris leans in closer. 'It's so fucking grainy ... I think they're arguing.'

'Is there audio?' I ask, straining my eyes to see their lips moving, but I can't make anything out at all.

Paris shakes his head. 'This is all we have.'

'What about magickal defenses?' Sie says, coming to stand next to me and staring at the screen.

'Nothing we can't handle.'

The screen flickers and, for a millisecond, I see something that makes my blood run cold. Was that ... 'Wait! What was that window that popped up right there? Go back.'

'Just a sec. I don't know how I did that. It's a secondary system. Just one camera going to a laptop maybe,' Paris murmurs, typing a bunch of stuff I don't understand on a black screen.

A window appears showing a dark room with shutters and one jury-rigged light hanging down from the ceiling.

Music blares through the speakers intermixed with sounds of screaming. Paris fumbles to turn down the volume.

'What is that?' Theo asks, pointing to the only thing in the room. 'Is that a cage?'

I don't trust myself to say anything, my fists tightening as a figure inside the cage moves. I see her dark hair, her pale skin. She's naked and dirty, curled up in a ball.

'It's a conjure cage,' Sie says, his jaw pulsing. 'The Order kept their fighters in them when they weren't in the ring. It nulls magick, even being close to them makes a shift almost impossible.'

'They're using it to stop her from changing?' Paris asks. 'What's with the music and stuff?'

'They're torturing her,' I say, somehow keeping my fury in check, but have to look away.

'Why?' Theo snarls.

'Because she already has a clan,' Vic says. 'Remember the stuff you said the books at Maddox's had in them? They think if they can break her, she'll submit to them and she'll be theirs.'

'This was what we were afraid of,' Sie says. 'We—'

'Fuck,' Paris breathes and I look up at the screen again. 'There's a folder of video clips here.'

He clicks on one of the first files and I see Lionel's clan holding her, cutting off her dress. Touching her. He clicks on another one. Two of them are standing close to the cage and I can't see what they're doing at first.

Then, there's an audible groan and Jane flinches as something splatters her.

No one says anything, our eyes glued to the horrifying scene, our collective fury palpable.

Paris closes the file. He doesn't click on anymore. 'Why would they—'

'We need to get her out of there,' I interrupt.

I need to kill them. I need to do something to help Jane right now.

'I'm the lightest on my feet so I volunteer to take recon,' I say, grabbing the master link key off the desk and tossing it to Vic. 'You've been there before, right? Let's see if that piece of crap will work now. Get me into that house.'

I slip a microphone into my ear and squeeze Paris' shoulder again. 'I'm on Channel 2.'

I think Vic is going to argue, but he surprises me. He puts the link key on the door to the kitchen.

'I'll try to get you into one of the bedrooms upstairs. The rest of us will come through in thirty minutes no matter what so get us everything you can.'

I nod, giving him the go ahead as I pull my gun out, but a thought crosses my mind.

'This is your father's clan. You've known these guys all your life,' I begin, but Vic stops me.

He glances at the viewscreen of Jane in the cage.

'They all need to die,' he says, 'but leave my father for me.'

I give him a cold smile. This is the Vic I can get behind.

He opens the door and peers inside. 'Looks like the pantry,' he murmurs apologetically.

'Is it the right house at least?' I ask.

Vic nods and I go over the threshold without a backwards look, the door closing behind me.

'Testing,' I murmur.

'We can hear you.' Paris' voice crackles a little, but it's good enough.

I don't waste any time. I crack open the same door that brought me in here and see a dilapidated kitchen beyond. No one's in there, so I make my way across the room silently.

I hear a buzz and footsteps.

Hugh's voice calls through the hall.

'He's here!'

For a second, I think he's talking about me, that they know I'm somewhere in the house, but all he does is approach the phone, pick it up, and press a button. He's opening a gate, I realize.

Who are they expecting?

Hugh leaves, stomping down the corridor to the foyer and out through the front door. I leave the kitchen, going the opposite way until I get to a wide archway that a quick glance tells me is the way into the living room.

There's a noise from above me. There's more than one body moving around up there. Someone starts coming down the creaking staircase and I go through the next door. The space is bare, but there's a transom window that opens into the living room with a shutter that's half-closed. Assuming they meet with their visitor in there, this should work out perfectly.

I look through the glassless window. Two of them are already in there. One is Lionel and I have to stop myself from shooting the son of a bitch before Vic gets here. My finger twitches on the trigger. It would be so easy. Right between the eyes.

But I slowly move my finger away. I told Vic I'd wait and that's what I'm going to do.

The front door opens and closes with a bang that rocks the house and a second later I'm floored by who comes into the living room with Hugh.

Don fucking Foley. I can't believe it. Looks like every fucker I've been wanting a piece of to avenge Jane is together in one room today.

Good.

I whisper all the intel I've gathered so far into the microphone so the others know what they're walking into.

'Why have you called me here?' Don asks, sounding bored. 'Your message was cryptic as usual.'

'Don. Buddy. How you doing?'

Don rolls his eyes. 'Just get to the point, Makenzie. Some of us actually keep our ends of the deals we make. I have work to do.'

Lionel laughs. 'Even after the Ten screwed you, you're still their little lap dog.'

'Not at all.' Don smiles coldly. 'I always knew The Order might only get a few days to stir the pot before they shut us down, and I still got to stick it to your son and his clan in all the chaos. They'll be in the Mountain 'til they die. You should be thanking me.'

Lionel scoffs loudly. 'As usual, Foley, you did exactly what I wanted you to without even knowing it. Anyway, we heard you were looking for your daughter.'

Something passes over his face. Fear maybe.

'You know where she is?'

Lionel waves someone into the room. 'As a matter of fact, I do.'

My eyes widen as Jane is walked through the door. She's wearing a rough sack with holes cut for her head and arms that goes down to her knees. There's a rope knotted around her neck that Stoke is using to lead her. He pulls her forward hard even though she's not fighting him. Her eyes are dull. It doesn't even look like she knows where she is.

'Jane, honey, look! Your dear old dad's come to visit.' Lionel's tone turns colder. 'Aren't you going to say hi? Don't be impolite, now.'

Her eyes flick to Lionel and then to Don.

'Hi,' she says, her tone somehow more bland than usual.

What have they done to her?

I check my watch to stop myself from rising up and taking them out, reminding myself that it's safer for Jane if I wait for my whole clan to arrive. Almost time to start killing.

Don doesn't move. He just surveys his daughter with an apathetic eye, not seeming to care how Lionel and his clan are clearly treating her.

'Your girl is a succubus. Did you know that, Don?'

Lionel grins as if he thinks Don doesn't know, but he frowns when he gets no reaction.

'Holy fuck. You did!'

Don shrugs. 'Might as well tell you,' he says to Jane. 'You must already know anyway. Your mother was a succubus.'

'What happened to her?' Jane says slowly as if it's difficult for her to form words.

'Don't you know, honey?' Lionel says with smirk on his face. 'Your daddy killed her. Ain't that right, Don?'

Foley stares Lionel down before he turns back to Jane. 'Yeah. I killed her. I found her fucking some guy, trying to feed off him in an alleyway like a—' He breaks off, his lip curling with disgust.

Jane blinks, coming out of her haze a little. 'So you killed her?' she asks, accusation in her voice.

'Aren't you listening?' Don says, looking at Jane like she's a bug he wants to squish. 'She was a filthy, immoral monster. She did it to herself.'

～

Jane

STOKE STUCK a needle in me before he let me out of the cage. It made me groggy, but my head is starting to clear. Anger is burning away the drugs.

'You killed my mom because she was hungry?'

'I did her a favor,' my father sneers at me. 'The fae were already watching her. It was all thanks to me that they didn't get you too!'

'What do I have to thank you for?' I sputter incredulously. 'You left me!'

Don draws himself up. 'I might not have been there in person, but I made sure you didn't feed off anybody like she did. I kept you from getting comfortable and letting the demon out. The fae never found you because of me!'

I try to shake away the last of the cobwebs in my head, but I don't feel right. My body is sluggish and weak. I'm swaying a little on my feet.

'It was you,' I say, in a lightbulb moment. 'You were the one who always made me move on. You killed Angie!'

'That woman from foster care?' He shrugs. 'That was regrettable. The Order boys I sent were told to send you a message you'd actually take notice of since you ignored the one I left in your locker at school. The woman found them in her house and they got a little overly-excited.'

'They beat her to death! They cut out her eyes!'

He shrugs again.

I stare at him, wondering if he was always this twisted, if my mom knew his true face.

'So you were just trying to keep me safe from the fae?' I ask incredulously.

'It would have worked if you hadn't started whoring yourself out to those incubi.'

'Now, now, Don,' Lionel laughs. 'Let's not forget, you've been working for the fae for over fifteen years. Are you sure you weren't just keeping your succubus daughter a secret so you could use her against them if they ever turned on you?'

My father doesn't reply.

Lionel shrugs. 'Didn't think anyone would connect the dots? But who cares, right? It's in the past. I just thought you should know, Don, your daughter is ours now. No more getting the Order to follow her around and make sure she doesn't feed. She will be feeding. From us.'

Stoke, still holding the rope around my neck, chuckles low.

Don looks like steam is about to come out of his ears. 'How much, demon?'

'How much?' Lionel asks.

'That's why you called me here, isn't it? You own a ton of girls. You don't need her. So how much do you want for her?'

I look away from all of them, blocking out the sound of their voices talking about buying and selling me like I'm not a person.

My neck is jerked and I see that Lionel has a gun out. So does Foley. Everything happens in slow motion, but both of them fire on each other.

I'm hauled out of the room and pulled down the hall by Stoke before he curses and picks me up, throwing me over his shoulder and carrying me up the stairs. He takes them three at a time.

My body is shaking from all the revelations and the fear of being put back in the cage. Something is telling me not to let him get me anywhere near that thing. Anger is finally blowing through me, igniting my core like a furnace.

I feel the demon side of me, fury in my blood.

I demon-up and I feel the change. Stoke falls to one knee as my weight drags him down, but heaves himself up and tackles me, shoving me the rest of the way to the bedroom where they've been keeping me.

'You're going to be punished with the belt again,' he

snarls at me. 'I swear I'll do it right now if you don't put your glamor back on and get in that cage!'

He rips off the burlap he put on me earlier and I'm ashamed when his words make me cower for a second. He stands over me, relishing the terror he's put in my eyes.

Assholes like him feed on it. I look him in the face and I push that fear away as deep as I can. That's how I functioned every day as a human. I can sure as hell do it as a demon if I need to.

I launch myself at him, grabbing his skull between my hands and squeezing it like a melon. He screams and it's music to my fucking ears. The laugh that bubbles out of me is hysterical and maniacal and I revel in the feeling of finally being able to fight back.

I'm free.

Maybe I'm insane.

'Don't you like that, daddy?' I shriek, squishing his head until he goes limp.

The door opens behind me and I turn with a snarl, dropping the body so my hands are free to keep killing.

But it's Vic standing behind me.

I'm torn. My slaughter spree has only just begun and I sort of want to kill Vic too while I'm at it.

'Hi,' he says, closing the door behind him. 'I'm wondering if we can start again. I'm Alex.'

Vic

She looks crazed and I'm sure she's going to try to kill me. And I'm even more sure that I deserve it, but she doesn't lunge.

'You came for me,' she whispers, the anger going out of her eyes.

'Of course we did.'

Her glamor comes down and I have to hide my reaction. She's bruised and battered. She looks thin and weak. Lionel and the others have hurt her. From the smell in here, they've done what we saw on the video more than once too and maybe more.

She turns her back on me and my body locks up in fury at the welts on her back, the closed wound on her thigh from where they shot her.

'Jane, I—'

She ignores me, walking across the room and through a door. I hear a shower turn on a minute later and I follow her

'Jane, we need to go.'

She shakes her head and begins to clean herself with the soap, scrubbing at her skin over and over again in frenzied motions.

I gently take the bar from her and work it into a lather in my hands. She watches me, unmoving as I take over, washing her hair carefully and moving down over the ridges on her back. Her skin looks sore in places too.

She turns around to face me again, watching me as I wash her front. I try to be methodical and gentle, not scare her or upset her. She stares at the wall behind me.

I finish up and drop the soap on the floor. She looks down at it for a second. Then she looks back up at me. Her mouth opens and closes, but no words come out. She's breathing hard.

Without warning, she launches herself into my arms, gripping me tightly and kissing my lips deeply. She's fumbling with the fly of my pants and pulls my hard dick out. She doesn't say anything, doesn't wait. She just impales herself on it with a groan, moving herself up and down on me. I know this is because she's weak and injured, but I'll take it. I feel when she begins to pull energy from me. She's insatiable, sucking what she needs to heal and I give it to her willingly. Everything I have is hers to take.

I know what this is. It's not forgiveness or caring. It's starvation. That's all. It doesn't matter who I am. I'm here.

I grab her waist and move her when she slows, pushing her against the wall and thrusting into her roughly, giving her more, making sure she's full to brim with power, and surprised when she seems to do the same for me. Her lips are still on mine and her moans are muffled. She tenses and squeals as I send her over the edge, her legs shaking around me and then she stares into my eyes.

She draws back, watching me while I silently struggle to come back down from the high she just gave me. I've never felt so strong, so alive. But I make my head clear. Right now, we need to get out of here.

'I feel better,' she whispers woodenly as I let her down.

I nod, putting my jacket around her shoulders and lead her out of the room.

She eyes the body of Stoke.

'I did that,' she mutters and I feel her muted sense of pride that she killed one of them.

'You did good,' I say.

'Where are the others?'

Her voice is little more than a whisper. She still sounds weak and I eye her worriedly even as I internally rail over her physical and mental treatment. Lionel's going to die today and I hope I get to be the one to do it.

'Hopefully beating the shit out of my father and his clan for all that they've done,' I tell her. 'Jane. I'm sor—'

She pulls back. 'You made me leave.' Her voice breaks and I find tears coming to my own eyes. 'Please take me away from here.'

I just nod because it's about all I can manage.

We go down the stairs and back to the living room where the others were fighting when I left to find Jane.

The three other members of Lionel's clan are dead and Lionel himself is backed into a corner. Kor is in front of him. They have guns pointed at each other.

Sie has Foley by the throat on the other side of the room. 'You've had this coming for years, old man,' he's growling. 'Remember when you burned my face for losing that fight? Remember that, Foley?'

Foley just scoffs and spits in Sie's face.

Sie wipes the spittle off his cheek. 'You're going to regret that.'

Foley sees that I have Jane with me and spits on Sie again. 'I didn't burn you because you lost a fight. I did it because a group of humans paid me to. They were watching the whole time. The more you screamed, the more money I got.' He sniggers.

Sie roars, drawing back his fist to finish Foley once and for all, but he catches sight of Jane too.

He focuses on her immediately, his fist falling to his side. 'Are you okay?'

'I just want to go,' she says, not even looking at her father.

Sie turns his attention back to Foley and lets out a laugh. 'Revenge on you isn't worth upsetting her,' he says, stepping back.

'It won't matter. She'll never care for a monster as ugly as you anyway,' Foley sneers.

I turn towards my own father. 'It's over,' I say. 'Every member of your clan is dead.'

'You were always such a disappointment, Vicious,' Lionel says.

'The name my mother gave me is Alex,' I say. 'I won't be using any other from now on.'

'You just don't get it, do you? When you're the leader, you have to make the tough decisions, the ones no one else can make. You and your brothers never understood that.'

His words make me freeze. How many times have I thought those words? Said those words? Used those words as an excuse to justify my actions no matter how terrible? How many times did I do something cruel to Jane and rationalize it with those exact sentiments?

I have been the worst of my father and I didn't even realize it. I glance at my broken mate beside me.

No more. I make the decision in a split second.

I won't be like him anymore.

'Come on,' I say to the others. 'Let's get out of here.'

'But Foley. Lionel,' Korban mutters, but then he looks at Jane.

'Do you want them dead?' I ask her.

She just stares at me. 'Do whatever you want.'

I nod and give her the link key that brought us here to let her do the honors. She puts it on the door with shaking fingers.

'Little bitch,' Lionel mutters.

He points his gun at Jane.

NO!

I jump in front of her and the bullet gets me in the chest.

Korban breaks my fall and shoots Lionel.

Lionel's gun goes off again as he sinks to his knees, clutching his stomach, but the bullet misses us.

I grip my wound with a groan. Blood is pumping out of it fast.

Theo's at my side in an instant, putting pressure on it. I'm feeling lightheaded despite the power boost I got from Jane a few minutes ago I know I'm going to need that magick she pushed into me to get through this. It might look as if I just saved Jane, but I'd be dying right now if it wasn't for her.

Korban checks Lionel's body. 'He's dead.'

His eyes find Foley who's still standing by the wall, his face looking smug.

Korban sees it too and he shrugs, gives Jane a wink, and shoots Foley between the eyes. Foley's expression morphs into one of surprise as he falls to the floor.

'That's for your daughter, you fuck, and for Dreyson. He might have been an asshole, but he was still an Iron I.'

Jane's worried face hovers above me and I try to smile, but it's hard. She takes my hand and ... it's not so hard anymore.

I close my eyes.

∼

Sie

WE GET out of there pretty quickly after Alex passes out. Jane's looking stoic as always, but I think she's in shock. The connection between us feels faint. I thought she'd be upset when Kor shot her father, but all I got from her was a vague sense of relief.

He'd never have left her alone. She knew that really. He would have been a thorn in all our sides, but we really would have let him live if she'd asked us to.

We portal back to the house in Metro and Theo and Kor get Alex upstairs to the clinic.

Jane watches them ascend, and I feel faint worry coming from her.

'He's going to be fine,' I assure her. 'Just let Theo do his job.'

She gives a faint nod and I draw her to me.

'We thought we'd lost you,' I murmur into her hair.

She holds onto me tightly, but her face is expressionless.

'What do you need?' I ask.

She doesn't answer.

Getting more and more worried about her by the minute, I lead Jane upstairs to her room and put her gently on the bed. She just sits and stares at the wall. I text Theo to come as soon as Alex is fixed up, and I start a bath, putting my soap in it.

I get her a few minutes later, taking her slowly across the room to the bathroom. 'Do you want a bath?'

She doesn't even look at me, but I see her nostrils flare as she smells my scent. She steps into the bath and starts to sit down.

'Wait,' I say, darting forward to grab Alex's jacket that she's still wearing.

But she rears back with a terrified snarl, clutching the sodden garment and I put up my hands.

'Okay, baby, okay. You keep it if you want.'

She settles in the bath, not moving at all, hugging her knees tightly.

I don't know what to do. Letting my glamor down and tearing someone's throat out isn't going to work here. How can I help her? The woman I love, my mate needs me and I don't know the first thing to do to fix this. For us, sex and feeding usually fixes just about anything, but not this. That will do more harm than good after some of the torments she's endured.

I back out of the bathroom slowly, taking out my phone.

I call Theo.

He picks up. 'What is it?' he asks impatiently. 'I'm still trying to get the bullet out.'

'Tell Alex to dig it out himself!' I snarl. 'You need to get in here. She's not okay, Doc.'

It takes Theo less than thirty seconds to appear in Jane's room.

'What's going on?'

I gesture to the bathroom. 'I thought a bath … but she's just sitting in it and she won't take off Alex's jacket and,' I let out a shaky breath, 'I can't feel her properly. She's not right.'

He gives me an incredulous look. 'Did you think she fucking would be? You've seen some of the footage. They tortured her mind and body. Even if she wasn't autistic, she'd be broken into pieces after everything they put her through.'

'I know. I didn't mean—I don't know what to DO, Theo!'

'Stay out here for a minute,' he tells me and goes to the bathroom door.

He goes inside and I hear his gentle murmur, but then Jane starts screaming and there's the sound of splashing. I rush to the door to find water all over the floor and Theo grabbling with Jane. She's demoned-up in the bath and launching herself at him. Her emotions are disjointed, in flux. Her eyes are flashing in fury. Her wings flap hard and the force of them propels her out of the bath and into Theo. They thud to the wet floor.

'Help me!' Theo yells as her hands go around his throat. Her claws bite into his flesh as she squeezes and start to choke him.

I lurch forward, not sure what he wants me to do because I'm not going to hurt her. She's been through enough pain on our watch.

'Shit, she's strong,' Theo grinds out. 'Get the case out of my pocket.'

I do it, opening it to find a two full syringes.

'What the hell are these?' I growl at him.

'Sedate her before she hurts herself!' he orders me.

I take a step back, shaking my head.

'We can't just drug her after everything she's been through!' I bellow, my hands tightening around the case. 'She's been hurt enough by us!'

I hear it start to splinter, but I stop squeezing before the syringes break.

We can't do this. Not like this.

'Do it!' he yells.

'NO!'

Theo succeeds is pushing Jane back a little so he can breathe.

'You think I want you to?' he pants. 'I can't help her if I'm dead, Sie!'

'What the fuck is going on in here?' Alex booms and I feel his power pushing me down, making me submit.

My knees buckle and the case with the syringes in it clatters to the wet floor. Theo head drops to the floor, and Jane's attack freezes. She gasps at the full force of Alex's power directed on us and for once I'm glad he's able to make us yield because I know nothing short of knocking Jane out would have worked.

I glance quickly up at Alex and then back down. He's still standing at the door. He looks angry, but I see how concerned he is. His eyes are locked on Jane still poised over Theo. She's stuck where she is until he lets her go and I'm pretty shocked he still has the reserves to pull it off after healing himself so quickly from the bullet he took considering how powerful she is.

The bathroom is silent except for the scared noises Jane's making that cut my heart into a thousand pieces. Alex's eyes move to me and the magick holding me eases off.

I breathe out a small sigh as Jane scrambles off Theo. Her glamor comes back up and she huddles by the wall. She hugs herself and starts rocking, her breath coming in fits and starts.

'She started having a flashback, or something,' I say quietly.

He says nothing for a moment, just watching our scared, broken female.

Finally, he jerks his head towards the door. 'Get out,' he growls low. 'Both of you.'

Theo get up, casting a tortured look at Jane.

'She needs—' he begins.

'What she needs,' Alex interrupts, 'is the lingering scents off her and rest.'

Theo gives a reluctant nod and leaves. I linger for a moment.

'What are we going to do?' I ask.

Alex glances at me. 'You're going to give her space. I'm going to act like the leader I should have been. Tell Theo I'll call for him after she falls asleep to discuss how we're going to help her heal from this.'

I nod, leaving the bathroom and heading downstairs. I go to the living room and I find the others there. Theo is sitting alone, researching treatments in one of his medical books it looks like. Kor and Paris are sitting together on the couch, their shoulders touching. No one speaks at first and I sit down heavily in my chair, not sure what to do now.

Paris is the first to say anything. His voice is subdued. 'Those fuckers.'

Kor puts his hand in his. 'We killed them.'

'Too late for Jane though,' he says bitterly.

Korban bursts to his feet. 'I need to see her!'

I'm up and barring the door before he gets two steps.

'Move or I'll move you, big man,' he warns.

I shake my head. 'No. Alex is with her.'

'All the more reason,' he sneers. 'I don't trust him with her after everything he's done and neither should you.'

I hold my ground.

'She demoned up and attacked Theo,' I tell him. 'She would have killed him. She's confused, not herself. You know how strong she is. She's dangerous to all of us except Alex right now.' I run a hand through my hair. 'I know you want to be near her. I want to be up there too,' I say more gently, 'but she needs time to heal and to rest and she can't do that if we don't let her. You might not trust Alex with her, but I do. He'll do everything he can to help her.'

'We can't just sit here and do nothing!' he snarls.

Paris stands, putting an arm around Kor.

'I agree with Sie,' he surprises me by saying. 'Alex is still the leader for a reason. He's been an asshole, but you saw him take that bullet for her.'

Theo nods. 'We need to give her time to heal and we need to give him time to connect with her the way we all have.'

He picks the book back up and starts reading again.

I put a hand on his shoulder. 'We can still help from afar,' I say.

We can help Alex and Theo. Caring for Jane twenty-four seven is going to take it out of them. We need to be there for them.'

'Fuck,' Korban hisses, but gives a nod. 'Fine, but if I think for a second that Alex isn't doing everything he needs to do to get her through this, I'll kill the sonofabitch.'

I snort. 'If Alex isn't doing everything he needs to do to get her through this, I'll help you.'

CHAPTER
TWENTY

Alex

I don't make any sudden movements as I watch Jane try to catch her breath.

I let out a small grunt as I cross the bathroom, my wound screaming at me to lay down. When Theo got Sie's call, I snatched the pliers from his hand, dug for the bullet myself, and ripped it out, none too carefully.

I kneel down beside Jane, keeping her quiet and her body immobile just in case she demons-up again, though I think she's exhausted herself. It takes a lot more to subdue her than it does the others, but I have the power thanks to her and if using it helps her, then I'm going to.

'You're very strong,' I say, 'but so am I, little succubus.

She doesn't say anything, but she's still making those scared little sounds.

'You're safe here,' I say. 'You're safe with me. It's all over now, baby girl.'

I ease up on the magick so I don't accidentally do anything she doesn't want me to, and she lets me gently take off the wet jacket. Her bruises and broken skin, as well as the faint scents of the other incubi, make a growl of fury erupt from deep in my chest, and she cowers a little, fear returning to her eyes.

I cut the sound off abruptly.

'Sorry,' I murmur. 'I'm going to wash you off, okay?'

She doesn't say yes but doesn't fight when I pick her up and put her carefully back into the water. I start soaping her body and the sounds she was making ebb. I wash her just as I did earlier, but this time much more slowly and thoroughly. She lets me.

'Good girl,' I praise when I'm finished and I feel a tiny sliver of contentment over the connection between us.

It's gone far too soon though.

I help her stand and wrap a warm towel around her. When I pick her up, she gives a cry begins to struggle. I'm forced to subdue her again and hold her firmly as she goes limp.

'I'm sorry, sweetheart,' I murmur, 'but I promise you you're safe, okay? Let's get you into bed. You need rest.'

'I thought you were shot,' she whispers, sounding confused. 'Was it a dream?'

'No, it wasn't a dream, but it takes more than one bullet to kill me,' I say with a small grin.

I lay her in her bed and tuck her under the covers, sitting next to her and holding her hand. She's fast asleep in less than a minute and I pull out my phone to let the others know how she's doing.

Theo enters a minute later with a glass of water and a couple of pills.

'They're just painkillers,' he says when he sees me eyeing them.

He puts them on the nightstand and steps back.

'I've started creating a treatment plan. We can discuss it later. How is she?' he asks.

'She spoke a little, but she's exhausted. I don't think she's slept in days. I suppose that's not surprising though.'

Theo's jaw tightens. 'I've told Paris to send me the clips of her that were saved on that drive.'

'Why?' I ask, my eyes narrowing.

'Because I want to know what they did to her. Everything they did. She could be broken from this. Recovery could take months, if not years.'

I nod. 'I understand. Tell me what you find.'

'I will. When she wakes up, see if you can get her to take the pills and drink the water.'

He leaves me alone with her and I drag a chair up to the bed to sit in.

Jane sleeps for a few hours, but fitfully, crying out and writhing on the bed. In the end, I get into it next to her, holding her in my arms and she quiets.

I stay like that with her all night, sleeping a little myself and watching clips Theo sends me of some of the worst treatments Jane was subjected to. I seethe in silence at what she endured. Death was too good for Lionel and the rest of those fuckers!

But Jane fought and she survived ... and she took the energy she needed from me when I found her just like a demon should. I hate that the past few days happened, but I'm also so proud of her. I have no doubt that she'll come through this. She has to.

She doesn't wake until the following afternoon and when she does, she just grips onto me and cries.

I hold her tightly, my chest hurting as I feel the worst of the emotions she's begun to work through.

'Everything's going to be okay,' I say. 'It's all over. They'll never touch you again, Jane. You're so smart, so strong. They could never break you.'

'But they did,' she sobs into my shirt. 'They did break me. I would have done anything to make them stop. Anything,' she cries. 'And then you showed up and I did ... that ... to you in the shower in that place! I'm so sorry! I don't know what I was thinking.'

She sobs quietly into my shirt.

'They didn't break you, baby,' I murmur. 'That's why they kept ramping everything up. They couldn't crack you. They underestimated you completely. You are so much stronger than they thought, stronger than they were, stronger than all of us.'

'It doesn't feel like that,' she says brokenly.

'Maybe not right now, but I'm going to tell you every day until you realize that it's the truth.' I make her look at me. 'And feeding from me in the shower was instinctual. You were starving. I'm glad you took what you needed from me to heal.' I stroke her cheek. 'And, the power you gave back is the reason I'm able to be here with you instead of in bed healing slowly.'

She hugs me tighter. 'You don't need to be here,' she whispers. 'You probably have better things to do. I'll–I'll be fine if you need to go ...'

Pain lances through my heart that she's even suggesting that I should leave her alone, that I've treated her so badly and been such a prick that she thinks anything is more important than she is to me.

'I would never have anything better to do, sweetheart.' I sigh heavily. 'I'm sorry I'm an asshole,' I mutter. 'I always have been. I thought I had to be. I thought that was what being the leader was. But it's not and I want you to know that I'll never hurt you again, Jane. I promise you that. We're your clan and you're ours. We'll always make sure you're safe and that nothing like this ever happens again. You will always come first.'

She closes her eyes and inhales deeply. 'I really thought I'd never see any of you guys again,' she says quietly. 'I thought none of you wanted—'

I wind my arms around her and pull her closer, relieved when she lets me.

'You were wrong,' I tell her, 'but that's on us.'

'But when you wanted me to leave, no one spoke up,' she whispers so quietly I can only just hear her.

'They couldn't,' I admit with a wince. 'None of them could. I wouldn't let them.'

She draws back and looks at me. I feel her trepidation, but she pushes it away.

'I know I've caused you a lot of pain,' I say, 'but I'm going to spend the rest of my life making it up to you, baby girl.'

'I guess if you fall short I can just beat the shit out of you,' she mutters dryly.

I smile widely, glad she's started to joke a little. It's a good sign.

'You definitely can.'

THE NEXT FEW days fall into a pattern of Jane resting, lying in bed staring at the ceiling listlessly, and sobbing in my arms. I stay in her room with her almost all the time, making sure I don't leave her by herself to face her fears alone. I failed her so many times before, and I refuse to do that ever again. Nightmares come whenever she closes her eyes, so I lay next to her while she's asleep, as she seems to find my presence comforting.

She sleeps a lot, which Theo says is normal, but she still seems tired all the time, so I tell the others to stay away unless she asks for them. I keep Theo apprised of everything she does and says, and he tells me that it's all encouraging, that I'm helping, and that I should stay with her unless she asks me to go.

Tonight, she demons up, tearing at me, screaming in anger and fear. Sometimes, I let her rake her claws down my flesh, for her betterment or for my penance I don't know. This time, I subdue her with magick. It calms her quickly, the demon part of her recognizing my authority in the clan. I can tell her human side hates being controlled though, so I only do this when I absolutely have to, if she's past listening to my voice and I'm afraid she'll hurt herself.

Her glamor comes back up, and she quiets as I wrap my arms around her, murmuring that she's safe, that I'm with her, and that she's not alone. She cries herself to sleep.

The connection between us is alive with pain and despair, and I make myself feel it all with her. This is my punishment for how I treated her so many times. I deserve it and more. If I could take every dark thought from her, I would and it still wouldn't atone for the past. But I can't do so; instead, I hold her close and never shy away from the memories she's carrying of her time with Leonel, no matter how it reminds me of my failures or how much it turns my stomach.

**

Another week goes by before she starts getting up and moving around the room, showering by herself, and getting dressed in more than pajamas during the day. Theo is in charge of her meals and brings them to the door for me to take inside the room. The others stay away for now to give her time, but they leave presents for her outside the door, too, little things like the tiny disco ball Kor got her, their soaps, and sweatshirts with their smells on them. I find her inhaling the scents and she puts the clothes in bed with her. They seem to help her sleep a little better.

We watch movies together, I comfort her when she needs me to. I make sure she eats. I try to be everything she needs me to be.

Finally, she turns to me one afternoon, two weeks after we brought her home, and huffs at me in annoyance.

I give her my immediate attention. 'What is it, baby girl?' I ask.

She looks annoyed. 'I'm going stir crazy.'

I frown at her. 'Then leave the room.'

Her eyes narrow, and she looks suspicious. 'I can just … go?'

I tilt my head at her. 'You're free to do whatever. Leave the room. Leave the house if you want. You aren't a prisoner, sweetheart. Just please let us know if you go outside, huh? We want to make sure we know where you are in Metro. It's still not a hundred percent out there yet.'

She looks at the door, and I feel her trepidation. 'What if … what if you're wrong and they don't want to see me?' she asks.

I fold her into my arms. 'That's ridiculous. They've stayed away because I told them to. Come on,' I say, pulling her towards the door. 'I know just what you need.'

'Pizza?' she asks hopefully.

I laugh. 'I'll message Paris to get you some pizza if you come downstairs with me.'

∼

Sie

I'M LOOKING up from my book before she even comes through the door, excitement getting the better of me. I haven't seen her in almost two weeks except for sneaky peeks through the door whenever Theo delivered food ... and through the cameras of course. I think all of us have been glued to the screens to make sure she's okay, watching her, making sure she's eating and that Alex is treating her right.

She looks better than she did when we brought her back, but her eyes still have shadows in them.

I give her a smile, but I don't stand. I remember how she was when we first got back and I don't want to scare her again.

She looks relieved to see me though and practically leaps across the room to sit on my lap and wrap her arms around my neck.

'How are you feeling?' I ask.

She doesn't say anything, but when I cast a questioning look at Alex, he gives me an uncharacteristic thumbs up. I frown and try to feel her. I haven't in two weeks, wanting to give her some semblance of privacy while she dealt with the aftermath of what happened.

She feels in a bit of turmoil still, but happy that she's with me, which I'll take.

'Where are the others?' she asks.

'Paris, Kor, and Theo went out to get pizza.' I smile as she brightens, relieved that she seems so much better.

She stays on my lap until the others arrive and, when she hears the door, she tenses a little.

'It's okay,' I murmur. 'Just the guys back with the pizza.'

'Sorry,' she breathes.

'Don't be sorry, little succubus. It'll take time, that's all.'

She gives me a small smile and stands up, taking a deep breath as we hear the others in the kitchen.

Paris comes into the living room first and grins. 'You're out of your room!'

In true Paris fashion, he lunges forward and grabs her, picking her up and twirling her around. He kisses her lips hard. I give him a warning look but relax when I see she's smiling.

Theo's right behind Paris and he rolls his eyes, taking Jane from him and hugging her. He puts his forehead to hers, not saying anything, just feeling her. He gives her a small smile.

'Ready for pizza?'

Her answering grin has Korban freezing in his tracks. 'Jane,' he murmurs, taking her hand in his and pulling her hard towards him. She falls into him, bracing her hands on his chest. His mouth is on hers, kissing her hard, palming her ass.

I clear my throat and he gives me the finger.

'Pizza time!' I say and Jane pulls away as I knew she would.

Korban gives me a smirk and leads Jane over to the couch.

'I'll get you a slice,' he says. 'Someone put on the TV. I want to watch Bake-Off.'

I go and sit next to Jane while the others set up the room and get the pizzas from the kitchen.

'Alex has been okay?' I murmur, not wanting to ask, but after he's treated her during the past weeks, needing to make sure he's not falling back into old ways.

She nods. 'I told him I'd kick his ass if he put a foot wrong.'

A laugh bubbles out of me. 'I'd pay to see you put that Makenzie in his place, princess.'

We eat pizza and watch Bread Week. We joke and talk,

and, for the first time in a long time, we share an easy camaraderie. It feels like we're a true clan, a family brought together by the woman we all clearly adore.

But, all too soon, I notice that Jane starts to look tired. I message Alex.

'She needs to feed … and so do I.'

He looks at his phone and catches me eye, giving me the go-ahead.

'How about a nice, hot bath, sweet?' I ask Jane.

She turns her drooping eyes towards me and nods.

I pick her up and take her upstairs, setting her on the bed while I draw the bath. I grab my soap, but hesitate, wondering if she'll get upset like she did the first night.

'That smells good,' I hear her say from behind me and turn to find she's already naked and seems to be a bit more awake.

I grin as my eyes move over her, pouring in the bubbles without looking away. Her body has completely healed, I note gladly.

She steps in immediately and lets out a soft sigh as she sinks into the water and relaxes.

I, on the other hand, stand by the side of the tub a little awkwardly, wondering whether I should join her, or not.

'Are you coming in too?' she asks, tilting her head.

'If that's ok.'

At her small, answering nod, I shuck my clothes and step into the big tub. Her eyes move over me, following the scars on my torso, up my neck, and to my face. I'm letting her see all of them exactly as they look, but she doesn't seem bothered by the marks at all. I didn't realize how afraid I was that she'd think they were ugly.

She smiles a little shyly.

'He was wrong, you know,' she murmurs.

'Who was?'

'Foley when he said I couldn't care about you. I do.'

'I know you do,' I say. 'I can feel it in here.' I touch my heart. 'I know it's dumb, but it's true.'

'It's not dumb. I can feel it too. I can feel all of you.' Her eyes take on a far-away look that I don't like. 'I felt so alone when I couldn't.'

'We did too, Jane,' I say, cupping her face with my large hands.

We wash each other slowly and I feel her relax as I lift her into my lap. I softly, savoring this time. But all too soon she begins to fidget and I know she wants more.

'Stop squirming!' I growl, hiding a grin.

I stand, taking her out of the water and wrapping a towel around us. I take her to the bed and lay her down on it.

'Demon up,' she says.

I frown. 'I don't think that's a good idea,' I mutter, thinking about how recently I killed that dragon shifter. I'd never forgive myself if I hurt Jane.

She fixes her eyes on me. 'I trust you. Please?'

As if I could ever say no to her. I nod a little jerkily and do as she asks, lifting my glamor. She lets out a breath as she takes me in.

'You're so fucking hot,' she murmurs. 'Touch me.'

I drag my sharp claws across her skin gently and she gasps, leaning into my touch.

I push her back and spread her knees, opening her labia wide to gaze at her core.

'Please,' she whimpers. 'Please ...'

I can feel the fear in her left over from her time with Lionel's clan.

'What will help?' I ask, only allowing myself to feel concern, not letting anger in for her to pick up on.

'Replace all their touches with yours,' she replies.

I nod. 'That I can do.'

I begin at her toes, running my large hands up her legs and around to her ass, over every part of her in between. I lick her pussy, making her gasp and get impatient before I move up to caress her abdomen and navel, picking her up and sitting her in my lap to touch her back and shoulders. I move my hands down and up her arms, kneading her breasts and making sure I don't neglect the tips. I put my hand around her neck and squeeze it just enough to be comforting before I cup her face and kiss her.

'Is that better?' I ask even though I can already feel that it is.

'Yes,' she breathes.

'That's not fair,' Theo says from the door, sniffing the air. 'I've been too busy to play Scent Our Mate.'

'How are the others?' I ask, ignoring his complaint as I keep touching Jane's body, making sure I erase every last fingerprint from Lionel's clan.

'They're fine. They went down to the garage to mess with Paris's new bike so they won't be tempted to come up here. They know she's not up for all of us right now.'

'I'm sure they'll get their time with our beautiful little succubus soon,' I say with a smile.

Theo approaches the bed. 'Mind if I join you?'

'I don't mind if Sie doesn't,' she says, but then looks away.

I shake my head. 'Whatever you want,' I tell her, frowning when I feel worry coming from her.

'This might not be the time,' she whispers, 'but I'm so sorry I attacked you, Theo. I didn't mean to. I was confus—'

'Don't,' he says, cupping her face. 'It was my fault, never yours.'

'Do you have any rope?' she suddenly asks and I wonder what she's thinking.

'I usually have something knocking around,' he says, his eyes roving over her. 'Feel like getting tied up, beautiful?'

He produces a cord from his pocket.

'Are you okay with this?'

She grins. 'It's not for me.' She falters a little. 'I don't think I'm up for being trapped so soon after ... after the cage. I'm sorry.'

'Hey.' Theo comes closer, putting his forehead to hers. 'No more sorrys, Jane,' he whispers. 'Not ever.'

He takes off his shirt and gets on the bed, giving Jane the rope. 'You're in charge, Miss Mercy.'

CHAPTER
TWENTY-ONE

Sie

She's surprised he'd give up the reigns so easily. But she's intrigued, too. She takes the cord from him and loops it over his wrists, tying them to the headboard.

'Is that okay? Not too tight?' she breathes.

'It's perfect,' Theo tells her. 'Just like you.'

I watch her blush at his words. She puts her lips to his, groaning a little as she peppers his jaw with kisses. She moves down, her teeth on him as she finds his nipple and worries it.

He gasps and then grins darkly.

'Doctor Wright,' she mutters looking up at Theo's face, 'it appears that you haven't been taking care of your needs properly. That's very naughty. Let Nurse Jane help.'

I see Theo shiver at her words and she grins, preening as she feels his arousal spike.

'Would you like that, Doctor?'

'Yes,' he whispers faintly, his gaze not moving from Jane and what she's doing as she moves down his body and

She pulls off his pants in one swift move, and he swallows hard, pulling at his bonds a little.

I drag my sharp claws down Jane's back gently, and she gasps, leaning back into my touch.

Then, she sinks down and begins to lick Theo's already granite-hard cock. I notice with surprise that her tongue is unglamored. It's dark and long. It flicks over him, twists around him and he arches off the bed with a moan.

She looks back at me and gives me a slow grin.

This girl.

I part her cheeks, drawing one sharp digit down her crease before easing it into her hot, wet pussy. She's more than ready for us.

She pushes her hips back, impaling herself more deeply onto my finger with a guttural sound that makes me want to fuck her into oblivion. I ache to pick her up and thrust into her hard, hold her, and not let her go until I've bred her.

But I keep my tight control. I don't want her to be scared.

She takes Theo in her mouth and bobs up and down a few times while Theo groans and writhes in pleasure, but she stops abruptly.

'I need more,' she announces, climbing onto Theo's cock and sinking down on it with a loud moan.

She doesn't allow Theo to move, she takes him at the pace she wants, her rhythm fast and her movements languid.

'I want you too,' she whimpers at me.

I climb on the bed behind her and dip down to lick up her ass, but she scoots away and makes a sound of displeasure.

'No,' she growls.

'I don't want to hurt you,' I whisper, caressing her face.

'What if I want you to? Just a little?'

Fuck ...

My cock is painfully hard as I pump my hand up and down my shaft.

'You tell me if it's too much,' I say, taking her jaw firmly and turning her face to look at me, making sure she's listening.

'I won't have to. You'll know how much I love it ... in here.' She touches my heart with a cheeky grin as she teases me.

With a growl, I push her forward over Theo's chest.

With the precision of a viper, he snatches one of her nipples with his teeth and she gasps, stuck between us.

'The tables have turned, succubus,' I whisper in her ear and feel her excitement mounting. She wants to escape, a tiny bit. She would if she could and it gives me an amazing idea for another time.

She's still as I ease my length into her slowly, Theo's cock and mine stretching her pussy wide. I pull out and gently push in. With a growl, Theo snaps the rope in two and takes Jane's hips, lifting her off him and slamming her back down.

She screams, arching back.

'This is what you're aching for, isn't it?' he grinds out. 'Our succubus wants to be taken by her mates, fucked hard and thoroughly.'

'Yes,' she whimpers. 'Please!'

I can't hold back anymore however much I wish I could. I thrust into her from above, pushing her forward while Theo holds her up, pistoning into her from below.

She squeals and bows, twisting on our cocks and under our hands, her body undulating as we make it sing. She screams with pleasure every time she's filled by us, whimpering meaningless words and sounds, sobbing in ecstasy.

She tenses with the ultimate pleasure, feeding from us as we feed from her. Theo yells his release a second before I roar mine, catapulting our succubus into another tumult of pleasure that has her coming all over our cocks for a third time.

I let her go and slip out of her, shuddering in the aftershocks of one of the most intense orgasms I've ever had in my life. Jane melts onto Theo.

I was worried it would be too much, that she wouldn't like my darker side coming out to play, but she's satisfied and content.

She rolls off Theo onto her back beside him, panting hard and staring at the ceiling.

I lay next to her and she curls into me. I think it's for a cuddle, but then I feel her teeth graze my neck.

'Do it,' I plead, my heart beating faster in my chest. I need her to do it, I yearn for it.

'It's okay?' she asks quietly.

'Yes,' I groan, my arms holding her tightly to me, 'I want forever with you.'

I let out a grunt as I feel her teeth pierce my skin, moaning a little at how right it feels.

She pulls back and gives me a wide smile as I drag her back for a deep kiss.

'That was nice,' she murmurs when my lips finally leave hers, and I chuckle.

'It was nice,' I agree.

'Yep,' Theo murmurs with a yawn.

'I like you tied up, Doctor Wright,' she says, 'but I think I enjoy it a little bit more when it's me and I'm on your special table of doctorly debauchery.'

Theo groans. 'Careful, Miss Mercy, or you'll find yourself there sooner than you think.'

Jane giggles, laying between us for a while, keeping her body touching us both as if she can't quite believe she's here with us, but then she sits up suddenly like a meerkat, sensing danger.

'I want more pizza. I'm going downstairs for some.' She narrows her eyes at Theo. 'I'm not saving you any if you don't get down there in time,' she says. 'Also, I hid my cereal. You won't find it unless I want you to, so you better be extra nice to me.' With that bombshell, she grabs a robe and leaves the room.

I grin at Theo and he smiles back at me. We lay there side by side, basking in the knowledge that Jane is here. She's safe and she's not going anywhere.

I feel more relaxed than I have in weeks until Paris bursts into the room a second later.

'Where's Jane?' He sounds panicked.

'Chill. She's downstairs.'

'Fuck!'

He races from the room and we follow, not bothering with clothes.

'What is it?' I call after him.

'I found out who it was. It just came up in the files I was going through from before the fire. I never even considered ...'

I stare blankly.

'Who betrayed us, who burned the house!' he says impatiently. 'It was fucking Stan!'

No ...

I feel sick. How many times was he in our house with free reign? How often did we call him to bring us take-out or to grab something from the store? He always seemed kind of weak and pathetic to be honest, even for a human. He even asked me about becoming a prospect once.

Traitor.

'Okay, so we'll get him. What's the big deal?'

Paris turns back, his eyes wide with fear. 'He arrived with groceries a few minutes ago.'

My stomach plummets into my legs like a cartoon anvil.

'Where are the others?'

'Down in the garage still.'

CHAPTER
TWENTY-TWO

Jane

It feels like it's been more than two weeks since I got back. I guess that's a good thing. It's not like I've been bored up in my room with Alex, but I did miss the others. Alex asked me a few times if I wanted to see them, but I said no. I was afraid they didn't really want me here despite Alex's excuses.

At first, I wondered why Alex was chosen to be my babysitter. Literally, any of the others would have been a better choice, I'd thought, even as I cried on him, and he held me whenever I needed him to. It took me a few days to understand that I kept demoning up without realizing it and Alex was the only one who could safely be around me.

I took that to mean that he didn't really want to be there. I tried to go it alone. I mean I was by myself for years. I didn't think it would be hard. I mean, I realized while I was in that cage that I wanted to be with the Iron I's but it's because I love them. I didn't think I needed them.

I tried to pretend I was okay in front of Alex for a whole day, thinking that he'd take the out that I was offering as soon as he could. But he didn't. And then something – I don't even know if it was a sound or a smell – took me back to that cage.

It was like I was there again with those sadistic assholes marking me with their scents in the most awful of ways, the dirt that was covering me, them laughing about what they were planning to do to me when I broke and became theirs. I could hear far-off screaming the whole time and I realized that it was me. When I came back to myself, my throat was sore and Alex was holding me against him, whispering that I was okay. I sobbed into his chest for two hours, and after that, I hoped he wouldn't leave me because I didn't want to have to go it alone anymore.

I hated Alex for how he treated me, how he made the others treat me. At least, I thought I did. I kept waiting for the other shoe to drop while he was with me in that room. I thought it was a mask, that he'd slip up and say or do something mean. But he didn't. He stayed with me all that time. He didn't try to feed from me. He watched movies with me and sat with me. He made sure I ate. He told me about his brothers and his mom. I don't know if I trust him yet. I think that might be a long road, but the past couple of weeks have shown me a different side to the Iron I President.

I take another bite of my slice, glad I'm finally getting something more than the 'healthy', well-balanced meals that Theo has been cooking for me for two weeks. Don't get me wrong, he's a great cook and everything he made for me was nice, but sometimes you just can't beat a decent pizza.

I turn the page in the magazine I'm reading. At first I picked it up because it was the closest thing to read and that guy from before, Stan, is in the kitchen putting away groceries. I didn't want to just sit here at the table staring at him while I was eating. Awkward. But actually there's an interesting article on sharks that has caught my attention.

I keep reading, and belatedly realize that Stan is standing close to me. He's hovering like he wants a tip.

My heart sinks. I'm not really in a place to socialize.

I glance up and wonder at the weird look he's giving me. It looks kind of ... malicious.

'Can I help you?'

He sneers at me. 'I can't believe you're Foley's daughter.'

Alarm bells start ringing in my head because I doubt any of the Iron I's would have told him shit.

'What do you care?' I ask.

'Foley had half the Order boys running after you for a decade. He used resources on you like you were some big deal and, the whole time, all you were was some retarded supe slut,' he laughs. 'Just some brain-damaged, druggy whore who loves to choke on demon cock.'

I raise a brow. 'Are you done?'

'That bomb was meant to kill you in that house,' he sneers. 'Vic wasn't meant to be bringing any of the on-call girls to Metro.'

'His name is Alex actually,' I mutter. 'So you burned down the Clubhouse.' Mansion. 'You were the one who killed Monique, Carrie, and Julie. Even if you hate the supes, they were human.'

He snorts. 'Barely! They were just supe slut addicts just like you.'

'You sonofabitch,' I snarl. 'So you were taking your orders from Foley, huh? You know he's dead, right?'

Anger erupts through my veins and I feel that other side of me start to awaken. I'm done with this and I'm done with him. I keep myself reigned in, but I'm already planning how I'm going to kill this no-good, traitorous fuck right here in the kitchen.

'I heard,' he says through gritted teeth, 'but I still have a job to do.'

'I mean, yeah, you won't get your Order merit badge unless you kill Foley's retarded incubus-whore daughter right, side-quest?'

'S-side what?' he stutters, his cheeks reddening.

'You heard me, you little bitch.'

I slowly inch my fingers into the wooden bowl in the middle of the table, my fingers closing around the link key I noticed in there earlier. One of the Iron I's must have just chucked it in there like someone would their car keys when they got home after a long day.

'You're an opening act, okay? In case no one's ever told you, you're not a main character.'

Stan looks just about purple now. Guess I struck a nerve.

'I'll show you a fucking main character, you dumb fucking whore!' he screams, digging a knife out of his pants and waving the business end at me.

Maybe a few weeks ago, that would have scared me, but I sort of wish I had a bigger knife to brandish so I could say those cool lines out of Crocodile Dundee.

I don't though.

'Gosh, side-quest, I'm totally unarmed. You got me.'

'Stop calling me that!' he cries in a high-pitched kind of whine that makes my lip curl in disgust.

Nope, this guy is not killing me after I survived the Iron I's and the fae and the nasty, incubi sex pests. It would be the dumbest death story ever.

I faintly notice Sie lurching forward, but before he can stop me or take over, I'm bouncing out of my chair and demoning-up, in control of it completely for the first time since they brought me back. I rush Stan, grabbing the hilt of the knife and keeping it away from me so easily it's pretty pathetic for the guy who thought he was dealing with a human. I push him across the kitchen and into the pantry door hard.

I relish his ridiculous struggle and see him beginning to realize that I'm not what he thought, what Foley told him I was. But that only lasts a split second before I'm remembering not only how he betrayed the Iron I's but also how their on-call girls died in that basement. We weren't BFFs, but they were three women just trying to make it in Supe Land, only to get cut down by one of their own. They didn't deserve that end. The fact that Stan destroyed Alex's childhood home as well, the only place where the Iron I president has memories of his mom, is less important as life and death goes maybe, but no less significant to me.

His eyes widen and I see the moment he gets it. 'You're a – you're a—'

'Yeah, bitch, I'm the main event.' I grin nastily, slapping the link key on the door. 'Oh, shit, Stan,' I say, 'looks like you brought a knife to a magick fight.'

I could draw this out for a lot longer, and maybe I should, but, to be honest, I'm not really the type for torture after everything that happened to me. So, I just grab a hilariously horrified Stan by the scruff of the neck and tear open the pantry.

'This is for Carrie, Monique, and Julia, fucker,' I hiss and I throw him through into the snowscape on the other side.

I give him a little wave and shut the door before he can try to get back in, breaking the connection.

'This is getting ridiculous,' I mutter half to myself. 'I mean, seriously, who else is going to try to kill me?'

I go back to the table and pick up another piece of pizza, getting back to my shark article. I glance up at Theo and Sie a few seconds later when they don't say anything. I find them just standing at the kitchen door in silence with our mouths open ... and their dicks still out.

I can't help my chuckle. 'Was that a little too cold,' I tease.

Theo cups his junk with a sardonic look, hiding it from my view. Sie just rolls his eyes at me. I see Paris standing behind them, looking surprised with a small smile playing on his lips.

'Where did you send him?' Sie asks, staring at the water on the floor from the snow that blew in with wide eyes like he can't believe I just did that.

'A frozen lake in the middle of nowhere.'

I look back down at the magazine and take a bite of my pizza.

'How did you know there was a door there that you could use?' Theo asks with a frown.

'Went there with Foley once,' I say after swallowing my mouthful. 'There was a derelict cabin on the shore.'

Paris sits down hard in the chair next to mine. 'Holy shit!'

I glance at them. 'You guys actually think I'm going to take any crap after my time with Lionel's shitty clan? Things are a little hard right now, but I'm still a badass mofo. I don't take *any* BS and I think I *might* be harder to kill even than you guys.'

I put out my hand and drop an invisible mic and then use it to turn the page in the magazine.

'Told you she can take care of herself,' Korban says and I find him behind the others, leaning nonchalantly against the banister of the stairs. I can feel his satisfaction when he looks at me and I smile. I belatedly notice Alex at the door to the living room and realize he must have seen what I did to Stan as well.

'Well, fuck,' Sie mutters at Kor. 'I guess so.'

I can feel how proud they all are of me and I can't help but bask in it, a small sigh escaping me as I go back to the sharks. I'm not quite right yet, but I know I will be.

EPILOGUE

Jane

'So they still think I'm dead?' I ask, chasing my potato around my plate as we sit on the deck in the evening sunshine eating dinner.

'So far, so good,' Paris says. 'I mean it should be fine. We made sure there wasn't enough DNA left to identify who'd actually been in the lake house at the time of the fire, so all the fae have to go on are the camera files I left for them to see. I deleted everything else. As long as you don't forget to put that orc stone on when you leave the grounds, they won't think anything different.'

My fingers find the smooth, blue stone that my mom left for me. How many years did I wear this thing, not realizing how magickal it is? All it took was Ada, The All-powerful, to touch it, say some creepy-sounding words, and TA-DA! One amulet that keeps my identity under wraps to anyone who'd wish me harm. It's pretty awesome. I thought I'd have to live in the attic, or something until we figured out how to get rid of the Ten, so I'm pretty stoked to have some powerful friends.

Alex's hands wander over my stomach and I feel his smile against my cheek as I shift on his lap and glance at the others around the table. They hardly take their eyes off me at all these days. I thought their constant attention and protectiveness would be too much for badass me. Maybe it would have been to the old Jane. But they give me space when I need it and it turns out I feel a lot better when they're with me. I rub my stomach. Just a little bump so far. No one would be able to tell if they didn't know.

The house was finished being rebuilt last month, but Alex said he wanted everything to be perfect, so we only just moved in a couple of days ago. It's beautiful. I've missed the open spaces both inside and out. I look around at the new wood and reclaimed bricks, the large lawn, and the woods beyond, and I see Theo smile at me.

'All the changes still bothering you?' he asks.

I shrug. 'I'm getting used to them. It just takes me a little time.'

The truth is that even though I love it here at the new and improved Clubhouse with the bigger pool and my own room, I can't help but remember what happened here, the lives that were lost because of Stan. I avenged the human casualties as best I could though. I thought leaving him in the middle of the frozen lake I went ice fishing at with my dad when I was a kid was fitting for that Order prick. He's definitely a popsicle now.

'You're not sleeping better though, are you? I can tell.' Alex says and I frown.

He chuckles. 'So grumpy these days.'

'It's not easy,' I admit. 'My back keeps hurting at night.'

His hands cover my shoulders and knead the muscles

gently. I lean into his touch with a sigh, letting my eyes drift closed.

He's so different than he was before. I still sometimes think I'm waiting for the penny to drop, but he seems to have let the Vic side of him go completely. He still lays down the law, but it's in a much more *fun* way.

'You know you can come to any of us no matter what time it is if you can't sleep, right?'

I nod.

'But you're feeling okay besides that?' Theo asks.

'Yeah,' I groan under Alex's expert hands. 'I feel mostly fine during the day so long as I have snacks, just tired sometimes.'

I feel a third hand drift over my stomach and crack an eye open as I tense at the unanticipated touch, scowling at Paris who leans in close and gives me a peck on the lips.

'Grumpy mate,' he chuckles as his hand is slapped away by Sie who plucks me out of Alex's arms and cradles me to him before taking me back to his seat.

He keeps his arms loose so I can get up when I want to, but I rest against him, and my abandoned mocktail is put in my hand by Theo.

I grin at him, remembering what we did last night in his clinic. He's definitely loving all the *checkups* he's having to give me, always finding a reason to give me an exam or take my temperature with his special thermometer.

That thought has me pressing my legs together and I feel Sie's answering rumble as a part of him hardens under my ass.

I turn to look at him and he kisses my lips gently. 'Are you feeling up to a little exercise?' he asks, his lips twisting up.

I don't return the smile. His idea of a little exercise is me and him sparring in the ring until I'm panting and sweating like a beast. Despite my condition, he's adamant that light exercise is good for me. Theo, that betrayer, agrees with him so long as I don't do too much and Sie is extra careful, which he always is although mine and Theo's definitions of 'too much' are wildly different.

My eyes narrow. 'It depends.'

'Well, how about a game of Hide and Seek?'

'I do like games,' I murmur and he chuckles.

'I know you do, baby girl.'

'Now?'

'Yeah. How about we give you a five-minute head start, and then we try to find you? First one to catch you gets to sleep in your bed with you tonight.'

I grin. 'What if none of you find me?'

'Well, then you can decide who you want to be with you.'

I put my drink on the table and get up from Sie's lap. He helps me to my feet.

I take off, leaving the deck as fast as I can. 'Time starts now!' I call. 'And no demon senses!'

I don't hear a reply as I sprint across the lawn and into the trees. I make sure I leave some footprints on the path as a fake trail before I veer off into the undergrowth, careful not to disturb the ground or the bushes. Once I'm far enough away, I start running again, although carefully, of course, because I don't want to risk a tumble. I keep going until I'm out of breath and then I slow down, looking for a good spot to hide in. There's a hollowed-out tree trunk, but it's home to way too many bugs for this autistic girl's senses.

I keep walking until I get to some boulders and rocky outcroppings, finding a good spot between them where I can't easily be spotted. I squat down to wait, wondering if there's a time limit for them to find me. I should have negotiated one. Ugh! I know better than that. I don't want to be out here all night.

I wait for what seems like hours, but when I check the time on the pretty fae watch that Theo gave me that monitors me and the baby at all times, it's only been fifteen minutes.

I stand up for a second because my legs are cramping, but as I do, I see Alex. I crouch back down with a curse, hoping he hasn't seen me, but a moment later a shadow falls over me.

'Got you!'

I squeal loudly, my heart in my throat, and I dart out, running into the trees, but he catches me a second later, picking me off my feet in his demon form. I scream, giggling hysterically and trying to get away from him, but he well and truly has me.

I stare into his eyes, the fight going out of me as he picks me up in his arms, his fingers delving under my skirt and ripping off my underwear. They love doing that, I've noticed.

'Those were my favorites,' I growl, squealing as two of his fingers impale me.

'I'll buy you some new ones. Exactly the same, I promise.'

He groans when he feels how ready I am. 'Good girl. Always so wet for me.'

And then it's not his fingers inside me anymore, it's his thick— My eyes fly to his grinning face.

'Is that your *tail?*'

He nods slowly, savoring my expression, his thick appendage wriggling and writhing like a tentacle inside me, making my legs feel weak. He hasn't done this before.

I realize he hasn't stopped walking. He's taking me into the forest.

'Where are we going?' I mewl, trying to keep my brain working while he's making it want to take a vacation.

His tail begins to move more vigorously.

'If you can talk, you can take more,' he tells me and my eyes roll back, my body tensing as an intense orgasm rips through me.

I'm clutching him, calling out his name. I shake as he draws out my pleasure for as long as possible and I realize how much I care about this demon. But he's not mine like the rest. Not yet.

I've made him wait long enough.

I sink my teeth into his shoulder suddenly and he freezes mid-step, his eyes closing as he draws a shuddering breath.

'You're sure?' he whispers.

'It's a little late to be second-guessing.' I let out a small laugh. 'I'm sure, Alex.'

Something changes in an instant, like a piece of a broken machine snapping into place. I feel him more powerfully like I did that time in the shower, but this is more than a glimmer of his feelings. I let him in completely and something I've rarely felt before coils in my chest and radiates outward.

Joy.

'This is what the others were talking about,' he murmurs in wonder.

He cuddles me tight, his tail slipping out of me to snake around me and push into my mouth. I suck on it with a hum and he lets out a groan of his own. I feel his spiny cock ease into me slowly, filling me in a completely different way.

We're at a building. It looks newly built, and I realize we're deep in the woods on the Clubhouse grounds.

'What is this place?' I whimper as his body torments mine.

He grins wickedly. 'I had it built for you. For us. All of us. It's so safe that it can't even be seen by anyone outside our clan.

'So it's like a panic room?'

He kicks open the door and carries me over the threshold. My eyes widen as I see a bed larger than any other I've ever laid eyes on, with Kor, Theo, Sie, and Paris all lounging on it with room to spare.

'If you think of a panic room as a secret clan sex palace, sure,' he mutters raising a brow.

'You bit him,' Kor says to me as soon as we're inside.

'How did you know?'

'We felt it. All of us. Like we became—'

'Whole,' Alex finishes with a nod. 'Like we're complete now.'

'Complete or not,' Theo says, 'put her down. Let me make sure she's okay after that run in the woods.' He frowns at Sie. *'Unsanctioned* run.'

'Spoilsport,' Alex mutters in my ear and puts his glamor back on as he pulls out of me and sets me on my feet.

I sway a little.

'Are you okay?' Theo asks.

I roll my eyes at him. 'I'm fine. The jellybean is also fine.'

'Let me check you over anyway.' He leans in closer. 'Shall I let the others watch?'

My breath catches and I give him a tiny nod. He whips my dress over my head and takes off my bra.

'That's better, Miss Mercy. Now, if you'll step over to this couch here ...'

He leads me to the leather sofa and bends me over the back gently so my ass is in the air and in full view of the others who are waiting on the bed.

He snaps on a pair of gloves and I practically gush at the sound. He probes my channel gently with one finger and then two before tutting.

'Have you been taking your vitamins, Miss Mercy?'

'You know I have,' I growl. 'You make sure every morning.'

He scissors his fingers inside me, making me whimper.

'You weren't talking back, were you, baby girl?'

Alex gives me a light swat on my ass and I look around, wiggling it a little as I shake my head at him, but I'm not scared. I trust him not to hurt me.

I feel his tail again, but this time it probes my ass as Theo pulls my cheeks wide, his fingers still playing with me.

Someone caresses my nipple, making it peak and I turn to find Sie. He pinches it, making me moan.

'Bring her to the bed where we can all play with her,' I hear Korban growl low.

I'm pulled into Alex's arms and lowered into Kor's lap. He lays down with me immediately. My knees are bent and spread wide. I feel my wrists being cuffed above my head and held there while Korban works himself into my ass and Alex thrusts into my pussy.

I'm panting and begging for more as they both enter me to the hilt. I vaguely notice Paris videoing this with his phone, getting close-ups as Alex and Kor begin to move their cocks in and out of me.

Kor picks me up and pumps into me in a frenzy while Alex grasps my hips and keeps to a more leisurely pace. My brain short circuits at the opposing sensations, and I scream their names, bursts of light exploding behind my eyelids as my body locks up with the kind of pleasure you don't forget ... like ever!

I'm still blissed out of my mind as I feel myself being picked up and filled again. I open my eyes to Sie holding me, already fucking me. I feel Theo enter my pussy too, stretching me in the most delicious way. My body isn't my own. I'm spasming in their arms. I see Korban kneeling by the bed, Paris fucking his mouth while he watches me and the others.

So hot.

I stare, watching Kor work Paris' shaft expertly, making him throw his head back on a long moan.

Sie releases inside me first, gripping me hard, his thrusts erratic as he pulses inside me. Theo follows a second later, biting my shoulder as he grunts his pleasure.

I'm placed gently on the bed again and I see Paris ease away from Kor, caressing his hair as he pulls him to his feet and kisses him.

Paris comes to me. He looms over me, kneeling next to my head and I take him in my mouth as far as I can. He grabs my hair and fucks me hard. I feel a vibration and I startle, looking down to find the others watching from between my legs. Theo has my pink sparkly dildo on my clit.

'Time to come again, Miss Mercy.'

I shake my head as Paris keeps fucking my mouth, my body protesting Theo's words. I've lost count of how many orgasms they've dragged out of me. I don't have anything left.

'Yes,' he says. 'At least one more. They're good for you.'

I plead with my eyes, but he doesn't give me an ounce of mercy. He turns up the vibe.

The others hold my legs wide as I struggle, Paris keeping my upper half subdued.

'Come, Miss Mercy,' Theo growls. 'Or you're going to spend your whole pregnancy in my clinic with a plug in your ass and a speculum making sure your pussy is as wide as I can make it ready for the birth. Maybe I'll have a pump locked onto those meaty nipples, twenty-four seven and if there's not a machine milking you, I will be!'

Punctuating Theo's words, Paris pinches and twists my nipples and Alex's fingers thrust into me hard, pistoning into my pussy.

I scream loudly, muffled by Paris' thick cock, my legs

shaking as one final peak is forced out of me at their hands and to Theo's filthy threats.

I feel Paris' release pour down my throat, and I swallow as his movements gentle. My mouth releases him with a pop.

I lay on the bed unable to make any part of my body move even an inch.

'I think she'll sleep okay tonight,' I hear Alex say.

I'm picked up and cradled, my eyes blinking in slow motion.

The others were right. Now that my mind is quiet, I can feel the *completeness* they were talking about. It's like the final piece of us is in place.

I'm placed under the covers on the bed in Alex's arms. Theo takes the other side after a brief argument with Sie, but he wins because he says he needs to monitor me. I smile a little at that but begin to doze as I'm enveloped by their warmth.

I'm tired, but my body feels so alive and my back isn't aching either.

'That was amazing,' I yawn. 'Can we do it again tomorrow?'

'We can do that as often as you want, baby girl,' Alex promises.

'Good.' I snuggle down in the bed, feeling how content they all are, how happy – just like I am. 'Night.'

EXCLUSIVE EARLY ACCESS TO THE FORBIDDEN?

The whispers in the dark are true – **a six-book spin-off of the tantalizing Dark Brothers series** is coming.

Which means... **I need you...** to reach into the shadows of temptation and be the first to feel every pulse-pounding moment.

My ARC Team is OPEN...

Yes, I need YOU to join my ravenous, Addicted Readers of Carnality.

If your heart races for brooding antiheroes and the fiery heroines who tame them, if your soul yearns for love stories laced with the sweet poison of passion, then *whisper your consent.*

Need More Demons?

Let's Talk Spoilers! Join My Discord!
https://geni.us/KyraSpoilers

VENGEANCE AFORETHOUGHT TRILOGY

When hearts are the real treasures to be stolen, can a con-woman outwit the demons of her past?

VILLAINS AND VENGEANCE

She stole from them, lied to them, and now they're her prison mates.
In a world without exits, trust becomes the rarest and most deadly commodity.
https://geni.us/VillainsandVengeance

VENGEANCE AND VIPERS

https://geni.us/VengeanceandVipers

I was supposed to be their downfall. They were meant to be my revenge. But the chains that bound me have now tangled us all.

VIPERS AND VENDETTAS

https://geni.us/VipersandVendettas

Six seductive demons, bound by venom-laced passion, teeter on the brink of salvation and ruin.

A former slave waging a final stand for a life far beyond her darkest dreams.

PART ONE
SNEAK PEEKS

VENGEANCE I AFORETHOUGHT

VILLAINS AND VENGEANCE

KYRA ALESSY

VILLAINS AND VENGEANCE

TRAPPED IN A DEMON-INFESTED SUPERMAX ALONGSIDE FIVE VENGEFUL INCUBI WHO'VE SWORN TO CLAIM MY BODY, SOUL, AND DARKEST SECRETS—TURNS OUT, LOVE MIGHT BE THE DEADLIEST CON OF ALL.
BUT WHO'S CONNING WHO?

I'M A THIEF, A LIAR, A MASTER OF DISGUISE—BIG DEAL. WE ALL HAVE OUR TALENTS, RIGHT? MINE JUST HAPPEN TO LAND ME IN A SUPERMAX SUPERNATURAL PRISON. BY CHOICE, MIND YOU, BECAUSE SURVIVAL ISN'T A GAME FOR THE FAINT-HEARTED.

AT LEAST IN PRISON I'M SAFE...WELL, AS SAFE AS I CAN BE AS THE ONLY WOMAN IN A PRISON FULL OF PSYCHOTIC DEMONS AND MONSTERS. UNTIL A CLAN OF INCUBI, I HAD A SOFT SPOT FOR (AND MIGHT HAVE STOLEN A SHIT-TON OF JEWELS FROM) STRUTTED THROUGH THE GATES OF MY SO-CALLED SANCTUARY.

CORNERED? MAYBE. THEY'RE THIRSTY FOR REVENGE, SAYING I RUINED THEIR LIVES. NOW I HAVE TO PAY UP. BUT THEY'RE NOT THE ONLY ONES WHO CAN PLAY THIS GAME BECAUSE, IN THE END? MY GOAL IS TO STAY ALIVE.

THAT'S ALWAYS BEEN THE PLAN, AT LEAST.
BUT SOMETHING SHIFTS—A SEARING GLANCE, A FORBIDDEN TOUCH, AND SUDDENLY, LINES ARE GETTING BLURRED.
MY BEAUTIFULLY CONSTRUCTED WALLS START SHOWING CRACKS, DRAWING ME INTO A GAME I NEVER INTENDED TO PLAY—ONE FAR MORE DANGEROUS THAN THE PAST I'M RUNNING FROM.

A BROKEN BODY CAN HEAL, BUT MY HEART?
WELL...THAT'S TO BE DETERMINED.

Chapter One

Jules

I shouldn't have come here.

I say this to myself at least fifteen times a day, but, it was kind of my last option. It's funny really. See, I have a ton of enemies, very persistent ones. The kinds who torture those who've wronged them for years before they finally let them die, the kinds who are able to work some nasty fucking magick on a human girl like me.

I can deal with it. That's on me. I mean, I'm a great thief, an even better liar. When you use those talents to make money off bad guys, well, enemies just come with the territory. And that's okay. I expect it and I can live with it. Plus, I can take care of myself in general.

Don't get me wrong, I didn't grow up dreaming of being a crook and a swindler, but we all have to make the best of what we got. I got an innocent face, decent smarts, and a raw deal that made utilizing my natural skills a no-brainer for me. Survival is what's important and sometimes that takes sacrifice. No friends, family, fun, or fucking for me. All the best f's, or so I've heard.

Maybe one day I'll have a life, but it's not going to be today.

See, the problem is that there are worse things than missing out on experiences other humans take for granted or having a few supes in your past harboring a grudge or two.

And that's why I'm in prison.

I know what you're thinking. You can't be that good at stealing if you're in the clink.

Well, I didn't get caught, smart-ass, and I don't intend to. That's why I'm hiding out in the most dangerous and inescapable supe prison there is. I'm not getting caught ... by being caught. Shhhhhhhhhhh!
My plan is genius. No one is looking for me here.

Well, mostly.

KYRA ALESSY

I poke my head out from the hole in the ceiling, making sure I have a good hold on the rope I'm half-hanging from. It's thick and strong, and it holds me pretty securely as I watch what's happening below.

The demon king is pacing. He does that a lot when he's not roaring loudly about some problem, or punishing a lowly supe who's displeased him. He keeps his subjects in line with fear and he's good at it. It's why he's been in charge down here for so many years. But I can't help but notice he's a little more on edge than usual. It's probably because of *that damned female* that he and some of the others with good noses get whiffs of through the tunnels from time to time.

Yeah, that'd be me.

And being the only woman, not to mention the only *human* in a maximum-security prison full of the worse supe criminals and monsters imaginable is as dangerous as it sounds. I'm literally trapped inside a mountain with over a thousand dangerous dudes who would love to get a hold of me.

In fact, that's what this place is called.

The Mountain.

Good thing stealth is my middle name.

'If you come back here without her this time, I'll have you all hogtied and left in the lower levels to be picked clean down to your bones!' Dante yells at his tracker team's backs as they sprint from his *throne room*.

That's what he calls it. Dude actually thinks he's a king. I guess when you're a demon strong enough to be in charge of a place like the Mountain, you can call yourself whatever you want, and everyone just goes with it.

I glance over at the corner of the room where a fresh body leans. I didn't know his name, but he was one mean mofo. This morning, he wanted to be the Mountain king. It took Dante less than a minute to kill him and that's only because he was entertaining himself.

He's not the first demon I've met by a long way, but if I ever fall into his hands, I hope Siggy does the decent thing and offs me quick.

Dante leaves the room and I take the risk without hesitation. I might not get another chance today and I'm hungry. I drop the rope I twisted together from Siggy's old silk and shimmy down it to the ground.

I keep an eye out for Silas, Dante's right hand vampire. He's almost caught me a few times, but I keep a can of garlic spray on me and I've been able to mist him in the face before he's sunk his teeth into me. It's not lethal for an older one like him, but it blinds him for a bit so I can get away.

When neither Silas nor any guards appear, I dance over to Dante's supply pile and open a box, grabbing some cans of peaches from the hoard he presides over. Supplies to keep prisoners alive are delivered through the one-way portal every other week. Dante and his people control everything that comes through, and it's not like I can ask him or anyone else here for food, so I liberate it when I can.

The next crate is full of twinkies and other packaged cakes with a long shelf-life. I start grabbing handfuls, shoving them into my backpack. If I can get enough food and ration myself, I won't have to take a chance like this again for a couple of weeks.

I'm on borrowed time. I know that, so it's best to take as few chances as possible. Getting captured because I needed an extra Hostess cake isn't how I want to go.

I hear steps outside the room and, my heart jumping into

my throat, I abandon my mission, launching myself back to the rope. I climb faster than a coconut farmer and pull up the silk just as Dante comes back into the room.

He sniffs and turns around in a slow circle before he throws back his head and roars. I make sure he can't see me as I peer down at the unhinged prick from the hole above him, unable to shake the idea that he's going to catch me. Every day he seems to get increasingly irrational, the search for me beginning to consume him. Every day he reminds me more of someone who, believe it or not, is even scarier than he is.

Shivering a little, I turn and climb back into the darkness. I can't see much in here, but I don't need to. I've been hiding out in the Mountain for a while, and I know the tunnels I frequent like the back of my hand.

I shimmy through the shaft until I get to an opening that leads into a wider passage. These ones are used by the other supes, so I wait and listen before I emerge. After that, it's a few hundred steps to relative safety.

I reach the main cavern and feel a tremor in the lines as she comes.

'It's just me,' I whisper and put my hand out even though I still tense and cringe a little in case this is the day she decides to eat her human buddy.

But she just brushes against my hand with her bristly pedipalps.

The first time she did that, I thought I was a goner, but she uses them a little like fingers to check things out and they're actually oddly soft and fuzzy, kind of similar to kitten paws ... *on a four-hundred-pound spider*.

She nudges me. I know what she wants me to do. I think she got sick of me sleeping on her web like it was a hammock, so she made me a kind of bedroom out of silk suspended in the middle of the cavern this morning. I call it the White Bunker.

'Yeah, I know. I promise I'll snuggle up in the bunker in a little while,' I tell her. 'I love it. Really. But it's almost time for the new meat to get here and I have to find out what kinds of supes are arriving.'

I need to be in the know to stay ahead *and alive* in here.

She nudges me again and then leaves me, climbing up into her web while I jump down to the bottom of her cavern. I put down my backpack and grab the flashlight I stole off one of Dante's guys last week. I'm not sure how it works exactly, but I've been using it for days and it hasn't shown any signs of dying so it's probably got a conjure on it.

I pick my way through the rubble, taking pains not to look at the dried up *remains* that are scattered around in various states of decay. Everyone has to eat and all these supes were dumb enough to venture into Siggy's territory. I sometimes wonder if that's why she keeps me around. She definitely knows that me being here draws in the supes who can smell me. They're lured right to her lair to be sucked dry like Capri-Suns, so it makes sense to give me room and board alongside her.

I slip down another tunnel and venture out of the web that defines Siggy's borders. I hear scratching, the tell-tale signs of another arania close by and I slow down. Siggy might be my friend and protector, but there are reasons she has a soft spot for me. There are others of her kind here and they definitely won't differentiate between the human guest and the supes they call dinner.

I make my way carefully, making sure I don't touch any of the webs that are spilling out of the other tunnels. I always count my steps, so I know I'm close. When I get to a small hole in the side of the tunnel just big enough for me, I climb into it, arriving at my look-out spot high in the wall of the main cavern of the prison.

This is the Mountain's hub after Dante's 'throne room'. The food gets delivered via a portal that opens in the stone circle at the center of the space. There are tables where the inmates play games and socialize off to one side. The fights happen in the high ring at the back of the cavern.

Dante presides over them like a benevolent ruler. To a lot of the inmates, I guess he is. He might be a psychopath demon, but he runs this deep, dark penal colony and keeps things ticking over relatively smoothly as far as I can tell. I mean, he has rooms for torturing his enemies or those he considers weak, of course. The pixies that are sent here are smaller than most of the others, so he uses them as servants and they get punished badly if they fuck up.

His throne room always has one or two half dead supes hanging in it until they expire and start to smell. He has a special way of gutting his victims so they stay alive for days. He lets his men entertain themselves with the unlucky ones and their screams usually make me retreat to Siggy's territory where I can't hear them so clearly.

I scan the cavern. As usual, a ton of supes are in here too, milling around and waiting for the portal to open even though it isn't supply day. New prisoners appear like clock-work from all over and it looks like I'm just in time to see the next group roll in.

A bright light momentarily blinds me and, when it recedes, a group of fifteen or so supes are in the middle of the stone circle. The ones who have a human form are mostly in them, except for a couple of the wolf shifters. There's also an orc at the back who looks pissed.

The ones who haven't been in the Mountain before look around like they're lost. They always do when they first get here. Dante usually gives them an audience with him during the first week and decides which supes he wants for his guard, his help, and the unlucky ones bound for his torture rooms.

But there are others in this batch who have probably spent time here before. They look confident, not terrified. One of them strides forward and I gasp, throwing myself up against the wall almost involuntarily at the sight of him.

It can't be!

Not able to help myself, I inch forward to look again. It's him. I'd know that aristocratic baring and that long, dark hair anywhere. Four guys stand at his back. Iron, Axel, Jayce, and Daemon. Ugh! He brought almost the whole clan with him.

I facepalm.

No. No. No. Shit. Shit. Shit.

When is this streak of bad luck going to END?

I peer down. None of them have even bothered to demon-up in the face of all the hardened criminals around them. They don't look scared to be here either though I don't remember ever hearing that any of them had been sent to the Mountain before.

'Relax,' I mutter to myself.

They couldn't know I'm here. This is a coincidence, that's all.

'Take us to the demon king,' resonates the imperious voice I remember all too well, the sound carrying throughout the cave and making all the supes here stand up and take notice.

It makes my skin prickle. That and the sudden silence in the crowd. I've never heard these guys so quiet and it's unnerving even though I'm safe up here.

A beefy looking shifter emerges from the crowd. He's one of Dante's guards. 'No one sees Dante. Who the fuck are you?'

He's on the ground a second later, not moving and I didn't even see what happened, the incubus' attack was so fast.

'Take us to Dante,' he says again.

Vampire Silas steps forward and I shiver. I didn't even notice he'd arrived, he's so sneaky.

'Who are you?' he asks.

'Julian Maddox.' The tone is arrogant, it's owner used to getting what he wants. 'Your lord is going to be very happy we've come.'

Silas looks Maddox and his guys over and then shrugs.

'It's your asses if you're wrong,' he says and starts leading them from the main room.

Maddox begins to follow the vamp, but freezes and tilts his head, sniffing the air. His clan does the same and Jayce whispers something to him.

'Smell some sweet pussy?' Silas chuckles when he notices they've stopped, and a rumble of assent goes through the crowd. 'Yeah, there's a female in here somewhere, but don't get your hopes up. When we finally get her, she's Dante's.' He grins. 'At least at first.'

I shiver, goosebumps erupting over my skin.

'A female,' Maddox murmurs, the acoustics of the cavern magnifying his voice. 'You don't say.'

And then he looks up – *directly at where I'm hiding*!

I scramble back, hitting the wall with a thud. I'm breathing hard but trying to stay silent.

They can't be here for me. They can't.

Shit!

I shouldn't have fucked with a demon clan like them, a supe like Maddox. The guy doesn't like to lose, isn't used to it. I knew better! But the payday was *big*, and they were so desperate it was easy to fool them. They were like shiny, ripe apples. I couldn't have resisted picking them even if I'd wanted to. Besides, I think sardonically, I couldn't have *afforded* to resist.

I've made my bed and now I have to yeet it out the window any way I can. That's how Julia Brand has survived and that's what I'll keep doing.

I back out of the space and into the tunnel behind it, deep in my own thoughts.

It's a dumb mistake to be so unfocussed on my surroundings outside Siggy's territory and I'm reminded of that when I'm taken in a painful grip. A large hand covers my mouth.

'Hush, girl. No screaming now. Wouldn't want anyone else joining the party just yet.'

One of Dante's scouts.

They don't usually come this far into Arania Alley.

I pry the fingers away from my mouth with a ton of effort. Whoever has me is like steel, feels big. Escape is not on the cards.

'Dante will kill you if you don't take me to him directly,' I hiss into the dark.

There's a low chuckle and I cringe when I feel a wet tongue slither up my cheek.

'Worth it,' he rasps in my ear.

I glance around, trying to come up with a plan while I berate myself for letting my dumb ass get captured.

I've been through these tunnels a hundred times and not one of the inmates has ever actually seen me until now. But I wasn't paying attention. I was thinking about Julian *fucking* Maddox and his crew.

I glance around, ignoring the scout's roaming hands … claws … shit, they could be tentacles for all I know. I have no clue what kind of supe has me.

But I do know exactly where we are, and it can't be more

than a couple of steps to Gargantua's tunnel. She's the biggest arania I've seen down here hence her nickname.

'Do you hear that?' I ask.

'Hear what?' he asks faintly as his hands continue to move over me and I feel a demon-sized dick at my back.

Fortunately for me, this isn't my first rodeo when it comes to some asshole feeling me up, so I'm not freaking out yet and I can think clearly.

'Someone's up there in the tunnel. They'll see you,' I say with conviction, and I feel him tense. 'What do you think Dante will do to you in his torture chambers if he finds out you defiled what's his?'

The fear gets to him just like I knew it would. He believes me.

'Over here!' I call and he swears, a meaty claw pushing hard at my mouth.

'Shut up,' he hisses, and he pulls me down the tunnel with him.

One step ... Two step ... It's got to be close!

I feel the wall of the cave at my right, and I throw my knees up, kicking off the stone hard with both feet like I'm in a swimming pool, making my captor stagger to the side even though he's much bigger than me.

I just hope we're where I think we are, or this won't do anything but piss him off.

But I hear the silk rustling under his shoes as he gains his balance on the other side of the tunnel and I give myself a mental high five, praying to every god I know of that Gargantua is waiting just inside her tunnel to dart out for her prey the way I've seen Siggy do before.

'Shit,' he mumbles, trying to get out of the thick webbing under his feet, sending multiple vibrations up the strands like a fool.

I curl around myself as much as I can, using him as a shield, and I feel something heavy barrel into him. He screams and we're dragged backward. Realizing I'm nowhere near heavy enough to anchor him, he releases me, and I sink into the soft silk that's all over the cave floor.

I hear his claws scrape ineffectually against the rocks around the opening that leads into Gargantua's domain. But then there's a dull thud. It's silent now except for his stuttered breathing and I know he got bit. The paralysis sets in quick.

I'm still on the ground and technically in Gargantua's web. It sticks to me, and I don't move a muscle while I listen in the dark.

There's a slight swish as the arania picks up her prey. She hunts the same way Siggy does, so I know that she's wrapping him for transport to her main web to save him for later. I just have to wait for her to take him and hope she can't make it back in time even if she does feel my movements when I unstick myself. That's a skill I've become pretty adept at since bunking with my spider buddy if I do say so myself.

'Over here! O'Toole went down this way.'

O'*Toole* was that asshole's name? Apt.

A light shines down the tunnel and I freeze.

'Well, where the hell is he?' a second voice asks.

'I told you I heard a ye— Holy shit! It's HER!'

A bright lantern is held up, blinding me.

'What are you—'

I peer up through my hair and wince. Two orcs. Dante's favored trackers. Both have blades and they're dressed in jackets and old jeans. Long hair hangs around their faces, but both of them have intricate braids and beads woven into their dark locks. As inmates go down here, they actually seem to keep themselves pretty clean and tidy.

They're just staring down at me, looking like they can't believe it.

Yeah, you and me both, guys.

Caught twice in one day. Luck isn't with me right now, that's for damn sure. My mind is racing, trying to figure out how I'm going to get out of this, wondering if I can use Gargantua a second time.

'Dante is going to give us whatever we want for this,' one of them breathes.

'Where's O'Toole?'

The two orcs seem to suddenly notice the webbing that's all over the ground and spilling out of Gargantua's tunnel. Both take a couple of steps back, looking wary.

That's not what I want, I think as I begin to pluck at the web under my fingers. I've experimented with Siggy's web and even a couple of little strums usually gets her attention. Here's hoping Gargantua isn't going to be lazy now that she's got her meal.

'Looks like an arania got him.'

The other one rolls his eyes. 'About time. That dumb cryptid was a liability.'

I keep playing with the web with one hand while I begin to unstick myself with the other and get ready to move. My shoes are well and truly embedded though, so I ease my feet out of them. This is why I keep my laces loose.

I feel a shudder in the silk.

She's coming back.

Fast.

'Can you help me, please?' I ask in my best damsel voice, keeping some of my attention on the entrance to the arania's home.

The two orcs look at each other and I swear I see their dicks start hardening at my helpless, pathetic state.

Orcs. Easy to read, even easier to play.

They both step forward at the same time to lift me up, practically tripping over each other to be the first to touch the female, but at the last second, I roll out of the webbing just as I see Gargantua out of the corner of my eye, getting ready to strike.

Holy fuck she's massive and so, so fast that she gets them both in one attack.

A millisecond later, the lantern is smashed on the floor and all I can hear is the breathing.

I'm out of the web, but I still stay where I am. The arania is clearly in a hunting mood today and the last thing I need is to get caught by her too. I definitely won't be able to talk my way out of *her* clutches.

I don't move until a minute after I hear her take them, getting to my feet and walking gingerly back down the tunnel. My shoes are lost for now, but maybe I can come back for them tomorrow morning when the aranias are usually napping.

I can't help but think that maybe it's time to get out of dodge. All signs seem to be pointing that way what with Dante clearly stepping up his search for me, and the arrival of that incubus clan whose money I *might* have run off with after I stole it out from under them.

I keep it together until I'm back in Siggy's territory and only then do I give in to the fear, sagging against the wall and practically hyperventilating with my hand clamped over my mouth to stay quiet.

I've been lying low here for weeks and I've been in my share of dangerous situations, but that was way too fucking close!

I have to face facts. It's not safe enough here anymore to be worth the risks of hiding out in an actual prison. I'm going to need to get out of the Mountain and, when I do, I've got to have another plan in place or all of this was for nothing.

I stand up, the terror already fading to the background as I go into problem-solving mode.

Siggy won't be happy I'm leaving.

∾

Iron

I'm hungry. Feeding should be the last thing on my mind right now. I mean, fuck! We're in *the Mountain* and the assholes who put us in here weren't overly forthcoming about when we might be getting out, so odds are this is for life. No one escapes from this place, not unless they have friends in high places and, considering we *were* those friends, there's no one on the outside who's going to help us.

I look around, not letting my gaze fall on anyone in particular although I know it's only a matter of time before I'm challenged. I'm a big guy and an even bigger demon and the order of the hierarchy is supreme in here. Plus, my tats show I was a marine once and there are plenty of supes who love to fuck with the guys who used to pretend they were normal to get by before the humans knew about us.

We follow the vampire down the corridors. I keep my focus on Maddox who's just in front of me. His first step is to introduce us to the power in the Mountain.

Dante. The name still strikes fear into many on the outside even though the King in the Mountain has been locked up for years now. I don't even remember what charge they got him on in the end. He had his fingers in a lot of pies on the outside both in the supe realms and in the human one. He's smart and violent, a powerful supe that embodies the old stereotype of what a real monster from the depths of hell looks like. He's an original demon who hasn't been tempered by his time outside the darkest realm where he was spawned. He has friends who'll do anything not to become enemies and enemies who'll do anything to become friends. Even after the years he's spent in this place, his influence on the outside hasn't waned. We need him to know who we are and then we need to become his friends too.

For now.

My first step will be finding out everything I can about this place and the inmates so that *we* become the authority here because there is no fucking way I'm about to live the rest of my life under that demon's heel no matter how powerful he is. Being second to Maddox is enough and I only tolerate that because he's earned my loyalty.

As we walk these shadowy passages, I'm already committing them to memory. My training makes me a great lieutenant in this clan and that's without even considering my size and other skills.

My nose, though, doesn't work so great. When they were talking about scenting a female earlier, I didn't smell her myself, and I didn't give Maddox's words much thought. So, when I catch a whiff of a tantalizingly sweet female, I almost stumble, my nostrils flaring. It's followed by the shocking realization that it's familiar.

I know that scent.

Victoria Styles.

I look up sharply at Maddox's profile. Did he notice it's her? He must have.

As impossible as this scenario is, I'll take it. I don't even care how she came to be in the Mountain. It's been a while since I had anything to smile about but knowing that somehow she's stuck in here with us, that we're going to have our revenge on that deceptive, manipulative, human bitch ... Yep. That'll do it. The ghost of a dark grin makes my lips turn upwards.

I'm still imagining all the ways I'm going to make her hurt when the vampire leads us into a large, round cavern. The ceiling is high and riddled with clusters of holes that would make a trypophobe freak the hell out.

The room itself is pretty bare except for a platform at the back with a door ... leading to another cavern, I guess. There's an empty, wooden chair in front of it and I belatedly notice the battered body of a pixie hanging high on the wall from its wrists.

A low moan comes from it and I realize the poor bastard is still alive. I wouldn't want to be in his shoes.

'Wait here,' the vampire says.

He walks across the room, his gait unhurried, and he scratches at the entrance like a rat.

Jayce is practically bouncing on the balls of his feet. 'Did you smell—'

'Yes,' Maddox says under his breath. 'We'll talk about it later.'

'But it's—'

'He knows,' I growl low, side-eyeing him and willing him to shut the hell up and act half-way sane for a minute.

I try to cut him some slack. I know he's hurting. We all are, but we're new here and we can't afford to be seen as a threat. Not until it's time.

The human in this prison is worth her weight in orc stones, maybe more to Dante since he'll own her when she's found. He has the most to gain ... and the most to lose. We can use her to our advantage in multiple ways and I know Maddox will see that too.

Jayce persists. 'But—'

I hear a thud and Jayce's muffled grunt of pain, and I give Daemon a reluctant nod as he steps back from shutting Jayce up. Daemon's only been back with us a few weeks. We were never all that close when he was part of the clan before. Then, Maddox had to kick him to the curb for his part in what happened two years ago. It occurs to me that Daemon likely blames *her* for that too. We might not see eye to eye on most things, but he'd be well within his rights to be seeking revenge too. I'll bet he wants to get even just as much as the rest of us do.

I thought being in here was going to be boring, but we're about to get the sweetest payback if we can keep the bitch alive long enough to suffer.

SOLD TO SERVE

THE DARK BROTHERS BOOK ONE

ONE WOMAN ENSLAVED. THREE CALLOUS MERCENARIES. AND SECRETS WHICH COULD DESTROY THEM ALL ...

Kora ran away to start a new life where she was in control of her own destiny and her own body. Instead, she was captured and auctioned to the highest bidders: Three former mercenaries with black hearts and a dilapidated castle.

Mace is their leader; harsh and unforgiving. Kade lives in the shadows and, if his snarls are anything to go by, may not be a man at all. And cruel Lucian's only delights seem to be drink and terrorizing their new possession until she breaks.

And she might.

Kora has never been a slave and she must keep that secret at all costs. If they learn who she is, she'll be forced to marry a man who terrifies her far more than these lords do.

Can she escape these three dangerous Brothers who have begun to show her that there is more to them than their tragic pasts? And if they find out her secrets, can she trust them not to throw her to the wolves?

CHAPTER ONE

It was hot for the time of year. The midmorning sun beat down on her fair skin, making her squirm in the ropes that held her to the wooden slaver's pole. If she survived the day, whatever wasn't covered would be well and truly burnt by this evening. She glanced down at her body. Her robes and shift were long gone, but thankfully some of her smallclothes remained. The wrapping around her hips provided at least some modesty, though her chest was bared to all. A good portion of her was still caked in dried mud from the night before. That might at least help with the sun, she thought.

A bead of sweat trickled down her scalp under her hair, leaving an itch in its wake. She pushed herself up onto her toes, but it was no use. Her wrists were bound too high to reach. The best she could do was to rub her head on her arm, spreading the wetness and dirt alike.

She scanned the busy street of Kingway, a typical market of trinkets and foodstuffs in a bustling town, large enough to get lost in, but certainly nothing like the mammoth cities in the north she'd heard about. She and two others, an unfriendly old man with a nasty cough and an equally hostile youth, were the only slaves for purchase, it seemed. Neither of them had spoken to her since she had found herself chained alongside them in the wagon.

Her lip quivered. Only yesterday evening she was saying the final rites, beginning the three-day ritual that would see her cast off her old life and step happily into the priesthood. Being a Priest of the Mount was – well, if she was honest, it wasn't as if it had been her fondest dream. She admitted to herself that she did not feel the call to serve the way the other novices professed to, though she had never spoken those thoughts aloud. For her, a life in service to the Mount was a means of escape and of safety. Complete and irreversible. Or at least it would have been in three days' time when she said her vows and swapped her grey novice's robes for the black ones of the priests. A tear tracked its way down her dirty cheek. For the thousandth time, she hoped to the gods that this was a dream, just a silly nightmare, and she'd wake up a bit late for morning prayer and be chastised as usual. But as she heard the tell-tale jingle of the coin purse at the portly slaver's belt, she knew it wasn't so.

She had been stolen last night as she slept in her narrow cot in the long room with the other novices. A tall, cloaked figure hefted her up easily, covered her mouth and threatened to kill her if she struggled. She was frozen; heart thundering, ears roaring. Her life had not prepared her for anything like this. It wasn't until she felt the thud as she landed on the ground outside the walls of the cloister that she finally came to her senses. After her months of hiding, they had found her … she couldn't go back! She pushed him as hard as she could, but he didn't let go. He grunted in pain and slipped in the mud instead, taking her with him and covering them both in it. He recovered his balance first and slapped her hard.

When she awoke, she was chained in the wagon and her abductor was gone. Her angry demands, questions and, finally, pleas were pointedly ignored by the other slaves and saw her gagged by the slaver; the smelly rag was still tied tightly around her head and jammed between cracked lips she wished she could moisten. She'd realised then that she'd been wrong. He hadn't taken her to bring her back to her family, nor to Blackhale, her betrothed. It had simply been to sell her. She'd never had to worry about this before. She knew it was done, especially here in the south, but the estate had been guarded and no one stole freewomen with property. She had been taken for no other reason than that she was nearest the window in the dormitory and she was no one. A part of her had been relieved – at the time.

Now, the slaver approached her, the wisp of a licentious smile on his face from the attention her semi-naked body was garnering, filthy though it was. He didn't seem interested in her except for the money she would bring him, thank the gods. He looked past her, into the crowd, and she jumped as he bellowed, 'Flesh auction! Midday!'

Flesh auction. She closed her eyes rather than see everyone's on her. She'd heard of such things, but of course never been to one. And now she was to be the main attraction.

She was left to braise, and after a while she couldn't help but drift, half-dozing and pretending she wasn't here, that this wasn't happening. The voices, noise and frenzy of the marketplace melted into the background.

'Is she alive? Looks like a dried-up corpse.'

Her eyes opened just a crack. They felt sore, swollen. She turned her head towards the voice and was ensnared by a man's gaze. He was older than she, with dark hair that was greying at the temples. He was a large man and wore a fine green tunic embroidered with a house sigil that she recognized but couldn't place.

He perused her body slowly from bare feet to chest, where his stare lingered, and she shifted uncomfortably, her face burning from more than the sun, which was now almost overhead. He smirked when his eyes met hers.

'I'll be at the auction,' he called – to the slaver, she

assumed – 'but looking at her, the price better be low.' Then he stepped closer and said, for her ears alone, 'You're going to be mine, girl.' His hand darted out and kneaded her breast, pinching her nipple hard. A hoarse cry erupted from her throat, weak and muffled by the gag, and she kicked out at him instinctively. He chuckled and pulled the gag down, taking in her face almost as an afterthought.

'Save your strength,' he muttered. 'You're going to need it before the day is done.' And then he was gone, leaving her shivering at his words even though she was absurdly grateful she could finally moisten her lips.

Looking out into the street, her eyes filled with tears. She wasn't sure what she'd expected, but, perhaps naïvely, it wasn't that. What was going to happen to her? She'd never even kissed a member of the opposite sex nor had the talk that she knew other girls had before their wedding nights. She wished her father hadn't kept her so cosseted. The most she'd seen were servants' stolen moments in stairwells when she'd snuck around at night. She had little idea of what to expect.

She noticed a man standing not far from her. He seemed frozen in the middle of the street – in everyone's way. People tutted as they passed him, but he ignored them. He was staring at her – not at her nakedness like the others, at her. She stared back, taking him in. He looked … *weathered*. That was the first word that came to mind to describe him. That and handsome, she supposed, in a brutish sort of way. He looked like a stable hand or a … *a mercenary*. Yes, that was apt. She'd never met a sell-sword before, but he was what she imagined them to be like. The look in his eyes was hard; dangerous. His hair was the color of wheat, cropped quite short. His shoulders were broad. He was a head taller than anyone else in the street and she guessed she'd barely make it to his chest. He wore black despite the heat of the day, and his dark leather boots were dusty and worn. He was no farmer nor merchant, that was for certain.

The slaver appeared in front of her with a bucket and, before she knew what he was about, she was doused in freezing water. She gasped at the sudden cold on her burning skin and screamed in shock. Then he began to sluice the water down her body, rubbing the worst of the mud and dirt away with his hands like she was a dog or a horse. She twisted and kicked, striking his shin with her foot, and he swore and took a short whip from his belt. He struck her twice in quick succession, and she squealed as it bit into her back and shoulder.

'Please, I beg you. Stop!' she whimpered.

'Shut your mouth, slave,' he growled at her and then, as if only just taking in her words, 'You speak prettily. He didn't tell me where he found you, but you aren't some village lass, eh?' He sounded surprised and then made a deep, horrible sound of satisfaction. 'They're going to be chomping at the bit for you.'

She stopped fighting, not liking the gleam that appeared in his eye. She held her breath as he continued with his ministrations. His impersonal fingers trailed up and down her skin until she could bear it no longer and then he poured another bucket over her head. She gritted her teeth and didn't make a sound, sagging in the ropes that bound her numb hands as he pushed the gag back into her mouth.

He cut the bonds moments later and she fell to her knees. The younger of the other two slaves picked her up at the slaver's direction and they began to walk down the road to the town square. She was glad of it. At least this hid her body somewhat and she didn't have to traipse through the town with everyone watching. Even if she was of a mind to walk, she didn't have the strength to struggle away from his grasp anyway.

She was thrown roughly into the middle of a raised platform. Grit dug into her knees, but she didn't move until the slaver wrapped his meaty hand in her long dark hair and dragged her to her feet. He began to speak loudly for the gathered crowd to hear.

'This slave comes to me from a ruling house. She's a hard worker. She can cook and clean. She can perform any menial tasks set before her. Who will give me five?'

'House slaves go for thrice that in these parts!', yelled someone from the crowd. 'Your words ring false.'

'House slaves are rarely sold,' another added from close by. 'Why has this one been cast out?'

'She was caught stealing,' the slaver replied smoothly, unmoved at being branded a liar. 'But she comes from good stock. Needs a firm hand is all.'

Kora gaped at his lies, looking at the men and women around her whose faces ranged from surprise to outright revulsion. The man was a fool. No one of means would buy such a house slave for their home. Short of killing their master, thievery was one of the worst grievances that a slave of status could have against them. It meant they weren't trustworthy and therefore useless to a noble family of any rank.

'I'll give you three for her,' someone called out, sounding bored.

She recognized the voice as the wealthy man in the green tunic from before and tensed. He didn't want a house slave, he wanted a pleasure one. If she knew anything at all, it was that.

'Five.'

'Seven.' *Green tunic.*

The voices sounded uninterested. This was very much not the frenzy of bidding the slaver had expected. She didn't look up to see who bid on her; she was too busy praying to the gods that this would not be her fate.

She realised dully that the number had stayed at seven. The slaver's hand tightened in her wet hair. She winced in pain as he pulled her head back, displaying her body more blatantly as if just realizing his blunder. His hand reached down to the cloth wrapped around her hips. He meant to pull it off! Here in front of everyone. He wasn't trying to peddle her simply as a house slave anymore. *No!* She twisted away from him with a cry and she felt his grip on her hair loosen, but he pulled her back roughly with a forced laugh that spoke of a nasty beating with that small lash he carried if she was still in his power later.

'Come, come, good people. She's a spirited one is all. Worth ten at least!'

'Twenty.'

The crowd hushed and the slaver's eyes gleamed. He was silent for a moment. 'Can you pay it?' he asked at last.

'I can.'

The voice was hard and gruff. She sighed through the gag in relief. That wasn't the man in the green tunic's voice. She opened her eyes and dared a look. The man from the street. The mercenary. She swallowed hard, in some ways more terrified. What could he want her for that was any different from the other one? Her eyes flicked to the man who'd been outbid, his crisp lime clothes a beacon in the crowd. He looked gracious, as if he didn't care, but she could see a barely contained fury in his countenance that no one else seemed to notice. He was anything but satisfied with the outcome.

The blond sell-sword came forward. Her new master until she could escape and make her way back to the Temple. She had a week, perhaps, before the moons moved out of alignment. After that it would be too late to begin the rites, and the door to the Mount would be closed to her for good.

The slaver waved him back. 'You can come for her later.' He squeezed her arm hard as he said it, his eyes promising more pain.

She turned her gaze to the mercenary, trying not to let the fear show in her eyes. The slaver wanted time for his revenge. No doubt he'd make up some lie about her trying to escape if asked.

The mercenary's hard expression didn't waver as he threw a bag of coins onto the dais. It landed at the slaver's feet. 'I'll take her now.'

Thank the gods. Her shoulders almost sagged in relief, but she didn't want to give the awful man any satisfaction.

The slaver's lip curled slightly as he maneuvered his body down to pick up the purse. He didn't let go of her, instead using his teeth to open the drawstring. Looking inside, he smiled coldly.

'So be it,' he said and pushed her hard. She yelled as she fell off the platform, but she was caught long before she hit the ground. She didn't need to look up to know it was him, her new master.

But she did look up, and her breath hitched as her eyes caught his. For a moment neither of them moved, but then his gaze flicked down, just a moment before she realised she was in a man's arms all but naked. She began to squirm and he set her down, his face hardening as he looked at her. Someone handed him the Writ of Ownership, which he took and pocketed, not even deigning to look at it.

Then he simply turned and walked away, what was left of the now-dispersing crowd parting before his long stride. Unsure of what to do, and feeling green tunic's eyes on her, she hurried after him, crossing her arms over her chest to conceal herself.

She caught up with him as he neared the outskirts of the small town. He never even looked back to ensure she followed. They came to a stable, where a large horse was tethered outside. He finally turned to her, a length of rope in his fist. He took her hands and looped the rope around her wrists, tying them together in front of her firmly but gently. The other end he tied to the saddle. He took the horse's bridle and began to lead it towards the forest road but hesitated. He turned and her eyes flicked to a knife he now held, wondering what he would do. She was surprised when the gag around her head went slack and fell to the ground. She immediately licked her cracked lips, grateful for this small mercy after the past day.

He mounted his horse in silence and it began to walk slowly, its gait steady. She was pulled forward and she gasped. She took a halting step and then another, wondering where he was taking her. Her skin was on fire, she needed water and she was this man's prisoner, but it was either move forward or be dragged, so walk she did.

They travelled for a time. She wasn't sure how long for, but the forest began to darken and still horse and rider showed no signs of stopping. She focused, as she had all afternoon, on putting one bare foot in front of the other. It was all she could do. Step. Step. Step. On and on and on.

Finally and inevitably, her toes caught a stone and she stumbled, her knees giving way in betrayal. At first he didn't stop, and she was afraid he'd let the horse plod on, dragging her behind like a felled deer.

'Please. Stop. I beg you.' Her voice broke and she hated the sound of it.

The horse drew to a standstill. She tried to stand up as he

dismounted and approached, but it was no use. Her legs just wouldn't hold her any longer. She fell back to the ground with a low cry.

'I can go no further. Please let me rest,' she implored, raising her eyes to his.

He looked surprised at her weakness, as if he hadn't even considered she might tire. She saw no kindness in his face, and for a horrible moment she thought he might simply continue, whether she was on her feet or not.

But he let out a long-suffering sigh. 'Very well. We'll camp nearby for the night.' He scanned the forest path ahead of them. 'But not on the road.'

She gave a squeak as he picked her up and set her on his horse's back. His eyes narrowed at her. 'He's a war horse. He won't obey you, so don't even try,' he ground out.

She nodded as she gripped the saddle with her bound hands and he led them into the forest. Soon she heard the trickle of water and they came upon a small clearing with a shallow stream running beside it. She looked around her. The trees here were old; thick and foreboding. She shivered and then inwardly chastised herself. When had she become so foolish? *They're just trees.* It didn't matter that the closest thing to a forest that she'd ever been in before today was a small hunting wood on her family's land. She'd spent time in nature as a novice during her training, after all. Though she'd never camped outside overnight.

The mercenary took her from the horse and set her on the mossy ground, pushing her down to sit with a heavy hand on her shoulder. She frowned at his back while he busied himself with his horse, ignoring her once more. She looked out into the forest and then at the stream. After the ride, she was feeling a bit better. Should she try to run while his back was turned or slake her thirst? Shaking her head at the thought of attempting to get away in her current state, she half crawled to the bank, gulping the cool, clear water until she felt sick. She wouldn't have got far anyway, she reasoned, and there would be other opportunities.

When she looked up, he was lighting a fire in the middle of the clearing. She inched closer to it. Her skin still felt hot, but her teeth chattered. Soon he had a small blaze going, and he turned his attention to her. He didn't speak, just watched her as she sat. She stared back at him, drawing her knees up so he couldn't see her nakedness. He'd had all afternoon to look at her breasts, of course, but he hadn't. To sit in front of him now like this made her feel helpless, and she didn't like it one bit.

He leant back against the tree behind him. 'What's your name?'

'Kora. What's yours?' she fired back.

His lip twitched. 'Master, I suppose.'

She tried to keep the sneer off her face, but she knew she'd failed when he raised an eyebrow at her. She wrapped her arms around herself, still shivering despite being quite close to the fire.

His eyes narrowed. 'How long did he have you staked out in the sun?'

'All morning until the ... the auction.'

He was silent, as if waiting for something more.

She gritted her teeth. '*Master*,' she choked out.

He snorted. 'My name is Mace.' He grabbed one of his bags and dug around inside for a moment. Then he tossed her a small pot. She fumbled, only just catching it. 'Your skin is burnt. Use the salve and drink more water or you'll get sun sick.'

'Why do you care?', she snapped and wondered where she'd found the gall to speak to him in such a way.

She saw his jaw clench. 'You were expensive,' he said coldly. Then he stood and walked over to where she sat, towering over her like a giant. She swallowed hard and made herself crane her neck to look him in the eye. She would not be cowed.

He leant down and she couldn't help but flinch. Would he beat her for her insolence? But instead he seemed to be inspecting the marks the slaver had given her earlier in the day. 'Use the salve on those lashes too,' he muttered, untying her wrists. When she was free, he straightened and marched into the undergrowth. She stared after him as he melted into the twilight.

For a while she watched the forest where he'd disappeared, wondering if this was a trick of some sort, but he didn't return. She used up the small pot of salve over the worst of her burnt skin and the ridges the lash had made and found that her body immediately began to feel better. There was none left for her feet though and she belatedly realised she should have tended to those first.

She went back to the stream, biting her lip as she looked out into the night beyond the dancing shadows cast by the fire. She should run now while he was gone, she knew, but the more she gazed into the darkness, the more she feared. There were noises coming from beyond the clearing and she didn't know enough to identify what animals made them. There were wolves out there at the very least. She went back to the fire, stoked it and fed it with some sticks the mercenary had left before lying on the soft moss and closing her eyes.

She woke groggy the next day. The fire smoldered next to her and she was covered in a blanket she hadn't had the night before. She sat up and looked around the clearing. The mercenary – *Mace* – was standing with his horse.

'Get up. It's almost time to go.'

A thick, dry biscuit landed in the moss in front of her. It wasn't much, but she hadn't eaten in two days, so it was a veritable feast as far as she was concerned. She gobbled it quickly and stood, keeping the blanket carefully around her. He turned away from her as he smothered the fire, so she quickly saw to her morning needs while he wasn't watching. Then she drank deeply from the stream again. She did feel better today despite sleeping on the ground. The salve he'd given her had done wonders. Her skin was still a bit red, but it didn't hurt anymore. Even the welts from the slaver's lash no longer felt swollen.

Her bare feet were a different story, however. They already hurt, though she was only walking on the soft moss of the clearing, and she knew that if she looked, they'd be a mess of cuts and blisters from the day before. She hoped they didn't have far to go today.

She clasped the blanket around her shoulders tightly as he beckoned her – as if that would offer her any real protection. 'Where are we going?'

Mace said nothing at first, and she thought perhaps he wasn't going to tell her. He gave one of his sighs.

'To the keep,' he said finally as he snatched the blanket from her.

She gasped, but he ignored her, rolling it up and stowing it on the horse without another word. He tied her hands as he had the day before and lashed her to his horse. He took them back to the road.

'Is it far?'

He muttered something about indulged house slaves. 'Walk quickly and we'll get there faster.'

She stared at his back with a frown as he mounted his horse and they began the trek anew. Before long, her feet were in agony as they travelled over the rough stones and sand of the thoroughfare. She took to trying to walk on the edge in the grass and moss whenever she could. She also began to pick at the knot in the rope. She knew something about knots; not the names or anything so involved, but her seafaring Uncle Royce had taught her some, and Mace had used one that was similar. She'd be able to get it undone eventually.

She didn't make a sound as they travelled and, again, he never once looked back. After a while, her deft fingers slowly but surely began loosening the rope around her wrists, but when it suddenly and very abruptly fell to the ground, she tensed, sure he would notice. She'd meant to hold on until the last moment, but now the rope was being dragged along the ground sans prisoner.

Her eyes darted to him, but he hadn't looked away from the road ahead. Without a second thought, she dashed into the undergrowth, trying to be as quiet but as quick as she could be. Ignoring the pain in her feet, she dodged trees and stumps.

～

MACE

Mace wasn't sure what prompted him to look back when he hadn't all morning. Perhaps he heard something and his finely tuned senses put him on alert, or perhaps it was just luck that he turned his head at just the right moment to see his newly bought and very expensive slave running into the undergrowth and the end of the rope trailing along the ground behind the horse. He gave an annoyed, rasping groan from deep in his throat. He should have known after what the slaver had said that she'd be trouble. And how had she gotten his knot undone so quickly?

He leapt from his mount and sprinted quickly through the trees, the horse's easy canter ceasing immediately. He knew this stretch of road well. The river wasn't far and it would slow her down. He moved much faster than her. There was no need for him to rush, though for some reason he did.

He hadn't been himself since Kingway when he'd seen her bound in the sun, skin burning, covered in mud. Ordinarily he wouldn't have looked twice, but instead he found himself staring at her, unable to tear his gaze away. Her bearing was not that of an owned girl. It made more sense when the slaver said she was a house slave, but he'd have known it at once by the lilt of her voice as soon as he'd heard it on the road. They always sounded like they were part of the noble families they served and were typically a bit above their station because of it, in his experience.

So he'd paid a ridiculous amount of coin for a potentially useless slave girl; one so intractable that, though he'd been a picture of respectability last evening despite wanting to give her a good hard fucking to put her in her place, she still ran at the first opportunity. She'd learn soon enough that he and the others were not like the noble family her kin served. Thieving and any other mischiefs would be punished harshly.

At least she'd be well-versed from birth in the needs of a large estate though. A house slave's domestic skills were valuable, after all. He grinned, remembering other female house slaves he'd come into contact with. Such helpful little things usually and always up for a bit of bed play in exchange for less work. Kora could try to seduce them if she liked. Gods, she'd probably succeed, but she'd get no special treatment for the effort.

His brow furrowed as he remembered how she'd felt in his arms when he'd caught her after the slaver had thrown her off the dais. Warm and perfect as if she fit him somehow, as if something was moving into place. It had been a curious sensation and not something he'd felt before. Perhaps ... No. He steeled himself against these odd thoughts. She was an untrustworthy house slave that would be useful in their endeavors with the estate they'd bought after leaving the Dark Army – well, as long as they kept her on a short leash anyway. She would be useful to them and the keep so long as she was watched closely. That was all.

He caught sight of her up ahead, her shorter legs no match for his. He let out a slow breath. Gods, even now he was tempted. He shook his head as he got closer and reminded himself that she was a slave who had been cast out. She would be devious and disloyal. They couldn't let their guard down around her. He had to remember that a slave who stole could never be reliable no matter where she came from and the only way he'd earn back even half of what she'd cost him was by ensuring well that she was never idle.

As he neared, he heard her labored breathing and sneered cruelly. Pampered little thing. They'd enjoy putting her to work in the keep; show her what it was to be a true slave.

Kora had been running for ages, branches tearing at her arms and legs, when the trees gave way to open space. A river. She skidded to a halt at the edge of a short stone cliff, wondering if she should run along it or jump in. But before she was able to decide, much less act, something hit her hard between her shoulders, plunging her into the surging water. Her cry was cut short as she went under. She flailed and kicked in the current, her head breaking the surface as she finally remembered to keep her fingers together as she paddled. She coughed and spluttered, trying to get her bearings. Then she heard someone clear their throat and looked up. Mace stood where she had been. She thought he looked amused at first, but his expression rapidly darkened and she cursed inwardly. She wouldn't get another chance before they arrived at this keep, wherever it was.

He pointed downstream, his order clear, though he said nothing, and she made her way to a shallow bank. He was waiting there, and as she clambered out of the water, he took hold of her dark, tangled hair and dragged her up onto the shore. Still he said nothing, but pushed her through the forest, using his grip to steer her in the direction he wanted her to go. She clenched her jaw and let him simply because there was nothing else she could do, but she hated every moment of it.

When they arrived at the road, he practically threw her onto the ground beside his horse that seemed to be awaiting him patiently. Her knees and hands slid agonizingly on the gravel. She turned over to find his hulking form a hair's breadth away, a length of knotted rope in his hand.

'My patience is at an end. You'll get no more kindness from me,' he growled, and she scrambled back in fear. Quick as a snake, he grabbed her ankles and, when she kicked out at him, he swung the rope. One of the knots hit her hard in the thigh and she cried out.

'You need a good whipping, slave. Shall I do it here in the road?'

Kora shook her head and ceased her struggle, tears rolling down her cheeks.

He made a sound of anger that had her shuffling away clumsily, afraid he'd make good on his threat, but he merely grabbed one of her injured feet and peered down at the mess of cuts and scrapes.

'You foolish girl!' he growled. 'Why didn't you tell me?'

She didn't answer him, unsure of what to say that wouldn't get her a cuff on the ear at the very least. Had he not realised she wore no shoes? Why did he even care?

With a shake of his head, he tied her ankles and wrists together quickly and swung her like a sack of grain over his horse's back. She landed with a grunt and they started on their way once more, his arm reaching behind to grab hold of her so she wouldn't slide off.

They travelled like this until the sun was high, the mercenary and his horse plodding along while she bounced around upon the demon beast's back, her stomach rolling despite its emptiness. At least her feet were being spared. *Small mercies.*

She was just beginning to wonder if he was going to keep her like this the whole way when they passed under something. She twisted her neck to see what was happening. It was a great stone archway and beyond it was a large and imposing fortress. *The keep.* It was grey and stark against the green of the valley behind. There were two towers and a moat as well as a thick defensive outer wall complete with ramparts, though parts looked as if they were crumbling from years of neglect.

They went over a bridge and under a raised portcullis into a bustling courtyard. She could hear the blacksmith's hammer close by and a thousand other sounds that reminded her of home. She wondered if her mother even knew she was gone and felt a sudden pang of sadness that brought tears to her eyes. Mama was probably sitting in her chair looking at nothing, as she did every waking moment. She never spoke, never did anything except stare at the wall and occasionally wander off. She'd been that way as long as she could remember.

She turned her thoughts away from *before* and steeled herself. It wasn't over. She would find a way to escape. She had to. She had less than six days, but she could still become a priest and, once she had pledged herself to the gods, neither her father nor Blackhale could gainsay it. She could visit her home without fear if she ever wished to. Provided she could find a way out of here within four nights, she could make it back to the Temple before it was too late.

WANT FREE BOOKS AND SPOILER TALK?

SIGN UP FOR MY NEWSLETTER AND DISCORD AND STAY IN THE KNOW!

Join Discord and be entered monthly for free paperbacks/hardbacks from yours truly. 😎

Members also receive exclusive content, free books, access to giveaways and contests as well as the latest information on new books and projects that I'm working on!

My Newsletter? It's completely free to sign up, you will never be spammed by me, and it's very easy to unsubscribe! Scan the QR CODE BELOW!

www.kyraalessy.com

https://geni.us/KyraAlessyDiscord

ALSO BY KYRA ALESSY

~

DESIRE AFORETHOUGHT COMPLETE SPECIAL EDITION HARDBACK

When Jane Mercy's path collides with the notorious Iron Incubi MC, the threads of desire, danger and destiny begin to unravel, and in a world where demons rise and love is the ultimate debt to pay, nothing will ever be the same.

https://geni.us/DesireACompleteSeriesE

~

<u>VENGEANCE AFORETHOUGHT TRILOGY</u>

When hearts are the real treasures to be stolen, can a con-woman outwit the demons of her past?

VILLAINS AND VENGEANCE

She stole from them, lied to them, and now they're her prison mates.

In a world without exits, trust becomes the rarest and most deadly commodity.

https://geni.us/VillainsandVengeance

VENGEANCE AND VIPERS

https://geni.us/VengeanceandVipers

I was supposed to be their downfall. They were meant to be my revenge. But the chains that bound me have now tangled us all.

VIPERS AND VENDETTAS

https://geni.us/VipersandVendettas

Six seductive demons, bound by venom-laced passion, teeter on the brink of salvation and ruin.

a former slave waging a final stand for a life far beyond her darkest dreams.

DARK BROTHERS COMPLETED SERIES

In a world of darkness, the intertwining fates of fierce women and brooding mercenaries challenge the very essence of love and war.

SOLD TO SERVE

In a game of power and survival, will she be the pawn or the queen?

https://geni.us/SoldToServe

BOUGHT TO BREAK

Liberation comes in many forms... sometimes in the arms of the enemies.

https://geni.us/Bought2Break

KEPT TO KILL

When your salvation lies in the hands of beasts, will you conquer or crumble?

https://geni.us/Kept2Kill

CAUGHT TO CONJURE

Unleashing the power within, a witch's redemption, or the world's doom?

TRAPPED TO TAME

In the arena of love and war, who will reign - the damsel or the dark fae?

https://geni.us/Trapped2Tame

SEIZED TO SACRIFICE

With forgotten sins and unseen foes, will memory be her weapon or her downfall?

https://geni.us/seized2sacrifice

∽

For more details on these and the other forthcoming series, FOLLOW ME ON THE ZON!

SCAN THE QR CODE BELOW

DARK REALMS SERIES

From the echoes of the Dark Brothers' legacy, the Dark Realms stir – a new saga of entwined fates and dark enchantments begins.

THALIA, GREY, DANE & KALLUM DUET BOOK ONE

SOLD TO THE FAE

In a city where magic cloaks darker truths, Thalia struggles to maintain her charade amongst creatures of power. When her false identity is stripped away, she becomes an unwilling captive of three Fae who would rather see her dead than alive.

OWNED BY THE FAE

Amidst a web of lies, can a spark of truth ignite forbidden love?

THALIA, GREY, DANE & KALLUM DUET BOOK TWO

Acknowledgements

For my kids, who will hopefully never read this book. I hope this series saves our house from the increased mortgage rates because I'd hate to have to go get another job.

For my grandkids, who I hope do read this and recognise how fucking epic their granny was when she was young and fun.

For me as an old woman. (If I've survived his kooky, fucked up planet). OMFG, stop being so fucking OLD and go tear some shit up!

xx 2024 Kyra

Printed in Great Britain
by Amazon